CW01590303

SISTER MORPHINE

CATHERINE EISNER's fiction has appeared regularly in a number of UK literary journals, including *Ambit* and *Mslexia*. She is an Associate of the Royal College of Art; this, together with her interests in anthropology and design, reflects in her writings, which extend from a study of sex-attractant pheromones in literature, to researches into the little-known 19th Century shamanistic culture of the autonomous Russian republic of Mariy El.

SISTER MORPHINE

Women's Narratives from the Case Notes of a Community Psychiatric Nurse

CATHERINE EISNER

SALT

CAMBRIDGE

PUBLISHED BY SALT PUBLISHING
PO Box 937, Great Wilbraham, Cambridge PDO CB21 5JX United Kingdom

All rights reserved

© Catherine Eisner, 2008

The right of Catherine Eisner to be identified as the author of this work has been asserted by her in accordance with Section 77 of the Copyright, Designs and Patents Act 1988.

This book is in copyright. Subject to statutory exception and to provisions of relevant collective licensing agreements, no reproduction of any part may take place without the written permission of Salt Publishing.

First published 2008

Printed and bound in the United Kingdom by Biddles Ltd, King's Lynn, Norfolk

Typeset in Swift 9.5 / 13

This book is sold subject to the conditions that it shall not, by way of trade or otherwise, be lent, re-sold, hired out, or otherwise circulated without the publisher's prior consent in any form of binding or cover other than that in which it is published and without a similar condition including this condition being imposed on the subsequent purchaser.

ISBN 978 1 84471 299 1 hardback

Salt Publishing Ltd gratefully acknowledges the financial assistance of Arts Council England

ARTS COUNCIL ENGLAND

1 3 5 7 9 8 6 4 2

'Tell me, Sister Morphine, how long have I been lying here?
What am I doing in this place?'

—M. JAGGER/K. RICHARDS/M. FAITHFULL, 1968

'Certain authors, speaking of their works, say: 'My book', 'my commentary', 'my history', etc . . . They would do better to say: 'Our book', 'our commentary', 'our history', etc., because there is usually more of other people's property in them than their own.'

—BLAISE PASCAL

Contents

INTRODUCTION

YOU MAY RECOGNISE the lyric, 'Tell me, Sister Morphine, how long have I been lying here, what am I doing in this place?'; it's composed, of course, by Marianne Faithfull (with Mick Jagger) whom I knew some years ago when we were both very young.

From her words I have derived my title for this collection of women's narratives which I have refashioned as fictions to delineate the effects of drug administrations on clients observed in psychiatric nursing.

To assist comprehension I have planted clues by prefacing each narrative with a summary of the common side effects of a generic prescription drug so, as you can probably guess, if there is a moral buried in these cautionary tales no diagnostician could ever have predicted it.

Such narratives reflect the growing popularity of self-narrative approaches towards a collaborative analysis of self-characterisation in counselling and psychotherapy. Diaries, letters, notebooks (including experiments in automatic writing), personal documents, news clippings, telephone conversations, and recordings in a variety of media are all identified as sources for experiential self-narrative assignments in psychotherapy, and this collection, I trust, explores similar sources to demonstrate how these theoretical exercises can enhance self-understanding in practice.

The themes of these fictions encompass:

Guilt,	Post-Adoption Trauma,
Incest,	Jealousy,
Infidelity,	Revenge,
Sibling Murder,	Illegitimacy,
Suicidality,	Morbid Self-Harm,
Betrayal,	Drug Addiction and Substance Abuse,
Child Abuse,	OCD (Obsessive-Compulsive Disorder),
Bereavement,	Grand Larceny, etc.

All of these cases are based on the experiences of a CPN (Community Psychiatric Nurse) in an outreach team with whom I have established a close personal bond.

As a CPN, she aims to establish therapeutic relationships among the mentally ill by implementing programmes of cognitive-behavioural therapy (CBT) intervention developed in consultation with the responsible medical officer. She also has autonomous responsibility for her caseloads which means she is in an unusually privileged position and, hence, sometimes uniquely placed to facilitate clinically significant symptomatic improvements in her patients.

As an experienced Registered Mental Nurse with a B.Sc. in Health Studies (augmented by a Supplementary Prescribing Course) her psychobiopharmacological knowledge permits her, under a Clinical Management Plan, to prescribe and administer mood-changing psychoactive drugs in pharmacologic interventions.

As the stories reveal, her individual interview-screenings of her women patients and monitoring of contextual stresses has, in particular, enabled her to conduct a special study of the side effects from such drugs—whether from antidepressants, tranquilisers or mood stabilisers—and the more bizarre asocial behaviour made manifest by these multifaceted side effects provides the substance of my fictions.

I cannot emphasise too strongly that these case histories are, indeed, fictions based on fact, their literary interest residing in their unconscious subversion of the classical rules of drama where—

unlike the dramatic unities—causality, conflict, transition and crisis cannot be neatly resolved.

Certainly, the CPNs regards her encouragement of her patients to record their experiences in 'creative sessions' (either as writings in the first person, or third person, or as audio-taped sessions when patients agreed to this) as a subtle psychotherapeutic interventionist technique; a technique which has been shown to often ameliorate prevailing levels of depression and self-harm, and to promote more effective stress and anxiety management, encouraging more adaptive responses to mental health.

By demonstrating a non-judgemental openness, and by communicating a willingness to listen (she is a Law Society Registered Expert Witness, incidentally), the CPN who recounts these stories is privy to remarkable confidences which often illuminate the psychopathography of a patient.

That said, the mental health problems of the psychiatric profession are also not neglected in her narratives. It should be remembered that—in a curious case of the biter bit—even doctors are not immune to 'white coat syndrome' and, on a graver note, it remains a sombre fact that, according to the latest available research*, one in fifteen UK doctors succumb like many of their patients to some form of dependence on drugs.

Perhaps little known is the predicament of psychiatric professionals when they are themselves prescribed a psychotropic medication (e.g. an antidepressant) for a mental health problem. Certainly, such a circumstance is not a bar to a psychiatrist practising. Indeed, it can be a valuable experience and mental health trusts routinely recruit employees with personal experience of mental illness. A former President of the Royal College of Psychiatrists, for example, discusses quite openly his own experience of mental illness, and how this has informed his practice.

So these fictions should not be regarded as indiscretions; nor should they be seen as representing substantially more than illustrative examples from case studies for stimulating self-reflection and further debate on treatment strategies.

* The British Medical Association

Rather, 'Sister Morphine', if it has any clinical use, could be considered as a therapeutic process towards a better understanding of dysfunctional personalities whose hopelessness or helplessness or hostility is so often a mirror of our own.

Yet, despite these resemblances, I reaffirm faithfully that in no particular in the text do these fictions breach the presumption of confidentiality or of legal privilege of information given to me.

CATHERINE EISNER

All the events in these stories are wholly imaginary, even the chance similarity of name; and no reference is made to any actual person.

SOFT SKIN

(*Felícia F.* — Alprazolam)

A Case of Grand Larceny in the Second Degree

Assessment Summary (extract): A 29-year-old, single woman requested admission to the emergency room. She claimed to 'hear voices' and reported seeing 'strange objects' ('robed figures afloat in the sky'). The patient sensed that souls of the dead were present in her body; not only was a 'good entity' in her body but also 'bad ghosts' within her, and her self-harm was due to her attempts to cut out the bad spirits with a knife. She reported auditory and visual hallucinations ('I saw my mother walk out of that mirror'), claiming to hear her mother's voice and to have a dialogue with her. She often appeared to talk agreeably with her mother. The patient had not had a job for many months and lived, without any apparent source of income, in a religious charitable institution. She also reported changing her handwriting frequently, and attributed this to the presence in her body of two persons, her mother and her father. It was impossible to correct the patient's false beliefs, many of which she committed to paper, writing in various hands. After 14 days, the patient was discharged into post-hospital care in a mental health community center. From her writings a composite account of her recent psychiatric history has been attempted but, although a psychopathological etiology was suspected, no definitive diagnosis was made.

Acknowledgements (written consent was obtained from the patient for publication of this Case Report): International exchange programs for cross-training of psychiatric/mental health professionals can yield profound insights into new psychotherapeutic interventions developed to enhance pharmacotherapy and improve outcomes in common psychiatric disorders. Abstracts prepared under these programs can be used for educative purposes, to teach an important clinical lesson, or to describe a diagnostic or therapeutic dilemma. Recent attendance, in Philadelphia, at a pharmaceutical corporation's sponsored symposium, for the reading of an abstract on specialty nursing, prompted an encounter with a South American *enfermeira psiquiátrica*. This psychiatric nurse's own paper on the clinical use of opioids had referred, in a brief digression at one of convention's sessions, to the following case. The respondent's American orthography in this account remains unchanged.

C.E.

SOFT SKIN

A Case of Grand Larceny in the Second Degree

Patient ID EP0841060170: Felícia F.
Occupation: Bank cashier.
Drug: Alprazolam.
Drug class: Benzodiazepine anxiolytic.
Common side effects: Release of hostility, decreased inhibition, light-headedness and other paradoxical behavioral effects suchas irritability and hallucinations may occur with benzodiazepines.

In the interview room she read her statement.

'Right,' she said coolly, 'I guess this is all true.'

She signed her full name. Felícia Epifania Ferreira.

'Thank you, Leisha,' fawned Mac, the chief cashier (in the bank they called her Leisha), and he squeezed her forearm with silken fingertips.

She arranged her lips into a perfunctory corporate smile, while thinking: *You creep me out, you jerk!* By a supreme act of will she suppressed a shudder of revulsion.

The older police officer nodded, and his partner opened the door which led into the bank's main lobby. Immediately after the robbery the two patrolmen had commandeered the bank's meeting room as a temporary operations center while they pursued their lines of inquiry. The younger uniformed officer, who was merely moderately cute, flexed his shoulders and winked at her with a preening self-regard she ignored.

As she crossed the threshold, Leisha was conscious of Mac's yearning gaze fixed on her figure in half profile—she knew perfectly well that most men surrendered to her dark good looks and she traded on this advantage.

She flicked a glossy strand of hair from her eyes in a practiced gesture contrived to be subtly flirtish.

Mac watched her return to her teller's station.

Before the door closed she heard him say in a hollow, defeated voice:

'Jeez. It's a disaster, all the way around.'

Sickened, Leisha sat at her position and folded her hands tightly on the desktop to control their shaking.

Across the polished marble floor of the lobby, behind the brass teller cages, she saw the bank's auditor was glaring at her. He weighed two hundred and eighty pounds and he now presented the appearance of a man who had been recently boiled in a bag. After all, the bank's hard currency reserves had just been depleted by more than a quarter-million dollars.

Leisha shrugged inwardly and told herself firmly she had nothing to fear. To calm her mind she once more reviewed the circumstances of her case.

The starting point had been when?

In her innermost ear a warm consoling voice answered: *It wasn't your fault. A culpa não foi tua.* Since the beginning of the fall, the words of her mother had been echoing inside her head like a long-distance trunk call.

Yet, despite her mother's comforting presence in her thoughts, Leisha knew that what she had done, in the opinion of all who would afterwards judge her, was wrong . . . irretrievably wrong . . . *except*, perhaps, in the opinion of her neurotologist, who alone among her few confidants would guess the truth of her motives.

She pressed her fingers to her temples as a jagged blade of raw light, zigzagging across her field of vision, stabbed with precision and temporarily blinded her left eye. Her hands and feet had somewhat cooled, she noticed, signaling an onset of nausea. She prayed desperately, indiscriminately, for the pain to recede and shaded her eyes under her palm.

With further gentle pressure on her eyeballs, she was rewarded by the pain fading in a multicolored phosphene, on whose after-image the pinched white face of little Sonny Kaminski now dimly emerged.

At the memory of Sonny, the corners of Leisha's mouth trembled on the brink of a secret smile.

Yes, she thought, she must not forget little Sonny Kaminski because, after all was said and done and denounced, Sonny, too, had shared her confidences, though unlike the good doctor he no doubt could not be trusted to keep them.

Leisha caught her breath, dizzy at recalling the mainspring of her audacious enterprise.

Yes. Before the arrival of Sonny into her life she had only dreamed and schemed, but after their chance encounter she'd seen at once that he had presented her effectively with the equivalent of a *fully collateralized surety* (to borrow a term of fiscal usage from her own bank) which could mitigate her operational risks. All Leisha needed to do was seize the opportunity.

That, at least, was true. *Opportunity makes the thief. A ocasião faz o ladrão.*

She remembered all too clearly the circumstances of their first unexpected meeting . . . it was not an occasion she was likely to forget.

A Small Man is Sly

Felícia Epifania Ferreira lived on the fifth floor of Mrs Kaminski's apartment building.

Three weeks earlier, on a Sunday morning she had cause to recall, Leisha had been kneeling on her prie-dieu outside her bathroom, poised to hang an advent calendar. The date was November 30th.

A votive candle was burning in the little shrine she had erected to Saint Nicholas. In Portugal, she thought, her young cousins would be counting the days to the Night of the Magi and the gifts they exchanged at Epiphany. (Her birthday was celebrated on January 6th.)

Each year, as the season of the Nativity approached, she struggled with a strange complication of emotions. Strong feelings of loneliness and homesickness threatened to overwhelm her. Hence, that morning, little by little, her prayers had turned to the Holy Mother, the refuge of sinners, for a blessing that would release her from the nine-to-five tyranny of a bank whose male-supremacist managerial ranks (she was convinced) conspired to grind her down.

Were her morning devotions answered? Certainly she felt her heart stumble as across the bathroom window fell a shadow. Behind the dimpled glass a hooded Blessed Virgin, immaculately white, seemed suspended, bowed in prayer, against the brightening sky.

She could scarcely summon the resolve to open the window . . . yet she did.

Framed by the open casement, Mrs Kaminski's only son bared his teeth and grinned at Leisha from beneath the cowl of a hooded ski jacket. Gripping a guardrail, he knelt precariously on the platform of a window-cleaning gantry he'd winched from the roof.

'You gotta be kinda crazy to ride this cage,' Sonny said flatly, in a poor attempt at nonchalance.

Yeah, kiddo, Leisha thought. *And let me tell you, you've got to be crazy to work in a teller's cage.*

She noticed there was no window-cleaning kit to explain his presence on the gantry. She could only assume his true intention had been to rob her. At her own eye-level, on the gantry platform, Sonny shuffled his stained high-top sneakers but he could not conceal a switchblade, and the shaft of a screwdriver sharpened to a spike.

'Come in, why don't you?' she said matter-of-factly. 'I can show you a way to make more cash than you have ever imagined.'

'This sure beats me all to hell. I thought you were in church today,' he muttered incautiously, not realizing that by these words he incriminated himself. He unclipped his safety harness and clambered through the window. A strong easterly breeze brought a chill into the room and she noticed her wind-chimes had been silenced by icicles from the eaves.

Up to that moment no man had entered Leisha's studio apartment. Sonny saw her bedroom was very simple and neat, with a Colonial rocking-chair in one corner beside a small wooden bedstead. Above the bed a hologram of the Holy Family was adorned with a sprig of palm.

At close quarters eighteen-year-old Sonny Kaminski could be seen to exhibit all the telltale signs of his narcotic dependence . . . the hopped-up rapid speech, the unhealthy pallor of a flesh clammy with sweat, and the drooped eyelids half-shielding narrow pupils unresponsive to light. As he had reached through the window, Leisha had noted hardened needle tracks on Sonny's momentarily exposed inner left forearm, along veins infected with weeping rashes.

'How much do you need for your next hit?' Leisha asked briskly.

Sonny produced from the patch pocket of his cargo pants his last five-dollar bill.

'More than this green stuff.' He sniffed. 'Yes ma'am, that's for sure.'

'Well, stealing from me won't support your habit.' Her manner was not so forbidding as to deny him altogether the glimmer of a ray of hope.

'So okay, I boost and shoot,' he countered defiantly, 'but truth is I guess I never got busted till now.' He began to shiver and shut the window.

(*The kid's gone cold turkey,* thought Leisha heartlessly. She had never dabbled in street drugs herself but she recognized his panic. In the bank, not a few young clerks with the shakes claimed they suffered from yuppie flu.)

She laughed out loud.

'You're not busted, Sonny. I'm not the fuzz. This an easy score.'

She handed him a ten-dollar bill.

'See. More than a dime's-worth of dreams for start-offs.'

Sonny extended his other hand and she added a five.

'You gotta be kiddin' me,' he whined. 'This'll buy nothin' 'cept flea powder.'

From her bureau drawer Leisha withdrew a bankroll of crisp new notes. Sonny's hooded eyes widened. The scared look was no longer there; but those eyes were full of greed.

'Wow! What's the deal?'

'It's very simple. You're going to be my gopher, Sonny.'

She then told him the precise details of his participation in her scheme. Sonny whistled. 'Hey, that sounds neat!' The sum of cash she mentioned amounted to the street value of four thousand quarter-ounce bags of dope.

'Is it for real?' He inclined his head and riffled the stack of banknotes against his ear. That's when Leisha knew he was hooked on the bait. As she expected, he could not resist a proposition so 'way cool', 'totally wild', and 'off the wall' . . . to quote his own impetuous words.

For more than an hour Leisha coached him in his shopping errands, then Sonny departed the way he had entered. His small compact form was ideally suited to breaking and entering.

A small man is sly. Far off, in her deepermost memories, she heard a familiar voice counsel her as if she were a small child again. *Um homem pequeno é velhaco.*

Since Sonny's last scam, during Mrs Kaminski's vacation overseas, when he had collected the rents for all fifteen apartments in cash and failed to deposit them, his mother had warned her tenants to be leery of her son.

Leisha watched Sonny ascend in his cradle like a clumsy *deus ex machina.*

Follow that cloud, kid, she thought. *This is no joyride.* But she ruefully admitted she could have been referring to herself.

As she closed the window the candle blew out.

She returned and relit the flame at the shrine of Saint Nicholas, the patron saint of thieves.

Now, as she sat at her desk, an hour after the holdup, she marveled at the nerve with which she had outfaced her co-workers who had scrutinized her every move.

She busied herself by filing an interoffice memo entitled, *Armed Robbery Prevention Strategies*. She glanced at a sub-section which stated:

> Unarmed 'soft-skin' operators, proportionate to armed security guards under special category instructions, should listen attentively to robbers, be calm, courteous, and patient, and treat the robber as you would a customer. *Do not resist*, but cooperate unhesitatingly with the robber, as this is the most reliable way to avoid injury. *Don't try to be a hero.* Take no action that would jeopardize your safety or the safety of others. Activate alarms *only* if you can safely do so without detection.

Well. As a vulnerable 'soft-skin target' she had acted accordingly. She hadn't resisted. On the contrary! Despite Sonny's tendency towards torpor when rehearsing thestick-up, he had come through on his promises to simulate a menacing rage. However, his true enthusiasm had been reserved for fashioning a 'funky' disguise.

When Sonny had entered the bank lobby precisely at 4 p.m., closing time, he was carrying a gray, nylon, carry-on flight bag from which he pulled a silver semi-automatic handgun. He was wearing black motorcycle-type gloves with red stripes running down the fingers. (They reminded Leisha of the burned out veins along Sonny's pitted forearm.)

He was also wearing a beige hooded sweatshirt, a black baseball cap, camouflaged battle-dress-uniform pants, aviator sunglasses, and a black and yellow bandanna over his lower face.

('I wanna bandanna,' Sonny had entreated her, when he had received his last briefing for the heist. He had acted like a sulky spoilt child who feared he might be denied a treat.)

The senior police officer had demanded a description of the robber but all Leisha could say she remembered of the incident were 'three eyes'.

She had rehearsed her statement and knew exactly what she intended to say. *Three eyes. I swear. That's all I saw. Two eyes leveled at me and the eye of the gun!*

She swallowed hard at the thought of the supreme trust she had invested in Sonny . . . those two eyes and that unwinking eye of the gun.

The descriptions of the unknown masked man given by the clerks at the neighboring desks had not been any more conclusive: 'a hideous little guy with creepy eyes' and 'a spaced out drugnut waving a pistol looking like a mad scientist.'

Leisha recalled Sonny's sallow face, slick with sweat, and rapid tongue darting to wet his cracked lips. His repetitive demoniacal screaming of 'Gimme all your money! *Right now!*' had achieved its desired effect. Leisha had promptly obeyed.

The subsequent bank audit showed that, during the two minutes in which the bank's lobby had been threatened at gunpoint, Leisha had handed over to Sonny one hundred and forty packs of twenty-dollar bills wrapped in violet color straps. Sonny had then swung his fully laden travel bag over his shoulder and escaped into the anonymous afternoon.

And to what destination was this 'hideous', 'spaced out' traveler bound?

Unless she was much mistaken, at this very same moment a stolen four-door white Dodge Neon, license plates unknown, was speeding some fifty miles south on the state highway in the general direction of their would-be rendezvous . . . with Sonny at the wheel, floating weightless, eyelids propped open with amphetamine uppers.

Out of sight, out of mind, she thought. *Longe da vista, longe do coração.*

But my own lonely masquerade is little more than half over and the last act has yet to play.

❀

She must strive to appear composed and *occupied*, she commanded herself, until the bank's closure and her release at 5.15 p.m.

Already the two uniformed cops were removing the yellow police tape which cordoned off the crime scene.

She glanced at her watch. 5.05 p.m.

Leisha straightened a sign above her desk: *Fight Fraud.*

She could not refrain from smiling. There was little she did not know about the varieties of defalcation possible in the practice of personal banking, since she had considered and rejected most of them over her long and systematic search for a deception that would confound her masters.

Leisha was well versed in the most frequent bank swindles and other so-called improprieties; from *salami*-ing (by shaving off fractional cents from thousands of periodic interest payments and crediting them to a single untraceable account), to fraudulent check *kiting* by drawing against insufficient funds.

Nope. She wanted no part in these activities since they were subject to the most vigilant monitoring. For her, a successful fraud to remove a generous portion of her bank's assets, she decided, would be best executed when obeying to the letter the conditions of her fiduciary duty . . . *do not resist, but cooperate unhesitatingly with the robber.*

She thumbed through the PVISP application form that Mac had insisted she complete, and she reread the passage which referred to the underlying purpose of the bank's Post-Violent Incident Support Program:

> Perceived criticism from an employer, a supervisor, or a co-worker can be a major factor in causing on-going emotional problems and loss of self-esteem after the psychological trauma of a violent incident.

She sensed the sinister, soft, gliding footfall which announced Mac's approach.

The contents of the PVISP, she realized, listed any number of anxieties dismissed by men as 'women's weaknesses' which could elicit Mac's sympathy or pander to his patronizing conceit. In such crises his determination to over-compensate by being 'nice' (in his own skewed estimation) was an observable characteristic she intended to exploit.

Mac placed a pitcher of water and a glass on her desk. Somehow he seemed to have guessed the nausea which at that moment had overcome her.

His hand squeezed her shoulder, then he cleared his throat. His breath smelled always of camembert and highland malt whisky.

She wanted desperately to draw back as from some unclean animal but she lifted her bowed head meekly, and met his moist gaze.

His face was rawboned, with deepset eyes, and his tall, gaunt frame brooded over her. Both his hair and his eyelashes were sandy colored and sparse, of a type she had heard some natives of Scotland describe as 'wanthriven'. His nose was pinched and pink, and his prominent adam's apple bobbed nervously above his tight collar.

(Leisha's father, a roadmender by trade, had nurtured a lifelong aversion towards Scotsmen. 'There is no part of the world where a Scotsman cannot be found,' he had repeated with resentment whenever the topic arose. 'Nor any place that would not be the happier without them.')

'Leisha, listen,' breathed Mac confidentially close to her ear. 'You shouldn't reproach yourself. You handled that little psycho real well. I can't see how any one of us could've acted any different. The low-life punk threatened to shoot your pretty little nose off, for gosh sake!'

In fact, Sonny's threatening note, which Leisha had drafted herself, was scrawled with these words in a disguised hand, unrecognizable as her own: *This is a holdup. This gun is NOT a toy. DON'T press the alarm. Give me ALL your money FAST.*

Mac's long spatulate fingers hesitantly circled her wrist. 'Right now, what you need is a diversion. How about a date to shake yourself out of this shocking business? Just you and me, huh?'

It was not the first time he had made advances to her as the solitude of another soulless weekend beckoned.

His smooth fingerti… her goosebumps. Mac ne… currency; the pads of his … cardsharper's from constan…

'What do you suggest?' Leis… chief cashier steadily. She notice… over his freckles with talcum pow…

'Well . . . uh . . . you know, it's … squirming with the effort to convey … planning on throwing some heavy can… was team captain in the inter-banks bow… …ne beer's cheap and there're no leagues until … …yasay?'

Although Leisha had predicted Mac's inv…, just as she had also anticipated her own answer since it was the very essence of her plan, she pretended to demur.

She waited for Mac to repeat his plea then she relented.

'Okay, big guy,' she said, 'lead on.'

❀

In the locker room, at the rear of the bank, Mac and Leisha prepared to leave the building.

Promptly at 5.15 p.m., the staff departed in a concerted rush leaving the chief cashier and an appointed deputy to set the alarms and lock up.

All that week Mac and Leisha had retained dual custody of the back-office keys. Mac's fellow keyholder was appointed on a rota basis, according to the bank's supervisory regulations, to discourage hostage-taking or kidnap for ransom singling out designated personnel. Accordingly, for no more than a month, Leisha had known with certainty that she and Mac would be the last staff members to leave the building on the Friday night she'd chosen for springing her long-overdue surprise.

Mac opened his locker and, with a grunt of exertion, lifted his bowling bag to the floor . . . it was a two-ball locker-trolley weighing twenty-eight pounds.

, suddenly sickened, and closed her own eeming with unwelcome thoughts. Earlier that embered reading in the local press, a woman's head n found in a bowling bag in the next suburb.

Pain again struck her between the eyes like a lightning shock, and bright scintillations behind the eyelids dizzied her to a degree of intensity that found her, slowly, almost unconsciously, clinging to the edge of the locker room door for support, willing Mac to depart.

There was a sense of impending danger in the very air, in the loneliness of her position, yet she turned to Mac with resolution and pretended to be brightly attentive to his every word.

The color had drained from her lips, but her mouth was steady and firm.

Mac slapped the contents of his bag, beaming with self-importance. 'My favorite strike balls!' he bragged. 'Last week I nailed six straight strikes with these little fellas. C'mon, let's get outta here!'

❁

When they double-locked the outer door they found the dusk was deepening into night, with the moon riding clear of the clouds. Seeds of snow stung her eyelids and sheshivered.

A silver hip-flask glinted in Mac's hand. He took a swig and smacked his lips.

'Weel, here's to gude company!' The toast was accompanied with a leer. Mac believed he acquired charm by affecting certain Scotticisms in his locutions.

One . . . two . . . three . . . four . . . five seconds, Leisha counted under her breath.

Thirty seconds was the time she'd calculated they would need to cross the asphalt backlot to where Mac routinely parked his car.

Six . . . seven . . . and there it was! The corny, two-door, scarlet convertible droptop was clearly chosen by Mac to fulfill a dream he'd harbored since his youth, in envy no doubt of some adolescent dude.

Leisha thought: *Yuk! Mac's idea of getting in touch with his inner child is a hot date for his Friday night passion-wagon at a drive-in movie with the top down.*

However, on this occasion—a clear but blustery evening—the car's retractable soft-top roof was latched shut against the cold. Placing his locker-trolley on the sidewalk, Mac unlocked the nearside door and jack-knifed his long spindly legs over the passenger footwell to reach his driver's seat.

Eight . . . nine . . . ten . . . eleven . . . Leisha congratulated herself on the accuracy of her month's-long surveillance when observing Mac's daily schedule.

Mac, a creature of unswerving habit, would unfailingly arrive each morning at the bank half an hour earlier than his bosses. Punctually he would reverse with a sidling motion into the most inaccessible parking space on the lot, a snug enclosure where two sheer blank walls met. This bay was so confined he could open neither his own driver's door nor the trunk. Such selflessness, Mac believed, would win favor with the senior bankers, little guessing that this obsequious act would provide Leisha with the most favorable conditions for bringing about his downfall.

Eighteen . . . nineteen . . . twenty . . . Leisha withdrew from her purse a neat stack of banknotes . . . or, to all appearances, a wad of bills no different from those she had thrust into Sonny's eager outthrust hands.

Twenty-seven . . . twenty-eight . . . no time to wait! Leisha hurled the packet into the interior of the car and slammed the door.

Thirty seconds! Her last clear view of Mac was of his craggy face turned to her in total bewilderment as the package detonated with a thunderflash and a vivid red dye sprayed the inside of the windshield.

From within the vehicle could be heard deep gasps and hoarse, frenzied chokings. The air quickly became tainted with an odor as acrid as a spent firework.

'Welcome to splitsville,' Leisha hissed.

She seized the handle of Mac's locker-trolley and sped away into the main street to flag down a cab. In less than a minute she was riding in a taxi to the airport, with the bowling bag safe in her arms, as though this one embrace warmed her heart as no other had in all her adult years.

She thought that she would never be happier than at that moment.

She turned briefly and looked back to see the canopy of Mac's convertible automatically lowering, and Mac—his long upper body stained the brightest red—leaping out, scorched arms flapping, like a demented jack-in-the-box.

'Confidential Disposals'

When they reached the turnoff to the airport, Leisha sat back in the cab and relaxed, dimly aware of the brightly lit buildings flickering past . . . fast-food restaurants, thrift shops, 99 cent stores, druggists, 7-Eleven outlets . . . very soon all these would be emptied of all meaning for her.

Never forget, a warm voice in her head affirmed, *you're a survivor. The greatest risk is not taking one.*

On the distant darkening skyline the colored neon of a casino spelled out: *Break the Bank for a Million Bucks!*

Well. What the heck, her haul had been only one quarter of that sum but Leisha was not dissatisfied with her afternoon's work.

She half closed her eyes and like a five-star general she retraced step by step the private campaign she had waged, and exulted in its successful outcome.

The idea for her deception first came to her when the bank introduced a cost-saving machine for the degradation of used notes in circulation.

The bank tellers were advised to cancel used banknotes of unacceptable quality by feeding them into the automatic cash-canceling machine after sorting.

Thus, in the past week, Leisha had been able to amass, in the 'Canceled for Collection' hutch of her cashier's desk, one hundred and forty packs of twenty-dollar bills, wrapped in florescent yellow color straps. Each stack, processed by the canceling machine, had been punched through in a domino pattern with six standard 12 mm holes.

Throughout the late afternoon she had substituted clean negotiable twenty-dollar bills in her till for the degraded punched banknotes, which, in turn, she rewrapped in violet color straps to falsely denote legitimacy.

Up until then her preparations had been mercifully uneventful.

And the transit to the back office of one hundred and forty packs of seemingly canceled twenty-dollar bills, now wrapped in yellow color straps, had attracted no remark.

Yet, there was no reason for her actions to excite interest; after all, 'Confidential Disposals' were part of her routine.

There had been a moment of alarm when she had transferred Mac's two favorite strike balls from his trolley-bag to her locker, and one had caromed off the rear panel with a metallic clash.

She had experienced an all-consuming rush of adrenaline. Fortunately, no one entered to see her load Mac's bag with the one hundred and forty bundles of oh-so-used-and-untraceable currency.

She had not miscalculated: a locker-bag containing two balls each weighing fourteen pounds is no different in weight to 280,000 dollars, all in twenties.

Certainly Mac had not noticed the difference.

Nor, for that matter, had Sonny in his frantic, drug-fuelled haste noticed the substitution of the punched bills. And to the gawking bank staff, observing the unfolding drama in appalled fascination, the regulation-issue violet color straps were signal enough of the notes' authenticity.

No doubt, at this very minute, Sonny was holed up beside a creek, on some dusty back road, sprawled in his getaway car, and opening his first pack of twenties to discover the notes were so much sausage-stuffing and punched right through with six fat zeros.

Nothing! *Nada!* Zilch!

She imagined his look of utter desolation as he toked up on his last joint of laughing grass. *Poor Sonny, definitely a classic weirdo! No more candy!*

Of course, Sonny and the bank security guard had never been in any real danger of shooting each other. She had assured Sonny that the guard visited the john like clockwork . . . on the hour. She had even taken a secret polaroid to demonstrate the fact.

Now, thinking of that final week—the anxiety and jittery suspense of it all—she shivered.

The worst moments for arousing suspicion, she had known from the very beginning of her stratagem, would be the vital seconds between Mac entering his car and her wresting the stolen dollars from his unwitting possession.

The solution had presented itself in the guise of the explosive dummy dye-pack, a cash degradation system designed to stain stolen cash indelibly. This special pack of real bills, in twenty-dollar denominations, was virtually indistinguishable from a regular stack of money except the dye device was concealed in its center. As Mac would learn to his cost, the stains from the red aerosol smoke and dye, when they came into contact with skin or clothing, would be embarrassingly difficult to remove.

He would have a hell of a lot of explaining to do; both his clothes and reputation were now in tatters.

Like the other tellers, Leisha had at all times, near to hand on her desk, a dye pack set in 'safe' mode attached to a special magnetic plate. Within the dye package was a small radio receiver that would be triggered when the pack was discreetly palmed by the clerk to be yielded up, among other wads of cash, to the robber. *But* . . . and this was the extra-cunning part of Leisha's plan . . . while the thief (in this case, *herself*) was still inside the bank, the pack would remain *dormant.*

Leisha knew that a small radio transmitter was mounted near the bank's entrance. Once the dye pack passed outside the building, and received the radio signal, it activated. She also knew her dye pack was set on a timer of thirty seconds to ensure any criminal was in his getaway car before the package exploded.

Mac had proposed a *diversion*; she had not disappointed him.

Did Mac deserve this act of retribution? Not for one instant did Leisha question the justice of smiting her foe.

A month earlier, when silently entering the locker room, Leisha had heard a gust of malicious laughter. A bull session with some of the guys from 'Confidential Disposals' had been in progress over which Mac had evidently presided. Unseen, she'd heard Mac confide lazily to a junior intern: 'Sure as hell that bean-eating euro-spic knows I have a crush on her, but what I want to know is has she one on me?'

Leisha thought: He's not worth my prayers. *When your boss is no good, you shouldn't waste good candles on him.*

Una Strada aos Esses

She arrived at the airport with ten minutes to spare to board her flight. She was traveling business class and the maximum weight allowance of her carry-on luggage was thirty pounds so, before she checked in, the absconding bank clerk stole a little time to buy mineral water and bitter black grapes.

Leisha thought: *These grapes are like eating the autumn.*

Who can explain the pangs of memory, and when they strike?

She remembered wandering as an infant with her father in his small vineyard and how his little sickle-bladed knife had separated the bunches . . . the succulence of those Portuguese grapes from his *vinhinha* of vines and flower gardens on the foothills of her village could never be recaptured.

The neighboring grower whose land surrounded her father's plot was a well-known port wine producer, a notorious drunkard of Scottish ancestry. His family had been established in the region since the early eighteenth century.

The face of the Scot had resembled a side of British beef and, following local custom, he was generally known by the name of Bife among the villagers.

According to family legend, Leisha's father, so she believed as a child, had been contracted by Bife to build a road through the landowner's estate. As the work advanced, the whisky-swilling *bêbado* had become progressively more drunk and uncommunicative. With each appearance of the drunkard the roadworks were halted while Leisha's father attempted to clarify instructions for directing the route. To her father's questions the Scot slurred an affirmative: ''Es, 'es.' So her father, a simple man, had put another 's' in the road until it snaked in and out of the terraced vines to double its intended length . . . *una strada aos esses*.

The cost of litigation against Bife to seek settlement for unpaid bills, and a frivolous countersuit claim, had been the source of her father's financial ruin, and his undying hatred of all Scotsmen.

Diabo daqueles estrangeiros! The voice of Leisha's father still raged in her head. *To hell with these foreigners!*

This bitter grudge had been compounded when her father was forced to sell the family *vinhinha* and Bife had outbid the other creditors.

Perhaps, Leisha reflected, as the aircraft leveled off over the ocean, she had been unduly harsh on Mac by making him the scapegoat for the hateful Scotsman who had so dishonored her family.

And Sonny, too, would never forgive or comprehend her betrayal.

The pity of it was that neither man would ever know her true motives for the crime. In recent months, the pulsating phantom voices of her dead parents resounding in her head had grown distressingly louder and more insistent until a visit to her doctor had confirmed her worst fears.

Her doctor had first diagnosed *tinnitus aurium* but a further audiometric examination by a neurotologist had identified complications: an acoustic neuroma, a tumor dangerously near the brain requiring surgical removal.

Her terror of the possibility of a botched operation had ignited in her the profoundest reaction: to seek out the world's most celebrated neurosurgeon, whatever the costs.

She had located her miracle-working surgeon in a gun-toting South American city, which ironically boasted the world's highest death toll from head wounds. However, against this inconvenience was weighed the advantage of an ineffective extradition treaty which failed to remove overseas criminals who sought refuge in the capital. Besides, her body craved comfort. In this new city she would again speak her native language freely, and enjoy a mild climate where windchimes sounded gently all the year round.

So when Leisha had added the surgeon's fees for microsurgery to the costs of her hospitalization and convalescence, and checked and rechecked the daunting sums required for her recovery, she knew she had but one path to take.

Once her course had been set there was no going back.

And yet, when all was said and done and ordained, had she been found so wanting in virtue, and so unworthy?

Sinking back into the softness of her fully reclining seat, lulled by the steady throb of the engines, Leisha heard again her mother's voice, sent like a tongue of flame to illuminate her inner darkness. *Ladrão que rouba ladrão tem cem anos de perdão*, her mother whispered reassuringly in her ear. *The thief who steals from a thief has one hundred years of pardon.*

MR & MRS CAMILLA REVISITED

(*Charlotte N.* — Buspirone)

Assessment Summary (extract): This patient participated in three hours of testing and a one-hour diagnostic interview. Neuropsychiatric tests were normal except for subtle memory deficits which were exhibited in her speech by inconsistencies in her confabulation of remembered experience. As this patient becomes more integrated and less dissociative she may become more able to clarify for herself the relative accuracy of her memories.

MR & MRS CAMILLA REVISITED

Patient ID CPN0304290749: Charlotte N.
Occupation: Market researcher for UK pharmaceutical company.
Drug: Buspirone.
Drug class: Anxiolytic azapirones.
Common side effects: Dizziness, light-headedness, nausea and headaches.

THAT MORNING I awoke to a smell of smoke as though our house was burning down.

In the event, the fire was a false alarm; my husband had merely burnt the toast—for him, an unaccustomed task — but, as I was soon to discover, my home was, indeed, doomed to spontaneous combustion, for on that otherwise special day, my birthday, my husband chose devastatingly to abandon me.

The date would have been memorable for quite another reason. Wednesday 29th July 1981 was a national holiday to honour the wedding of Prince Charles and Lady Diana Spencer. That's why my husband was, unusually, at home on a weekday.

The occasion, then, was a double celebration—a champagne TV-viewing party with a circle of our closest friends.

All our guests arrived mid-morning in good time to see Lady Diana leave Clarence House in her fairytale glass coach. That's when my husband began pouring the bubbly.

I shall always remember he had frosted the rims of the glasses with sugar; to sweeten the bitter pill which came half an hour later, I wonder?

I regret now the impulse which compelled me to assent to the absurd entre-acte which my best friend (?) then proposed. We were all *ooh*ing and *aah*ing at the Emanuels' bridal gown, an ivory silk confection which practically enveloped Diana like a collapsed parachute, when my 'friend' urged me to dress up in my own bridal finery. Just for a lark, she said.

So at 10.55 a.m. I floated downstairs in my own dress of Brussels lace. It was a copy of a gown from the 1930s, a princess-line strapless dress with a dropped waist and the under-skirt cut in figured panels of taffeta the colour of Cornish cream. The thing still fitted perfectly (36-29-46) and I received a tremendous ovation. But I saw the face of my husband darken; his eyelids were hooded and he strode out into the garden puffing furiously on a black cheroot. (At that time he was a civil servant, a Grade 5 Assistant Secretary, and, in the pecking order, he docilely followed the practice of his principal who smoked half Coronas.)

A garden must be a place that resonates with the animus of betrayal I would afterwards conclude because, out of the corner of my eye, I saw him flick his cigar butt into my flower border and crush it decisively underfoot.

Nonetheless, later, in the kitchen (by that time, Princess Di, her own dress a crushed meringue, had been debouched from the carriage), I was wholly startled when my husband whispered harshly in my ear the astonishing words: 'You may keep your lover, damn you, and good riddance to you both!'

He was holding a scrap of paper torn from my diary. Ridiculous man! The scribbled phrase he objected to was an idly unscanned parody of mine derived from Elizabeth Barrett Browning's 'How Do I Love Thee? Let Me Count The Ways.' You may judge the gravity of my crime. The objectionable couplets were: *'I love thee for thy depth and breadth and height/I crave thy soft embrace just every night/On thy pale form I long to rest my head/My comforter, nay, my saviour! My bed!'*

There had recently been an acrimonious running dispute between us concerning my unremitting fatigue. (A little later I was diagnosed with an overactive thyroid. Indeed, my hyperthyroidism accounted not only for my muscle weakness but for also the weight loss that granted me the frame to pour myself into a dress a decade old.)

I remember I shook my head in disbelief as he marched out of my life there and then to the strains of an organ voluntary.

There was the sound of a clockwork oven timer, too. I had been baking a *tourte bourguignonne* (without garlic, for my husband had a parochial palate and abhorred the taste; as likewise does, I believe, Her Majesty the Queen).

Not a confidence did I betray to my friends on that day.

Much later, there was an attempt at a reconciliation. Our meeting at a marriage guidance counsellor's was a charade. My husband would not say anything, not a word, and insolently read the Court Circular column as though he were still in his office.

Only, remotely, on the phone, did the source of his disaffection become known to me. My anaemia had become repugnant to him. My hair at that time was lank and greasy. He said I had a revolting habit of screwing my hair up into an unbecoming tuft and soaping my ears. It turned out that, when a child, my husband was the fond owner of a sleepy tortoiseshell Japanese bobtail cat named Neko with a kink in its tail . . . my appearance seemed to insult the memory of Neko.

(I have my own memories, too. My grandfather and his clubland chums used to breathe cigar fumes on me when I was a toddler, half sleeping in my cot.)

Of course, I never mentioned to my husband his own soft breath on my face at night tainted with hickory-cured Kentucky tobacco.

A 'Blip' on the Graph

The following year, 1982, we were divorced. If you look carefully at Britain's national statistics you'll see that, funnily enough, 1981 saw a significant decline in the UK's divorce rate yet divorces rose to pre-1980 levels in 1982. A pronounced 'blip' on the graph of marital discord, wouldn't you agree?

Surely those statistics show that I was not alone in becoming a divorcee on that momentous day? I was one of many victims as the brilliance of a much-wished-for fairytale romance threw the flaws in vulnerable marriages into stark relief.

Don't they say Diana's glass coach turned into a pumpkin because Charles, after their exchange of vows at the altar, forgot to kiss his bride?

So it's fair to say we both shared bad omens that day.

'If only,' I sometimes chide myself, even now. If only I had not so timorously fled the danger signals of my condition. (Eventually, I underwent radioiodine therapy successfully to control my hyperthyroidism without side effects.)

If only I had glared like Miss Havisham, when told, 'How well you look!' and answered, 'I do not, I am yellow skin and bone.'

At least Miss Havisham was honest about her cobweb-festooned bride-cake. She did not shun, but rewrote, her tragedy as a jilted bride. And, curiously, as I recall, Miss Havisham rejected the sentiments of certain vapid wellwishers, Camilla and her husband, and their false solicitude.

As Camilla's husband, 'Mr Camilla' (styled thus by Dickens), sycophantically soothes: 'Camilla, my dear, it is well known that your family feelings are gradually undermining you to the extent of making one of your legs shorter than the other.'

According to her own account, Camilla suffers sleepless nights, remorseful for the abandoned bride, relieved only by ginger and sal volatile.

Camilla confides that 'Mr Camilla' is witness to the nocturnal nervous jerkings of her legs. 'I have taken to the sofa with my staylace cut, and have lain there hours, insensible, with my head over the side, and my hair all down, and my feet I don't know where . . .' ('Much higher than your head, my love,' says Mr Camilla.)

And mentioning 'Mr and Mrs Camilla', as two of a kind, reminds me of another significant day far earlier than that royal wedding almost a quarter of a century ago.

Much farther back in time.

A Mirror Misting Over

When I was a child in Sussex, I attended Dumbrells school in Ditchling. ('A Dame School,' my grandfather called it. Because of its nearness to the wild heathland of Ditchling Common the local rector labelled Dumbrells a 'Hedge School'.)

A fellow pupil was a girl by the name of Camilla Shand.

So you can see the affinity I claim with the fortunes of Princess Diana and Camilla Parker Bowles (née Shand) is not as tenuous as you may imagine.

Two memories stand out from my early schooldays.

There was a fashion, I remember, to affect a languid school drawl, a certain slanginess when addressing individual girls.

The fad was something after the Russian manner of stressing the second syllable with trochaic emphasis, then adding an 's'. Lucinda became 'Cinders', for example, and I knew a girl named Theresa who, by extension, became 'Razors', even.

As I recall, a 'Camilla' was transposed through two tonal keys from 'Millers' to 'Dusty Millers', and then to plain 'Dusty'. This progression was quite natural, given we were mostly Sussex folk, dwelling beneath the Downs where windmills are commonplace.

That Camilla was kindly disposed there can be no doubt. On a Nature Drawing class on the Common, a vicious older girl once jabbed my forearm with a deadly sharp 4H pencil. (I still bear the mark.) Camilla patched me up with an impeccably creased handkerchief she produced from the top of one of her lisle stockings (a repository then customary).

Forgive me, but now, when I hold a mirror up to the past, I find the glass misting over.

In recent years I have lived in constant dread of panic attacks and every so often I am overcome by a terrible sense of something terrible about to happen. My fingers become numb, my heart races, there's a buzzing in my ears, and I'm conscious of such an overwhelming heat within me that I fear any moment I'll burst into flames from the very core of my being. However, my dosage has been increased to 45 mg a day and I'm assured that my condition will be stabilised after another week of treatment. Well, we shall see.

But to resume.

I do remember one other school outing when Camilla was present.

The walk in our crocodile file was very short. Just a few yards up the road, to be accurate.

We were visiting a dark, red-bricked benevolent institution which Dickens might have conceived himself in one of his more misanthropic moods.

The place stands there to this very day, among the furze bushes and fern-brakes, on the edge of Ditchling Common: a Rest Home for Distressed Thames Lightermen (dockers and bargees) founded by a wealthy local silk merchant. There is a vast anchor on the portico.

An ancient bargee was expecting us. Somehow his rooms evoked fog-bound wharves. (They were painted a dark green with surplus paint once destined for Thames barges.)

We small girls each sat on the bargee's knees while he demonstrated the hazards of unloading cargo in the West India Docks.

'Stand from under!' he boomed, and we fell between his legs.

I remember one little girl, perhaps of a more refined class, maintained a dutiful snootiness, and refused to participate.

Breaking the Unlucky Spell

So what remains of my tale? A keepsake box with a champagne cork tagged '1981'. A nervously bitten cigar butt. A clockwork oven timer fixed at forty-five minutes (that *tourte bourguignonne* in 1981 was set at Regulo 5).

At such moments I remember Miss Havisham and her once white dress, all yellow and brittle, in a state that crumbled under her touch. The withered bridal dress which looked so like grave-clothes, or the long veil so like a shroud. And, of course, I think, too, of the clocks in Miss Havisham's unchanging rooms all stopped together.

While everything else outside Miss Havisham's rooms grew older, those clocks just stood still.

So you will not be surprised to learn that I've devised, at long last, a ruse to thwart this run of bad luck.

It is superfluous to relate that my daughter never wore my bridal dress at her own (civil) ceremony, but my elder grand-daughter insists she wear it. She is marrying a Frenchman.

He, knowing of the dress's baleful history, says that French custom will break the unlucky spell as it's traditional to auction the bride's veil, etc., for the benefit of the married couple.

With my permission, bride and groom are planning to dismember my wretched bridal dress of all its rosettes and frillings and trimmings at the reception by auctioning it.

So like, perhaps, the stage-managed photocall of the royal ceremony, in this Year of Great Expectations* for crown and commoner alike, a memory of a former unhappy marriage may be dispelled.

* Written by Charlotte N. in 2005 and published as 'A Case of Literary Prochronism' in 'Ambit', Summer Issue 181, 2005. (The narrative was prompted by the announcement of the marriage of Prince Charles to Camilla Parker Bowles in a civil ceremony on Saturday April 9 2005 in the Guildhall in Windsor.) Her scurrilous quotations in reference to Pip ('Philip') and his prochronistically libellous views of 'Mrs Camilla' have been excised from this text.

YOU BETTER GO NOW

(*Zoë W.* — AMITRIPTYLINE)

'Let us love dogs, let us love only dogs!
Men and cats are unworthy creatures.'

— MARIE BASHKIRTSEFF, feminist painter (nom de plume, PAULINE ORREL)

Assessment Summary (extract): For this patient, delayed recall of traumatic experiences, and their accompanying emotions, have triggered a regression in her treatment and, in consequence, the process of grief has been much prolonged. To limit the duration and severity of this regression the patient should be assisted, with the aid of a balanced view, to evaluate the fallibility or accuracy of the recollected traumatic material that emerges during treatment.

Note: Specialist readers may remark on what appearsto be a not unadventitious recurrence of a tape recording as a convenient exegesis of this patient's history (cf. CPN0319141245 Esther G.); however, in both cases, the similarity of method and coincidence of widowhood reflect the growing popularity of self-narrative approaches (such as journals, correspondence, or autobiographies) encouraged by psychotherapists in the analysis of self-characterisations. As may be noted in comparing these cases, this theoretical approach can provide the means to self-understanding in practice. One of the psychotherapy approaches devised for restabilising the patient, and bridging the gap between inner and outer worlds, is as follows:

Five Adaptive Tasks for the Recently Bereaved

1. Establish meaning and personal significance of the bereave ment;
2. Confront reality and respond to it;

3. Keep communication flowing and maintain interpersonal relationships;
4. Maintain emotional balance and hold on to hope;
5. Preserve satisfactory self-image.

(See my Course Notes, *Grief Has Many Guises*, Experiential Self-Narrative Assignments in Psychotherapy.)

YOU BETTER GO NOW

Patient ID CPN0291070651: Zoë W.
Occupation: Charitable trust fundraiser.
Drug: Amitriptyline.
Drug class: Tricyclic antidepressant.
Common side effects: Blurred vision.Orthostatic hypotension. Depressive-like symptoms if taken with alcohol.

AFTER MY HUSBAND died I refused to set foot in our living room. For three weeks I roamed the house collecting every keepsake of our marriage for storage in grocery cartons. Then I packed them rafters-high in the garage and padlocked the doors.

My doctor referred me to a psychiatrist who treated me for a severe depressive illness.

During the winter I virtually hibernated, lying hidden by a coverlet, drugged half comatose by Amitriptyline, my ears plugged by radio headphones, as earthlings from the BBC World Service called to me across immense spaces.

I had been warned of the side effects—delusions, confusions, nightmares, hallucinations, hypomanic reactions of deranged elevated moods—but any memory of such cautions had no power to constrain my impulse when, one rainy day in late spring, I packed the hatchback with the wreckage of our marriage, bound for the vicarage car boot sale.

Reversing, I observed a splash of petrol on the wet driveway. An iridescent peacock's tail, I thought. An evil eye: the augery of bad luck. The petrol tank had, in fact, a pin-hole leak due its long-neglected wintering.

I marked that day with another black stone.

❁

There is a great burden of sadness overhanging car boot sales, those sellers of the flotsam and jetsam from a hundred marriages.

In fact, the event was in aid of the belltower restoration fund; we had been married in the church. Ironic, I mused, that a collapsing institution should be supported by another, for, looking around me as I set up my stall, I recognised the majority of visitors to be divorcees.

I was fearfully tired; for months I had neglected to eat; my weight loss had been dramatic. I examined my appearance in my compact mirror; I barely recognised myself — since the turn of the year I had lost fifty pounds — so there was every chance I could mingle unseen.

At first I traded briskly: Mike's rowing machine, his squash racquet, his collection of Patrick O'Brian's novels, his box of unused chisels, his orienteering Lensatic compass, and his bone-handled clasp knife, among others, were swiftly snapped up.

Then people drifted away and my fatigue became all-consuming. I was just on the point of admitting defeat, and decamping unremarked, when a familiar voice called, 'Debs! Hold the fort!', and I shaded my eyes to follow Deborah's aunt, the very woman I was most anxious to avoid, setting off, bargain-hunting, counter-clockwise, round the avenue of stalls . . . to be distracted for an hour, at the very least.

I crossed the grass to Deborah's stall. I was not mistaken — sullen Deborah was the long-dead Isabel's sole surviving daughter, and the child's likeness to her father was uncanny. At the thought of Hugh my breathing quickened. Mercifully, there was no danger of Deborah attaching my name to the stricken face before her. Besides, poor Debs was moodily reading a glossy magazine and paid no attention to the shadow who picked over her departed mother's trinkets on the makeshift trestle table.

Another broken marriage!

I bought Isabel's Kenwood mixer, her electric sewing machine, and a stencilled linen tablecloth with chainstitching which Isabel had not lived to complete. The tragi-comical impropriety of it! The worldly goods of Isabel, the *home-maker*, purchased as momentos all these years later by myself, the villainous *home-breaker*!

As an afterthought, I bought three of Hugh's C-90 audio cassettes — his recordings from *'Bop for Kerouac'* (tracks typical of Hugh's vintage, I recalled). Mike had played muted trumpet to Hugh's slinky lead alto sax in their amateur septet when they had studied together at medical school.

Forbidden memories began to stir within me and a pricking of tears blurred my sight.

The public-address speakers announced an unintelligible event.

In my hasty retreat, I almost blundered unseeing into the wheelchair of a stately nonagenarian who was demanding autocratically of her companion the meaning of the announcement. The tannoy was annoyingly intrusive.

'Mama, dear, they're publishing the fete,' answered a septuagenarian. In speech and manner they were *positively* eighteenth century, I reflected, and thought no more about them.

Once safely unobserved in the car, and driving from the fete, I glanced at the three cassettes: *'Ballad of the Sad Young Man'*, *'You Better Go Now'*, and a hand-labelled recording, in Hugh's practically indecipherable prescription-writing scrawl, overscribed with my name, the date of my birthday, twenty long years before, and the legend: *'You Make It So Hard To Say No'*.

If my heart gave any sign that I was touched by emotion I was indifferent to it. I thought: I have no heart to break so I should have no more tears to shed.

I inserted the cassette into the dashboard-mounted player.

A Whistling Jazz-Dog

Extraordinary! Two voices, each one once dear to me!

I heard the voice of my late husband, laughing, then the voice of his oldest friend, Hugh, chiming in.

There was the background roar of Hugh's rattletrap of a jeep revving. *Then I remembered.* That day, when twenty years' younger, we had all been going to the pub for a lunchtime birthday drink. I had driven with Isabel; the two men had followed together, with Hugh driving.

What was Mike saying to Hugh? I tuned down the bass notes and turned up the volume.

Mike (laughing): *I was watching his face when you were playing Art Tatum last night. Whistling he was!*

(Transmission of the men's talk was scrambled by loud asthmatic breathing.)

Hugh: *Yeah! Shame they didn't tape Arty on the Steinway.*

Jazz! Our husbands seemed to talk of nothing else!

(Resumed sound of whistling. That wheezing must be Isabel's ancient King Charles spaniel, Mopy; it was prone to a congestive respiratory condition; the microphone was amplifying the vibration from the dog's chest wall.)

Hugh: *I've belted him, and belted him, but he won't stop.*

(A whistling jazz-dog! They were all jazz-dogs, I thought.)

Mike (shouting at dog): *For pity's sake! Give it a rest! He's worse with the indicator on!*

Hugh: *He behaves better in the front seat, in the well of the car. Put him on that blanket in the well.*

(The blanket! I remembered that blanket. Hugh and I had lain on it under the stars the night before my birthday.)

Mike: *Can I go a week without washing my armpits?*

Hugh: *Depends. Nudge nudge, wink wink.*

Then the remark about Mike's armpit became clear. There was a conspiratorial exchange.

Hugh: *You still got it on?*

Mike: *Yeah. In stereo. Got it under me armpit. Not pleasant.*

(So Mike was the secret sound-recordist! An accomplice under Hugh's orders! How entirely characteristic of Mike—dominated by Hugh, as always. The device must have been hidden under my husband's arm with a trailing microphone.)

Hugh (languidly): *Isabel's knitting a bird for your Christmas tree.*

Mike (feigning interest): *Yeah? She's a super lady.*

(There was crunching of gravel. Evidently they had arrived at the pub to be greeted by the publican, Old George.)

Old George (familiarly): *You are in trouble, my son!*

(Now I recalled the scene. Arriving early, Isabel and I had been kept waiting at the bar.)

Hugh: *Go away, you horrible little man!*

(A gust of laughter.)

Hugh (ordering two more wines): *Best get them in. The same again but with an accent . . . Gewürztraminer.* (The squeak and popping of a cork.) *And a brace and half of English.*

(Mike and Hugh drank beer. The odd half was the 'usual' for George.)

Hugh: *Happy days!*

(They were, I thought. God! Those days were so blissfully happy, when I had been in love with Hugh!)

Hugh: *I'm gonna put Boz Scaggs on.*

(Footsteps as Hugh walks behind the bar to the pub's music system. Then a flood of mellow sound momentarily drowns our voices.)

Mike (murmuring to Hugh): *Uh-huh. I notice. I get it! 'How Long Has This Been Going On?' Nudge nudge, wink wink.*

(*The fool!* My husband always was such a fool! *'I notice!!!'* When, all along, *un*noticed, his own wife was conducting an affair with his best friend, under his very nose!)

Hugh (fingers tapping): *Quiet! I'm appreciatin' the good sinds!*

(Now Hugh was affecting his Prince Charles 'silly ass' voice. I couldn't help smiling. At this very instant, just as then, all that time ago, I found Hugh's sly superficial humour unaccountably attractive.)

Mike (confidentially to Old George): *No kiddin', the guitarist when he turns up for sessions always has a dozen gold labels in his guitar case. Hands shaking, nine o'clock in the morning, isn't that right, Hugh?*

Hugh: *That's why he does that pub gig down the Old Kent Road.*

Mike: *He counts all his wages in pints. When he's paid he takes out all his wife's money then sees how many pints he has to last the week.*

(I thought: Being the guitarist's wife might have been no bad thing; at least one knew where one stood.)

Hugh (interrupting): *Listen! I can't work out the changes in the first three bars!*

(Hugh and Mike attempt to sing them. Then Hugh resumes, whistling, pitch perfect.)

Hugh (to Mike, in muttered aside): *That pub. They've got an art-eestes' bar backstage. 3.30 till the morning. Can't tell what's daylight.*

Mike (admiring undertone): *So that's where you've been? Their singer, Evie what's-her-name?*

Hugh: *What could I do? After she'd finished singing they were still strumming their set. She was all alone, poor kid, looking for a sugar daddy, cos' of the aggro from her agent.*

(Sickened, I halted the car so abruptly cars hooted. I drove into a lay-by. My breathing was no less rapid than the long-lamented Mopy's. Now the soundtrack had switched to one of Hugh's classic Charlie Parker recordings: *'Gonna take a sentimental journey to renew old mem-o-ries.'*)

Hugh was still softly crooning (*'Got my bag, I got my reservation . . .'*), when I jabbed the car's tape-deck to switch it off. I wound down the window and swallowed great gulps of cold moist air.

Evie! A jazz singer! Hugh's *other* other-woman! And, until this precise moment, I had not once suspected that young woman's existence.

Distantly, the belltower rang.

Then, at the final stroke, so many of the mysteries from my muddled past fell away into dissolution.

a) The mystery of why no hint of suspicion had ever once been breathed abroad to betray my love for Hugh.

b) The mystery of Hugh's abrupt hurtful termination of our affair.

c) The mystery of Isabel's suicide; a suicide for whose provocation I had secretly held myself responsible for the past twenty years.

Over two decades I had harboured my guilty secret, for guilt is always jealous, guarding against exposure . . . yet, in the event, how falsely had all those years of unconfessed self-recrimination blighted my thoughts, and how unjustly had that ghost from my past hounded me into paranoiac fear.

A Pillow in Her Greenest Field

I slunk home to my self-imposed captivity, the more sombre for my brief release.

In the abandoned borders, dwarf pansies nodded their tragicomical pierrot masks in the rain.

Beneath my modest apartment was Mike's clinic; his practice had been sold but I still retained the key.

The night of my return from the vicarage fete, more heavily burdened with a basket of troubles than when I'd departed, I wandered through the darkened rooms of the old surgery.

Hugh and Mike had been business partners, as well as best friends.

After Hugh's flight from the chaos of his devastated marriage whose final reckoning had been Isabel's suicide, Mike had mourned as though for a lost brother. Hugh had never once telephoned, nor written. Not even a postcard. He must have dropped out of sight with that scat-singing Evie and all hell to pay.

The septet became a sextet, but everyone agreed the seductive notes of Hugh's special, stifled, velvety sound were beyond recapturing.

Hugh's own room in the surgery was locked permanently; Mike had not had the heart to reassign it.

Now I placed the key in the lock of the door to that unforgotten room.

The contents of Hugh's consulting chambers were unchanged.

Under a Petri dish was trapped, for some reason, a blackened, half-eaten biscuit—a crescent moon, with Hugh's bite mark out of it.

(I thought of Hugh's mouth on mine.)

I approached Hugh's leather-topped desk.

A framed snapshot of the devoted Mopy. A blotter. A date stamp. An ink pad.

I stamped the blotter. I calculated the date in June was ten days later than my birthday, twenty long years before.

The date of Isabel's death and Hugh's departure.

An entire, intimate, integrated world had been shaken and shattered in ten days.

I steadied myself on the edge of the desk and a metal kidney bowl containing tongue depressors clattered to the floor.

Uncomprehending, I began to read a notice on the wall: *The Misuse of Drugs Act. A list of controlled drugs: Amphetamine and Dexamphetamine. Benzphetamine. Chlorphentermine. Mephentermine. Methaqualone. Methylphenidate. Phenmetrazine.*

My vision swam.

I attempted to focus on the faded calendar still affixed to the wall.

Hugh had circled my birthday with three concentric red rings.

Above the chart chronicling that month of June so long ago, a photograph depicted an Alpine village hemmed by flower-decked fields (the calendar promoted Geigy Pharmaceuticals).

A sob caught in my throat when I read the calendar's verse: *'When the night and morning lie . . . will be time enough to die; then will yet my mother yield a pillow in her greenest field, nor the June flowers scorn to cover the clay of their departed lover.'*

Isabel's body had been found on June 17th in a field, four miles from the surgery; she had placed herself at the very spot where Hugh and I had lain as lovers.

Isabel had swallowed 500 mg of dexamphetamines (Hugh at that time had been prescribing for a patient diagnosed with narcolepsy); as a doctor's wife, Isabel was fully aware of the quantity for a lethal overdose.

Isabel's spaniel, Mopy, lay dead at her side.

I sank awkwardly into Hugh's chair, head buried in my hands.

The incident in the field that warm June night still made very little sense to me.

On the eve of my birthday, that night, we'd all four of us been drinking a good deal but both Hugh and I had the stronger heads and could sink more than the others; or so we had supposed.

Isabel and Mike had retired to sleep, whoozily overcome from sampling Hugh's ten-year-old, eighty-six proof, unblended malt whisky.

That's how our illicit tryst was made possible; Hugh had even taken the blanket embroidered *Surgery One* (stitched in red thread by Isabel) from the examination couch which still now stood in this very room.

That June night, to be gathered in the fold of Hugh's arms had been so languorously satisfying. Hugh had given himself unselfishly, considerately, and the marvellous rich sound of his voice, deepened by drink, and his whispered endearments so close to my ear had the effect of pleasurably delaying our impulsive journey to that place of no return some lovers call Remorse.

Hugh said, 'I cannot break away from you.'

To tell the truth I had experienced those moments of touch from other men which felt as animated as wood on wood; but with Hugh I entered a realm of touch which was totally different. In his satin hands my flesh became satin skin.

Hugh had very beautiful hands; doctor's hands. And very fine teeth.

I must have been seduced by his strong, amusing voice, his loving smile, I afterwards concluded.

We played catch with a tender phrase all night long, I remember, reworking the words to suit the night's exertions.

Hugh had been pitch perfect.

Only near daybreak had we heard a car braking swiftly, skidding in the country lane. Footsteps had swished in the grass and then, after an agonising pause, the person hastily withdrew.

Hugh had been nonchalant; I was terrified.

A farmer visiting the beasts of the field, Hugh had said, and laughed.

And thus an aching lust was turned into dust.

A sober Isabel, setting out on a dawn patrol for her errant husband, had discovered his jeep.

In dew-stained footsteps in the grass, I remember, I had singled out one of June's late-blown dandelion heads . . . a globe half-shattered as sign of Isabel's fleeting presence.

When I returned home and slipped into bed, Mike had been still sleeping, snoring like a chainsaw.

Now, seated in *Surgery One*, I reasoned that Mike must have, after Hugh's desertion, bitterly blurted out Evie's name to Isabel because by not a glance, nor glimmer of a remark, did either of them appear to suspect my own betrayal.

So, after all, *another* woman had been the scapegoat for the affair! It was *too* absurd!

Carelessness with a Handbag

I remember distinctly my last conversation with Isabel while we had waited in the pub for our husbands.

As events proved, it was to be the last conversation we were ever to have together in our lives.

Isabel had complained heatedly of the contempt for women displayed by the habitual unpunctuality of men; and she related an incident which illustrated how Hugh's negligent attitude towards his wife was apparent from the earliest days of their marriage.

On the first anniversary of their honeymoon, Hugh had been tasked to travel by train alone carrying Isabel's overnight bag containing her jewel scase and the only item from her wardrobe she regarded as truly haute couture: a dress which had once belonged to her mother.

They were to meet at a hotel in town. At Paddington, Hugh had blithely walked off, leaving her bag in the luggage rack . . . he'd clean forgotten it! She never saw the bag or her family jewels again.

Isabel, who had studied social anthropology, had then bizarrely interpreted the episode of Hugh on the train in terms of Levi-Straussian matrilineal societal theories because, as she explained, she was far wealthier than Hugh.

'Good my leech,' I once heard her declaim with a Shakespearian flourish, in a furious aside to her doctor-husband, 'you shall not have my blood to suck!'

Isabel cited as her *belle ideal* the wealth-holding women in the Cewa tribe in Central Africa, who, so she maintained with ill-concealed relish, treated their husbands virtually like pitiable beggars whose social valuation was zero.

In that tribe, a Cewa husband trailed after his wife bereft of any assets, and his welfare rested entirely with his wife; his relative position was one of inferiority and he had no standing in his wife's village.

In Isabel's view, Hugh had not only profoundly resented the disparity of their respective personal fortunes but, from the outset, literally, had not ever wanted to carry the 'baggage' of wedlock which he associated with the threat of dominance from Isabel's highborn matrilineage.

Well. *That* was Isabel's story, of course.

I knew better.

According to Hugh, such was Isabel's sense of her own deification as an all-knowing domestic goddess, never once had it occurred to her that she had looked perfectly hideous in her mother's Dior dress and pearls.

❀

At these memories of the futility of so many wasted lives, I am ashamed to relate I began to weep in earnest, then to succumb to helpless, hysterical laughter.

Feeble of me, I know, but, as I explained, confusion is one of the side effects of Amitriptyline.

My hands were shaking worse than that dipsomanic guitarist's; I realised my hair and collar were wet and I was shivering from the rain.

Later, in my flat, after I'd changed into my loose bathrobe, I poured myself the stiffest gin-and-tonic straightener ever of my making. That this was the first drink of the day I regarded as rather a downy little feather in my cap.

I lit several candles and turned off all the lamps; in these days of my seclusion behind drawn blinds I preferred candlelight; its soft gleam was more forgiving. I had not washed my hair for a week; I know I must have looked a terrible fright.

I confronted my reflection in the pier glass above the drinks cabinet.

The candlepower was redoubled in the mirror.

I could not deny I'd grown old; an ancient relict. The dark aureolas of my nipples, I saw, had come to resemble two perished rubber sink-plugs.

'Horror, horror, on the wall,' I intoned to myself in a husky stage whisper, 'who is the horriblest of them all.'

Then I replayed the remainder of the tape.

(Twenty years' ago, no different from today, Old George, the publican, continued to drone on about a late-night movie he had been viewing on the television.)

Old George: *Look. I was watchin' the last reel of 'What Ever Happened to Baby Jane' from videoin' it, then the tape ran out. They're on the beach, the two of 'em. So do you know the ending?*

(I had a sudden vision of those two ancient women at the vicarage fete. Had the autocrat in the wheelchair been a prefigurement of what I was about hear?)

Mike (a whispered complaint to Hugh): *Dammit, I've had it on my shoulder since we left the house!*

(Muffled crackling, hissing and auditory distortion, as Mike's hand begins to detach the microphone.)

Involuntarily, twenty years' later, in the here and now, I cried out to my dead husband: *'Don't!'* I wanted so desperately to hear Hugh's voice again, you see.

Mike: *I've had enough! I'm closing this show down!*

Hugh: *Hang on! Just a moment! Happy birthday, darling!*

(Rustle of paper as I unwrap my present: a sinister scarlet knitted bird embroidered in silver thread with *diamanté* eyes and flame-shaped wings of an ethno-spiritual character that recalls Isabel's studies in Afro-anthropology. Mopy barks as he tries to snatch the strange winged creature.)

Me (laughing): *Why, it's wonderful! Whatever is it?*

Isabel (menacingly): *A firebird, of course. Haven't you heard the old fable? It flew about in Paradise quite happily until it was brought down in flames because of the Fall.*

Hugh (warbling; a mocking, extemporary whistle): *Don't they say its song can cure the blind?*

(Hugh continues whistling, pitch perfect.)

Old George (plaintively): *Look! Bette Davis and Joan Crawford, they're on a beach . . . so do you know the ending?*

All (in chorus): *No!*

Old George: *Can't someone please tell me the ending?*

ONE MINUTE APART

(*Elenore S.* — LORAZEPAM)

Assessment Summary (extract): Despite initially accepting the need for supportive counselling to address her anxieties, the patient has paradoxically attempted to avoid treatment during recent crises, and, after her major loss, is increasingly preoccupied with suicidal ideations, at which times she refuses to make the emergency call. At these times the patient, by rejecting appropriate increased levels of care and emergency interventions, remains acutely agitated and overwhelmed by self-destructive thoughts. The patient appears to be unconsciously seeking to avoid taking responsibility for symptom management or life changes and, until these issues are better clarified, a state of almost continual crisis is predicted.

ONE MINUTE APART

Patient ID CPN0268191058: Elenore S.
Occupation: Geopolitical cartographer.
Drug: Lorazepam.
Drug class: Benzodiazepine anti-anxiety sedative.
Common side effects: Confusion.Changes in vision. Memory disturbance. May impair judgement.

I AM A MADWOMAN. This is a story of vanity and foolishness yet I am not so mad as to name those who have made a fool out of me.

The beginning was innocent enough. 'Pen Pal's Plea', I read in the letters column of our local newspaper. 'Schoolgirl, 18 years, seeks friendship with similar through exchange of letters. Will you be my pen pal?' The letter was signed C. Beauclaire; the address was a P.O. Box number in a small town in West Africa.

But what prompted me to clip out the item and fold it into my purse? It was an involuntary act, I rationalised to myself long afterwards; I had been powerless to repress such a capricious impulse, I reasoned, as I reflected on those first desperate lonely months of abandonment which had followed the death of my much-loved partner, Christina. (She had first won my devotion at university, when she had dwelt in the rarefied air of her final year and I, a fresher, had worshipped her from afar, unnoticed, on the outer fringes of her coterie. Then, years later, both working on our doctorates, we had rediscovered each other and our long enraptured journeying together had begun, our intimate desires so intuitively attuned that I believed, rightly, that such rare tendresses could be ended only by my perfect lover's death or the death of love itself.)

The case being the former, and, at that time, madly inconsolable, I had been prescribed, absurdly, over 5 mg of Lorazepam daily (for hyperanxiety; I was sleeping alone at night as the sole occupant of a house for the first time in my adult life), and thus I had entered that long dark vale of misrule, where my waywardness and the erratic querulousness of my grief had ultimately estranged me from most of our friends; indeed—I admit—eventually, even by my favourite niece was I shunned.

So, that evening, when I smoothed flat the folded press clipping on the tabletop, I believe I can truthfully swear there was no sinister intent in my opening my writing case and reaching for my pen. I thought, merely, selfishly, with the drug-induced twisted logic of the newly bereft: 'Why not make amends for all those lost lonely youthful years before I met Christina?'

Those schoolyard years, more than thirty years before, when the insides of pencil boxes smelled of pine trees. That blazing summer afternoon when suddenly—out of the blue, out of thin air—a bundle of thin blue airmail letters arrived in our classroom bearing intimate intelligence of girls like us, who, our English mistress burbled, belonged to our great Commonwealth family across the sea. (Her voice thrilled as she quoted from Blake: 'O African! Black African! Go wingèd thought, widen his forehead!' She handed us *Par Avion* stickers for our envelopes.)

The most ardent, diligent penpals had soon proved—predictably—to be members of 'the pack', an exclusive clique of boarders (I was a day-girl) who a year before, not long after I had first arrived in the town, had bowed cravenly to the dominion of their simpering goody-two-shoes gangleader to shun the coltish newcomer.

While the sun that summer was brass played loud on the carroty hair of my more popular younger sister, those new classmates of mine cold-shouldered the brash tomboy who could outrace her older brothers, the scapegrace who would rather climb a tree.

No. I never in those schoolyard years could write a coherent line except under compulsion, and, only then, my inky-fingered compositions were in prose as fractured as the breaking voices of my adenoidal brothers.

Yet the truth was I could not have listened to the boasts of those superior girls in that coven wholly without regret as they exchanged their vividly coloured foreign stamps. Their exclusion must have wounded me to some degree. Yes, I thought, the explanation for my revival of this long-forgotten schoolgirl craze was now plain. This was a pang of retrospective envy. Unknowing, I was eager to relive the keen anticipatory thrill of sharing their secret, guileless correspondence with a remote child who had bathed in Africa's sunny fountains or run along India's coral strand.

So I wrote to the mysterious C. Beauclaire. And I was wrong.

And my folly is in what I wrote. For, if I've learnt anything from this episode, I know, now at least, that a fool who starts out in conscious pursuit of artlessness is destined to trip headlong into the snares of artifice, as you can judge for yourself.

It was all there in my first letter.

I Make a Prediction

When I first took up my pen I had decided at once that a sure-fire way to begin would be to make a bold stab at predicting my future penpal's character and history.

On the atlas, I traced the Greenwich Meridian (its white straightedge, incidentally, is incorporated into our town borough's coat of arms; Christina was born here) and I followed its vapour trail as it migrated south from London through Peacehaven to stream out across the Pyrenees and the Gulf of Valencia, until it joined Route Tanezrouft for its 1800 km journey across the Sahara Desert on a direct bearing for the post box of C. Beauclaire.

Who was this schoolgirl with her face hidden behind that shimmering veil of distance?

I thought I would take a chance and guess.

'C', I foretold, wants to be a doctor or a dietitian (Christina had later qualified as a nutritionist); 'C' is, I surmised, an elder daughter, as I am, and, like me, she has older brothers. Oh, and, for good measure, she was born between mid-August and late October. I posted the letter, first enclosing a picture postcard of the town where I live (in a house, by the way, which was once Christina's childhood home). I turned again to the atlas. I measured the distance between the schoolgirl 'C' and myself. Over 4000 km! At a longitude of almost 0° 1′ 30″ E. Looked at like that, we were hardly more than a minute apart.

❁

My New Schoolfriend Replies

When I returned home some two weeks later on the hall mat there was not the tindery blue *aérogramme* I expected but an envelope of the faintest taint of yellow, the colour of bleached bones. I sniffed it, seeking human traces. It was post-marked eight days earlier and inked in one corner was a sketchy sun with hastily scrawled rays. As I began to read, my face burned with shame at my deception. It was clear she was captivated by my interest in her.

'I think you are a clever girl because all what you guess and tell me are true. Please, Elenore, about my birthday you are right. I am going to celebrate my birthday on 21st October. Also, my ambition is to be doctor and I am elder daughter but have two older brothers.' Her other remarks made me blush more furiously. 'From your letter I find out you like best wild animals. In my country there are python, tiger [*sic*], big snak [*sic passim*], cobra snak, lion and many others. I like cinema, reading, letter writing and swimming.' She signed her name: Comfort Beauclaire. (Not so unusual, as I afterwards learnt, as she later mentioned some of her schoolfriends' names, 'Praise' and 'Deliverance'—'Della' for short—and 'Peace' and 'Perpetua'.)

'As we have starting our friendship,' she went on in her broken English, 'I hope we can meet in either your country or mine.' Her final remarks made me feel even shabbier. 'Do you work, Elenore, or do you go to school? Try and tell me more about yourself.' I vowed I would. This time without fudging.

SHE ENCLOSES A PHOTO

My next letter told her the truth about myself and contained a birthday card with a bank note.

Unbidden, I drew a 'Daddy Long Legs' spider on my envelope (a talisman which, like her sunray motif, only we would recognise). I asked her for an account of her daily routine. Comfort's reply was delightful. 'In fact much happinesses were found when I received your letter and learn about you. I hope it was God who gave you up to me. Every morning when I wake up from bed I wash my face and clean my teeth. After that I go for water then I sweep my father's room and clean the chairs, centre table and coffee tables. I go to market to buy food and vegetables for our supper. After supper, I take my library book to read before I go to bed at about 10 o'clock. I must stop here with much looking-forward to hearing from you. I send my picture with this letter.'

The colour snapshot was of a strikingly pretty girl (her forehead was high and noble) in what appeared to be a cotton nurse's uniform with a wide clasp belt. Her gaze was disarmingly frank and her mouth hesitated on the brink of a smile. Could it be that she was a part-time nurse? For she wrote: 'Please my dearest Elenore, the details of my Junior Secondary School study course which I want to follow are Home Economics Management and Food & Nutrition. I have passed my basic education examination but due to financial problems I'm at home unable to continue to higher level.'

Disinterring Christina's archived address book, I dutifully wrote to the International Committee of the Nutrition Society for a recommended text, resulting in my sending a large official manual to Comfort, together with some lighter reading. She was pleased. 'I am with much pleasure to inform you with this humble words. I like your nice study book and everybody also like it to enjoy.'

Clipped to her letter was a testimonial signed by 'Master Justus' who wrote: 'When Comfort was in school she proved to be a serious student, moreover, she was respectful and obedient. Kindly assist her in anything you may give.'

❁

'You'll One Day Hear My Death of Hunger'

There was an interval of some months before I heard from her again, this time from a new city address. 'Please, the reason for taking too long is that I was admitted to the central hospital when I was attacked by disease. I was released only last three days. Please, Miss Elenore, right now there is no money with me. I has to struggle before I get money to feed myself. Oh, please I need your help, if not you will one day hear my death of hunger. I am using new Post Box Number so if someone tell you I had again using old address it is never true. Since you started sending the books some of my friends are jealousing about me. No please, it is not to get to go and marry but I am suffering is why I gone to the city. Why I gone to the city is I am looking for work. Hoping to hear from you soon. Stay sweet and take care. P.S. Hopes our love lasts long and never dies.' I sent her some bank notes slipped into a Get Well card.

❁

'I Have Some Crucial News for You'

'It is a pleasure to drop you this my few humble words,' Comfort next wrote. 'It is me, Comfort, calling you at this moment for help. Elenore, I have some crucial news for you. My headmaster Mr Justus S. Erasmus told me that he received a letter from Education Section stating that the pupils should contribute admission fee and actual study classes fee, total £100 per term so please I need your assistance. I can't conceal this issue to you and that is why I am writing you this letter to exaggerate matter to you obviously. I kindly blow you a kiss in the air. Bye-Bye.'

'The Brightness of This Day'

Some time passed because my workaday life had suddenly become frantically busy (the settlement of Christina's disputed estate and her business affairs had so consumed me that for the first time in my life my fingers trembled from nervous exhaustion).

Nevertheless, I wasn't idle on Comfort's account since somehow I found a moment to write to her Education Section for details of her courses, fees payable and name of payee and drawee bank. After some months, and receiving no reply from the department (her school like others was closed down during a period of political turbulence) a message arrived rebuking me for my silence. 'The brightness of this day has given me great opportunity to pen you this letter. It harasses me, Elenore, I am astonished why for so long period I have not received your letter. This baffles me a lot. I intentionally use school address to signify the school has been reopen. The method of payment can be two. Either you can despatched the money to me then I will send you receipt or I can give you school account's number.' The letter was distinct from her previous air mail in that it was of the palest shade of faded blue and was headed by yet another new P.O. Box number.

Significantly, enclosed in her letter was another from Mr Justus S. Erasmus, himself. 'Hi Elenore. I am head master of Saint Boniface Secondry [*sic*] Technical School and I have admit Miss Beauclaire as a student of this school but she have not yet paid her fees in question. (A lengthy syllabus report followed.) If Comfort pays her fees we will give her receipt confirming she has made full payment concerning the first term fee. I think I am done. Thanks for keeping me in work during my leisure time! If you are able to assist her God will bless.'

Master Justus's P.O. Box number was the same as Comfort's.

I Send a Foreign Draft

So the matter of her fees seemed taken for granted. It was natural I felt there was no longer a need for further enquiries and I confidently sent a foreign draft for Comfort's first term. Her reply was ecstatic. 'Hi Elenore. This is the voice of your friend Comfort calling you at this moment. I was entirely mesmericed [*sic*] when I received your letter. May God help you to restore what you have given out. Elenore, I have a little matter to discuss with you. According to Mr Erasmus he said you have enclosed Banker's Draft but there is some little problem with this. Mr Erasmus and I went to the Commercial Bank and have chat with the manager and he said there will be an inconvenient in this situation. So try as much as possible to turn draft into physical cash and hide in Wishes Card and in envelope by the methods that I have just tought [*sic*] you. Because the manager said that the draft will take a lot of time to withdraw and the post master will try to steal it so try to make good use of the plan above. We will send report and receipt at end of every term according to what you plead.'

'Hinc Lucem et Pocula Sacra'

Before I had found time to 'make good use of the plan' the Ministry of Education at long last replied from its offices which, it turned out, were in the very same city where Comfort now studied. They enclosed a letter typed smudgily on embossed notepaper, headed 'Saint Boniface Secondary Technical School'. (How odd that their coat of arms—a rising sun peering over an horizon bisected by the Meridian—was so similar to Christina's own home borough's. The scroll beneath St Boniface's embossed shield was inscribed 'Hinc Lucem et Pocula Sacra'. *From this source we receive light and draughts of sacred learning.*) The letter's contents were brief. 'I wish to inform you that, as far as our current records show, there is no member of staff who goes by the name of Mr JUSTUS S. ERASMUS nor do pupils obey any headmaster but me. Perhaps, if you give us the name of the student to be sponsored, we may be able to furnish you with more useful information. Yours Sincerely, Samuel C. Ephraime, Headmaster.'

'Forget Me Not'

Only a madwoman would hurl recriminations at an enchantress who signs herself 'your darling friend forever Comfort'. Yet I must admit a certain exasperation has crept into my latest retorts to her entreaties. 'As regards your continued schooling,' I last wrote, 'why not talk to Mr Ephraime about the offer by Mr Erasmus to teach you, since two heads, surely, are better than one.'

Her replies are plaintive, decorated with her sunray motif which is now embellished with scribbled tears. 'Please, I have take you as my sister, my schoolfriend, my guardian and even my provider. I am having sleepless nights these days. Forget me not. I end here with my appreciated words.'

Comfort, I have not forgotten.

I have begun yet another curious, tortuous correspondence with the rulers of your looking-glass land that lies at the end of our shared Meridian. Your name isn't mentioned, of course. On no account do I want you further incriminated in the double-dyed duplicity of that doppel- gänger Mr Justus S. Erasmus as I am convinced you are just one of many pawns in his looking-glass game.

As Comfort, herself, says: 'All the money you have posted to me came to Justus Erasmus as a gift and when I went there to collect it he told me he will not give it to me so you should endeavour and emphasise to make your ambition to post me another money card by the grace of our almighty God very soon with love, hugs, kisses to you forever Comfort.'

The Cape of Misfortune

Recently I have become so thoroughly distracted that, without warning, I can burst into tears at the most inconsiderate instant; or, unbeknown, I'll leave a dinner party wearing a friend's coat; or I'll even absentmindedly walk off clutching a handbag not my own.

My CPN (the community psychiatric nurse assigned to me) has had the satisfaction of weaning me off my Lorazepam and she has now increased my dosage to 9 mg daily of Diazapam; mercifully, she is unaware that I have secretly hoarded Christina's pharmacopœia of controlled drugs whose power had so pitifully failed to assuage the anguish of my beloved's final hours.

Yes, I console myself, Christina's most thoughtful bequest to me has been, after all, two rattlingly fine pillboxes of 100 mg of grey morphine sulphate tablets and an entire handful of her—'diffies' her dihydrocodeine DF 118s.

They are heaped in my hand at this very moment.

Ever since, as an impressionable girl of fourteen, I first read 'Paul and Virginia'—and roamed with them over their tropical isle to gaze from the Mountain of Discovery, beyond the Point of Endeavour, to the Cape of Misfortune where, in the eye of the hurricane, the boy Paul stood powerless to save his true love from engulfing waves—the dream has lingered with its promise of an idyll of chaste devotion unalloyed and remote from a western shore.

The dream does not fade.

Due south from Greenwich the Siren of my lost girlhood calls and I am irresistibly lured by the distant clamour of her lamentations. And though I know that the end of our Meridian is bathed in weeping sunlight I am certain that before too long I shall retrace my steps to that beckoning land where 'forever Comfort' may be found.

CONFESSIONS OF A KISSEE

(*Eveline* M. — Buproprion)

Assessment Summary (extract): By her own account this patient has grown up in abusive situations where personal boundaries, albeit strictly established, were invaded in a number of intimidating life-changing experiences. When challenged on the vagaries of 'pseudomemories', she denies any propensity to fantasise details of her autobiographical memory report. In the therapy of this patient there is a significant potential for her unconscious urges to precipitate reenactments of earlier boundary violations in her trauma history.

CONFESSIONS OF A KISSEE

Patient ID CPN0241090556: Eveline M.
Occupation: Speech Therapist BSc/SpPT.
Drug: Buproprion (Sustained Release).
Drug class: Bupropion hydrochloride; aminoketone class antidepressant; psycho-stimulant and mood brightener for lowsex drive (trial treatment discontinued).
Common side effects: Hallucinations. Confusion. Nausea. Dream abnormality. Insomnia. Dizziness. Dry mouth. Anorexia. Anxiety. Mood instability.

WHENEVER HER HUSBAND kissed her, she would at once imagine him kissing her own mother, and she could not prevent herself from succumbing to the nausea that those memories of maternal kisses aroused.

For, you see, she had been taught the 'Art of Kissing' by her mother, just as she had been taught the 'Art of Being a Good Hostess' by the Holy Sisters at the Priory School for Young Ladies she had attended as a child.

She even to this day preserved the Prospectus of the 'select' convent boarding school which she had first entered as a toddler, to be immured in the 'exclusive' crèche the Sisters supervised for favoured fee-paying infants.

The Sisters' curriculum was not devised, perhaps, to comprehensively expand young minds:

> *The Little Order of the Faithful Redemptoresses for Jesus and Devoted Sisters of Christian Instruction*—The Course of Education comprises Tuition in All Branches of English; Analysis & Parsing; Plain & Fancy Needlework; Drawing from Nature; Conversational French; Singing, Dancing & Music; Preparation for Local Examinations.

No, as she remembered those days, the Sisters' curriculum seemed, more, to comprise a series of exquisite, subtle chastisements.

Of course, the Little Order's punishments of tiny children were never in the category of *Jane Eyre*; she was never bidden to stand on a stool and denied all speech for all of her play-hour.

Her earliest memory was of an Arithmetic class; the younger children still puzzled over long division on slates.

She was whispering in class to her special friend, Verena, when Sister Clothilde addressed her silkily, with no hint of the entrapment which was to follow.

The subject on the blackboard was 'Length'.

'Eveline, dear child, if you would deign to grace us with your undivided thoughts, what is an ell?' Sister had asked disingenuously.

Fortunately, the sempstress at their Sewing class, in a task to measure false hems, had explained the unit the previous day.

'Forty-five inches, Sister,' Eveline had answered without delay.

'Mmm,' Sister Clothilde smiled mirthlessly, 'we shall see.' She took a chalk and commenced to write on the board.

'Ev + el + in'

Sister Clothilde turned to face the mystified class.

'Remember, girls,' their teacher glowered, 'evil comes to us in ells and goes away in inches.'

Eveline felt as if she had been seared on her forehead by the Inferno's brand.

'Mark it well, Eveline, evil that comes out of your mouth flies into your bosom.'

There was a general outburst of unseemly tittering, prompted by Verena, and the maths class was condemned to an hour's detention.

But Verena had the last word.

In her intense fury, Sister Clothilde had leant hard against the blackboard and the rear of her gown was criss-crossed with chalk.

'Well, at any rate,' idly mused Verena, who was well travelled, 'there goes one piece of baggage who'll pay no duty through customs.'

❀

Eveline was a day-girl. A pallid child, she lived with her mother alone in a cramped basement flat that smelled of musty bedrooms. Often, after the autumn rains, their lodgings flooded.

When Eveline considered her mother's faults there were many she heartily detested: the fact that her mother was a divorcee; the fact that Eveline was forbidden to be seen in her mother's company without wearing gloves; the fact that, in public places, Eveline's eyebrows were often smoothed with her mother's own spittle and thumbs; or the fact her mother, quite unabashed, would pinch Eveline's cheeks to induce a fraudulent schoolgirl bloom.

There were other, profounder, causes for blame.

In her infancy, Eveline had not been breast-fed (her mother had regarded the procedure with unfeigned repugnance); as a consequence of a calcium deficiency, the baby-Eveline's lower limbs had grown everted and, because of a continuing tendency to curvature, throughout her early childhood Eveline had slept at night with her legs confined by dual-tubular, metal calliper-splints with buckled webbing straps.

Confusingly, in Eveline's infant mind, the circumstances of her parents' divorce were not unrelated, somehow, to her eventual release from the fettered torment endured in those leg-irons.

After the final visit of the paediatrician, the callipers had been unstrapped and stowed in an upper compartment of her parents' double wardrobe.

Secrets of a Double Wardrobe

On that fateful night of her father's absence, Eveline had been reclining full-length, luxuriating on the quilted eiderdown of her parents' bed observing her mother apply cleansing lotions—a sombre face framed by the dressing-table mirror.

Then rising suddenly, her mother, in a shimmer of chemise, had chanced (or determined?) to abruptly wrench open the door on her father's side of the wardrobe.

There was a gasp. A curse.

Peering under her mother's arm, Eveline saw the withdrawal of three objects: a pair of silver cufflinks in the shape of miniature trowels; a strangely configured silver lambskin apron with sky-blue-coloured moire silk trimmings and rosettes, folded into a square; and a leather pouch on which (she later learned) were inscribed the words, *The Most Worshipful Brethren of the Amitie Temperance Lodge.*

That Eveline's errant father had not attended the masonic Lodge meetings for some six months prior to his exposure, and that he had been seen—by a 'concerned friend' of her mother's acquaintance—in the company of a minor poetess in the residents' bar of a riverside hotel, after hours, had provided grounds enough for an uncontested divorce.

Thus, the fate of Eveline and her mother was more than hateful banishment to furnished rooms with a dismal half-view over mudflats; their shame brought a harsh-learnt new knowledge of a thrifty purse.

Her mother wore black, as if in mourning.

Money came from her father like drops of blood.

Eveline hungered on the slenderest diet, for her proud mother soon taught her that feeding upon charity is a cold dish.

Her mother brooded on the smallest slights. Her face would darken, for instance, when she—a divorced woman — would be introduced *first* to a married lady, as though she, herself, was of a lower rank or from a different set.

But Pride does not buy food for the table; and before very long, Eveline's mother made a virtue of necessity and prevailed on the Sisterhood to make her name known, discreetly, to the school as one willing to accept pupils for Elocution lessons.

Fees were to be paid in guineas, of course.

'A giddy giggling girl, her kinsfolks' plague, her manner vulgar and her converse vague,' Eveline's mother taunted.

Eveline repeated the worn lines lingeringly, reciting from an exercise sheet.

Eveline's mother taught polish and social veneer; and, after the private classes, Eveline would remain behind to practise her lingua-gutturals.

'Ritardando!' her mother would shriek, bringing her amber-coated lips close to Eveline's mouth to demonstrate the application of a moist tongue to palate.

'*Pause* for feeling!'

The instruction of Eveline did not end until she had been corrected for a persistent fault of careless syllabication.

'Now, *staccato!*' commanded her mother.

'Her crime moved me,' attempted Eveline indistinctly.

The school-ma'ama slapped her daughter's face.

'Her *cry* moved me,' articulated her mother, very fast, with a sardonic glance, unmoved by her child's reproachful eyes, as tears brimmed.

Eveline's slapped cheek looked like an apple with one red side.

'A ripe *pippin*,' her mother said through pursed lips, as though the smack had been no more than an exercise in plosives.

Behind her mother there was a vast mirror for the dancing classes.

Eveline gazed at her reflection, as though she saw her face for the first time in a true glass; and it was at that precise moment she lowered a fireproof curtain between her own inner dramas and the world.

Thinking Day

In contrast with Eveline, the character of her special friend — Verena — could not have been more distinct.

Verena, a boarder, was a heroi-comical creation seemingly sent as a fiendish trial to test the Little Order's redemptive powers. Verena's rebellious tongue, so the Sisterhood avowed, was as cloven as the devil's foot — and sharper than the Serpent's tail.

Verena sang like an angel, but the Sisters knew that even though God was in the girl's tongue, the devil was in her heart.

Schoolgirl crushes and 'special friendships' were frowned upon by the Sisterhood, and certain girls would be separated to be rid of bad company.

So Eveline and Verena were deliberately parted when, one February morning, in a shearing wind, their faces raw, they walked out for a period of Nature Study into a white fog after frost.

'The fog is a blank canvas half-unworked,' pretended Eveline.

From heights above the mists unseen birds gave voice to swoops of song.

'Skylarks but no sky,' she thought.

February 22nd was 'Thinking Day'; a pilgrimage of reflection was to be followed by a service for the girl guides in the chapel.

In the rear of the phalanx of Priory girls trailed Eveline, alone, followed by Sister 'Bow-Fronts' Benedicta.

(The title, 'Bow-Fronts', had been bestowed on the voluminously gowned, amply-bosomed Sister Benedicta by Verena, the previous term. 'It's simply too divine,' Verena conceded languidly when all the class had agreed it was a terrific name.)

In the vanguard of the crocodile, Verena's skirt rustled and bounced defiantly, with a sound crisper than the frozen grass crunching under her feet.

Verena had a natural antipathy to Nature Study.

Starched petticoats were strictly forbidden to boarders by Sister Consuela, the Monitress of Discipline, but, typically, in breach of regulations, Verena had starched hers to stiffness with stolen sugar.

Eveline tried to ignore the laboured breathing of Sister Benedicta at her back.

In fact, Eveline did not mind her solitude; she preferred it.

Above her, in the boughs of a bare oak tree, ungathered balls of mistletoe hung, she fancied, like forlorn bundles of Christmastide endearments, unrequited in someone's embittered lovesick past.

The fronds of the hedgerows were frozen rigid, she thought, as though Nature had received news of a tragedy and turned white from the shock. She was reminded of her Great-Aunt May who was quite maddened with grief when she learned of her sweetheart's death in the early days of the Great War. Her hair was said to have turned white overnight, and the next day she had torn up her beloved's letters. That obsessive act of tearing-into-quarters was to become the habitual shredding motion of Aunt May's wasted hands for the remainder of her life in a Closed Institution.

(Behind Eveline, some distance down the path, Sister Benedicta—who hailed from County Limerick—stumbled and muttered to herself in her rich Irish brogue, 'Lord, when ye get so old, ye're heart don't tick over so easy.')

❀

The school bell sounded as the young pilgrims, shivering, returned to class from their expedition, bearing specimens for dissection.

On the Nature Table the girls disposed their finds.

Eveline arrived last, with no wilder exhibit than a perfectly oval mound of darkest green moss which had blown off the Priory roof in a gale.

The windfall seemed to quicken a memory of moist Hibernian greenness because Sister Benedicta nodded approval as though the mossy clump was nothing less than a holy clod from her native soil. 'Why, 'tis made more fair than the rarest emerald velvet!'

Eveline committed the fatal error of allowing herself a modest smile of self-congratulation.

Verena's hooded glance could not conceal the viciousness of her disdain.

Each article for their Object Lessons the girls arranged with care on a polished mahogany case with a glass top under which was displayed the life cycle of the silkworm.

On a stand, beside the case, was mounted a selenoscope to illustrate the phases of the moon.

Beneath this instrument, Verena placed the enormity of a misshapen pine cone, resembling a twisted church spire.

'Wow!' Someone swore and a classmate sniggered obscenely.

'For shame, child,' Verena intoned, simulating through pursed lips the sonorities of Sister Clothilde, and looking pointedly at Eveline. 'Have you no love for cripples?'

The Home for Deformed and Incurable Girls founded by the Sisterhood had been defunct for many years, but Sister Clothilde was fond of reminding her pupils that, in her youth, she had begun her apostolateship there.

The Arts of Love

The collar of Eveline's new guide's tunic chafed the nape of her neck, but until the homework supervised by her mother was complete she was formally obliged to remain in uniform, even though certain unspoken matters stood stiffly between them.

All the more surprising, then, on Eveline's return from the guide troop, given the circumstances of such undaughterly loathing, that her mother should—after concluding a particularly torturous elocutionary session—choose to introduce an entirely new topic: 'Social Graces'.

Wistfully recalling the etiquette of her own induction into Garden Parties, Bridge Teas and Subscription Dances (where she had first met her future husband), Eveline's mother instructed her daughter in the correct manner of eating slowly, noiselessly, with her mouth shut.

The fussy business of negotiating a finger-bowl was also explained; Eveline learned that convention demanded she should place the bowl on the doily provided, always at the left side of her place setting.

She was further instructed to pull on her gloves immediately she finished her dessert.

❁

But there was more.

Was it the effect of those misty recollections of distant party-going or some deeper, unfathomable impulse that made that cold February eve of Thinking Day the propitious moment for Eveline's mother to launch into, at length, her astounding new discursions on the 'Arts of Love'?

Why else did Eveline's elocutionist so dreamily exhale, apply tongue to fore-teeth, and, in a caressing tone, recite one of her favourite exercises in lingua-dentals?

'Soft as *the th*rill *th*at memory *th*rows across *th*e soul . . .'

For Eveline, bound by duty to her mother, every day brought a new light.

Without warning, Eveline was kissed firmly on the lips by her mother.

'Love's tribute . . . the kiss,' her mother announced sourly, 'tenderest pledge of future bliss.'

Eveline then learned that her mother had married her father because a man should be taller than a woman so that he be better able to kiss her.

Mother towered over daughter to demonstrate the ideal disparity in heights.

She cupped Eveline's chin in her fingers. Eveline was ordered to slightly part her lips.

(Eveline's mouth was habitually dry; now unreckoned fears parched her tongue.)

'Essential to practice,' Eveline's mother insisted. 'I shall be the kisser, and you the kissee.'

Face to face, in such strange intimacy, Eveline found her mother's breath to be a not unpleasing blend of cachous and an essence of cloves, applied to relieve toothache.

Her mother's perfume was a familiar undersong of *L'Aimant*, extracts of roses, orchids and jasmine rising from her skin.

(Many years before, Eveline's mother had satisfied the curiosity of her little daughter by indicating the points where best to apply perfume: places where a heartbeat could be felt; inside the ankles; on the wrists; behind the knees; at the nape of the neck and between the breasts. 'But *never* behind your ears.')

As the fragrance enveloped them, Eveline's mother nuzzled her own lips along Eveline's jaw-line, breathing gently into the child's ear, in a manner suggestive of long practice: a series of downy feathery calculated sippings, as it were, until she reached the corner of Eveline's mouth.

At her mother's tightening clasp, Eveline's shoulders began to stiffen; she felt faint as the blood in her veins rushed furiously into her entire system and away from her head; she was unable to think; her nerve ends prickled and she would have swooned had not her mother held her.

'There!' said her mother matter-of-factly. 'The first lesson in kissing is "The Love Nip".'

Her grip on Eveline did not weaken.

'Let me see now,' her mother considered, pausing for greater expressiveness, 'then, of course, there's what tradespeople vulgarly call "The Vacuum Kiss"—the baleful influence of the American cinema, I fear—but in this country, women of the fashionable class, in a *suitable* engagement, often prefer "The Eyelash Kiss",' she continued, almost fondly.

Eveline's mother pondered. Her voice became stern.

'There is, even, I am given to understand, an activity called "The Soul Kiss"—a *grande egoism à deux*—but *that* is an abomination of the French and should not be the concern of a properly raised English girl.'

Face flushed, Eveline had heard quite enough and she stamped hard on her mother's foot and was instantly dismissed to be sent to bed without supper.

❀

That night, Eveline skimmed the surface of sleep.

Had she misheard her mother?

Had her mother truly whispered, *'Who wants a kiss, and a bite like this?'* and nibbled Eveline's ear?

Coquettishness did not suit her mother, Eveline decided; and Eveline's distaste was shared evidently by her father, in a pattern of irreconcilable temperaments which extended far beyond her parents' religious differences.

She pressed her head deep into the pillows.

In the past, when she had heard her parents' quarrelling, she had devised a means of escape to another—hallowed — realm.

She would imagine the white, unsullied ceiling above her bed as a wendy-house of celestial calm of which she had been wrongfully dispossessed—an otherworldly refuge that would some day be refurnished in the manner she was rightfully heir to, if only she could believe in praying to God.

She composed herself for sleep, as she had been taught by the Sisters when she was five years old during her rest period on a rush-mat, her arms enfolded on her chest—in a cross—lest in the night she should be taken to meet her Maker and never again awake.

❀

Dux Femina Facti

Early next morning, unbreakfasted, Eveline set off for school before her mother stirred.

The terraced street of shops in which they lived was long and, not for the first time, as she neared the Priory School gates, Eveline reflected on how the parade gradated—according to an almost uncanny rationale—from dry goods premises to wet.

A milliner's, a haberdashery, a tobacconist's, a grocer's, a baker's, a fruiterer's, a butcher's, a dairy, not to mention the fishmonger's.

Faithful to its name, the Priory of the Little Order of Redemptoresses was not a branch-house of a larger order but an entirely modest establishment, founded in the days of Sister Clothilde's novitiate, by an eminent patroness from a wealthy old recusant family who lived locally.

In exchange for her substantial fortune, this devout — now ancient—heiress was able to live in revered seclusion within the Retreat House she had endowed.

Under the enduring rule of Mother Evangeline, the Little Order had become virtually autonomous and, for all practical purposes, beyond diocesan jurisdiction. During his long episcopate, the Bishop had not visited once.

When Eveline entered the gates she heard the trebling of the Boarders from the chapel led by the dwindling small band of Sisters who supervised the girls' matins.

Eveline crossed an inner court and approached a niche which hid a spiral staircase leading to the dormitories. The Boarders were housed in what had once been a Charitable Reformatory for Homeless Girls.

As she neared the first floor landing, she heard a breathless voice chanting:

'I must, I must, I must,
'I must improve my bust.
'The bigger the better,
'The more to fill my sweater.'

In the corridor she surprised a plump girl in an Aertex vest earnestly swinging a pair of Indian clubs. At the sound of Eveline on the staircase she blushed furiously. Their eyes met and, for a second, the girl's unshielded look sent darts of purest loathing; then she ran off.

Eveline entered the first of the dormitories.

A familiar lanky figure was standing by the window arranging her hair with the aid of a hand mirror.

'Hunnish nuns and bickering Vicars of Christ!' exclaimed Verena, tossing her hair when she saw Eveline watching her (it was an expression of her own she reserved for times of extreme exasperation).

Verena reluctantly began to change for the Boarders' prescribed early morning Swedish calisthenics. Her shoulder blades were as sharp as cuttlebones. The Sisters believed less in a girl's supple knees than in the certainty that a soul in a fat body is loth to rise.

Cursing expertly in an undertone, Verena drew on the red sash of her school House's colours. (Eveline wore yellow.)

The Sisterhood discouraged sketchy blouses but Verena, as a matter of principle, had managed a plunging neckline.

Together, Eveline and Verena descended the stairs to the Games Room.

At the door, barring the entrance, stood three grim-faced Sisters —the Faithful Redemptoresses: Consuela, Clothilde and 'Bow-Fronts' Benedicta.

The gravity of the occasion soon became clear.

A girl in Eveline's class, Mary-Ann-Louise, had reported a theft.

Mary-Ann-Louise was shunned by most of her classmates who regarded her as a high-strung colourless prig; however, she was esteemed by the Sisters as a subject of mariolatry (not to say *annie*olatry) in respect of her good conduct marks and the sanctity of her given name (she was the niece and namesake of the Foundress).

Sister Benedicta peered keenly at each girl, her eyes narrowing with suspicion as she addressed the class.

'Attend!' she ordered sharply. 'I'm hearin' a cruel thing from one o' ye!'

Mary-Ann-Louise wrung her pudgy white hands and began to sob.

'My whah-whah-watch,' Mary-Ann-Louise wailed.

Mary-Ann-Louise had been awarded a water-resistant gold Cartier watch for winning the Foundress's Prize Essay Competition on the subject of '*Arma Christi* and the Iconography of Torment'.

('*Creeping Judas!*' Verena hissed and mouthed an obscenity. She could not conceal her revulsion. Squeamishness would overwhelm her at the very thought of the physical agonies of Christ and, on the day of the prize-giving ceremony, she had painted the toes of the Saviour's statue in the assembly hall with baby-pink nail varnish to 'lighten the mood'.)

'The elegantest article! Taken it was from her desk entirely,' continued Benedicta. 'Faith, with a thief in our midst it's to wrack and ruin we're goin', and when I find her she'll pay smartly for it!'

The girls responded with silence and an exchange of sulky, injured looks.

'*Dux femina facti*,' quoted Sister Clothilde, darkly, 'one of our young ladies is the leader of the deed.'

She declared the crime an instance of turpitude unequalled in her experience.

Sister Benedicta's vast bosom heaved with indignation.

'Which wilful sinning girl is here among ye? Which *divilish* wretch? Ye'll confess! And, if ye don't do it of ye're own free will, I'll soon find a means of makin' ye!' With her Irish up, Benedicta was a sight wonderful to behold.

Eveline dug Verena in the ribs.

'*Divilish*,' she repeated with relish, and giggled.

Verena whispered cattily in Eveline's ear: '*Don't mock the afflicted! If all the world were ugly, Benadicta would be a beauty. But I wouldn't touch Bow-Fronts with a pair of tongs.*'

As Verena had cunningly calculated, Eveline could not stifle her laughter.

Benadicta pounced, seized Eveline by the ear, and dragged her down the corridor to set her at the feet of the Sisterhood's inquisitors.

An accusatory finger was extended and Benedicta pointed at Eveline.

'Ye vicious intriguer! Girls, shrink from her as from the viper's fangs!' she roared.

Eveline was more afraid than hurt.

The Sisters began to speak all at once; it was like being pecked to death by hens.

'Do ye not blush at ye're vileness? Snail ye were born, and snail ye'll end!'

'She was born odd—an egg of the devil's hatching!'

'A slut not good enough to show her godless face!'

(Eveline thought: *'They're not all saints who use holy water.'*)

When Eveline protested her innocence, justice was roughly administered. Benedicta applied cold water to the forehead of any girl who was bold-spoken.

The Monitress of Discipline, Sister Consuela, pronounced Eveline's sentence with a stinging rebuke.

'We take no great comfort to catch a thief. A viperous spirit must be converted by confession.'

'Aye! Confession! Tomorrow!' Sister Benedicta agreed eagerly. 'The longer she lies in the dirt, the dirtier she is!'

Verena grinned, regarding Eveline as a mousetrap that smelled of fresh blood.

'Didn't I warn you?' mocked Verena under her breath. *'Don't cross Benadicta Bow-Fronts. If she were the Queen of Rome she'd fight with the pope.'*

Eveline composed her face carefully to convey a nonchalant forbearance.

'How fearfully amusing,' Eveline murmured to her special friend.

❁

During the long schoolday which followed Eveline lived in her own shadow.

That evening she madly polished her lunch-money with *Brasso* to appear virtuous and bathed in water purged with disinfectant, but it was as useless, she thought, as throwing rosewater into the sea.

(Benedicta had decreed: 'Ye who deal in dirt defile ye're fingers.')

Eveline shuddered at the malediction. She had a vision of herself forever walking the earth with blotted hands.

Not all the finger-bowls in England, she thought, could wash away the stain.

❧

'You look so used and worn, darling,' had been her mother's only brittle comment on Eveline's declaration the following morning that she was to attend confession that day.

Eveline's apprehension was compounded in so far as, up to the very hour appointed for her atonement, she had *never once* attended a confessional.

(Concealed from Eveline, her father's influence had prolonged her childhood years of discretion—*anni discretionis*—and the Sacrament of Penance, at the adulterer's insistence, had been withheld.)

Now all such privileges had been overruled.

On Eveline's departure from Assembly, Sister Benedicta pursued her charge through the cloisters, as angry as a wasp.

'All saint wi'out, all devil within!' the Sister jeered. 'Why, ye're worse than Herodias, so ye are, ye sullen child!'

Eveline was hustled to the chapel door, the leaves of her note-books fluttering as if the pages were the perturbations of an impenitent heart.

'Beware the foul corrupter-worm! With naught but ill thoughts in ye, ye'll injure innocency itself!'

They stood together in the freezing air at the door's thresh-hold as Sister Benedicta halted to catechise her:

'Lies and deceit are like tempest and hailstorm. Tell me, girl, what is a lie?'

'We tell a lie when we wish to deceive others and say what is not true.'

'*And*? Speak up!'

'And pretend to be better than we are,' completed Eveline, cravenly.

Her inquisitor exalted.

'Exactly. The properer the girl the less she should know conceit.'

Sister Benedicta appraised Eveline's figure in one withering glance.

'Even a deformed body may have a beautiful soul. But not an impious one!'

The Sister glared.

'What leads to the sin of impurity?' she demanded.

Eveline's tongue was almost paralysed.

'Persons that are . . .' Sister Benedicta prompted menacingly.

'Persons that are indecently clothed, immodest books and moving pictures and . . .' Eveline faltered.

'And too much familiarity with the opposite sex!' Sister Benedicta completed savagely, prodding Eveline through the door, in the direction of the confessional-box.

''Tis a tainted child that needs contrition of early corruption, and ye can tell the good Father I told ye so!'

Eveline was thrust into darkness, the door closed behind her, and her tormentor was gone.

Pudor Ille Vincendus

There is no religion that cannot boast of its martyrs, and Eveline, that morning, entered the Priory chapel as staunchly as any of the martyrised to outface her spiritual physician, and the wounds soon to be made to her soul.

From out of the gloom emerged the outline of the confessional-box, as vast as her parents' double wardrobe.

Shadowed in its recess, with its gleam of polished rosewood, the massive double cabinet was all but indistinguishable.

A curtain covered the upper half of her confessor's booth yet Eveline knew who was seated there. A printed card in a slotted mount informed her of that fact.

'I'll imagine it's one of those Black Forest weather-houses,' Eveline counselled herself. *'When the little man pops out of his own door holding a black umbrella you know bad weather is coming.'*

She entered her own cubicle, closed the door and knelt.

A crucifix hung above a latticed screen. From the other side of the grille the priest emitted a dry cough—the false hemming which was prelude to a penitent's unburdenings.

'BlessmefatherforIhavesinned.' Eveline modulated a syllabified 'Low Tone' which, according to elocutionists, conveys 'fear', 'caution' and 'secrecy'.

The rasping utterance which responded was frail and wavered, weakened by great age.

'The Lord be in thy heart and on thy lips . . .'

'. . . not forgetting Mother's, too,' Eveline added silently, sickened in her throat, remembering amber lips glued to hers like birdlime, sticking fast.

❁

Eveline had no fear of Father Bertrand, her confessor, whose parchment flesh was as blemishless as a disinterred saint's—as spotless as the Lamb of God.

If he had any weakness of the flesh it was his unbeatific dandruff. 'A scrofulous cleric,' Eveline's mother had described him. 'A man in a black cassock with *his* scalp condition would do better to hang a clothes-brush on his back. Or ask his barber for a friction-rub.'

From behind the grille there came another hesitant cough.

'It is never too late to mend,' Eveline's Father Confessor prompted gently.

A silence.

Eveline glimpsed a luminous dial as Father Bertrand consulted his watch.

'Come child, conscience cannot be compelled,' he intoned, 'a guilty heart needs no accuser but itself.' (The old man spoke in riddles, she thought.)

'Sin-angels fell from heaven,' Father Bertrand recited mournfully, 'but great virtue-angels have built up heaven on earth and not at teenage bottle-parties.'

'Well, honestly!' Eveline bristled. *'B-minus for baloney and two measly cheers!'*

'If you do not open the door to the devil's foul works,' resumed Father Bertrand gravely, 'he will go away.'

'His foul works, father?' Eveline asked, inwardly fuming. 'What are they?'

An embarrassed pause.

The delicacy of his reluctance to elucidate was conveyed with another discreet cough.

'Misconduct with schoolboys is considered an occasion of sin.'

(Eveline roundly damned Sister Benedicta:*'The poison she's poured into this priest's ear! It's enough to infect the purest well.'*)

'Oral sanctity is mental piety,' Father Bertrand cautioned obscurely. 'How true it is that a kiss on the mouth so often touches not the heart.'

(*'Too true! Too true!'* Eveline wanted to yell.)

Timid hints and suggestions from her confessor followed, with allusions to the dangers of mingling indiscriminately in the society of modern young men flushed with lust and wine and casting licentious looks.

It was a dark page in Eveline's history when, in the end, she bowed her soul in the dust and endured her first surrender to the degradation of prying eyes probing deep into the secretest recesses of her being.

'Pudor ille vincendus,' urged Father Bertrand. 'Vanquish your modesty, child, and make a full avowal. It is by nature a girl's way, as the Sisters remark, that when you do as you *will*, it is not as you *ought*.'

(*'Except when one's a properly raised English girl,'* scoffed Eveline.)

'A girl's innocence is a jewel of the finest water,' her confessor concluded. 'Stolen virtue is a vice more abhorrent than *theft* itself.'

The word, 'theft', echoed in the the little chamber like an unequivocal accusation.

Eveline, unblushing, vehemently denied theft of any variety and sought absolution.

Her worst crimes, so far as she knew, she told Father Bertrand, were leaving lacquered hairspray on the bathroom mirror; and dropping her hankie in the street in the forlorn hope that some *galant* would return it (instead, an errand-boy on a bike had whistled without stopping and thumbed at the gutter).

And beyond these transgressions, the only flirtatious exchange she'd ever experienced with a *real* boy was when an older pupil from the neighbouring school had, behind her back, tied the belt of her bottle green gaberdene macintosh to the platform-handrail on the circular bus into town one Saturday morning, and she'd had to travel on the complete circuit before she could disentangle herself to jump off.

Father Bertrand chided as though she had confessed to saying her prayers backwards and hellish fires were about to devour her.

'You must avoid bad company. To have fallen by your own desires is a sin greater than seduction by others.'

Over the chapel roof the wind shifted. The stained-glass window above them brightened and the priest's face assumed a darker hue, his domed head red-lit like that of a pantomime Demon King.

To overcome a young lady's sensuality the Father decreed that Eveline's penance was to entrust her prayers to Saint Aloysius (' . . . who had passed unscathed through the temptations of his youth . . . '), and commit herself to a number of devotional exercises for a fortnight, including Extra-Biblical Studies.

'By the merits of the blessed Heavenly Mother and all the Saints, whatsoever evil thou has endured, be they to thee for the remission of thy sins. Amen.'

At her dismissal, Eveline swiftly withdrew. She glimpsed beneath the curtain the arthritic righteous hand of Father

Bertrand turn the pages of his breviary (for it is a good divine who follows his own instruction).

She heard the priest mutter: 'It's too early for a wee girl to be partaking of Eve's sins. We pray Eve's fallen daughters receive not her plagues.'

A moment later, Eveline, eyes streaming, was standing shriven in the chapel porch gasping for air, her feelings harrowed, her mind confused and overwrought by the ordeal of premature initiation into the mysteries of her own iniquity.

She despised herself. That she had knelt at the feet of an old man whom she knew to play cards under the holy and white mantle of the most exalted piety on the Sabbath excited her unqualified self-contempt.

For it was known in the school that the virginal Father Bertrand—who, due to his transparent virtue, was an inmate of the Priory's Retreat House—had been entertained for many years in the afternoons by that venerated old lady, the Sisterhood's highborn benefactress.

He took tea with the Foundress in her rooms and, together with her faithful lap-dog, a barbet-poodle, they measured out their lives in apostle spoons.

After their tête-à-tête, the priest allowed the Foundress to cheat him at cribbage and he was rewarded in the evening by a glass of Montrachet.

❁

'Salaam,' greeted Verena ironically when Eveline, with tear-swollen eyes, subsided beside her in their favourite hideaway behind the drying racks, in an alcove off the cloakroom.

On rainy days in study-time they often sought the warmth of the heated pipes which snaked from the slow-combustion stove in the chapel. The room was filled with a robust fug. Several pairs of woollen stockings were drying on a radiator.

Verena was smoking a du Maurier filter tip, if only because she adored—as she was so fond of reminding her admirers—the smart red box.

She was wearing a pair of new, red striped espadrilles contrived to enflame her classmates to passions of envy.

('All strut and show,' was the censure of Benedicta.)

Verena spoke of 'her people' in the South of France and ostentatiously carried air-sickness tablets in her purse to impress the other girls who were made to feel hopelessly démodé.

For Eveline a cigarette was a forbidden fruit; but forbidden fruit is sweet, so she accepted one.

'You look the last word, my dear,' Verena mocked.

'Thanks awfully.'

The sun broke through a cloud and penetrated the skylight.

'Self-glory in a shaft of sunlight,' thought Eveline resentfully. She dissembled a smile; hatred sometimes has need of a mask. *'The rich are different,' Eveline seethed. 'Ever since she was very little, Verena's behaved like a natural leader, and I've always acted like a peasant lucky enough to rise to the level of servant.'*

Verena knew all about power; it was instinctive within her.

Once and forever it was borne in on Eveline that she had been striving vainly against Life's stream, and all along her special friend had regarded her as someone's poor dupe.

'Yes, I suppose I am bound to forgive her,' she said to herself, *'but I'm not bound to trust her ever again.'*

A thrill of loathing ran through Eveline when Verena cocked her head to one side, blew smoke expertly through her nose, and submitted her victim to critical examination.

'How shall I put it?' Verena began, eyes agleam with malice. 'You're not so ugly as to be altogether frightful, nor so beautiful as to entirely appeal.'

Eveline was conscious of her upper lip beginning to tremble and she tried to suppress the quiver in her voice.

'Have I no redeeming features, then?' she asked lightly.

'Darling, don't you see?' Verena drawled. 'We've *both* absolutely none!'

She then ran her tape-measure-eyes over Eveline again and pronounced:

'According to Sister Clothilde, we're both equally bad so the devil has put us together. Two blacks make no white,' she says, 'that's why she keeps us apart!'

They heard the brisk footsteps of Sister Clothilde approaching down the passage to the cloakroom and they sprang up and stubbed out their cigarettes.

Verena winked.

With two fingers she touched her own lips and, in benediction, brushed Eveline's brow to make the sign of the cross.

'Go in peace, my child, and sin no more.'

❁

'How was school today?' Eveline's mother enquired, later, with uncharacteristic interest.

'Oh, wonderful fun,' answered Eveline carelessly, her expression blank.

❁

'Hands on heads!' The class obeyed.

Sister Benedicta stared pointedly at Eveline who insolently redirected her gaze at the rafters. (For a reason only she could account for, Eveline felt fortunate and unassailable. Earlier that morning at breakfast, she had begun the day lucky when she'd eaten an egg with a double yolk.)

Sister Benedicta slowly ascended the aisle which divided the tiered galleries of pitch pine benches where the girls sat. As she passed, she flipped open each desk lid to inspect the contents.

When she reached Eveline's desk Benedicta lunged in triumph.

'My soul to the saints if I know what to do wi' ye!' she screeched as she withdrew a commemorative enamelled tin pencil-box emblazoned with the Royal Standard and an embossed popular portrait of Queen Elizabeth II in her ceremonial robes.

Sister Benedicta spat on the box.

'Why, it's convertin' her it is, God help us all!'

The offending article was swiftly consigned to the classroom stove.

'A heretic! An' not a bit o' shame in her! Merciful hour! Never have I seen a girl fall into such a sin as this!'

Flames crackled, and the monarch's imperial crown bubbled and dissolved into the embers.

''Tis a scandalising disgrace to the one true church when ye threaten the throne of God!'

Eveline's protestations were met with another ferocious outburst.

'Unnatural child! Not a word from ye! Ye'll see the Monitress after Mass and, please God, she'll be improvin' ye're blasphemious manners!'

But the matter of the missing wrist-watch was not forgotten.

Mary-Ann-Louise's plump shoulders shook with unrestrained weeping.

Benedicta searched the girls' faces, her small angry eyes flashing sparks.

'Shame on ye're impudence. Ye may sit there and defy me! But, if none of ye sinners are after confessin', we shall seek intercession from He who knows the secrets of the most wayward heart.'

Verena, unintimidated, removed her hands from her head and wiggled her fingers.

'May we ask what you intend with us?' she asked, coolly supercilious.

'Ye'll know the worst soon enough.' Benedicta grinned malevolently. 'Aye and, before ye lie down, pray for ye're souls tomorrow!'

(*'Bedad, and may we all be safe in glory,'* sneered Verena.)

❀

Events then followed swiftly.

After morning Assembly, the Reverend Mother announced that Eveline's class was to gather in a secluded enclosure set aside for the Sisters' meditation between the chapel and the Retreat House.

'Come with me this minute, all of you!' Sister Benedicta unlocked an iron-railed gate and herded the class through an arched entry.

On the other side of a low wall could be glimpsed a children's playground. On Sundays the swings were chained up and secured with padlocks.

The class passed from shadow into subdued sunlight where a small lawn was encircled with a brick path flanked by *relievo* stone panels depicting the Stations of the Cross.

Eveline noticed Verena shiver on seeing the Instruments of the Crucifixion: the hammer, the pliers, the iron handcuffs for the scourging, the spear, and the crown of thorns.

Benedicta, her mouth severe, pointed to a laurel grove.

'Every girl will go to the Little Garden of Reflection, and there she'll meditate on her misdeeds. Be sure ye're sins will find you out! God is all-seeing and from his punishment no sinning girl can hide!'

Within the grove, a metal blade plunged in the ground flashed like a sundial from the centre of the grass.

'In the garden beyont ye'll find the sword o' Michael the Archangel. Ye'll each draw that true blade and replace it. Do ye hear? And ye're to crave aloud before the Captain of the Heavenly Host: "If I am the thief then strike me to death O God my Judge and all the Saints of Jesus."'

One at a time, each suspect entered the concealment of the grove and returned to the Sister.

To all appearances, Eveline seemed markedly unconcerned, but Verena was blushing furiously, flushing uncharacteristically from her chest to her throat.

On Eveline's return from the grove, Benedicta turned on her like a harpy and forced her to her knees.

'To struggle alone with Satan is the blackest curse o' Protestant shame. Confession is truthfuller altogether than breakin' the Eighth Commandment wi' ye're guilt lyin' on ye're stubborn soul forever!'

But Eveline obstinately remained silent, so, when the agony of the other girls in the garden was over, Benedicta ordered them all to kneel before her with outstretched hands, whereupon to their collective astonishment she smelled their palms.

'There's no escapin' the mark o' sin,' Benedicta berated Eveline. 'Once touch vice and ye'll be defiled!'

But her dismay was plain to see as she futilely inspected again and again Eveline's hands for evidence of the corrupted soul she sought.

With increasing frustration, Benedicta redirected her attentions to Verena, pressing her pale pudgy nose into the haughty schoolgirl's extended hands in pursuit of her compulsive olfactory palm-readings.

There was a yelp of satisfaction as Benedicta yanked Verena by the scruff of her neck and harried her to the chapel where the Sisterhood waited, heads bowed in a dark assembly of bearers of sorrows.

The clock chimed, striking the hour of reckoning.

Verena's proud chin remained uptilted as she faced her accusers.

'You didn't grasp the sword, because you were afraid,' Sister Clothilde lamented. 'Isn't that right, girl? Afraid you might die, because you are guilty! Guilty because you are the thief!'

Eveline began to shake through her entire frame when she heard the harshness of Sister Consuela's auto-de-fé.

'To a bad character good doctrine avails nothing. There appears to be no end to your transgressions! Go you must, Verena! You are a reproach to all who stand in God's grace!'

From sheer relief Eveline was laughing and crying in the same breath.

Mary-Ann-Louise smirked.

Verena merely shrugged.

Eveline's last glimpse of her special friend, before Verena's excommunication, was of Verena smiling inscrutably, raising a hooked little finger in an intimate wave, then blowing a final kiss.

Eveline was the only girl to blow her friend a rueful, renunciatory kiss in return.

Of course, Verena fell into Benedicta's trap because of her fastidious refusal to handle the sacred sword, as Eveline had predicted when conceiving her defensive stratagem.

A danger foreseen is half avoided.

That Eveline had personally exposed the cheap magic sideshow was known only to herself; for, late the previous evening, she had learned the secret of how Sister Bow-Front's trickery was done.

At nine o'clock, Eveline had awoken from a dream portending her salvation in the garden and she'd slipped out of her bedroom unobserved. Under cover of darkness, she had shinned up a yew tree growing by the Priory chapel wall.

Perched on a bough, she had viewed the Sacristy through a small quatrefoil window, just in time to see Benedicta enter and fetch Saint Michael's sword of truth from its velvet-lined casket. Casting apprehensive glances over her shoulder, Benedicta had then fetched a flask of incense, with its spoon, from a cabinet.

Thereupon, the Sister had plunged the sword's handle into the incense-flask and smelled the result. She had recoiled from the pungent fumes of the aromatic gums.

At the moment of her replacing the sword in its casket and withdrawing from the Sacristy, Benedicta's sly smile was seen to broaden into a wider grin.

'Anyone who holds it will have the scent clinging to their hands,' Eveline had whispered in wonder.

The scene enacted had comforted her. There had been no reason, after all, she had considered, loftily surveying the Little Order's precincts spread out beneath her, why she should ever have questioned her own long-held scepticism for the supernatural beliefs under which the Redemptoresses ruled.

Needless to relate, not a word of her discovery did she breathe to Verena.

Verena's expulsion did not surprise Eveline's mother.

'That girl will likely turn into a really bad woman,' she sniffed.

Verena had been sent to a finishing school in Switzerland. A classmate had reported last seeing her, before her departure, 'jumping a red light, and looking perfectly splendid in the dinkiest little sporty two-seater.'

Verena, Eveline reflected, would—like the cat she was—always fall on her feet.

Fortunately, Eveline's mother had never enquired too closely into the loss of the commemorative pencil-case bearing the portrait of the Defender of the Anglican Church, which—in defiance of her Romish husband—she had secretly conveyed to her only daughter.

When Eveline had discovered Mary-Ann-Louise's Special Merit Prize Cartier watch, fallen from the budding young gymnast's pocket on the dormitory landing, she had selected its place of concealment with extreme care, reliant on the foreknowledge that the fervency of the Sisterhood's simple sectarian precepts would have been an interdict persuasive enough to prevent Sister Benedicta from opening *that* particular Pandora's box.

The Kissing Machine

Many years later, on the day of her mother's funeral, Eveline stood with the Superioress Consuela among moss-grown tombs outside the chapel after the Service of Committal.

Glancing at her feet, Eveline read uncomprehendingly a dedication engraved early in the nineteenth century on an infant's headstone:

Little Lips Once Sweet
Now Seal'd for Heaven
by a Mother's Kiss.

Eveline was suddenly reminded of her mother's Frosted Orange lipstick, and of a bizarre newspaper clipping, dated 1939, she had discovered in a drawer among her mother's effects. Eveline shuddered. As to why her mother chose to squirrel away such an item was beyond her understanding: the faded text from the column of a popular women's beauty magazine recorded the fact that Max Factor had invented a 'Kissing Machine' capable of pressing two sets of rubber lips together, under ten pounds of pressure, in order to test the indelibility of his lipsticks.

Eveline's father, whom she had not seen for more than thirty years, approached, leaning heavily on a rolled umbrella, clinging to the arm of his companion, the minor poetess.

Mother Consuela gently pressed Eveline's fingers in condolence and withdrew.

'Much religion but no goodness,' Eveline's father grunted, nodding in the direction of the departing prioress. 'Much praying but no piety.'

'I thought the service went swimmingly,' the minor poetess gushed.

Eveline felt every particle of loving kindness shrivel within her. (Eveline's mother had drowned in an exercise pool during a session of hydrotherapy for her crippling osteoarthritis.)

The minor poetess extended her hand, but Eveline pretended to be pulling on her gloves.

Then Eveline reached up and breathed gently into her father's ear, tilting his head back, nuzzling his jaw-line in a series of downy feathery calculated sippings until she reached the corner of his mouth.

(Her father, Eveline was reminded, had a distinct blue vein across the bridge of his nose, which her mother used to say was a sure sign of a man likely to die by drowning.)

Scarcely within hearing, Eveline whispered, *'Who wants a kiss, and a bite like this?'* and nipped his lower lip.

'The d-d-deuce!' Eveline heard her father mutter in total bewilderment; his face was a deathly pale.

At the very end of that day, all she remembered through her tears was a pure white magnolia petal on the gravel drive, impressed with the treadmarks of the hearse's tyres.

THE CHEATED EYE

(*Miriam R.* — FLUOXETINE)

'No woman . . . seriously wishes to be male and have a penis.
But most women would like to have the privileges
and opportunities that go with it.'

—ELENA GIANINI BELOTTI, *Directress, Centro Nascita Montessori di Roma*

Assessment Summary (extract): The patient's physical examination was remarkable only for intermittent fasciculation of the left eyelid. In this, her second one-hour diagnostic interview, the patient intimates an early impairment of her sexual response cycle, and a consequent decreased libido, due to interpersonal problems on which she does not care to elaborate other than to refer to a 'chronic disharmony' in the sexual history of her marriage. Her level of personal insight appeared to be good, as evidenced by her pointed reluctance to indicate specific psychosocial stressors, since she is unconvinced a solution exists to resolve problems she insists she is capable of identifying. A more complete history is recommended to identify predisposing illness or conditions and elicit any history of prior sexual trauma.

THE CHEATED EYE

Patient ID CPN0198271154: Miriam R.
Occupation: Montessori preprimary teacher.
Drug: Fluoxetine.
Drug class: Antidepressant (selective serotonin reuptake inhibitor) for the treatment of bulimia nervosa.
Common side effects: Insomnia, headache, anxiety, nightmares, taste changes, vision changes, decreased sex drive, dry mouth, skin flushing, loss of concentration.

OF COURSE, HER first emotion, when she learned her husband. was living with his Russian interpreter, was utter relief. No longer was he to be found brooding in his garden room, amber decanter glinting by his side, wearing that wintry smile whenever their eyes met.

Then new feelings of resentment seized her. Looking from her study window to his room below, she could see, under the lattice of the glass roof, her husband's whorled crown of dark shaggy hair—thinning in the centre, she noticed—where he had slumped forward, beard on chest, feigning sleep. Playing possum was invariably his ruse when unwelcome questions remained unanswered. And those he had answered had been matters of fact, cursorily conveyed with his face turned from her.

He had said no more than that he was living in his unleased town flat with a young woman named Nadezhda. He called her Nadia, a Russian from Saratov who had never visited the West before. He said she was unworldly, and in the city she was endangered by a childlike inexperience. At heart, he said, she was an unsophisticated, provincial girl who was prey to primitive superstitions. Without too much thought he had bestowed on her his protection.

'All that you imagine is probably true,' Leon had said. Beyond that he would say nothing more.

She slammed the window and saw his eyelids flicker. So be it, she decided. If he chose to retreat behind a carapace of calculated indifference, then she would contrive her manner to be no different from his—yet, she vowed, before the week was ended it would be her intention to unbeard a lifetime of manifold deceptions.

First Report — 'The Stakeout'

The next day she obeyed her new resolution by seating herself at the street frontage of a Greek café opposite the city mansion block where, behind the pane of a first-floor window, could just be glimpsed the tip of a dismantled 'To Let' sign—a visible token of the collapse of any pressing interest Leon might have had in selling the lease.

She had rejected the baklava and had been drinking slowly from a single glass of bitter tea for over an hour, watching the lemon slice sink as the sun westered behind the roofs, when she saw a young woman mount the steps and pause outside the apartments' entrance.

Nadia. Unquestionably. A tall, slender, doleful girl with whispy, duckpondbrown hair, very short skirt, early twenties, wearing, she was certain, Leon's newest black leather zipped jerkin.

The girl with the duckpondbrown hair unlocked the door and entered. Within a few moments a light was switched on in Leon's flat and Nadia, if indeed the shadowy form was hers, appeared at the window staring down at the street and the square beyond.

The café had emptied. (*Establishing shot, exterior, day,* she thought. *Location: Moscow Road leading to St Petersburgh Place, London W2.* She jotted a note on the last pages of her 'Activities Report'. *Time: 17.30 hours. Shadows long.*) She rose to leave. The sign above her read: *Thank You For Not Smoking PIPE or CIGAR when café doors are closed.*

As she walked to Bayswater Station (*tracking shot*), she marshalled on her fingers her next manoeuvres. [i] The over-ruling strategem was to gain entry to the flat. (She had lived in the flat with Leon practically all their married life, but, when they had moved permanently to their pied-à-terre cottage, she was certain *her* keys had been sent to the estate agent; a request for them now would be bound to alert her husband); [ii] the problem of temporary leave from her work must be overcome—she would need many spare hours for surveillance; and [iii] she must make certain Leon had no hint of her actions.

Her last thought was jolted by the sudden emergence of Leon crossing the station concourse towards her. Mercifully undetected, she ducked out of sight beside a kiosk and observed her husband hasten by, his eyes set on a more distant quarry. His long hair blew in tufts, a moving plant. (*Fadeout.*)

The Keys

(Flash forward.) That evening, she again reviewed the obstacles. Unless she could recover the flat's keys—covertly—she was lost.

The telephone rang.

Leon.

When she said, 'Why don't you hang up?' Leon said, 'Where's the difference, you're hung up, whatever,' and slammed down the receiver.

And then, reluctantly—had Leon's words goaded her? — she remembered the plastic holdall on the top shelf of the hall closet. Memories surfaced and resubmerged. The lightning darts of her mind were like so much cross-hatching that had begun to etch a picture of her predicament, until she saw, as yet indistinct, the semblance of the path she should take.

(*Cutaway. Over-the-shoulder shot.*) Mounted on a pair of steps, she withdrew the holdall from where it had lain, unopened, for more than five years. (*Reverse angle view.*) She bit her lip, tears brimming. She felt as weak as water.

(*Cue close-up.*) Holdall.

(*Medium shot.*) In her bedroom, door locked—yet there was no other in the cottage except her small dog—she hesitantly unzipped the contents and tipped them on to her bed.

Item 1. Two latchkeys with sticking plaster labels overwritten with her own name—*Miriam.* (So it was as she suspected; Aunt Wilma *had* kept their flat's keys — entrusted to her more than fifteen years before. Leon would almost certainly have forgotten.)

Item 2. A military flashlight. (Her mouth dried. An uneasy memory stirred, swiftly suppressed.)

Item 3. A soiled surgical corset, the elasticated panels begrimed and buffed glossy with human spoil. (She was riven by a prolonged shudder and fell to her knees beside the bed.)

Item 4. A baby's pink crocheted woollen blanket, frayed at its edges, with an embroidered initial *M.* As she fingered the soft, familiar fabric—smelled its sour lactic traces—her heart broke and she wept. (*Wipe.*)

SECOND REPORT—'CHILDES MASS'

At first light, Miriam crossed the allotments to the schoolyard. Her little white dog trotted behind her. She noticed the sky was in the likeness of blown glass cooling; soon the horizon would be entirely clear.

She descended into the crypt and entered the classrooms—a giant striding among the child-sized furniture. She made sure all the sensorial materials and equipment for her exploration classes —the activity trays, the wooden blocks and plastic containers—

were correctly arranged in their places along the wall. From above she heard the nuns at their matins.

As the strains of the harmonium and their earnest voices reached her, she was drawn to the entrance porch, hands exploring the dusty ledge immediately below the warm-air duct. She pulled down the flaps of a cardboard box to stroke the bedraggled feathers of the injured starling Andrea had rescued. The youngest in her class, the boy alone was charged with the duty to feed the foundling. A glass pippette for the purpose lay in the straw. Andrea was just five years old yet appeared younger. His lustrous black hair was brilliantined and smelled of oil of roses. He was astigmatic, viewing his world though spectacles fitted with a frosted lens. He taunted the other children to attract their scorn, which, once gained, reduced him to tears. He wore a black armband.

In the front of her 'Activities Report' Miriam had jotted, 'Mother dcd. No siblings. V. critical to orient *A* towards self-reliance through personal work-cycle to gn snse scl rspnsblty.'

Under her hand the bird protested feebly, emitting a mournful 'Krrrr,' then, wing drooping, rolling with a bandy-legged gait, teetered away from her grasp. The smudged feathers, she noted, reminded her of foxed crepe; a visual pun, à la Buñuel, whose self-conscious knowingness did not escape her.

(*Dissolve.*)

(The Sister Directress looked searchingly into Miriam's eyes when the subject of leave was broached. Miriam hid her hand under the pages of the Duty Roster; she had developed a telltale scar on the first two knuckles of her right hand from inducing vomiting. But the Sister Directress discreetly refrained from probing into the underlying reasons for the request and she agreed willingly enough to a proposal of staggered time blocks to suit Miriam's absences. They had known each other since Miriam's early days as a film student. An ardent admirer of *Potemkin*, Miriam had chosen to film a homage to Eisenstein's erratic staccato style at this very school. The result was *Childes Mass*—a 16 mm B/W single reeler of bleached fades and clumsy defocussed transitions with rapid heteroclite jump-cut frames that documented the playgrounds of an urban childhood. In the end, despite an Hons, Miriam was irresistably drawn to the wisdom of the Sisters' teaching traditions, and had remained at the school—a convert of a kind—like a genre painter who saw no reason to stray from her first subject.)

Third Report — 'The Pushkin Club'

The evening was cool so the out-of-season dark wool cape she threw over her shoulders granted her a plausible concealment to melt into the dusk. Thus seven o'clock saw Miriam striding after two distant linked shadows as they crossed Leinster Square. This quarter of London was familiar to Miriam and she found no difficulty in keeping pace with the couple as they turned the corner of the Westbourne terraces and entered Ladbroke Grove.

She halted and drew back at the gateway of a peeling townhouse set in a neglected garden. A doorbell sounded and Miriam heard a gutteral murmur in Russian as her husband and his paramour were admitted by a hulking grizzled usher. When the door closed Miriam inspected the illuminated bell escutcheon. 'The Pushkin Club.'

Standing in an angle of the garden, in a quadrant of shade, Miriam found she could observe—through a slit in the shutters—the company of discussants within.

This is what she saw. A fine, high-ceilinged drawing room with flaking lemon-coloured plaster. (She thought: *"Lemon Peel"—wasn't that the title of an unwritten sketch by Chekhov?'* It was.) There was a large copper samovar on the sidetable and a framed photograph of Osip Mandelstam. A frayed electrical flex holding a shaded bulb was suspended from the ceiling's crumbling plaster rose.

Sub rosa, in front of the vast library stacks which formed the far wall, a half circle of ill-assorted chairs had been drawn up to face the window. A row of émigrés with expectant faces drank tea from unmatched china teacups which appeared to be the only items they'd saved from their country houses before their decadent *burzhuaznyi* drawing rooms were converted by the Bolsheviks into grain stores.

There was much laughter and clapping when an actor wearing side-whiskers and an old, worn frock coat darted between the chairs and stood before the window.

'A monologue in one act by Anton Pav'lich Chekhov,' he announced in a heavily accented, corncrake rasp. There was scattered applause. The mock lecture commenced.

Leon's hand, she saw, was resting on Nadia's thigh, but when the actor came to the passage where the deranged hen-pecked *soi-disant* lecturer wrings his hands and rails across the footlights ('. . . my wife runs a boarding school. Well, not exactly a boarding school, but something in the nature of one. My wife doesn't give parties and never has anyone to dinner. She's a very stingy, bad-tempered, shrewish kind of lady, so no-one ever comes to see us. If only I could run away from that stupid, petty, spiteful harridan of a wife who's made my life a torment . . .'). Miriam saw her husband reach out and grip his mistress's knee. Nadia, however, did not smile.

Fourth Report — 'Componential Analysis'

Miriam clenched the infirm key with its taped plaster dressing and unlocked the door to the familiar vestibule. She sniffed and recognised the brand of floorpolish that Mrs Bryce used for the tiled landings.

As she mounted the lower treads, she heard the first-floor flat door open and voices rebounded in the stairwell. (*Ambient sound: footsteps, exterior traffic movement.*)

She retreated into the shadowy recess beneath the stairs. (*Canted dutch angle shot with limbo lighting.*) Her husband descended with Nadia in tow. (*Continuity note*: Leon wears a dark suit, black shirt, no tie; Nadia wears forest-green nylon parka with jersey shirt of matching colour and tan chinos.)

Crossing the lobby, Miriam's husband laid his hand on Nadia's shoulder and gave a coarse laugh.

'In the right hands it could be hilarious,' Leon said, and snickered once more.

Nadia disengaged his hand as she opened the door.

'Tell me, *Lvyonok*,' said Nadia, inconsequentially, pronouncing the words thickened, as though her teeth were grinding on ice, 'who is that *Amerikanetz* whose name sounds like a sneeze?' They closed the outside door before Miriam heard Leon's answer.

(*Boom crane shot*.) Inside the flat, from the street window, she watched them depart towards Bayswater. She switched on the tape deck of Leon's recording console. (*Indo-Jazz Fusions* by Joe Harriott and John Mayer.) She felt another wound opening; she had an image of a third tongue savouring their shared pleasures.

In the bedroom she slid open the fitted wardrobe.

She examined the labels of Leon's new clothes. A Zegna silk tie. A zipped leather blouson by Cerrutti (his *studied* jacket, he had joked) and a pure cashmere overcoat by Brioni from Beal & Inman, both black. Plainly, Leon's arduous three-month assignment in Russia, constructing colossal sets for the 2nd Unit of a pan-European shoot-'em-up actioneer, had not been without its consolations—or without its *trophies*. She recoiled at the hateful sound of a scented silk slip slithering from a hanger.

But Leon's nature she knew—intimately. It was the hidden dossier that recorded the lineaments of Nadia's desires that she had entered this room to read; to turn each page of her Russian soul. She smelled the pillow then tracked Nadia's perfume to its source—a philtre of *Krasnaya Moskva* in the bathroom cabinet. She stood by the unmade bed, turned to the penultimate page of her 'Activities Report', and began to write:

1. *Nadia's note on bed to Leon:* 'Lover-Lyova-Lyovka! Remember collect eggs, saffron and fizzy candles you promised. And Lyovushka! All must chill until tomorrow. Wait! Be tempted not! Yr N.' In the kitchen, Miriam opened the fridge to find it crammed with covered glass dishes of

vivid, exquisitely prepared *zakuski* and a towering *Charlotte Russe*.

(*Freeze frame.*)

Miriam scowled. A pang of childish envy. A celebration? But of what? On the fridge door was taped a picture postcard from Bournemouth. She turned one corner to read the message in a familiar scrawl.

2. *Postcard*: 'Still soaking up the photons. *L. L.*' (*Love Laurence* . . . Leon's best friend, was a confirmed bachelor and xenophobe and would not have dreamt of holidaying anywhere but on the south coast. He was a linguistics specialist—a pedant, but a passionate one. Once, he had attempted to explain to Miriam his theory of ambiguity in contextually sensitive componential analysis, but when she had stifled a yawn he had given up.)
3. *Icon of St Nadezhda* (devotional print mounted on card above bd) & stub of burnt candle in cndlhldr in frame.
4. *Extract:* Paperback copy of Mikhail Bulgakov's *The Master and Margarita*, with passage from Chapter 13 on page 149 marked in yellow fluorescent highlighter pencil. (*N.B.* Book on table on Leon's side of bed, but flyleaf inscribed *Nadezhda Stepanovna Cheremisovna. N.B.* Xanthichromatic quotation beginning: 'Here his eyes opened wide and as he whispered he gazed at the moon.')
5. *Textbooks:* Copies of *Learn to Interpret by Interpreting* byG. G. Yudina, Москвá, and *Grammaire de la Langue Russe* by André Mazo, Institut d'Études Slaves, Paris (with dedication penned on title page: '. . . *ma nouvelle camarade d'armes adorée—aujourd'hui nous avons trouvé les mots . . . et il y a tant à dire et tant de lendemains!*')
6. *Draft letter from Benedict* (Leon's solicitor) to the Home Office applying for a 'special extension to Miss Cheremisovna's work-permit' due to her 'indispensable services' which were 'essential to a major motion picture's successful post-production.' (Miriam silently pledged never to have dealings with Benedict ever again.)

7. *Pocket English Grammar* edited by Laurence and dedicated to Leon. (At her wedding, she was sure the entire congregation must have known, except for Laurence perhaps, that Leon's best man had long carried a torch—as a flame is attracted to a brilliant, self-applauding butterfly—for the shockhaired bridegroom at her side. When Laurence's *Grammar* was at last published, Miriam believed that she, alone, understood that much of the text was a kind of *roman à clef* to be decrypted by no one but Laurence and herself.) She flipped to page 237 of **Adverbial Clauses** and read 'Joyce wandered in, **the way that she does**,' and **Modal Verbs**, page 47, 'Leonard **must think** about the consequences of his actions.' (Then there was a catch in her throat.) **'Since Joyce's father died**, she has not been able to sleep.' and 'Joyce' reappeared on page 233 under **Joining Clauses** as 'Joyce is **either** ***desperate***, **or** ***just silly***' and, again, under **Possessive Pronouns** on page 187, 'Leonard's wife is so beastly I think they must have bathroom towels labelled **his** and **its**.' (Joyce had been Miriam's maiden name.)

She closed her 'Activities Report'.

Upon such slender data she was now confident she could conduct a bloody but decisive campaign.

❀

The Glove

The doors to the Reading Rooms were still open when Miriam arrived an hour later. As she approached the portico, she hesitated to enter. Beside the door squatted one of the city's pavement bedouins, huddled with his traps under a filthy military tarpaulin. The upturned collar of the waterproof concealed the lower face but deep-set eyes swivelled after her, eloquent with reproach. On the ridge of the dado above his head, an abandoned elbow-length silk evening glove (heraldically *appaumé*) pointed (*sinister*) to the hunched figure below.

Steeling herself, she crossed the threshold, rejecting the silent appeal. (Leon, one year shortly after they were married, when blessed with abundance, had invested in the entire print sequence of *Ein Handschuh*, a cycle of 10 etchings by the symbolist, Max Klinger.

'To look back,' she mused, 'and see ourselves goodlooking,' for the characteristics of Klinger's discarded glove as erotic fetish had not escaped her; her mouth lifted in her defining smile, her eyes somnolent yet watchful as a cat's, 'when we would forget the days and think only of the nights.')

Again her secret smile—pondering the futility—the folly—of attempting to revive past happinesses—and the lines composed themselves . . .

They had always found the equation yield.
Nightly, a certain figure over
the denominator gave the proof.
Now it's impossible to believe they held
that there was ever
an alchemy that could equal love.

The Reference Annex shut at half past four and already the keeper was cranking closed the fanlights beneath the cupola.

A reader, a scholarly young Welshwoman with brown eyes so dark they were almost black, helped her to locate the correct stack.

In her 'Activities Report', under the heading of *Russian mentalität*, Miriam wrote, *Izlivat dushu*—'pouring out of the soul; the mingling of two lovers' souls, for example'; *Stradanyie*—'mental suffering due to unrequited love or coarseness of lover or spouse'; *Toska*—'melancholy homesickness'; *Grekh*—'a sense of sin only removed when sinner reaches a state of highly emotional repentance'; and, finally, *Tyomniye sili*—'dark or sinister, evil forces'; the latter she thrice underlined.

Fifth Report — 'Dead Letter Box'

The following morning—a Wednesday—Miriam resumed sentry-go at the Greek Café. Routinely, she had skipped breakfast so she felt only a mild sense of *Grekh* when she chose the *Siami* honey-cake and ordered a cappuccino.

Beside her, on a plinth, a bust of Hippocrates counted each calory.

She hid the honeycake in her handkerchief for disposal later.

(*Available light*.) Across the street, Nadia emerged, alone, with Leon's leather Cerrutti slung over her shoulder. The girl narrowed her eyes against the harsh sunlight and sauntered off towards St Petersburgh Place.

(*Long take*.) The two women, ten paces apart, traversed the Park towards Kensington Gore. Laurence's 'photons' danced between the leaves of the sycamores and winged seedpods spiralled down to meet the paving. There had been heavy rainfall in the night and pink worms had been flushed out of the grass and lay wriggling on the drying paths.

Miriam tasted sickness in the back of her throat. The sun scorched her shoulders and she removed her jacket . . .

So hot
the bench
in the park
carries its shadow
draped over

one arm

(*Close-up*.) A brilliant green leaf caterpillar landed on Miriam's breastbone where it remained, a bright enamelled emerald clasp.

Behind her, out of sight, Miriam heard a childish treble shout, 'Nat! Donchawannatunabagel?' and she knew, with absolute certainty that, if she turned around, she'd see a small school-boy on whose dark head of hair, attached by a hairgrip, would be a *yarmulke*.

She turned. A small boy, wearing a red blazer, ran past in the heat haze.

Perched on the back of his head was a skullcap. ('All that you imagine is probably true,' Leon had said, yet, if Laurence's context-sensitive theory was to be believed, in a blind test no ambiguity concerning the derivational history of the boy's utterance could be admitted.)

Nadia paced across Rotten Row, her shoes making clear impressions in the dampened sandy gallops.

Miriam carefully trod in each of Nadia's footmarks—a sequence of steps that, with practice, she believed she could learn.

(Rapid clips.) A soldier cantered by, his horse kicking up a delighted pair of heels, obliterating Nadia's tracks.

(*Master shot. Church Square. Exterior. Day.*) After Nadia had produced a headscarf and entered the church, Miriam examined the noticeboard, squinting, as the sun bounced off the virdigris of the copper canopy. For several moments she remained puzzled by the Cyrillic characters and the Julian Calendar dates—then she fathomed that some two weeks separated the Old Style and New Style entries. By counting the days backwards she realised that this morning—at this precise moment—a 10.30 a.m. liturgy for St Nadezhda was being observed within.

(The saffron, Miriam suddenly surmised, was for Nadia's cake. A cake to celebrate the feast of her saint's day.)

(*Interior.*) Choral singing. Votive candles shone through the incense billows. Miriam choked on the fierce acridness, took two paces forward and entered Holy Mother Russia. Instinctively, she sought the concealment of a stone pillar. *Cut to . . .* The arch-priest's hairy eyebrows like an imperial spreadeagle. Cut to . . . Nadia threading a path through the worshippers, approaching before the iconastasis to genuflect, bowing low, the heel of her right hand pressed against the floor. *Cut to . . .* Nadia rising to kiss the censed icon in front of the screen—first the hem of the Virgin, then the holy robe of the Infant. *Cut to . . .* Sparkle of candlelight as a tear (*Toska?*) brims and trickles down Nadia's jaw. She sniffs, and wipes her cheek with her palm.

(Nadia's pursuing phantom, unabashed, followed directly behind her.) And here was experienced a sense of *Grekh* Miriam knew she would never, never later relate — Miriam stooped, and planted her own lips where Nadia had impressed hers.

(Lipsync.)

Then a surge of émigrés, making obeisances, drove Miriam to a far alcove where a cloth-covered table was laid with neatly classified mail from abroad.

So, Miriam reflected, what better place for Nadia's *Dead Letter Box* than a Russian church in the heart of London?

The name *Nadezhda Stepanovna Cheremisovna* leaped out at her from the cover of a flimsy, faded blue envelope. She withdrew the airmail from the stack and looked for the name of sender. *Stepan Alexievitch Cheremisov*. She released her suspended breath. '*Learn to Interpret by Interpreting*,' she thought. Clearly the father was sending his mail to his daughter here at the church, *poste restante*, and not to Leon's flat! Surely that very fact suggested an impermanence in the girl's relations with Leon? Then she softened. Perhaps Nadia feared her father's censure. Perhaps the deception was devised as a propitiation more to confound patriarchal suspicions than Leon's. Then Miriam saw there was another letter for Nadia—with a London postmark and hastily pencilled address—and abruptly she was not so sure.

(Pan.) Nadia halts on the steps. She removes her headscarf as the Archpriest departs through side entrance. Looped through his fingers he carries twin gold crowns haloed with sunbeams (evidently a rehearsal for a wedding). Nadia pockets her father's letter, unopened.

(Reaction shot.) Miriam's mouth twitches and tightens.

(Medium close-up.) Nadia opens letter with London postmark, reads contents, smiles. Applies lipstick. Adjusts sunglasses. Examines watch. Struts towards Knightsbridge.

(Tracking shot.) The pursuit was shortlived. Past the barracks—the air ripe with the sweetness of straw and warm ordure—the two women strolled in the sun. Then they were gone—last seen entering *Maxies* cocktail bar and restaurant—buried in the traffic blur and wavering fumes. *(Ripple dissolve.)*

(Mirror shot.) In the mirror behind the cocktail bar, Nadia could be observed seated at a table talking intently to a young off-duty

waiter (or so Miriam judged)—one of London's tribe of hollowed-cheeked nightworkers, whose circles of dark flesh beneath the eyes (Miriam noticed on closer inspection) had tautened like blackened drumskins.

Then unbreached custom translated—in a trice—the waiter into diner, for he drew out a chair to seat himself at Nadia's side and waved familiarly to the bar for drinks. *Honey Dew Screwdrivers.* Vodka, orange juice and melon liqueur. (Colour? Verdigrisgreen.)

Nadia's companion possessed no discernable earlobes, a certain sign (according to Aunt Wilma) of unregenerate criminality. (Miriam's own lobes were vestigial.)

At the bar, Miriam nibbled from the remains of a dish of *zakuski* —a hint of red and black caviar on toasted roundels—and discovered the waitress, impatient at indecision, had ordered her, unbidden, a Virgin Mary.

(*Close-up.*) At the table, Nadia and her khol-eyed suitor communed with clasped hands. (*Voiceover*, cigarette-roughened, compelling, 'Mais Nadine, je t'ai dit que je prefere le vert,' etcetera.)

Miriam drew near, hurrying towards the exit. As she brushed past, her elbow toppled a sugarbowl and fluted glass saltpot. (*Slow motion.*) In the disarray—as the two lovers flailed at the linen cloth—the spilt seasoning was passed from palm to palm. Very soon the lovers began to quarrel and 'Nadine' gnawed nervously the ragged ruby chips of her varnished nails.

One last glance at the bar mirror reassured Miriam that any sense of *izlivat dushu* between the couple had now been satisfactorily dispelled.

The Graze

Secure beneath a chainmail of suds, the steam condensing on the ceiling, Miriam searched through veils of mist for the familiars and revenants who at bathtimes would always revisit her.

First she read the star-map of her knees, the pink domes with their constellations of blue grit embedded beneath the skin.

(*flashback*.) There had been heavy rain. They had gone to the Fair, she, her father and Aunt Wilma—idly following the cinder tracks that had been sprinkled on the sodden turf—until they heard the barker calling them to 'The House of Cobwebs'. Glimpsing the painted ghouls of the Grande Guignol, she had struggled to turn back.

But Miriam's hand was held tight by the Old Man (for thus, with a mixture of fear and affection, aunt and niece secretly referred to Miriam's father).

The Old Man had paid ninepence, and drawn Miriam into the dark. Then his hand loosened and he was gone. Too frightened to cry out, she had blundered down the blacked-out maze of passageways, cobwebs brushing her face, banshees screaming from the speakers above, until pulses from a welcoming green light beckoned her on.

Then, in the darkest depths of the corridor, she saw that the light issued from beneath the bearded chin of a gargantuan gargoyle, the green rays fringing its throat, eyes glittering with malevolence. She gazed up in terror. The light turned red and the face erupted into a roar of jubilant laughter. She ran. Stumbled against musty canvas, fumbled for an opening in the tentflap, and, heart pounding with fear, fell upon the cinders.

Aunt Wilma drew the child to her feet, and inspected the plump flesh speckled with fresh blood. The Old Man emerged from the tent, a shamefaced grin buried in his beard. A cold wind sprang up. He hugged his armpits, banging his limbs—a wild semaphore.

(*Still*.) But, face impassive, still Miriam refused to cry.

'No sense no feeling,' muttered Aunt Wilma, 'the girl has a face like a yard of pump water.' But she bent down and whispered, 'Bloodied but unbowed, eh? That's right. If the Old Man wants to act the goat there's no call for tears.'

The Old Man, soldierly, shrugged deeper into his army trenchcoat and buttoned his upturned collar. He switched off his flashlight with its sliding coloured gels and, stiffbacked, he, too, knelt at her side.

'I was only signalling in the dark,' he explained, and held her to him. She clung tightly but felt only the palisade of unrelenting ribbed stays beneath his coat pressed hard against her; until he pulled away, his eyes clouded with pain. Then her tears welled.

The Graze

Children weep for their future lives.
In the cinder grit beneath the skin,
in the nettle's spite and wasp's sting,
apprehend a lover's griefs,
and husband spurned.
And the infant, sobbing,
fallen from her swing,
chants
a lament for wives
abandoned.

(*Flash forward.*) Now, in the bath, tracing again her star-map, she could see the blue flecks had not faded.

(*Flashback.*) That night, Aunt Wilma had sent Miriam to her cot early, unable to outstare the clearsighted, unblinking gaze of the nursery's newborn assessor whose tiny fingers entwined and disengaged so compulsively in the open stitches of a coverlet from which, as she slept, she never withdrew her grasp. When Aunt Wilma switched on the nightlight and padded to the stairs the child nestled down and felt for the edge of the blanket. Not until she had performed her comforting ritual of packing a frondlike fringe into one nostril did she sleep.

Later she awoke and heard the Old Man's stockinged feet shuffling on the linoleum as he passed her door to his bedroom. She could hear him muttering, *'Slither'n'slip to the Land of Counterpane,'* and his pillbox rattled in the pocket of his dressing-gown. Only in the very last letter from Aunt Wilma did Miriam learn that her father's counterpain had been 10 grains of Barbitone rising, in his final years, to a dosage of 30 grains per night.

Next morning, when Miriam opened her eyes she discovered that someone in the night had removed the safety bars of her cot and the pink coverlet with the embroidered letter *M* was gone.

❁

Sixth Report — 'The Cherry Orchard'

Despite the changed circumstances between husband and wife, Miriam was reluctant to refuse Leon when he telephoned from the Studios and invited her to roam those vast halls of illusion to view his startling new sets.

When she entered the sound stage she was amazed by the audacity of his vision.

(*Scene. A forest track. Night.*) Leon couldn't dissemble his self-applauding grin when he approached to greet her. He pointed to the huge boles of the oak trees, encrusted with lichen, that he had caused to grow in three weeks to the nightsky. A dense tangle of branches wove a web on the dark vault above them where electric stars glittered in their courses. Leon buried his finger to the knuckle in the bark of a tree.

'See, they're hot-wired sculptured in polystyrene then sprayed and linked together in sixteen-foot lengths right up to the "reds".' Leon pointed to the lighting grid—zenith distance—above their heads.

'The sky's a diorama but those branches are real. They're full-grown trees hung upside down. We bought up an entire cherry orchard in Kent.'

Leon described how he had hired 400 lb chainwinches to harvest the remains of mature trees—the remnants of a hurricane—and how he had assembled a scenedock in the orchard. Now, inside the Studio, the set dressing crew applied the finishing touches.

He nodded towards the director of photography who all morning had been testing a new 'swing-and-shift' lens designed to extend his depth of field.

'Remember,' Leon confided, as the cameraman packed away the 35 mm blimped Arriflex, 'all the lens sees is the last coat of paint. It's our job to reorchestrate the values of scale to cheat the eye of the camera.'

His beard brushed her cheek, and he casually, proprietorially, kissed her temple.

(Under the stars, she thought.)

'The object is to cheat the shot,' he said.

When Miriam paused at the exit to glance back at her bearded woodcutter husband at ease within his own sylvan scene—the starlit enchanted forest, the velvet blackness of the painted backcloth—she could not be certain she had not glimpsed a hooded figure clad in dark green moving in the shadows between the trees.

(To see the cherry hung, she thought.)

❦

The Running Noose

(*Resume on interior of ironmonger's shop.*) Her speech placid and measured, Miriam bought four yards of three-strand hempen rope and—in an access of secrecy to ensure her visit should pass unremarked—she purchased a number of other needless hardware items.

❦

That night, for the first time, Miriam placed the events of her life in order, as she had promised herself four days before.

❦

(*Flashback.*) They were passing a country churchyard, Aunt Wilma and Miriam (who could not suppose why her aunt had chosen this path). Miriam must have been no more than eleven because she recalled she was wearing her new high-school blazer and she remembered its constriction and unaccustomed weight on her back. They walked to an open patch of grass at the far reaches of the graveyard where Aunt Wilma pointed to a plot where there were no headstones.

Later, Miriam had sat on the tomb of the first rector (he was buried with his head to the churchyard wall so on the Day of Resurrection he would be facing his risen flock). Then, immersed in the sickly scent of flowering laurels, she had cried for the mother she had never known.

The Sociogram

Miriam had been taught the techniques of schematics by the Sister Directress. When she examined her own sociogram she saw it conformed in practically all respects to the classic corelative patterns of the classroom most frequently encountered in her textbooks. Leon was without question in the category of class *Star*, forming an exclusive *Mutual Pair* with Nadia, whilst Laurence could be clearly classified a *Rejectee*, leaving Miriam, herself, labelled with the lamedog-tag of *Isolate*, shackled irretrievably in a halter-led, one-way *Chain* of dependence to her father, the Old Man. And, between them, to complete the schema, holding Miriam—as always—at arm's length, stood Aunt Wilma who, though yielding never to her niece, had yet submitted to her station as docile bondservant to her older brother.

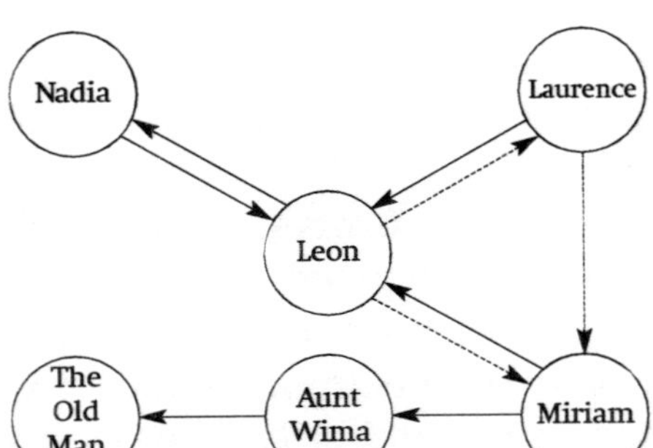

Seventh Report — 'Russian Montage'.

(Miriam's point of view from car parked opposite entrance to Leon's flat.) Nadia and Leon emerge and walk away arm in arm.

(Travelling shot.) Miriam makes rapid U-turn and parks outside flat entrance.

(Props note.) Hempen rope with running noose prominent in view above dashboard.

❁

(Exterior. Day. Resume on iron staircase to Mrs Bryce's rooftop flat.) Sign with arrow points upstairs to *Caretaker*. Old Mrs Bryce limps down staircase. (She labours from the weight of a metal caliper affixed to one ankle, the result of having fallen, two years previously, on treacherous ice on this very staircase.) She wears a patched housecoat; and her crimped hairdo is protected by a faded cotton headscarf. She grunts with satisfaction as she encounters two brand-new galvanised zinc buckets placed at the foot of the stairs.

(Medium close-up.) Mrs Bryce carries buckets into the Ground Floor rear of Mansion Block.

❁

(Cut-in . . . extreme close-up.) A hand attaches hempen noose to wooden crossbar.

❁

(Découpage in manner of 'Russian Montage' cross-cutting on steps leading to first-floor flat.)

(Cut-in . . .) The hallway, alcoves and first-floor landing are dazzled by a profusion of resplendent YELLOW FLOWERS. Bowls, vases, urns are dense with preternaturally glowing blooms.

(Cut-in . . .) Mrs Bryce enters from ground-floor rear, exclaims with astonishment, shaking her head in wonderment at the

all-enveloping field of gold, as, muttering, she carries the empty pails and mounts the stairs to first floor.

(Cut-in . . . close-up.) A hand presses steadily on Leon's doorbell.

(Sustained ringing of bell as automatic door-opening device erratically whirs on and off.)

(Cut-in . . .) First-floor flat door is flung open and Nadia, eyes wide, face pale and distorted with fright, runs to the head of the stairs . . . whirls, as she sees, for the first time, the golden petals that fall across her face. Her fingers describe a crucifix over her mouth.

Nadia:
Svjataja deva Mariya!
(*Subtitles:* **Holy Virgin Mary!**)

(Cut-in . . .) Brushing aside the yellow blooms, the old *babushka,* Mrs Bryce, breathing heavily, turns a corner of the stairs burdened by the weight of the two buckets.

Nadia:
Poshel k chertu!
Ubiraisya k d'yavolu, staraya ved'ma!
(Subtitles: **Go to the Devil! Go to Hell, old witch!**)

(Cut-in . . . extreme close-up.) Icon of St Nadezhda engulfed in flames.
(Cut-in . . . extreme close-up.) Nadia screaming.

❀

(Roughcut . . . Resume on steps to schoolroom crypt . . . Extreme close up . . .) Little Andrea screaming with infant heartbreak as he stumbles down the stone steps, tears streaming from beneath his shattered wire-framed specs.

(Softfocus.) One eye is enlarged and startled behind the lens, the other blind under frosted glass.

❀

The Mancub

(*Interior. Crypt schoolroom.*) There were no words Miriam could use to comfort the boy. The cardboard box lay empty at his feet. A single black feather drifted across the polished floor. But the bird was gone. How this was so the boy could not know, but he knew he had failed her. He howled at his own betrayal. The other children looked askance with scorn. Miriam gazed at the little mancub, deaf to his imperious rage. (*Lvynok,* Andrea's teacher pronounced to herself, *Little Lion.*) Looking closely, she could see the incipient growth of dark down that furred his cheek along the jawline.

A frost touched her and Miriam allowed the icy crystals to grow around her heart until her resolve was fully made and she was certain she would not soften. Then, since the children had begun to clamour for attention, she restored order by surprising them with a complete change of routine.

Eighth Report—'Unravelling'

(*Interior. Miriam's fire-lit study. That night.*) There remained one last task—the destruction of Miriam's 'Activities Report'; the removal of the final pages. One by one she tore out the sheets of notes and tossed them on the flames.

(i) *In the Cheremis culture of the Volga-Don region it was believed that the wrath of a saint can be invoked by burning a candle upside down before its icon.* (The sparkling candles Miriam had lit, inverted under the framed print of St Nadezhda, had succeeded beyond her modest expectations. A pity Leon's leather Cerrutti had been scorched in the blaze.)

(ii) *An engagement can be prevented by entangling the legs of a table with a rope. Should the girl's father hear of this spell he can break it by chopping both table legs and severing the rope*. (But Stepan Alexievitch Cheremisov had been asleep over two thousand miles away.)

(iii) *An omen of impending misfortune is sight of an old village woman carrying empty pails*. By good fortune, loyal Mrs Bryce had sustained only a mild sprain from her second fall. (She had required little prompting to begin the long-neglected spring cleaning of the first floor. As agreed, Miriam had placed the new buckets for collection by the stairs.)

(iv) *When salt is passed from hand to hand these persons quarrel*. True. And the lovers had continued to quarrel shortly after Mrs Bryce had been sent tumbling by Nadia who had jumped into a cab conjured by her khol-eyed summoner. (*Flashback. Travelling matte. Taxi rear window.*) Nadine sobbed on his shirt-front while he mocked the *ingenue*, but she *had* seen a witch, she had, and it would drive her to the Devil. Nadine's quivering finger points to the *ved'ma*, old Mrs Bryce, hobbling after the cab, hurling imprecations.

(v) *The Devil can get in your mouth*. That is why you must make the sign of the cross over your lips.

(vi) *A bird flying into a room is an ill omen*. Andrea's starling had not stirred until Miriam carried the box into Leon's bedroom. She had cradled the tremulous bird in her hands, perching it on the bedside table. Later, when Nadia had entered, the first thing she saw in the candle's flare was a dark fluttering presence like a bat hammering at the window in confusion.

(vii) *Yellow flowers are a sign of infidelity*. Miriam had referred the extract from *The Master and Margarita* to Laurence who had provided an unexpected exegesis of Bulgakov's text which immediately followed the phrase, '*. . . as he whispered he gazed at the moon*.' On the telephone she could hear Laurence riffling the pages, then he quoted, '*She was carrying some of those repulsive flowers*,' and crowed in recognition. '*It's an ugly colour*,' he read, 'that's because it's Russki semiotics for an unfaithful woman, it's central to the text, don't you see?' Then she heard a carillon of mordant laughter. 'Forgive the emotional histrionicism, but I warned Leon . . .' But Miriam hung up.

❁

She had taken her secateurs and gone straightaway into the garden. First the Yarrow (*Achillea millefolium*) and plumes of Golden Rod, then the yellowish Lilies (*Enchantment*), and finally she chose the yellow Aster; not the species plant but the low-bred cultivars that had strayed to the kitchen door — the Aster*asters* — for these she considered the most fitting tribute of all from the philosoph*aster*, poet*aster* and ciné*aster* she knew herself to be.

❁

The fire subsided, a flame guttering on the last fragment of paper. The room had grown dark. Miriam switched on the Old Man's army flashlight (how curious that the dusty *Empire* bulb could function still after remaining inactive for so many years) and a beam of green light was cast on the pink coverlet she had placed on a chair. (*Mise-en-scène*.)

❁

Miriam began to unpick the threads of the blanket, unravelling the pink wool, until she had formed a skein. (To be Penelope at Ithica, she thought, forever fated to disentangle swaddling clothes to make a shroud.)

❁

In the gloaming, the little dog grew restive on Miriam's lap and leapt in the firelight to the hearth; then, in the singsong voice she reserved for the animal, she crooned:

'If I were as pretty as you,
as quarter as pretty would do.'

A ball of wound pink wool rolled from the table edge. (The little white dog **snarled** when the ball reached it. When the little white dog reached it the ball **snarled**.) She must remember, she smiled sleepily, to relate to Laurence this oddity of contextual sensitivity.

❁

From the garden room below, Miriam heard Leon's discreet, suppressed sneeze. The sound grated. The truth was that the frequent muffled explosions did, indeed, sound remarkably like *Kissinger!* and, in time, the apprehension as one waited for the next convulsion began to attack one's nerves. (She could glimpse Leon through the glass roof as he poured unsteadily another amber tumbler and the spirit spilled. She was reminded that tomorrow the first Montessorian lesson in 'Isolating the Variables' was an exercise devoted to *differential visual-tactile-muscular perception of form.*)

❁

She stepped out on to the terrace above the garden room and in her peripheral vision she had a prickling sense of the planets teeming above her. She stared up at the over-arching night. She whispered as she gazed at the crescent moon which appeared to her as the half-closed stopper of a dark urn in which she had been irredeemably entombed, and the scattering of stars seemed to her as light dimly penetrating the filigree of an abandoned design; fragments of an unfinished frieze chased on the outer surface of her sepulchre. Yet what the subject of the original pattern could have been—strain her eyes as she might—she could not possibly begin to guess.

COUSIN LUDWIG'S SUBTRACTION GAME

(*Grete B.*—Imipramine)

'And he said: "Thy brother came with
guile, and hath taken away thy blessing." '

'Irrlichter:
Von dem Sumpfe kommen wir,
Woraus wir erst entstanden . . .'*

Assessment Summary (extract): An earlier counselling session with her sister, Isolde (see *The Eleven Surviving Works of L v. K*), unusually for any case, allowed a trauma disorder shared by siblings to be compared and cross-referenced. The current course of Imipramine, as a palliative to suppress symptoms through chemical interaction, should be viewed as a medicinal therapy preparatory to a drug-free approach. The next steps towards improved health are the introduction of detraumatisation and relaxation techniques and desensitivity therapy to review calmly the perceived threats.

* Will-o'-the-Wisps: From the marshes we appear, where we originated . . . (Goethe's *Faust*, Part I, Scene XXII.)

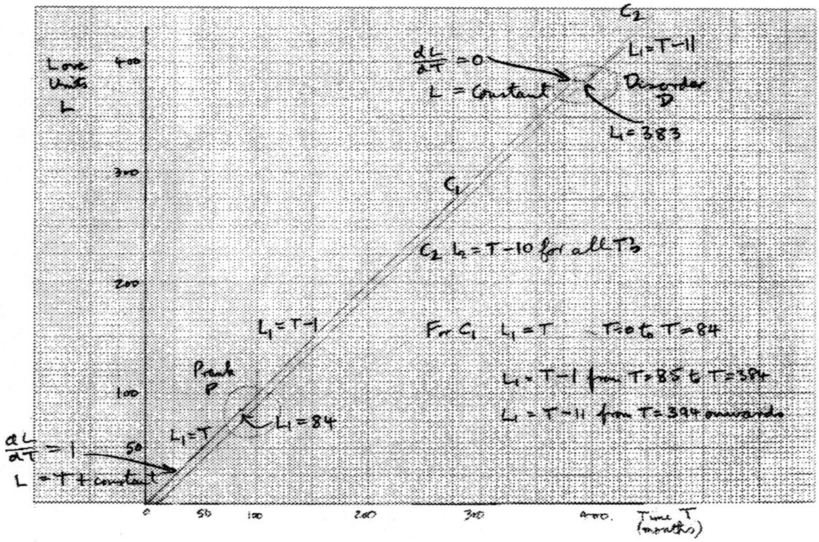
Love Units L
C_2
$L_1 = T - 11$
$\frac{dL}{dT} = 0$
L = Constant
Disorder D
$L_1 = 383$
C_1
C_2 $L_2 = T - 10$ for all Ts
$L_1 = T - 1$
For C_1 $L_1 = T$ T=0 to T=84
$L_1 = T - 1$ from T=85 to T=394
$L_1 = T - 11$ from T=394 onwards
Peak P
$L_1 = T$
$L_1 = 84$
$\frac{dL}{dT} = 1$
L = T + constant
Time T (months)

COUSIN LUDWIG'S SUBTRACTION GAME

Patient ID CPN0308270743: Grete B.
Occupation: Private tour & travel operator.
Drug: Imipramine.
Drug class: Tricyclic antidepressant for treatment of panic attacks and agoraphobia.
Common side effects: Increased heart rate, blurred vision, constipation, dry mouth, weight gain or loss.

When the dead speak their speech is often banal.

For instance, I once overheard two aged nuns whispering together in a French railway carriage. The older *religieuse* said: 'But you must remember Beatrice, she died two years before me.'

The voice she lowered from within the darkness of her hood was a kind of liturgical gurgling.

Perhaps, then, you'll believe my claim when I tell you I'm convinced my ear is finely attuned to register similar occasions. And of those events there can be none more strange than the case of the loss of my father.

An Errant Light

When I was a small child my mother would repeat, with curious emphasis, a family saying whose true significance I was to learn only much later.

'The love that lasts the longest is the strongest,' she used to say, placing her hand devoutly over my father's when he was in one of his black moods; yet, before she died, I was able to prove her conclusively wrong.

My father was a proud, stiff-necked character and, in the days of my early girlhood, he worked as an under-forester for a cadet branch of the Hohenzollerns.

In those desperate years of hunger and suspicion he was grateful for the job his friend, the Count, had granted him. I remember my father wore an old forest-green wool jacket of the Count's with ribbed-cloth knee breeches of a matching colour. His cap was of wolf-skin and his wide embossed belt and field-boots were of buff leather. As befitting a forest steward, my father carried a shotgun as his badge of office. His pockets bulged with acorns for sowing among the thickets on his forest patrols.

(In respect for our benefactor's memory I shall refer to my father's boss as the 'Count' but that was not, in fact, his title. As a youth, my father had been a medallist student at the State Summer School of Forestry which the Count hosted each year at the *Schloss*.)

So we went to live in the shadow of an ancient palatine forest, a place where hardly a yard of light was admitted; where continuous black darkness had strangled all the light.

'We live out our days in shadowlight,' my grandmother would complain gloomily. (She used the word, *Schattenlicht*, whose mysterious ambiguity conveyed so well our sense of strangled light and oppression.)

Ours was a little hamlet composed of timber shanties by the forest edge, hidden from the Count's castle by kitchen gardens, embankments and shrubs.

With my sister Isolde (who was ten months my senior) I would explore the forest tracks, which were mostly so narrow we had to walk in each other's footsteps. Sometimes, gathering mushrooms, we would walk as far as the swamplands where the river's watermeadows began.

One evening we followed a dark, beaten track which ended at the margin of a marsh. Around us the scrub swarmed with mosquitoes and hornets.

In a clearing we were overcome by a stifling odour of resin compounded by the mustiness of leafmould and decay.

All was silent save for the sound of a dog-badger brushing about the forest.

Isolde drew back in fear but, before I followed, I saw in the gloaming a dancing ring of little points of light as bright as the brightest star.

'Look!' I exclaimed. *'Irrlicht!'* And I pointed to the 'errant light' we called the will-o'-the-wisp in our corner of the province. But Isolde had fled.

I would have thought no more of this incident had I not, a half hour later, heard my father's roarings echoing from the timber-yard.

When I approached I could see he was shaking with fury. When he erupted into one of his carpet-biting rages his nose would glow like a danger signal. Now his face seemed to be turning all colours.

From inside the heel of his boot my father withdrew from a secret sheath his hunting dagger and brandished it at the throat of a terrified young woodcutter who covered his face and ran off.

'Take your idiot face out of my sight!' my father shouted. 'You're not wanted here!'

On a makeshift stretcher formed by poles and lashed great-coats lay a figure I recognised as my young cousin Ludwig. Ludo was the son of the *Oberforst-Meister*, my uncle, the chief forester.

A half-hewn tree had fallen on the boy and killed him.

Isolde ran to my side, clutched my hand and burst into tears.

I gazed, passionless, at Ludo's small still face. That a local superstition was proved true was my only thought. In those parts they believe that sight of a small corpse-light in the marshes indicates the death of a child.

❦

After that tragedy the fury of my father scarcely abated.

Yet, as it turned out, it was not to be myself but his cherished older daughter, Isolde, who was to bear the full brunt of his foul temper.

Here I shall explain why my father turned on my sister.

You should know that Isolde was a finicky eater, and even in those lean times she would pick at her food. Hunger and hardship compelled us, like the other forest dwellers, to grow what crops we could, yet, perversely, potatoes were in short supply due to marauders stealing them to distil into spirits.

Up on the highest point of the forest, in the glades of the charcoal-burners, were said to be huts harbouring their illicit stills.

Every scrap of food and fuel was precious. You would not see any fragments of timber lying about. Every chip of bark remaining along the logging roads was carefully gathered by the locals; they even collected sawdust as a fuel; and every piece of stray brushwood was sorted into billets, according to its state of rottenness, dampness and, for the more fastidious, its stench.

My father, too, was a fanatic who abhorred waste.

So you can imagine his wrath when, returning home late for supper one night, he was assailed by the acrid smell of burning food and beheld the unaccustomed sight of Isolde's platter completely licked clean.

Father had a nose for scenting trouble, as I mentioned.

In her terror Isolde was blushing most unbecomingly.

Father stared fixedly with suspicion at her tidy plate then turned in anger to wrench open the hob of our kitchen stove.

I held my breath. My tongue dried and my mouth tasted of chewed string.

Peering into the fire's heart, Father started with a yelp of pain as a spurt of boiling white pulp stung his cheek. The pain dealt from a hot potato bursting from its skin is agonising.

Thenceforth there was a red wen where Father's face was burnt, over which, at length, he cultivated side whiskers.

He blamed Isolde's faddishness for his misfortune and did not talk to her for an entire month. His silence fell like a dead frost.

No one dared to tell my father that I was wholly to blame . . . I loathed those potatoes no less powerfully than Isolde but I dutifully ate them. (On hearing Father stamping his boots at the door, I had switched our plates and deposited Isolde's wilfully uneaten portion in the stove.)

Between Isolde and myself any mention of this prank was a matter which was under several interdictions through the years.

My grandmother was not blind to my misdeeds.

In her counsels she spoke with care, choosing her words as if she were matching silks.

She privately reproved me: 'You laugh when your sister weeps, and weep when your sister laughs.'

In all truth I was guilty as charged. Quite simply, my grievance sprang from envy of an older sister whom my father had loved *a whole ten months longer than myself*. And the envy would have remained an unrelieved grudge had not my little cousin Ludo, shortly before his death, confided to me certain secret instructions for applying a remedy he had discovered, which, if followed precisely, he said, were guaranteed to redress forever this deficit of love.

The Secret Game

Cousin Ludwig (like my uncle) was maddeningly methodical.

Ludwig was an inventor of fiendishly complicated board games.

When he won he would wrestle me to the floor with more enthusiasm than was entirely proper for a nine-year-old.

'The player unable to move loses!' he would shout in triumph, twining his scrawny legs in mine until our pelvic bones ground together.

He hated his more favoured older brother, Ernst, who bullied him. There was a deep scar beneath his left eye where Ernst had hurled a missal with metal edges after church. Ludo wore it as badge of honour like a duellist's bragging scar.

One hot afternoon in the forest, Ludo explained to me his theory of 'The Subtraction Game'.

We were seated on a warm knoll overlooking the river valley. Deep-voiced cattle-hounds were baying from the upper pastures.

Above us, battalions of pines marched up the ridge, their bark as smooth as the mast of a ship, their branches as regular as a ladder. Below us, meticulously ordered columns of firs, spruce and larch converged on an overgrown grove of state birches, a plantation once harvested by a military department for experiments in extracting asphyxiating gases.

Ludo leant forward (though there was not another soul in sight) and whispered in my ear.

'This is a secret,' he said. Despite dropping his voice, he could not conceal a tremor of unease. 'Swear you won't tell.'

His breath smelled of yesterday's bratwurst; he twisted my hair.

'As God is my judge,' I whimpered.

He withdrew a crumpled diary from inside his shirt and spread out two pages of scrawled calculations.

'D'you see that?' he asked eagerly, pointing to a declining curve labelled 'E' plotted over the 'Time' axis of an intricate graph. 'That's Ernst!'

For a minute Ludo was convulsed with silent laughter.

He then pointed with a nail-bitten finger to a steep growth curve marked 'L' projected along the same axis.

'That's me!'

The longer I looked the more puzzling his squiggles seemed because I could see the time-line of Ludo's rough graph extended merely across the previous fortnight and abruptly terminated before the week after next began.

'What does it all mean?' I demanded impatiently.

'You'll see,' he teased. 'Just ask Ernst who's Pa's favourite fair-haired boy after Friday, that's all.'

Resentful at the web of mystery woven by his spidery scribblings, I tore the pages from his notebook and raced down the hill.

There was no pursuit; my last glimpse of Ludo alive was of him seated on the knoll, loosely clasping his knees as though hugging a secret that he could scarcely contain.

Now Friday had dawned and little Ludwig was dead.

In the lamplit refuge of our porch I studied again Ludo's calculations and tried to penetrate his meaning.

Only when I remembered the distraught young woodcutter whom Father had blamed for Ludwig's death did the truth strike me.

Of course! Why hadn't I seen through his woodman's disguise when he had blundered past me, eyes glittering, swollen with tears? The young woodcutter was Ernst!

I remembered suddenly the youth's muttered protestations as, shoulders shuddering, he had fled the death scene.

'B-b-but why won't they listen to me?' the fleeing figure had sobbed brokenly. 'He ran deliberately into the path of the tree b-b-before it fell . . .'

Now, with a fresh understanding, I knew what Ernst knew: that the two brothers had been fooling around in the forest and the stunt Ludwig had pulled on Ernst must have gone tragically wrong.

I knew then, with absolute certainty, that, for the remainder of his life, Ernst would be held culpable for his younger brother's death, while Ludo, unto the last, would glow bright in his father's memory as the favoured child. Yes. Ernst the older son, like Esau the firstborn denied his Abrahamic blessing, would fall further and further from grace.

I compared once more the plunging descent of the curve marked 'Ernst', predicted on Ludo's smudged gridlines, with the degree of curvature expressing the peak of his own ascendency at point 'L', where the graph abruptly terminated.

Doubtless, Ludo had not truly foreseen the potentially fatal outcome to what he called his 'Subtraction Game' but, in a perverse way, I was proud of my young cousin's dogged absolutism; for, in the differential equation he had plotted on his secret balance sheet, in his scheme to reverse his deficit of paternal love, he had, after all, contrived to magnify his brother's transgressions, by the simple expedient of eliminating his own from the final reckoning.

In short, his last recourse had been to wholly subtract *himself*.

Go With Great Precaution in the Fog

'The younger sister is often the ancienter,' observed my form mistress at our new school, with more prescience than she could have possibly imagined.

In England I was to discover I was more quick witted than my older sister and my teachers soon learned I was naturally good at numbers.

'She's as lively as a parcel of snakes,' I overheard the maths master murmur to a colleague after quizzing me on my figure work.

(I'll abridge the troubled years of our family's wanderings and gloss over the humiliations my father endured in his attempts to evade the governmental Red-Tapeism of post-war Europe, except to record that, thanks to the benign influence of the Count, we pitched up at last as displaced persons on the Sussex coast, which has been our home ever since.)

In the hurly-burly of a new school year—in a strange land that was not ours—the epic sibling rivalries of Ludwig and Ernst were swiftly forgotten.

The other day, Isolde showed me one of her school exercise books which recalled the anxieties of those early months:

'I am not very accustomed with the English language,' Isolde wrote. *'It is eight months now that I left the continent. In the beginning we founded not quite correct our way and we must often ask the policeman which are here very kind. A policeman answer me in German because he was as a prisoner during the war in Germany and has learned there some words. He was very please to use them.'*

True. English people were very kind to us.

The same could not always be said of some of our teachers.

Because only ten months separated us (Isolde had been born in October while I had arrived prematurely at the end of the following July) I was positioned as the youngest girl in class and she took her place as the oldest.

'The younger sister is often the ancienter,' Miss Sharp, my acid-tongued form mistress, would repeat pointedly with a piercing glance, as though she would take cold satisfaction in driving a wedge between Isolde and myself.

'Never were two sisters more dissimilar.' Miss Sharp was galled, I think, by the fact that we sat, without rancour, where she had slyly seated us, at the same desk.

That there was a profound truth in this observation is evinced by the series of misadventures that next befell us both. Aptly, Isolde's (fractured) English compositions for her school homework remain as a crib to prompt my memories of those times:

'November 3rd. Autumn remembers us of cold and wet days. Then the trees loose their leaves. Today I had the first time my new winter coat on. Because I am born in the north of Europe I sometimes am longing for the grey skies. Who has been on a mountain immidst snow will never forget it. You can hear the chiming of cow bells in the pasturages. I always have liked to think on those days.'

The moment I scanned those innocent words I felt a queasy pang of realisation as I recalled with astonishing vividness that remote November day and our trudge along the muddy bank of the River Ouse in search of mushrooms and of our lost past.

'It has now rained during some days,' Isolde wrote. *'England is surrounded of the sea and is quite different to the place I am coming from. Fog is everywhere. The trains go with great precaution in the fog. The fog is not well to breath.'*

A furry vapour hung like a wet pelt over the watermeadows as we followed a tributary into the fog. Inch by inch, we felt our way along a raised footpath, imagining we were deep in the forests of our fatherland.

A railway engine whistled far off.

Below us, pale, dim, rippling lights beckoned us through the grey mist shrouding the marshes and I continued to shiver with a familiar sense of foreboding until the path turned uphill and trees resolved themselves in gradually increasing distinctness.

We did not recognise the terrain but the skyline seemed just a few strides away so Isolde ran on ahead to regain our bearings.

Less than a minute passed, then I saw her drop from view.

I next, simultaneously, heard two dreadful sounds: a pitiful cry of pain and panic from my sister, and the hiss of breakers straining to reach the shore.

We had strayed on to the headland! A place forbidden to us by Father.

I ran to the cliff's edge and looked down at a dizzying wall of chalk falling away from my feet. East and west stretched nothing but an expanse of low grey sky clouding the waters of the English Channel.

On the sheer cliff face Isolde clung to a perilous handhold already crumbling under her grasp. Her left foot was twisted at an unnatural angle.

'My ankle!' Isolde groaned. 'It's broken! I can't use my feet to climb back!'

She stared into my eyes with an intensity that seemed at once to strip away the emotional distance that for so long had existed between us.

Knuckles white, her grip was loosening.

Frantically I searched the ground for a makeshift support. I tugged at a fence post but it snapped midway.

In that great extremity some instinct past reasoning made me untie the braided draw-strings of my dirndl apron and knot one end to my wrist.

Lying full stretch, I wound the other end round Isolde's forearm. The mushrooms we'd gathered tumbled from the apron pocket into the sea.

Whatever happens, I thought, our fate will always be bound together.

Isolde was breathing rapidly; her upraised face was as pale as any Undine's, and her eyelids fluttered like snatches from a flickering silent film.

My efforts were not in vain for, the instant we were strung together, she fainted, and her grasp weakened, and I found myself bearing her suspended weight by one arm.

I felt an immense, tearing pain from my arm socket and, despite digging in with my feet, my body started to slide forward on the springy turf.

Isolde's eyes opened and she shook her head, rising to consciousness.

'Save yourself!' she cried out harshly.

(We both knew of a young schoolgirl who had died that year at that very spot; the series of rocky ledges above Splash Point were notorious as the hunting grounds of 'eggers' who collected gulls' eggs for local fishermen who sold them as delicacies to London hotels.)

What brief span we had remaining before I was to be dragged over the cliff edge I cannot judge because we next heard our names echoing off the headland and we shouted at the top of our lungs in response.

My father had a strong carrying voice.

His vast hand closed on Isolde's slender wrist and lifted her clear.

I saw the blade flash from his hunting dagger and he cut through the braid where Isolde's forearm was cross-gartered with bright red welts and birdlime streaks of an eerie white.

Then Isolde was clasped in Father's embrace, weeping harrowingly, face buried in his chest and mumbling explanations.

Her words completely exonerated me of any misconduct.

But as I gazed at my father's broad back, and at Isolde's raw fingers twisted tight round his neck, I will tell you truthfully that, at that critical hour, I felt I resembled nothing so much as an amputee reaching out for my father's blessing with phantom arms.

❁

Death-in-Life

'There are in England the opposite customs as they are in use in my country,' wrote Isolde shortly afterwards. For a school task we were instructed to compare aspects of Englishness and Germandom.

I wrote in my winning essay: *'In England the Jack-o'-Lanterns in the marshes are thought to be the souls of children who have died without being baptised. In my own country we believe the erring light is a ghost following an invisible funeral procession. Of course, your poet Alexander Pope, a Londoner, claimed Nature "remains the same, unerring" but, for those who have been lured on a dark night towards the death lights that foretell the traveller's doom, this belief has no currency.'*

I did not mention to my teachers that the rippling lights I had seen in flight above their Sussex marshlands had actually been the slow-moving reflections of the channel Boat Train, hidden by fog, leaving the harbour and weirdly distorted like moonshine in the standing pools of the watermeadows.

Clearly, as our survival of our ordeal on the cliffs bears witness, the 'Dead Man's Candles' we thought we saw glimmering from the marshes had not been harbingers of another death, after all.

Yet, if not a mortal death then a 'Death-in-Life', I dare to suggest, was heralded by the fake apparition of that luminous phenomena.

Over the succeeding decades my father's health declined until he was laid off work altogether. From time to time his benefactor, the Count, wired him international money orders or sent him crushed food parcels damaged in the mails (even now I recall the taste of salvaged glacé cherries coated in coarse, scented tea leaves).

The Count's fortunes had improved manifold, he informed my father in a letter. (During the war the Count had been placed under virtual house arrest with round-the-clock surveillance by the Gestapo. He was regarded as an Imperial Pretender.)

The post-war years had been tough. 'Like ploughing with dogs,' wrote the Count. But now he had charge of six mounted forest guards and twenty foot guards, and he had added a first-class planing mill to his estate which, as I described, was bisected by a floating river, lined with flumes, for rafting the timber to his sawmills downstream. I remembered poor Ludwig tagging after the sawyers returning from the mills, balancing on a plankway across a sluice, ever in search of mischief.

'The nation never dies so long as it has forests,' the Count wrote, imparting as much meaning as caution allowed, 'even if the benefit is only to be reaped by our great-grandchildren.'

These guarded remarks must have heartened my father who had cleaved to a more principled notion of 'blood and soil' which, like the Count's views, anticipated the concerns of modern ecologists.

❁

The first sign of my father falling into decline was his slurring of speech. When walking, he shuffled and his gait was impaired. Then, early one morning, we found him wandering outside the house in his nightshirt, barefoot in the snow.

When we spoke to him, he plainly had no understanding of where he was, and he said he wanted 'to go home'. But when we returned to our house he refused to accept his surroundings as his own. Believing he was in the wrong house, he then lurched off down the drive much to my mother's distress.

More troubling still he failed to recognise Isolde. He became convinced that my sister was in fact 'the other woman', and that somehow she had tricked him into getting married, whilst he was meant to be betrothed to someone else. He preened himself in front of a mirror and warned my mother that young women found him irresistibly attractive. It was as if he had retreated in his mind, we suspected, to his years of courtship before his marriage.

Isolde, his favourite daughter, was desolated; but he continued to act considerately towards me, perhaps with more affection than I had ever hitherto enjoyed. I began to positively bask in the warmth of his greetings.

My mother was also wounded. My father denied he was married, even when Mother produced their wedding album to demonstrate their union.

Curiously, Father was confused by gender and would constantly refer to my mother as 'he' or 'him'; for he had fallen victim to a bizarre dissociative disorder termed 'Systemised Amnesia' which is characterised by loss of memory for certain discrete types of information, including complete loss of memory relating to a *particular person*. In his case, that individual was *Isolde*.

Often he was verbally aggressive but never to me.

Isolde began to fear him.

Once he shouted when Isolde entered his room: 'Take your idiot face out of my sight! You're not wanted here!'

To our horror he reached under the bedclothes and scrabbled at his heel as though unsheathing a spectral dagger.

These attacks were doubly painful for Isolde as she was just ending a souring love affair with X, a famous British painter (German-born, I should add, and an acquaintance of my father's). She had learned accidentally from one of X's models that it was the practice of the painter's daughter to issue invitations to the prettier of her girlfriends to meet her celebrated father for lunch, *then not herself show up*. In effect, she was a *procuress* for her father. That was how Isolde met X (whose belief in his own irresistibility far exceeded my father's).

'Beware! It's an evil trade!' the model had winked ironically.

How long my own father would have suffered his dementia, believing he was living in the wrong house with the wrong woman, I cannot begin to imagine because after ten months had elapsed my mother arranged for him to be hospitalised for a rehabilitation programme.

His specialist believed there was every likelihood of a sudden recovery; he concluded that the confusion associated with my father's disrupted identity was the result of psychological stresses underlying his reluctant bilingualism. That there was a higher incidence of mental disturbances among polyglots, the shrink claimed, was evidence of the trauma of assimilation.

This absurd diagnosis proved to be so much quackery when, by a piece of luck, my father was evaluated by a visiting professor of psychiatry who demanded a detailed family history.

That's when the truth (which you've probably guessed) emerged.

From his dossier it appeared that my father had made an early first marriage which my parents had kept a solemn secret from Isolde and myself; my father had been a widower when my mother married him and the father of a two-month-old baby girl, *Isolde*. No wonder he mistook Isolde for his first wife! At thirty-two years, Isolde was exactly the age of her true mother when she died in childbirth.

(The shadow cast by the forest of our homeland seemed to grow blacker every moment. I remembered the trees crowding together, the branches touching, forming a domed mausoleum which the sun never penetrates.)

Her pledge to hoard this family secret without betrayal must have weighed heavily on my mother, who was prey to dark repressions. No wonder she attempted to soothe my father with her neurotic reassurances: 'The love that lasts the longest is the strongest.'

A Numerical Error Amended

Well, call me a calculating woman, but my first reaction to this bombshell exploding our family myths was to delve into my bottom drawer of mementos and retrieve cousin Ludwig's juvenile theorisings on the nature of parental love.

(Among my treasured memorabilia was stowed my father's old wolf-skin cap, another poignant example of his tendency to fabulate tales of often Munchausenian proportions. In my childhood he had boasted that he had despatched the wolf with the butt end of his huntsman's whip . . . a feat hardly possible as the last reported sighting of a wild wolf north of the Danube was more than one hundred years ago. I replaced the cap beside the scabbard sheathing Father's hunting dagger where I'd hidden it for safekeeping. The elkhorn handle, I noticed, had yellowed with age.)

The faded sheets on which Ludwig had figured out his 'Subtraction Game' I arranged on my worktable in my study, a room I confess I rarely leave these days.

My lips were dry—from anticipation or my medication I cannot be sure.

I fixed myself a long drink (forbidden by my doctor) and then set about applying Ludwig's differential equation for modelling reality to the events I have just related. The result was both astonishing and deeply satisfying.

To redress the balance of paternal love (since Isolde had been denied Father's natural affection for ten months), I have, like Ludwig, drawn a simple graph to aid understanding, and formulated the properties of the solution thus:

Where the derivative (d) as a rate of change of paternal Love (L) is a function of the variable, Time (T), then L varies with T (in months) for both Child 1 (C_1) and Child 2 (C_2); note C_1 = Isolde and C_2 = Myself.

For C_2, since $L_2 = T + $ a constant (−10), due to difference in age (10 months) between C_1 and C_2, then it follows that $L_2 = T-10$ for all values of T (greater than 10, of course).

However (for C_1), $L_1 = T +$ a constant (0), so from $T = 0$ to $T = 84$ (C_1 at 7 years) then it follows that $L_1 = T$ for all values of T. But, from $T = 85$ to $T = 384$ (C_1 at 32 years), $L_1 = T +$ a constant (−1), due to effect of my Prank (P), when Father didn't speak to Isolde for a month, and ∴ $L_1 = T—1$ for all values of T in that range. From$T = 384$ to $T = 394$ (C_1 at 32 years and 10 months), $L_1 = T +$ a constant (—11), due to the effect of Father's dissociative Disorder (D), and $L_1 = T—11$ for all values of T henceforth (unless a further incident ensues). There has been none, as my father recovered his memory following the ten months that Isolde was deprived of his love.

So:

∴ L_2 (for C_2) will be greater than L_1 (for C_1) by 1. (Paternal Love is thus exceeded by one month for C_2, i.e. me!)

I repeat. Paradoxically, due to the effects of my Prank (P) when paternal Love (L) was withheld from Isolde for a month when a child, and of Father's dissociative Disorder (D), when paternal Love (L) was withheld from her for ten months when an adult, I discover that the love bestowed on myself, the younger child, exceeds that bestowed on my sister *by one whole month!*

That's correct. I'm a stickler for accuracy and I have simply amended a numerical error.

Now I reflect on it, that morning of family revelations at the hospital was like a decisive battle of a civil war and we all made our names that day, as though, until then, no one knew the value of who they really were.

Isolde said meekly in gratitude, upon Father's recovery when he recognised her, 'It was as if a man I thought was dead had come home upon his feet.'

And as for me?

When the heart is full the tongue speaks: 'The blessings intended for the firstborn have gone to the younger, and the one will be stronger than the other,' I tell myself, remembering young Ludwig.

My glass is raised.

'So I declare that the love that *favours* the strongest is the longest.' And I smile blissfully as I'm embraced in the firmament of my father's love.

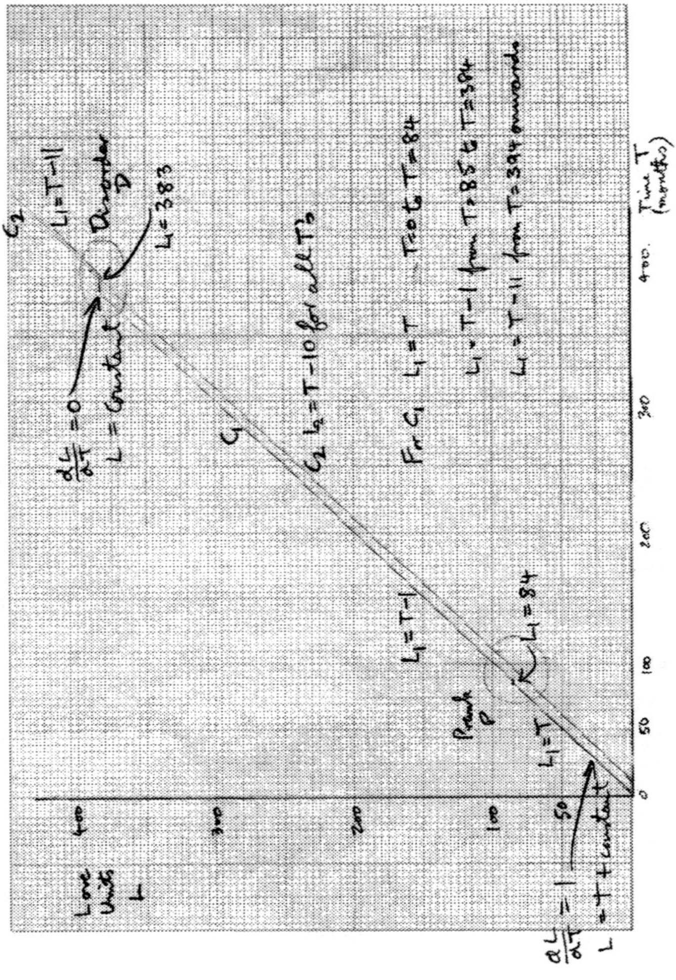
Love Units L
Time T (months)
C1
C2
L1 = T−11
L = 383
L1 = T−1
L1 = 84
L1 = T
Panic P
Disorder D
L = Constant
L = T + Constant
C2 L2 = T−10 for all T's
For C1 L1 = T T=0 to T=84
L1 = T−1 from T=85 to T=384
L1 = T−11 from T=394 onwards

HONEYMOON WITHOUT MAPS

(*Esther G.* — THIORIDAZINE)

'. . . all the appliances of pleasure. There
were buffoons, there were improvisatori,
there were ballet dancers . . .'

—*The Masque of the Red Death*, by EDGAR ALLAN POE (1838).

Assessment Summary (extract): Measures of patient and carer satisfaction were devised for the purposes of this assessment, and currently the burden of care has shown to be improved in the second week of treatment, producing clinically detectable improvements for the patient linked to higher carer satisfaction. In the CSQ (Carer Satisfaction Questionnaire) the answers, in relation to the carer's rôle, reported no further increase in this patient's depression or suicidality, yet, conversely, no pronounced advance in coping with personal hygiene was noted, nor was insight improvement observed.

HONEYMOON WITHOUT MAPS

Patient ID CPN0319141245: Esther G.
Occupation: Dance coach (Merited Practitioner of Choreography).
Drug: Thioridazine.
Drug class: Phenothiazine derivative, antipsychotic tranquilliser (at low and medium doses) for treatment of agitation, depression and sleep disturbances.
Common side effects: Drowsiness, vertigo, nocturnal confusion (bizarre dreams), lethargy, headache, dry mouth, blurred vision.

I'M ALONE A good deal now, which is why I have all the time I need for this attempt to make sense of the puzzling events which last year were so difficult for me to understand.

But, then, I suppose, the episode I am about to describe is not exactly a state secret since you'll have read something about it in the newspapers. At the time the story made quite a splash; except (hollow laugh), those dramatic front-page headlines were entirely false.

The real story behind the story, as it were, is altogether stranger; as strange, you might say, as that queer fish, my husband, who on more than one occasion was responsible for leaving me totally in the dark, too.

In fact, when I reflect upon my past, I find that even on the night of our honeymoon I was literally left in the air as to his intentions.

Let me explain. As a special bridal gift, the house of a great aunt had been lent to us, complete with servants, for a long weekend in St. John's Wood.

We'd had a good send-off from the wedding party and, naturally, I was elated, but on the evening following my marriage we emerged from the Tube into a suffocating yellow fog—the 'London Peculiar' as my aunt used to call it.

Within minutes, the actions of my new husband proved no less odd because we had barely walked ten yards before he was lost from view.

My calls met with silence.

'Howard!' I repeated. 'Where are you?' My voice became shrill with alarm.

There was no answer. I felt like a ghost; I felt invisible in a murk lit only by the aureole of a distant street light.

Then Howard's hand gripped my arm and he guided me towards the dimmed lamps of a cab rank outside a pub.

'What happened?' I was trembling. I could smell whisky on his breath.

He switched on his Lost-Boy-Seeks-Little-Mother smile, which up until then had retained a degree of charm.

'I sh-sh-sure needed a stiffener,' he stammered, dabbing his lips. 'No need to turn all moody on me.'

That was the first layer of deceit I was to uncover that night. Of the other deceptions my brief honeymoon disclosed I cannot bring myself to speak.

Let me just say that Howard may have cut a fine figure of man in his hired morning suit but I soon realised the effect was all in the tailoring.

In the master bedroom, deprived of his padded shoulders and fully unclothed, he looked far from prepossessing.

'So this is the playpen,' he murmured po-faced, testing the springs of the mattress.

I pretended to busy myself at the dressing table but I sneaked another glance in the mirror; I could see, only too evidently, that it was Moss Bros. who had made him a man.

In fact, now I further dwell on it, I had half expected swords raised in an arch at the church porch, among other desiderata, but no members of Howard's old regiment had attended. His reluctant best man had been my younger brother.

At Howard's insistence the reception had taken the form of a tooth-pick-supper (or *souper aux curedents*, as my matron-of-honour, Delphine, had contemptuously referred to it, as though neither of our families had sufficient silver table-plate for the buffet or the means to hire any).

The day before the wedding I had erupted in an irrational rash. The bridal gown Howard had chosen accorded to his own brash taste and did not suit me.

'Flash girl, flash geezer,' I heard a guest mutter, as I walked up the aisle.

In my aunt's house, the drapes above the bed were the colour of burnt orange, I remember, and there was a stale, cupboardy odour throughout the apartments. The carpet smelled of ancient spilt perfume.

'Smell's like a whore's handbag,' Howard complained.

His last words before he slept were: 'And another thing. You know I hate wearing those grasshopper things.'

For a moment I was thoroughly perplexed.

'You mean you hate wearing tails?'

'Yes, and that b-b-bloody top hat.'

That night I wept into the small hours.

❈

I daydream for hours and pictures from my past just fall into my mind like projector slides in a carrousel . . . and often out of sequence.

Consider the circumstances of our first meeting: a Saint Valentine's supper dance. My first impression of the dance hall was of a room hung with cane hoops over which were stretched fragile hearts of crimson tissue paper.

I had arrived late escorted by my brother in a party got up by Delphine.

Howard was haw-hawing with one of his pals at the bar. He had obviously just reached the punch line of some well-worn story: 'And then the Adj found him in flaggers!'

Evidently he thought himself an absolute hoot but, personally, I deemed the joke howlingly unfunny.

Yet I smiled with the rest of them. Who wants to be known as an uppity party-pooper?

The moment the band returned at the end of the interval Delphine roped us all in for the first dance (a smoochy number, I remember).

I was aware Delphine regarded me as a Plain Jane so when Howard turned to me with a careless certainty, extended his hand and grinned, I suppose I felt flattered . . . he was the star turn, obviously.

Then, of course, he asked for the next dance . . . and the next. He danced divinely, but then men of his generation from before the war invariably shone on the dance floor.

Delphine tried to put me wise about Howard and warned me he was a no-hoper.

While Howard fetched drinks she whispered: 'He's a randy devil and thinks you have oodles of money. Nuff said.'

So when I agreed to meet him later the following week Howard must have though he'd hit paydirt.

My mother's views on this misalliance I was to learn a few days later when I finally plucked up courage to tell her that Howard was twenty-six years my senior.

Mother shook her head as though to dislodge an improper remark and hissed: 'It's as though a mouse has fallen in love with a cat!'

'My treasure,' he would sometimes whisper, in the first bewildering days of our marriage, but very soon I began to suspect my husband's sincerity in these attentions extended solely to the very modest inheritance I had received as a dowry from my grandmother's estate.

I was only three days into my nineteenth year when we married; Howard expected me to be submissive and take on the colour of his opinions and, for some years, to humour him, I would indulge his prejudices with fairly good grace.

His pet peeve was the perceived private wealth of my own social circle and the absence of the allowance he expected me to grant him.

On the subject of money (his family's lack of it) he would talk at great length and in arcane detail like the sleeve notes of a long-playing record.

Should I ever object, or disagree with him, he would call me stuck-uppish or label me as 'niggly'.

Goaded, whitefaced and spiteful, I would snipe back and accuse him of plebbishness.

Pretty soon I was made aware that my husband was a cadger and a sponger. Too late I learned that his colleagues (or, more properly, his foppishly-dressed drinking cronies) questioned his capacity to hold down any job for more than a month . . . indeed, it was a remote possibility they, as remittance men, regarded with half-amused scorn.

When I confronted Howard with the housekeeping book he simply greeted my entreaties with a sullen look. He glanced at my column of figures and declared the expenses 'piffling'.

'Listen!' I shouted. 'I'm damned if I'm skivvying and scrimping while you swagger about town like a king in velvet!'

'Spare the sermon,' he sneered, 'I won't be saved.' Howard was the son of a parson and, like his father, he did not actively seek preferment.

Very early on in our marriage I learned that any affection from Howard was dear-bought. Ours was to be a marriage of rewards and punishments.

I contemplated divorce, of course, and confided in my mother.

'In a hundredweight of law there's not an ounce of love,' Mother recited sententiously like an accusation, as though I were the guilty party and wanting in warmth.

My mother's words stirred me to seek a rapprochement.

Regrettably, the next evening I chose the wrong moment when I found Howard sitting, as usual, in idle silence, somewhat soused . . . I mean, if he were not actually saturated, then he was sodden round the edges.

'Look. I've been thinking,' I temporised, 'I know you've thought me cold . . . '

'Th-th-thought you *cold*!' Howard exploded. 'Dear God! You're practically freeze-dried!'

His childhood stutter always returned when he was roused to anger.

He poured himself another drink.

I took his hand but he shook it off. However close, I thought, he was never the nearer.

After our rows I would lie in the cold spare room feeling like a marrowless bone that had been thrown to the dogs.

Sleepless, I would search the past for happiness but saw only how sadness and gladness succeeded each day until only sadness remained.

❀

Then, as now, my reaction to Howard's insufferable piggishness was to fling myself into my studies.

At that time I was in my final year at the dance academy and early each morning, before our class work, Delphine and I rehearsed for the Leavers' Concert. With the other girls in our troupe I practised my steps at daybreak in front of the long mirror in the rehearsal room.

Delphine was our little company's soloist and principal dancer in three separate divertissements in a programme of sugar-coated spritely dances devised to satisfy the sweet tooth of the Dean.

Despite my blistered toes, and the unbroken frozen silence I daily endured under Howard's resentful gaze, I began to look forward keenly to the night of the show.

But on the actual day I grew apprehensive. For a week Howard and I had acted like strangers and my sleeplessness and a sudden attack of first-night nerves had conspired to make me feel strangely light-headed.

But nothing could have prepared me for the performance itself, for I was soon to find myself embroiled in a humiliating *coup de théâtre* where, not for the first time in my life, an act of idiocy on my part was to make headlines.

❀

An hour before our performance I waited breathlessly in the wings, my senses blurred by apprehension. I was in a wretched state. My limbs trembled and I nervously flexed my feet and ankles. Like my fellow performers I suffered from black toenails which bled, and tendinitis, due to the excessive repetitiveness of our class exercises.

There was a sickness in my throat; the stale backstage reek of painted canvas, laden with the beeswaxy smell of the rosin tray, nauseated me.

I was about to seek the coolness of the washrooms when a commotion outside the prop store drew my attention. I found Delphine slumped on a replica of a fallen column, clutching her stomach from cramps.

A rippling whisper reached me.

'Touch her head! She's sick with fever!'

I took Delphine's hand; it was wet from perspiration. I dabbed her forehead which was flushed from an intense heat.

Our *maîtresse de ballet*, whom ever since we were juniors we had addressed familiarly as our *petite maman*, was summoned and there was a hasty dressing-room powwow. Maman suspected a case of chronic gastritis brought on by Delphine's erratic diet, so our senior year's prima ballerina assoluta was divested of her costume and removed to the boarders' infirmary.

In a few moments a scene-shifter approached me.

'She says, quick change!' he reported, jerking his thumb at Mme Maman.

Then he cheekily advised me to cut my fingernails so as not to scratch out my new partner's eyes.

I was simply astonished at how Maman assumed unhesitatingly I would dance in Delphine's place. As I mentioned, Delphine had always considered me her lame duck. She had no understudy, but somehow Maman must have known I had spent all my spare hours with Delphine helping her memorise her rôle.

So, within a few seconds it seemed, the wardrobe mistress, her mouth full of pins, was stitching me into Delphine's costume still warm from her recent incumbency.

'You might pass in crowd,' the wardrobe mistress said.

'So I might,' I murmured, thoroughly confused.

She fussed with a last minute adjustment and attempted to prettify my reddening throat with calamine powder.

In borrowed plumes I felt a perfect fraud.

I walked to my chalk mark and drew a deep breath just as Maman had taught us to relieve the pressure on the solar plexus.

Delphine's partner, the *jeune premier*, a sly upper-echelon boy of eighteen in a silver tunic, bestowed on me a false musical comedy smile.

Behind the footlights the rustle of the audience subsided.

The conductor tapped his baton.

And so my fatal *début* began.

❁

My strength returned as soon as I set foot on stage; the future seemed to smile on me, and I judged my performance to be near perfect in grace and brilliancy of execution.

Our *pas de deux* was an energetic double act from a dusty old ballet but demanding, nonetheless, intricate steps which were difficult to fit to the music.

Throughout, I sustained a clean silhouette in my carriage that I was convinced rivalled Delphine's, and the series of vertiginous pirouettes I exhibited, which climaxed in my tour de force of over thirty *fouettés en pointe*, was a feat of daring that drew on reserves of stamina I never knew I had . . . at every step before I'd half thought of doing it I seemed to have done it.

When the curtain fell at last I was certain I would never attain the technical virtuosity of that consistently high level ever again.

Yet what followed was the ominous void of a stunned silence.

Centre stage, I, too, paused, blank and dumbfounded. I looked around me. The corps de ballet, who had assembled for the next item, were staring, transfixed.

'Well, a new variation, certainly,' I heard the conductor pronounce, sotto voce, from the orchestra pit.

Then, from the auditorium a roar of coarse laughter signalled a general stamping of feet, and the whole company clapped and cheered.

Maman, approached grim-faced.

'Voyez!' she said archly, raising one eyebrow. *'Elle est la belle assassine!* The very image of Therese Raquin! Where do you think you are, to dance quite naked?'

Then, I realised what had happened. Not only had the strap of Delphine's bodice slipped off, leaving more than my shoulder candidly uncovered, but I had cut myself against the edges of the metallic spangles of my partner's costume, a hazard Delphine had been spared since there'd been no dress rehearsals.

Blood was trickling down the inside of my arm. My long, white, bell-shaped skirt was also spattered with blood while my partner, not to mention the stage, was spotted with blood-flecks which glistened under the hot lights.

At this moment of damning realisation, I heard Delphine's voice, offstage:

'Truly, darling, from the stalls,' she drawled, 'you looked as leggy as a painted clothes-peg.'

She was dressed in an elegant wrap and carrying a pair of opera glasses.

'Now, now, miaow-miaow!' laughed one of the girls.

She fetched a mirror but my appearance was beyond repair.

'You look like nothing on earth!' the boy in the cheese-grater tunic taunted.

I was not surprised. I had not expected him to behave otherwise than awkwardly . . . he smirked as he wrestled with what little better nature he could own and then praised me with faint damns.

I thrust aside the mirror; I knew I was deathly pale despite the rouge on my cheeks.

I was on the verge of bursting into tears when I saw Maman motioning to us to move downstage.

The audience was baying for our curtain call as the stage faded into darkness, and I found myself caught in the cone of a spotlight, with hundreds of eyes upon me and no possibility of escape.

I padded in my blood-filled pointe shoes towards the footlights to be greeted by a storm of applause and encoring which mercifully drowned the hoots and catcalls from the gallery.

In fact, to the chagrin of my abrasive cavalier, the audience in a frenzy of enthusiasm sprang to their feet, as if their seats were on fire, and the curtain rose and rose again I don't know how many times.

❁

That same day the late edition of the evening newspaper carried a small notice in the first night review section:

Baptism of Blood

Surprise understudy kicks up a storm

in evening of dash and charisma

> Tonight, in an evening of high drama—not to say melodrama—the capital's moribund ballet season was jolted into life by a much needed flying kick-start when a graduation performance ended virtually in a bloodbath. A last minute switch in the gala triple bill meant we were privileged to be present at the debut of a highly original talent who, despite being almost flayed alive with sequins, in a blood-letting due to the flail-like action of her partner's faux-constructivist doublet, made a real hit with audi-

> ence and press alike. Technically assured, this blood-imbued vampiress injected sexuality and emotional urgency into her portrayal, dancing fluently with the unassailable dignity of a highly promising dancer tipped to be one of our future primas.

Praise indeed! But, as you know, that overnight sensation — the *blood-imbued vampiress* thought to be long buried in the press-cuttings files of our national newspapers—was to be dusted off for resurrection over thirty years' later, at the height of my notoriety, in headlines screaming a *cause célèbre* that is still vociferously debated by ethical hair-splitters in medico-legal jurisprudence, even today.

❁

This same clipping from my own scrapbook, I notice, is dimpled from raindrops (since they cannot be my tears); for I have a distinct memory of jauntily approaching home that evening with a naïve *élan*, determined that no downpour would dampen my spirits nor less the wily snideries of Howard.

In those early years of our marriage we lived in a service flat on the upper floor of an Edwardian mansion block, and I remember my mood of unquenchable glee as I greeted the sleet beating on the skylight above the stairwell and hobbled on bruised toes across the top landing to our door.

The flat was in darkness when I entered. In the living room the radio was rebroadcasting a rainswept state funeral, and I was consumed by the dismal sounds of muffled drums, the rumble of a gun carriage and a dead march.

At my entrance the first words I heard were: 'Dammit! I've had just about a basinful of your brazen effrontery!'

Howard was seated opposite me, brooding, sunk in a deep armchair. He then held aloft a bouquet which he tossed to me across the room.

Mockingly, I stood in 'first position' and bobbed to catch it.

Howard snorted. 'Fella's not fit to wipe my nose!'

I glanced at the attached notelet in the dim light filtering through the window; it was signed by my mischievous reviewer.

> You are a star! Your future is safe and my heart is yours! I love you always, darling. I think you're lovely and absolutely wonderful! Godspeed and may your luck come true.
>
> R x x

'What *are* you talking about?' I demanded, groping for the light switch.

Rex was well known as one of the *balletomanes* in a claque that followed our company on tour. At one time he had attached himself to Delphine, from motives purely of disinterested devotion, I should add. Now it appeared he had redirected his adoration to me.

(Actually, I later came to know Rex quite well—in so far as one can ever *know* anyone—and he turned out to be more epicene than libidinous, and if not exactly queaned-up then queerish.)

Outside, the rain fell without slackening like the hissing of a hostile audience.

'You've landed yourself in a pretty mess this time,' Howard growled in an odd gruff voice, 'you mark my words!'; but whether he was referring to that gala performance of mine or my supposed faithlessness I was never to learn, because he violently wrenched himself out of his chair and advanced towards me.

I'd seen Howard snap before. We'd be having supper and conversing easily enough, and all of a sudden he would snap and a dish would end up flung against the wall. But I'd never seen him snap quite like this.

His eyes were fixed on me like fierce points of light. He took three steps forwards, his left arm lowered with a balled fist, and right hand raised threateningly just like the villainous sorcerer in *Swan Lake*.

He began to curse me with a special vehemence.

'For heaven's sake, Howard, you're behaving like the Dark Ages,' I entreated, my fingers joined in involuntary prayer. By now his profanities thoroughly frightened me.

He then grasped my clasped hands, dragging me, caveman-style, across the floor—so my feet slithered on the polished parquet—until he broke my grip by powerfully thrusting my arms to my sides as though they were his spring-loaded chest-expander.

Then I bit his ear lobe.

'You bolshy young viper!' he snarled.

(But enough of words. *Satis verborum!* Even after all these years the foregoing scene is still so distressful I find I'm compelled to render on a stave the first traumatic six seconds of its action in *Benesh* notation. *Benesh*, if you weren't aware of it, is the rhythmic and spatial vocabulary used by choreographers like myself for reanimating significant dances in our modern repertoire.)

I never intended to write a he-said-she-said narrative in every salacious detail so I'm not sure how much more of this improvised marital mauling I should transcribe to my reluctantly notated score. However, you'll observe that, by the end of this first sequence, my feet have returned to 'fourth position' with my right leg crossed over my left leg in a defensive 'scissor movement' to block Howard's attack.

In the following sequence I was at a loss what to say or do next.

Howard once told me that, during the war, he'd had 'a hot time of it in a hush-hush show' and there was no doubt that he was well versed in the art of unarmed combat; he knew no end of ways to torment me.

Against those odds, my words were as futile as trying to talk a fanatic down from a ledge. We were struggling in the dark and Howard's eyes were staring like the dead.

And as we fought, in ponderous slow motion to the grave measure of that dead march, all the while the falling rain laid a soundtrack of background static . . . a dirge-like 'music prompt', you might say, to propel the dancers in a masque for a defunct marriage.

My hair, which had been pinned up for my performance, was loosed, as he threw me like a flying turkey on to the couch.

I shudder now at the sheer tackiness of Howard's seduction technique. My mother had called him *feline*, which was perceptive of her because once we were married he soon made it known that he expected me to act a leading part in some endless puerile romance he'd envisioned, in which, apparently, a *distingué* worldly playboy enslaves a fluffy sex-kitten who's supposed to grow up to be a glamour-puss.

He began to beat me with an olden-style pointe shoe (one of a pair that the previous evening I'd been 'breaking in' by jamming the heel in a door).

At which point I said indulgently, 'It's no use, Howard. Why don't you give up?' as though the entire squabble was a childish game.

'The devil I will!' he said between clenched teeth; he was eaten up by rage.

I then placed a cushion between my legs and squeezed hard.

(Perhaps I should tell you that, measured by the norms established in male sporting circles, female modern dancers are graded above average for lower body strength and, in extremity, our thighs can exert a crushing force which compares favourably with the biting capacity of a wolf. Although petite, I'd been schooled in my exercise routines to be ruthlessly competitive, and I was no longer a timid neophyte.)

Howard tried to catch his breath; my remarks seemed to have had the effect of only further infuriating him.

Until that evening he had behaved at home no worse than an average savage, but now I saw him for the brute he was.

'You're crushing me,' I groaned.

He gripped my chin and whispered: *'I could take these two f-f-fingers and rip out your throat with my hands.'*

His grip tightened.

'What have you got to say now?'

His hand was clamped over my mouth; I could not breathe, let alone speak; I could not look him in the eyes.

Then the longest, darkest day of my life turned the deepest black.

Slowly my strength ceded to his unyielding need.

(At that craven droit-de-seigneurial moment I recalled the quaint words I had once read in an agony column: *Forced love like an over-fanned fire refuses to burn.* Squalid but utterly true.)

He was calm when he finally released me, soothed by a reaffirmed belief in his god-like power.

(I thought: *'An old sin and a new shame.'*)

He turned away and did not have the courage to meet the reproaches in my eyes; he knew he had committed a great offence and there was no possible way he could improve the occasion.

'I don't ever want to see your face again,' I managed to blurt out.

After that enormity I was sick at heart, and nothing he said could have comforted me.

He sought refuge in the shadows of the unlit kitchen.

'You better put some ice on that,' he said levelly, pointing to my lip which had swelled to twice its normal size.

He then said it was better if we travelled apart for a while.

'Under separate cover,' he said.

❁

'Depend upon it, dear—when a man knows he is in danger of losing his wife it concentrates his mind wonderfully,' my mother twittered with a brittle smile.

But I was not so sure. Three months had passed since Howard had decamped, and he'd left no trace.

We both felt very uncomfortable talking about him. After all, Mother had suspected Howard's cut-glass accent as not being quite top drawer and told me as much, so she must have realised there was no point in forcing the issue.

'A long streak of misery.' That's what Mother called Howard.

Therefore, I decided I would not inflict any further misery on myself by even hinting at the bleak truth of our breakup . . . particularly to Delphine. To entrust a secret to Delphine was like confiding in a magpie for the whole world to hear.

But, though I confessed to merely a trifling contretemps, Delphine, ever alert to misfortune, at once appeared to detect more than a discordant note in the marriage she claimed to have brokered, and spoke as if we'd had a major falling out.

'He sounds perfectly horrid,' she declared. 'How can you possibly go on living with a militant doctrinaire?'

I shrugged off any further probing by retorting that Howard, when it suited him, could be extraordinarily charming, a point which her silence seemed to concede.

In a gesture to cheer me up she suggested a shopping expedition.

❁

It was a poisonous kind of morning, I thought malevolently, as we walked together across the park, early, to the first day of the sales. I retain a very clear impression of that dank Wednesday . . . the very flanks of the trees seemed dipped in green ink and, I recall, in the heavy morning mist even the moon, withdrawing behind the shopfronts, appeared mildewed.

During the night there had been a gale and, above me, a bough was rent along its length like a twisted grin.

In the jewellery department at Harrods I chanced upon an adorable little Art Nouveau love-knot brooch, set with cornflower blue sapphires, which I felt certain would provide a subtle foil to the fabric of my favourite cocktail dress . . . a pale coral sheath in shot silk that I wore with a twisted bandeau of a similar colour.

I hurried down to the banking hall on the ground floor to cash a cheque, but when I returned I was mortified to learn the brooch had been sold only minutes before.

I stood there alone for a moment, feeling like a lost lemon, then I sought out Delphine who I found, as was customary, in one of Harrods' gilded phone booths, chirruping intimately, unconcerned by the impatience of a file of shoppers fuming outside. She must have seen my look of distress because, with a few rapid words, she terminated the call.

The next in line, a small spare man, impeccably dressed, of Middle Eastern appearance, opened the booth door for her and was instantly captivated, I could observe, when she swept out and bestowed on him her most imperious smile. The man beamed; for some reason, Delphine had a penchant for small men as her adorers. The man said something unintelligible but Delphine was undisconcerted . . . her eyes spoke one language everywhere.

With Delphine her power was all in the eyes. She could make a man's pulse race at five paces. Even a half glance from Delphine can be a passing bewitchment with an imprecise promise as to when she will reverse her spell.

'Cut orf 'cos I wos aht of change, dearie,' she rasped loudly, in a hoarse cockney accent, heedless of the waiting onlookers. She shrugged and snapped the clasp of her purse. 'Got nuffink, Lor' love yer. Not even the price of a cup of tea nor a fag neivver.'

I said that, actually, there was nothing I'd like better, and that my feet were killing me. Which is how we ended up in Delphine's little mews flat around the corner.

❀

I sat in Delphine's bright chrome kitchenette feeling undervalued, overlooked and out of luck. We each toyed with a glass of plonk ordinaire.

'Did you get that brooch,' Delphine asked, examining me intently while lighting her second cigarette with her first.

'No. After all, I decided it was rather common,' I replied stiffly.

I looked at the chrome clock as it struck two. (*'This is a dark hour,'* I thought.)

Delphine—absurdly beautiful—had removed an artificial fingernail and was pensively scratching her elegant nose with its tip. In the harsh winter sun, her skin seemed translucent—the effect of a favoured crash diet of cabbage leaves and camomile tea. Her secret was a permanently empty refrigerator.

My own fingers beat on the chrome table until Delphine smiled warily, and clicked her tongue in irritation.

'One more cigarette,' she said pointedly, 'then we'll leave,' while in fact meaning that very shortly I should take my leave.

To occupy my hands I turned to a woven wicker cutlery tray and began to listlessly polish a fishknife with an oven glove.

There was something sombre and immense, I thought, behind all this glittering triviality.

Then my eyes settled on two objects stowed in a section of the tray. A chill ran through me and I felt an inward stirring of dread.

Side by side, two napkins of fine lawn linen were folded, origami-style, into bishop's mitres.

(*'Got nothing.'* Delphine's words resounded in my head as I outstared her interrogative gaze. *'You were truer than you knew, my friend. We've both got nothing, just as you said.'*)

No one of my acquaintance, except Howard, had ever folded napkins in that particular fashion. It was a private joke between us. Howard's father had taught him, when a child, to fold them for the rectory's breakfast table. Howard used to quip that the preoccupied air with which his father unfolded his napkin was the nearest he ever came to contemplating an episcopate . . . the very idea of his father with 'a tulip on his head', he said, amused him.

'Have you thought of taking him back?' Delphine asked blandly. Delphine always hid her claws. Her voice issued through a cloud of smoke from a Balkan Sobranie as she reapplied her nail extensions.

'Of course,' I said, hoping my voice did not betray my inner struggle. 'But they'll have to be some changes.'

Delphine reached for my coat.

'Yep. Natch. I can see that.' She walked with me to the door.

Wordless messages passed between us in the seconds before we parted.

'So long,' she sighed negligently, without looking round.

I couldn't despise the flawless Delphine; she was, unfortunately, just one of those girls who attract bad husbands.

As Rex once crudely observed, in a remark satiric of Howard: 'He's incorrigible, sweetie, let's face it. He'll always have an eye for a tasty-looking bit of skirt.'

I also correctly deduced that Delphine had swiftly tired of having Howard sleep under the same roof.

A prized object, when possessed at last, seldom retains the same charm it had when pursued.

I had no doubt that Howard had been Delphine's confidant at the receiving end of her intense telephone conversation at Harrods, and rung only to be summarily banished from the mews in anticipation of my arrival.

So, at the end of that treacherous day I retraced my steps across the park, my emotions whirling, and feeling as though I'd been tortuously making my way out of a wind tunnel for the past three months.

When I returned home I took a bath—a balm to my wounded spirit—and reflected on the concurrence of so many audacious betrayals. I thought also of that sapphire love-knot brooch, almost certainly acquired by Delphine behind my back according to her perverse, dog-in-the-manger impulses, and equally coveted as another self-denying object of desire, regardless of the cost.

Blue has never been Delphine's colour, you see. Not her colour at all.

Curiously, that night I dreamt not of the brooch but of a lost silver buckle—a symbol which I have since learnt can indicate an impending broken engagement or that one's affairs are beset with danger of chaotic confusion.

When I awoke next morning I saw Howard's shadow in the hallway . . . his crooked shadow running ahead of him.

I heard the drinks cabinet open softly in the next room, and the clink of a glass.

'Just fixing myself an eye-opener,' he said unsteadily when I entered.

'Surely you've had enough.'

'Enough there isn't.' He shook the empty bottle.

(*'He looks ruined,'* I thought, *'utterly ruined . . . God! I married a train smash.'*)

He collapsed into his chair and stared at me defiantly.

'Your pal, wossname. In a twink she's kicking me out in the street without so much as a b-b-by-your-leave. I'd as soon be pally with a wildcat as call her my friend.'

'You don't say so,' I said. 'I weep for you.'

'A wildcat,' he repeated meditatively and, indeed, there were traces of Delphine's nail-marks along his jawline. 'A wildcat in b-b-ballet tights.'

'Then you were very stupid, weren't you, to be caught by the same bait.'

❁

You may have seen, many years ago, the premiere of *Fugue for Two Misfits*, my short tragi-comedic *divertissement*, now an accepted standard repertory piece, and you may have also recognised my earlier transcription (see my notation) as the score of that ballet's selfsame opening sequence. If you are a ballet aficianado, then you'll know that my *Fugue*, like its musical counterpart, is a contrapuntal development between a male and a female dancer, with a short, repetitive, irritating theme. Insistent and incessant, the dance climaxes like a barber's pole and ends as it begins, da capo.

You will not be surprised to learn, therefore, that—over all those many years of our marriage—Howard kept a string of mistresses and continued to betray me with faithful regularity in innumerable affairs.

Yes, I can state the blunt truth now, quite dispassionately, as if it were a scientific proposition . . . The truth is Howard regarded me merely as his meal ticket . . . and he was perfectly docile just so long as he was content to believe I was in complete ignorance of the fact that there would always be some plummy vowelled popsie of his, in reserve, giving him the wink.

But since I suspect you are eager to learn more about the events of last year, and of how I gained such unearned notoriety as to be branded in the scandal sheets with a revived blood libel (*'Blood-imbued Vampiress' Returns from the Dead!* etc.), perhaps I should now describe Howard's final rendezvous with another speculative 'mistress' shortly before his death, and its tragically laughable aftermath.

I may have mentioned that Delphine had a predilection for small men. The year following her entanglement with Howard (who was exceptionally tall) she married a celebrated Irish jockey; a charming man.

As a matter of fact, there is a close affinity between classical dancers and professional jockeys; they both tend to have similar psychological traits; they both are disciplined by the toughest trainers to improve performance through punishing dieting regimes; and, to maintain their low body weight, they're both prone to anorexic starvation and anæmia.

So, fragile bulimical Delphine and her diminutive husband were both, as it were, hoofers, and, in a certain sense, were both either compulsively cantering or banting.

I don't want to pitch it too strong, but sometimes I suspected there was a pronounced degree of calculation in Delphine's choice of husband. In the actuaries' mortality tables, professional horse riders are estimated to be at higher risk of death than even motorcycle riders or drivers of racing cars. And so it proved. Delphine became a very wealthy widow.

In the years before that unfortunate man's death, he and Howard struck up a friendship. Howard, who loved the Turf, thus became privy to the hottest tips from the courses, and thrived for a time quite providently as a professional gambler.

Ascot, Cheltenham, Doncaster, Goodwood, Haydock, Kempton, Lingfield, Newmarket . . . by simply referring to the racing calendar, I could invariably distinguish between Howard's womanising itineraries for frivolous pleasure, and the circuits he followed for the serious business of on-course betting and ready money. (Howard liked to walk away without complications and insisted on tax-free winnings.)

That's why I was surprised early last year when, a day before the onset of his final illness, I discovered, purely by chance, that a big race meeting he led me to believe he had attended had been abandoned due to bad weather.

Howard had developed a deep, barking cough. Unusually, he had taken to his bed before the pub opened, complaining of chest pains. In his room I found him sleeping in his underclothes—jacket and trousers flung on the floor—with what appeared to be his race card fallen from his back pocket.

His race cards he normally filed in a bedside letter rack, so I was on the point of tidying away his scattered items when I glanced at the folded card and read:

In Memoriam — Aileen Una Maccaber

Fideli certa merces—To the faithful there is certain reward

Fraud and deceit are ever in haste . . . for Howard to be caught out in a hastily forged lie, by fabricating the alibi of a race he knew to be cancelled, clearly indicated to me that he must have had some uncommonly shameful secret to hide.

Judging by the hymns on the reverse side of the sheet, the *Order of Service* had been for a Low Church funeral, conducted the previous day, at a chapel for expatriated Scottish evangelicals who'd settled in the next county.

I was intrigued. It struck me that, if the lately deceased had been one of my husband's last flings, then his choice of mistress appeared distinctly un-Howardian, particularly in respect of Howard's deep-rooted religious prejudices, which were a product of the high-toned domestic piety of his peculiar upbringing.

Paradoxically, sometimes Howard could be more pi than his father.

I listened to Howard wheezing. He had fallen into a deep sleep.

On an impulse I decided to drive to the chapel that afternoon, intent to learn the character of the devotional obligation that had supplanted his love of a race day.

❁

The church, as I expected, was an austere mission hall built of undressed granite, set apart amidst fields, whose interior was half-clad in panels of dark, fly-mottled, varnished pine. There was a calm aspect of pleached hedges hemming the plot.

I found the minister in his vestry. His face and person, I thought, were as splotchy as his dusty woodwork. His eyes were lachrymose and hollow with fatigue.

His handshake was dry and papery.

I pointed to a black-edged placard, fixed to a stand beneath the lectern, on which he commended the prayers of his congregation to be offered for the soul of Mrs MacCaber.

He wrung his hands.

'Unhappy woman. God ca'd her at last. She mourned before her time and grieved fu' long to see her ain man gone.'

He extended an arthritic finger, and touched a brass memorial tablet set in the wall beneath a stained-glass window commemorating two world wars:

To the Slain

To the Glory of God and in Loving Memory of
Sgt. Major Wm. Alexr. MacCaber
this window is dedicated
by his faithful and devoted wife.
He Laid Down his Life that We May Live.
His Name Shall Live for Evermore.

The minister sighed.

'A lady steadfast to the last. A man has ne'er been mourned as she mourned that poor laddie . . . an' wi' gude reason.'

For a moment he fixed me with such a penetrating look that I felt utterly exposed. Then he drifted away, lost in thought, and I heard him mutter morosely:

'But, nae man has a lease on his ain life, and he can soon weary o' it.'

I clenched my hands together, and walked out into the dusk without even feeling the ground I trod. Against my cheek I felt a cool caressing breeze.

Plainly, no woman had mourned as Aileen had mourned (she had grieved for more than five decades) so Howard's relation to her had been, to all intents and appearances, for once uncharacteristically blameless.

Yet I remained baffled. I started in alarm as an owl in blundering flight swooped over my head into a wood. I felt I was in a flat spin. Directionless.

'An owl he would a-wooing go,' I sang senselessly under my breath in the moonlight.

Like many women before me, I had gone into the country to hear news of the town, expecting rumours of my husband's philandering, but I had come away with distortions and half-truths.

Even so, somehow, in this case, although my grievances were imagined, my own grief was real.

My mystification deepened as I drove back to town; but any advantage I had gained to surprise Howard with my suspicions was lost when I returned to find him collapsed on the living-room floor. His face was ashen and contorted with fear and pain. He was mantled in cold sweat and barely able to speak, straining to breathe.

'Not feeling quite the thing, old girl . . .' he faltered before closing his eyes.

Though gaunt, Howard was heavy-boned, so it is a lasting tribute to Mme Maman's unremitting class exercises that the muscle strength of a trained dancer's pelvic floor enabled me to move him to his bed, unaided.

Exhausted, weak, and with continuing chest pains, he lay in bed for the following seven days. He had suffered a mild stroke which, for a time, semi-paralysed his right arm so he was powerless to fend for himself. The doctor forbade him to eat, smoke or drink coffee.

I insisted he drank water regularly.

'I love water,' he croaked, 'as much as a cat loves mustard.'

During that week, he had, perforce, to crawl slowly across the floor when he needed to reach the lavatory because walking was too painful.

Deprived of sleep, I nursed Howard through broken nights of agitation and anxiety, until my own health, too, declined and I sank into a nervous depression.

Foolishly, I confided in my own doctor, in the belief that, only by sharing my impressions with another person, and voicing the disturbing intuitions which nightly preoccupied me, could I restore to myself some semblance of calm after my return from that grief-darkened chapel and my brush in the graveyard with that night-heralding owl.

My doctor dismissed my premonitions as a 'heightened emotionality' due to prolonged sleep disturbance and prescribed Thioridazine.

I now curse my unquestioning docility when I consulted my doctor, for my compliance was to have a disastrous outcome; it was as though a sheep had made a wolf her confessor, because —as you shall see—I was afterwards to regret so willingly falling prey to the power of a prescription drug. (As I told Delphine, only a few days ago, 'With a few of those magic pills and a glass of malt, you could fly without a plane.')

Certainly, at the beginning, I succumbed to a blissful lethargy, and the befuddled drowsiness which smothered me was deep enough to soften my sorrows and distress during my long vigils at Howard's bedside.

And it's true; I began to neglect myself . . . what few cosmetics I possessed I kept in a rusted biscuit tin. I shuffled about the flat in a pair of old ballet slippers; I'd painted nail varnish around the edges to stop them fraying.

I took to wearing an old Bokhara fringed shawl which I clung to for comfort; I became so superstitious I was never seen to be separated from it. (One of my backstage rituals before a performance had been to comb my fingers through the fringes as though it were a prayer shawl.)

I thought we'd hit rock bottom when, one morning, Howard said:

'It's the end of the line, isn't it?' He raised one eyebrow, roguishly. 'And I'm the last of the tribe.' (Which was true; he was an only son.)

He complained of a crawling pain which, he said, was creeping insidiously up his spine, like some dread cunning germ making a slow but sure journey to his brain. He felt the world was closing in on him, and he had a craving for alcohol.

So while I slept, and against doctor's orders, he began his tippling again. He could always rustle up drinks from nowhere; that was his forte.

'No need to get in a strop,' he said with a wink, when I sniffed his glass and gave him a severe wigging. He knew he'd been rumbled.

'Just a snifter, darling.' He was sitting on his chamber pot at the time. 'Without a drink I'd be squatting with the squitters.'

I relented.

Besides, Howard had become obsessive about his bowels, and, when he became egg-bound—or 'stodged up', as he put it—due to the morphine, he would expect me to remain in attendance while he desperately pored over each stool as though he were making a plaited loaf.

He simply wasn't cut out for idleness. He became morose, cantankerous and filthily offensive.

He would pee last thing, with the lavatory door open.

His 'dearest member' was his no longer, he said, and he gloomily mourned the loss.

When I objected to his disgusting expressions he yelled idiotically:

'Phooey! Phooey! Phooey! Don't come that lah-di-dah manner with me!'

And he'd become confused. One night he'd almost electrocuted himself when—sleep-walking—he had mistaken the electric fire for his chamber pot.

In the mornings, when the newspapers arrived, he would resume his drinking, which never failed to incite him to rail against the bloodshed in Iraq, cursing the invasion as a *débâcle*, no different from his own war in the Western Desert, and anathematised as 'another misbegotten adventure'.

'D-d-damn you D-D-Dubya!' he would stammer, and with a despairing swipe, he'd sweep the newspapers from his bed.

But his chest pains gradually diminished in intensity and frequency, so maybe the booze helped, after all.

❁

Yet Howard seemed always to complain of 'a sort of all-overish' febrility.

'Festering hot, dammit!' he would say and take another two tablets.

'Pink pills for pale people,' he would mutter.

Life with Howard was driving me scatty, not least because his humour had grown quite mordant.

One morning there was a sharp rapping on the front door.

Our caller was a postman, delivering registered mail addressed to Howard.

When I took the letter into his bedroom, Howard asked with a grin, 'Is that Death knocking at the door or is it just the sound of a skeleton sabre-rattling?'

He examined the postmark eagerly before he tore open the packet and read the contents. Then he touched the side of his nose with his forefinger.

'Hot tip. Had it straight from the nosebag.'

'Whatever do you mean?'

His sudden affability surprised me. Usually, after breakfast, and his shredding of the day's headlines, he would bury himself behind the racing pages, as if in a shellproof bunker, and sometimes he would not speak for the rest of the day.

'How do you fancy getting away from all this?' He waved his left hand at the debris of medicine bottles and his picked-over breakfast. 'A trip abroad? A night on the razzle? Think of it as a second honeymoon sort of caper. Same destination, see?' He pointed to the Swiss postage stamp on the envelope. 'What d'you say?'

I thought he was going clean out of his mind.

'Our first honeymoon was not exactly the stuff of roses and raptures,' I said. 'Remember?'

'You're sarky all of a sudden.' But he said it without rancour.

(After that first weekend together in St John's Wood we'd flown to Switzerland for five days in a ski resort.)

Suddenly, with a strange fervency, he gripped my hand.

'You must come,' he said urgently in a low voice. 'It's meaningless without you.'

I hesitated, but since I didn't relish another slanging match, I said I would think about it.

'Just going to get some shut-eye,' he said contentedly, and carefully refolded the letter and placed it under his pillow.

❁

'It may take days, if not weeks, for you to understand the concerns that were accented by the recent full moon,' I read in my magazine horoscope on that winter morning last year when I flew out to Switzerland with Howard. *'While you may wish these hadn't surfaced, they cannot be ignored on your travels. The holidays of joy are the vigils of sorrow.'*

Certainly, our first honeymoon in St Moritz had been brief and blessed with few delights, I reflected, as we drove in the shuttle service from Zurich airport.

And, when I began to think of that first blighted night in the bridal suite at St Moritz, the very notion of celebrating a second honeymoon seemed ludicrous . . . there was the matter of his ski-case, for instance.

I remember so well Howard's anguished look, all those decades ago—of helpless rage subsumed by persecuted suffering—when we unpacked on the first night in the hotel and he found his skis missing from their case. He behaved just as if he were a victim singled out for special torment by some vindictive oppressor.

Curiously enough, before that first honeymoon trip, he'd boasted of those skis—they were military-issue metal-edged wooden skis, he had told me, designed for Mountain troops during World War II, he was extremely proud of them.

When he unpacked his ski-case we were amazed to see two planks of unplaned, raw wood slide out. On the upper plank a cryptic message of five words was chalked, one of them unprintable. *'See how they run, **** !'*

'Nice friends you have!' I exclaimed, as I snagged a fingernail on a splinter.

He had looked shifty for a moment, then shrugged off the entire episode as the mischief of 'some jokers' in his old unit (which at that time was stationed with the British Army of the Rhine) who must have somehow intercepted our luggage, he claimed, with the intention of ragging him.

Howard was raging drunk that night; he collapsed in the lobby and, to my shame, the bellboy had to assist him to our suite.

'Give this man air!' the maître d' directed smoothly. 'M'laddo's out on his feet.'

❁

I might well have accepted that rigmarole of Howard's and cast it from my mind had not an incident occurred, of a similar sinister nature, in the third year of our marriage.

I had come into another small windfall, a dividend from a family trust, and I'd decided to splash out on a new car. To please Howard I had allowed the final decision to be his . . . which is how I came to be the reluctant owner of a canary yellow convertible, a sick-making colour so hideous that it reminded me of naval quarantine flags I'd once seen flying off the Bay of Biscay.

Two weeks after the car had arrived from the showroom, I discovered, on leaving the flat to cross the square, a set of footprints stencilled in white paint on the tarmac, leading from our front steps in the direction of our parking bay. And those ghostly footprints did not simply pause at our new motorcar but walked right over its roof and across its bonnet to where was daubed, in crude slashing strokes, another cryptic message which read: '*A nice little runner, ****!*'

That second unsettling act of vandalism, I remember, turned out to be a costly joke, which was not so lightly shrugged off by Howard.

Ever since I'd first met him, he had given the impression of being a hail-fellow-well-met sort of man, so I was puzzled by this act of spite, suggestive of some grubby subculture, and so evidently calculated to hit him where he lived. What other surprises were lurking in the woodwork, I wondered.

Afterwards, I noted, Howard came to have a haunted, hunted look of someone constantly glancing over his shoulder, as though he knew a frightful fiend was close behind him and he recognised its tread.

Now, so many, many decades later, as we drove the final kilometre to our chalet village, with Howard lolling against my shoulder where he dozed, I pondered bitterly on the elusive character of the man I'd married and, while I strained to distinguish the half-formed words which punctuated his laboured breathing, I concluded that I still had only the haziest notion as to the true nature of this riddle of a husband, behind whose false face, I had no doubt, another mask was determinedly hidden to wrap with deceit the man's final enigma inside an impenetrable mystery . . . the perennial conundrum, as Rex had once so sagely put it, of 'a regular snakes-and-ladders man.'

❦

We arrived with our luggage in the lobby of our agent's chalet at the appointed time, whereupon a naïve-looking, waif-like liaison man in thick pebble spectacles descended the stairs. His hair was parted precisely in the middle and combed down over his forehead in a cowlick. He bowed, and announced diffidently he was our representative, and began to call out the individual names of our group. There were some ten other couples who had travelled with us from Zurich. (They were a mixed cargo; 'a funny bunch', as I remarked to Howard; I found the whole shebang distinctly odd.)

Our 'Induction' would begin with a 'Preliminary Talk' we were told; the young man spoke with precision and pronounced 'preliminary' in a niminy-piminy voice.

My ears hurt because of the change in altitude, my legs felt wonky, and such was my fatigue my vision blurred until I could barely keep my eyes open. My clothes clung to me like a boiled rag.

When I travel overnight I double the effective dose of my tranquillisers, so I conclude my mind must have been in neutral from over-sedation for me to have agreed to attend what was described as a 'presentation', yet which sounded to my buzzing ears—through my dizziness and nausea—as more likely a lesson in high-pressured salesmanship . . . but what commodity the young man was selling I could not precisely determine.

Our sales rep led us into a large meeting room where about ten small tables and chairs were arranged. The group leader was a young woman with a high domed intelligent face which reminded me of a light bulb; she was wearing black ski pants as tight as eelskins.

A very meagre 'breakfast buffet' was set up on a sidetable; none of the fare appeared very appetising.

I hinted at my misgivings, which prompted a characteristic put-down from Howard.

'What d'you want?' he scowled. 'Jam on both sides?'

I looked around me at the weary faces of the other members of our group who had been called from the lobby to the meeting . . . it seemed the group leader's presentation was solely for the attention of married couples.

She raised her hand for silence. Her clipped voice was heavily accented, and mesmerising in its intensity.

'Quiet everyvun. May ve haf your attention. Mr and Mrs Harry Trenton all ze vay from Toronto haf just signed up vit us.' There was scattered applause as our sales rep confidently led the clapping . . . the Trentons half-rose from their seats in sheepish acknowledgement.

I found the entire proceedings squirmingly embarrassing. All the same, at that moment, my eyelids drooped andI became inattentive . . . after all, Howard and I had been travelling for more that twelve hours so it was only natural for me to drift into a reverie. Strangely, Howard, who was listening intently with an alertness I'd not observed since his stroke, did not prod me awake . . . indeed, for him, unexpectedly gentlemanly behaviour.

His upturned face was like a child's; the intake of knowledge was like a fledgling's open beak.

(What was the group leader saying?)

'. . . zo be assured zat you haf sympathetic people supporting you at all times zo zat it can be a gute journey, not a bad journey.'

(Ah! So that was it! So the free buffet was the enticement for enduring her hour-long sales pitch. She must be peddling a special Alpine excursion at a discount, I thought.)

'. . . and wrong to deny zat journey to zose people who *do* zink zey know zeir own minds clearly, ven zey haf ze legalised right to make zat decision venzoefer zey zo vish it . . . '

(Now the group leader seemed to be talking about some trading standard or other, applicable only under Zurich's Cantonal Law.)

'. . . vit our special team to assist you to make ze most of zese final days together vit us. I hope ve all are to haf a vunderful time, and find ze peace ve all seek, on zis vunderful journey ve vant to take, here in ze mountains.'

Ms Eelskins apparently had concluded her introductory remarks because she inclined her head to acknowledge a polite round of applause, and each couple was assigned a rep to hasten the completion of a bundle of forms and, at her prompting, to witness the signing of a 'Declaration'.

Ms Eelskins, who had elected herself to be our personal counsellor, then prepared us to answer some questions.

The zing of her perfume was disturbingly musky and the heavy fumes seemed to overcome my senses and immobilise my limbs.

'OK. Shoot,' Howard urged impatiently. 'We have no need of your twaddling reservations.'

'Ven vould you both like to go,' asked Ms Eelskins.

'Well, as soon as possible,' I said. My mind was so befogged I was anxious not to prolong this unwelcome interlude.

'It's her decision as much as mine,' Howard murmured, an edge of asperity entering his voice. 'Of course she's mentally competent to sign.'

I signed. The forms in triplicate seemed a needless fuss for a day's jaunt out.

'Zo. Any special requests?'

'Champagne.' Howard said. 'Veuve Clicquot.'

❀

In the small hours I awoke in our chalet room. My throat was parched.

This sparse and functional room included a television, a refrigerator in an alcove, a coffee machine, and assorted champagne with wine glasses on a shelf, beside a lone packet of camomile tea.

I examined with disdain a diet sheet pinned to the door, above a roster of staff duties.

In the fridge was nothing but a blackened jar of honey and two undercooked artichoke leaves. *'Like eating razor wire,'* I thought. *'Honey is sweet but the bee stings.'*

Outside my window, tremendous white-clad peaks overlooked the valley, as forbidding as a race of druids gathered to perform a ritual sacrifice.

I shivered; I could not quite discard a sense of unease.

The silent ski-runs and the cables of the ski-lifts looped the upper slopes, receding into the moonlit ranges as if a monumental game of the snakes and ladders had only lately been abandoned.

Our chalet was just above the snowline and, below me, a byre of wintering cows grew restive; I could see the darkness of their muzzles inside the shed, their breath condensing. I noticed their tails were tied up to prevent their soiling.

Behind me Howard slept fitfully, his right forearm at rest on the coverlet.

He was wearing his black velvet sleeping-mask, and his spectacles still rested on his forehead. His face looked roasted. In his own words, he'd been 'too befoozled by knockout drops' to properly undress.

I poured a glass of water and switched on a subdued light above the fitted vanity unit. As I drank, I idly riffled through the glossy company prospectus Howard's Swiss agent had mailed to England: *'Mayer Life Cycle Programs,'* I read, *'committed to facilitating personalized services to suit your own schedule for departure.'*

I saw Howard had been scribbling on the cover; since his stroke he'd taught himself to write with his left hand in an awkward rudimentary scrawl.

He must have been listening to the racing fixtures just before our departure, I deduced. (Howard was a devotee of steam radio and, as his sight began to fail, he turned to the tipsters and live commentaries on the wireless in preference to television.)

This is roughly the manner in which Howard had jotted down, in his private shorthand, the racing venues for the preceding week . . .

Ascot
Hayd'k

MAYER
LIFE CYCLE
PROGRAMS
Zurich

Mayerling! In that instant the truth struck me! *Mayerling!* The classic suicide pact that brought about the end of an empire!

How trusting I'd been to have so misread the situation as to almost become the unwitting partner in Howard's crazed double suicide attempt!

And a rapid skimming of the *Mayer Life Cycle Programs* brochure confirmed my worst fears, and told me all I needed to know about the aims of a Zurich-based organisation that proclaims every citizen's 'Right to Die', and promotes the controversial practice of assisted suicide for the incurably ill. The subtitle was: *The Practicalities of Self-Deliverance and Assisted Suicide for the Dying.*

How extraordinary that Howard's scribbles had, by association, led me to recall the sordid suicide pact between Crown Prince Rudolf Habsburg and the beautiful young Baroness Mary Vetsera at the Mayerling hunting lodge.

Apropos of which, I was in the first-night audience at Covent Garden, when the ballet *Mayerling* had its world premier, and I remember reading then about the doomed, depression-prone Rudolf. And had not that drug-addled rake, according to his biographers, exhibited a pathological fear of living alone? And was that not why the poor booby also feared death alone . . . too afraid to die without a witness?

Mayerling! As if shaken awake by that shock of recognition, I considered the coincidences with new insights.

Of course, it was the fate of the baroness, full of life and aged a mere seventeen—half Rudolf's age—to be the 'chosen one', his Companion-in-Death, in the adulterous prince's insane plan to attain self-deliverance . . . except he allegedly shot her first before he shot himself.

Howard and Rudolf.

So alike in base motives.

I can compare these two men for I feel I knew them both.

I could so clearly understand the psychology of Howard . . . his primitive fear . . . how essential it was for him to know that he had a secure exit if he needed one.

But . . . for Howard to have actually schemed to dupe his *own wife* and lure her as his unwitting companion on that dark journey to oblivion . . .

On this none too comforting reflection, I packed my bag and prepared to make my departure as my enigmatical husband slept.

I paused for a moment at the head of the bed, and removed his spectacles.

I murmured my farewells.

'Confine your tongue, damn you!' Howard muttered in his sleep, grinding his teeth. His cheeks had the heightened colouring of the painted dead.

Distraught, I picked up the phone and dialled 117—the number for the Swiss police—then I rapidly replaced it, leaning my forehead against the handset to cool my brow . . . and my anger.

However close, I thought, Howard was never the nearer; past hope, past shame, my husband would always lie like the truth.

So just how the story of my abandonment of Howard leaked out to the British press I can never be sure.

It makes me tired to contemplate the convolutions of such deviousness . . . it makes me queasy to put a name to that ultimate duplicity.

And I don't have the energy to write it down.

I don't want to.

I don't feel capable, somehow.

Nevertheless, a week after my return to England, the first of the screamer headlines appeared in the gutter press; a vicious character assassination which, as I mentioned earlier, raked up the entirely blameless incident of my stage début and attributed to me the reputation of a heartless woman with a scarlet past.

'Vampiress' Survives Failed Double Suicide Bid

Swiss assisted suicide 'may be illegal'

A campaigning Euro-MP is calling for an investigation into whether the planned deaths of a British couple who travelled to Switzerland to commit suicide were illegal. 'It is my belief that it is a crime in Switzerland to help able-bodied people to commit suicide,' he said last night. 'It is the inevitable consequence of the new trend towards Suicide Tourism.' The couple were not thought to be terminally ill, and concern has been raised about the death of the husband who is thought to have swallowed a lethal dose of barbiturates at a chalet supervised by voluntary euthanasia charity, Mayer Life Cycle Programs. The search for the wife of the dead man has intensified since it was learned that she signed a release document authorising their joint deaths. The whereabouts of world renowned ballet coach and former Prima Ballerina, . . . etc, etc.

❦

I am, at present, in hiding at Delphine's truly divine duplex penthouse apartment in the heart of Mayfair, safe from finger-wagging editorials and the tongue-wagging of my detractors.

I am quite alone. Neat as ninepence and wearing a false hairpiece, Delphine is presently presiding over one of the highly worthy charity bashes she organises with Rex—ever the socialite—in Kensington.

(Contrarily, both Delphine and Rex plead dire poverty these days. Delphine herself declares she's positively a 'pauper'; so quite how she intends to fund her jet-setting social calendar—never mind her Botox treatments—or sustain her fortnightly supper soirees and the lavish entertaining of her select circle of grandees, I dare not hazard a guess.)

Whatever the case, for the moment I am Delphine's guest and she's made arrangements for her porter to collect my mail from my flat.

This morning there arrived the airmail packet I had been dreading . . . the 'last effects' of Howard's. For a while I fingered the bulky outline of the five objects sealed inside the package but I could not conceive of its contents.

And now they are spread out before me I touch them with apprehension.

Item. A cash receipt for three handkerchiefs, purchased the previous week.

Item. A newspaper cutting chronicling the sixtieth anniversary of the suspension of Special Operations Executive's advanced operational base as an independent station in Algiers at the end of World War II.

Item. Howard's dictation machine (Howard had compensated for the loss of use in his right hand by recording his racing tips on this pocket-sized tape recorder as an aide-mémoire when instructing his bookie).

Item. A single unmarked microcassette.

And . . . *Item.* A scuffed, creased chocolate wrapper.

I draw a deep breath to relieve the pressure on the solar plexus, and load the cassette into the machine . . .

I hear a hissing of static, then certain sonorities . . . the deep lowing of cows, quite near . . . then, from the depth of the lungs, a shuddering, sepulchral smoker's cough which I recognise as Howard's . . . then Howard clears his throat . . . and he begins to speak . . .

D-d-damn you D-D-Dubya!

This is my suicide note.

I've disconnected the TV set. I'll hear no more lies.

What does Bush know of 'crusades' when I've executed five hundred of my own men?

In the North African Campaign they told us the same old lies, too. *Dulce et decorum est pro patria mori.* And wasn't our crusade also against the evildoers?

Last week, at the funeral of poor MacCaber's widow, I vowed to end another long-lived arrant lie.

Who could forget our giant RSM? MacCaber was his name and he was every inch as tall as one.

But MacCaber is a name of abject shame in our reconnaissance battalion.

Why? I'll confess.

No one else living knows the whole truth, and within the hour I shall join the inglorious dead.

Not a day has passed in the last sixty years without my thinking of that night with MacCaber in the shell-hole.

We were two hundred yards from the Ahmar bridge where our Assault Platoon had laid eight tons of explosive.

A mile away at Thahabi bridge our second platoon had planted a similar charge.

The plan was to cut off the enemy after their advance with simultaneous explosions.

I had sent MacCaber for a final reconnoitre of the field.

Through my night-glasses I could see the dust cloud raised by the advancing Panzer division, a third of whose armoured column had crossed the bridge.

I consulted my watch. MacCaber had still not returned.

So be it. MacCaber or no MacCaber the psychological moment had arrived.

Five minutes past midnight. *Zero hour, plus five minutes.* Those were our orders. Those extra five minutes of suspense had been recalculated for our special night ops by Command HQ, to keep the men on their toes and to confuse the enemy with an element of surprise.

There was no going back.

I depressed the plunger of the detonator.

In one second the geography changed.

Yet there was no answering thunderburst from the Thahabi flank.

A Verey-light shot across the ridge and I saw MacCaber stagger towards me, blindly retracing the detonator cable looped through his fist.

'Ye limb o' the divil, man!' he roared. 'Ye yellow-livered bastid!' Those were the last words he spoke. His upper face was a shattered death's-head under his steel helmet.

I placed MacCaber's dead hand on the detonator and retreated in a moonlight flit to the rear.

I found refuge in one of the 'slits' our sappers had cut into the hillside.

The corpse of a boy-soldier was my only companion. Someone had covered him with a dirty groundsheet but it couldn't conceal the sickly scent of death. His hobnailed boots protruded; hobnails worn bright as burnished silver by contact with the sand. I could mentally adjudge the miles of trudging their dead wearer had endured only to meet a German bullet.

Did you know that during Richard the Lion-Heart's Crusade his knights used to polish their armour by rolling breastplates in barrels of sand?

In that 'slit' I trembled at the lips, and shivered. In my distraction I dislodged little stones with ragged nails from the hard crust which formed the defensive wall.

Then by chance my fingers closed on a scrap of wastepaper discarded by one of the sappers. An army-issue chocolate wrapper.

A sixpenny bar. Fry's 'Five Boys'.

Do you remember the faces of that famous fivesome? Their features were devised to express the gamut of infantile appetites: 'Desperation'; 'Pacification'; 'Expectation'; 'Acclamation'; and 'Realisation'.

After Father took me to the speech therapist in Harley Street, Nanny gave me a bar as a reward.

The specialist had treated King George for his stammer, too; he dressed in pinstripes and tails like one of those 'doctors in sneezles' from A. A. Milne's '*Now We Are Six*'.

I was told my affliction was an 'episode in my speech'.

Father was the last of five sons so he had been pushed into the Church; his eldest brother was a brigadier.

That's why Father wanted to make a soldier of me. I was his only child.

So he was no timid vicar.

'A contumacious boy.' That's how he regarded me. 'Capricious and superficial.'

In his tiger's lair, my widower father would sit brooding in a mohair chair.

He was a martyr to colds and he smelled of *Friar's Balsam*, and of a peculiar pomatum specially formulated for clerical hair.

Each evening I would visit him for five minutes, and he would rise in his robe from composing his sermon to upbraid my wickedness in failing to master my aspirates. And each night my father would touch my head to little avail for signs of phrenological developments.

'S has its aspirate sound,' my father pronounced sternly, 'as in sin.'

I was afflicted with a lisp not to mention a stutter. I was naturally left-handed but he drilled me to be a right-thinking son.

In his dressing-gown, like a pillar of basalt, he would overbear me, bawling endless homilies: 'A *Battalion* consists of ten *Companies*, my boy!'

Or he would assume the mantle of his envied older brother and shout: 'A vicegerent is an officer ruling in place of another!'

He'd make me march with a kettle on for a helmet.

'Mark Time! Change Step! Right Wheel!'

Then, abruptly: 'Who taught you to sprawl? You may retire to amend your ways, sir!'

Should I protest he would seize me by the collar and propel me from the room.

'Confine your tongue, sir!'

He instructed Nanny to torment me with tongue-twisters. She armed herself with a little book of exercises composed by the King's doctor. I cannot forget thetitle:

> THE REMEDIAL ELOCUTIONIST: *Sentences in which Anomalous Words of the English Language are so Classified as to Indicate their Pronunciation, and to be Fixed in the Memory by Association.*

In my schoolroom the blackboard was used by Nanny with good effect to drill her class of one.

'She sifted seven thick stalked thistles through a strong, thick sieve.'

That was her favourite shibboleth. She was a rare oddity, my Nanny. Her appearance was semi-rebarbative; her depilatory spoiled her bushy eyebrows.

'You shall forfeit your chocolate!' she would threaten; the termagant had no mercy.

Once, Father thrashed me after Nanny reported my misconduct when returning a book of holy scripture to his shelves upside down.

'The serpent deceived me!' he roared, when I refused to own up.

'He says anything but his prayers, and those he whistles,' smirked Nanny.

A docile learner, I submitted to Nanny with extreme lassitude disturbed only by fits of panic when the uric odour of tansies wafted through the schoolroom window. I imagined that distinctive smell to be mildly improper and often when it acted upon my system I was in an agony to relieve myself.

Above the blackboard Nanny had caused to be mounted an angled mirror so she could observe her pupil and magnify his merits—or thwart a false boy's flagitious conduct.

'A streak in the east. A fleet steed. A sleek fleece,' she would enunciate with prissy correctitude, her erect whaleboned back presented to me, as she spelled out the words in chalk.

'A thleek fleethe,' I would attempt hesitantly, only to see her mirrored eyes sear mine and I would desperately seek the comforting hands of the bracket-clock which beckoned solitary nursery tea.

Only at Christmastide, returning in gaiters from his parochial visits, would Father halt by the front door, his face pale against his black cloth, and reconsider.

The grade of the street made him breathless.

There was a scraper for his feet; beneath the clean snow his boots were still as black.

Then he would say to Nanny: 'Bid the boy bide with us and dine.'

So once a year I dined with the laity and the clergy. I folded the napkins for the table the way my father taught me, so they'd adopt the shape of the rectory's narrow gothic windows, and an ill-assorted company would gather at our cheerless hearth. And for that single dinner-hour the grown-ups would assay those pleasantaries their natures denied them at other times of the year. Nanny, the old frog, was fond of a drop and would become quite giddy on half a thimbleful of sherry.

D-d-damn you N-n-nanny!

At the funeral last week of Mrs MacCaber any fond memories I cherished for Nanny gave way to hatred.

At the haberdasher's, before I set off, I bought three new handkerchiefs.

The till receipt reads '3 × Hanks . . . £2.97'.

Yes, the Widow MacCaber's funeral I knew would be a three-hank weepie. I'd traced her through the Dead Men's Shoes Department of my Recce Regiment, but no other member of my old outfit was present to salute Mrs MacCaber's coffin or extol her husband's conduct.

Scarcely surprising. My reminiscences do not accord with theirs, given the spurious coin of my exploits.

On the night of that Panzer attack, I afterwards learned, two of our companies with relief troops totalling some five hundred men were ordered to take up positions in the depths of a natural scar to avoid lying down in open country.

Before they reached the safety of the ravine my premature detonation of the bridge scattered the guts and brains of the majority of those unfortunate men.

The blast caught them in open ground, scorching the desert's western horizon with burst upon burst of scarlet flowers. Those who survived were mown down by firepower of unimagined intensity from the tanks of the Afrika Korps.

I alone heroically escaped in the single remaining undamaged halftrack truck . . . many more would be cowards if they had courage enough.

A chimerical scheme could yet retrieve my fame and achieve great things, so I told myself—I tell you truly that's what I thought then.

After all, history is written by the victorious . . . otherwise Command would've hung me out to dry.

So I obeyed the Eleventh Commandment. *Thou shalt not be found out.*

I wear a digital watch today, as you know.

Seven o'clock has passed, and I've almost reached zero hour. 19.42.

An entirely proper time for my death, don't you think?

It's going to be a four-hank weepie, after all.

Father taught me to reverence the Omniscient One for He is my judge.

I shall not fail. There are incalculable losses to reverse. The noose I've tied in this hank of sisal sash-cord I'm wholly confidant is serviceable.

Not for me the Black Draught of fable. I've dodged that last cocktail hour with the Swiss medicos and their mini-bar of barbiturates.

Though any modern child psychologist would tell you Father was ill-advised to curb my left-handedness with such a harsh rod, the blame for that massacre in the Western Desert must lie squarely with Nanny.

When I was six, the schoolroom clock was fixed on the wall directly behind my desk, do you see.

And Nanny strictly forbade me to turn my head.

But in Nanny's mirror I swiftly learned to read time right to left.

In times of panic, thanks to Nanny, a clock dial was always to be read arsy-versy.

The attack on Ahmar bridge was ordered for five minutes past midnight.

My fatal error was to depress the detonator at twenty-three *fifty-five* hours.

Five minutes *to* midnight! I'd jumped the gun a full ten minutes before our timed attack!

In Death I shall wear Life's last expression: 'Realisation.' D-d-damn you N-n-nanny!

❁

EPILOGUE

To resume (and conclude). Delphine has tried to encourage me to leave this room to take a bath—her intention was all too clear!

It's true my unwashed hair has become quite mousey.

But I said on no account was I to be disturbed. I said I found the room so hushed and soothful that I believed I'd sleep all I could, and that she was not to wake me, even for dinner—I would call her, I said, when I awoke . . . but, actually, I wanted very definitely to complete these apologetics, if only for my private satisfaction.

What further aspects of Howard's character can I illuminate, I wonder?

Well. Have I mentioned he was fearfully jealous?

When we first married he took a razor and ruthlessly cut out of my little black book all those phone numbers of close friends of mine whom he considered threatened his proprietorial rights over his new wife. In an access of morbid jealousy he cautioned me against contacting them ever again . . . even Delphine and Rex.

My God! Howard was a man to be handled with kid gloves! One could earn his indulgence only by guile or flattery and, until such clemency had been won, how his twanging tones and haughty voice alienated my family and relations, and unnerved my loyalest friends! With the exception of Delphine, naturally, who, as I have attempted to describe in all fairness, in tribute to our unwavering friendship, is one of those rare people who disarms with every smile.

Late last year, even that nice young doctor of hers she recommended—a conscientious chap who still troubles to make house calls—was caused to bristle by that persistent prickly manner of Howard's, a measure seemingly of my husband's abiding feelings of insecurity and worthlessness, to which his belated confession attests.

Howard said he was 'choked off' with the young doc and his hesitant prognosis.

'Cut the cackle,' Howard had grated, 'and come to the point.'

The point being that the young man thereupon licked his dry lips and bluntly stated that Howard was terminally ill with a degenerative condition and had less than six months to live.

'No kidding?' Howard had answered, unruffled. 'Yes, that's about the size of it, I suppose.'

Then the doctor inveighed against Howard's drinking and prescribed rectal paraldehyde (an unfortunate side effect of which was that he began to smell of burning sulphur).

'Yes, sir. Yes, sir. Three bags full, sir,' Howard snapped back rudely.

That brusque manner of his—inconsiderate and resentful—was clearly a product of an upbringing and young manhood unleavened by any affection.

His infancy had been tragic. Howard's mother had died of TB shortly after his birth and she'd been barrier-nursed. It's a melancholy fact that Howard never once as an infant was cradled in his mother's arms.

As to the brutality in his later years in the Services, those hair-raising stories he related of the indignities he'd suffered were—I became convinced after a number of retellings—actually to be viewed as blow-by-blow accounts of humiliations he himself, in reality, had inflicted on lesser fry.

He spoke of a 'bastard squad' who roasted 'new scum' at the military academy he attended . . . of 'beastings' and inventive punishments for trumped-up crimes such as 'serving warm toast', meted out to victims who'd find themselves 'counting dirty laundry with their teeth' . . . and it was that fœtid claustral atmosphere of oppression and intimidation that nurtured the young officer who was finally gazetted.

As it is, when I think of Howard now, as you might just possibly bring yourself to understand, there are few recriminations . . . for I'm learning that Time can tame the strongest grief . . . as can *thinking* . . . or, indeed, day-dreaming

The sinister folk at *Mayer Programs* have yet to confirm or deny the true manner of Howard's death in Switzerland so I still remain in the dark. But turn over a stone and you'll uncover more than you care to find.

No doubt it's bad for business for them to admit to an occurrence of self-murder at their clinic in a manner other than of their own devising . . . certainly, if it's not a cover-up, there's no sign yet of them coming clean with the true circumstances.

So when compared with these specious, ultramondaine Swiss metaphysics, Howard, the unhinged Englishman, does not, I believe, on the grand scale of things, deserve moral opprobrium. Foolishly, I'm still expecting him to show up—Howard as I knew him, as large as life and twice as natural—with that rueful, rumpled face of his . . . the rector's son with the look of a wounded lion who has somehow strayed off the set of *The Wizard of Oz*, having despaired of ever discovering the knack others acquire to suspend disbelief.

Already my memory of him is beginning to fade, yet when he's viewed from a critical angle some details remain in sharp focus. For example, Howard superficially appeared nattily turned out but, on closer inspection, a keen observer would notice that he'd directed his tailor to sew knife-edged creases into his trousers; a sly dodge he had learned in the army.

There is a recent photograph in my hand, as a write, that's quite telling in its capturing of the quirky nature of Howard's character.

In bright late autumn sunlight, at a racecourse picnic, are seated myself, Howard, Delphine and that a frightful old snob, Rex (who had continued to amiably regard Howard as something of a spiv). Howard has placed himself between Delphine and myself. I am seated on his right, yet the fingers of his good left hand are twined with Delphine's, while his right hand dangles, useless, at his side . . . it is I, his wife, who am obliged to sit on his blind side, as it were, and perhaps that has always been my place.

How long Howard had known he was cancer-ridden, or been possessed by the wild idea to plot our final exit from this world to the next, I shall never know.

Still, I *do* recall he once wrote a disputatious letter to a national newspaper, some years ago, citing the philosopher 'K' as a lifelong advocate of euthanasia, and refuting claims that the wife of 'K' was an unwilling partner in their suicide pact. (In her suicide note, Howard quoted with emphasis, she wrote: 'I cannot live without him, despite certain inner resources.')

'Hogwash! Tommy rot!' Howard had shouted when he'd read another correspondent's counterclaim on the letters page hinting at foul play.

Curious, but I've only just this minute recollected that odd fact . . . maybe the result of my meditations, yesterday, at that Scottish mission hall of Aileen MacCaber's.

I don't sleep much at night so, in search of spiritual nourishment, and to contemplate my *own* inner resources, I repaid a visit to Aileen's church, in the hope of rediscovering the calm the place held, havened by those pleached hedges.

But though directing Fortune may have led me there, I'm afraid to relate that the cure for my soul's unrest I was not to find.

The mission hall was locked when I arrived, and you'll scarcely believe it, but the absurd truth is that a one-eyed gravedigger at work in the churchyard paused from his labours to inform me the minister had died the previous week—*suicide*—hanged by his own hand.

I cannot say I was astonished . . . I remember the minister's last words:

'Nae man has a lease on his ain life, and he can soon weary o' it.'

Why, I mused, should we expect a soul's physician to cure himself?

Personally, in my own case, friends have ladled out condolences yet I am still possessed of perverse thoughts . . . I suppose it's the continuing effects of my medication. And I can't stop speculating—in a 'what-if' kind of way—imagining an alternative outcome to Howard's tangled plot to have me sign my own death warrant.

Just suppose I had died *first*, like the crown prince's naïve young victim?

According to my current will and testament, Howard would have inherited my entire estate.

So if he planned to die *after* my death, even delaying his suicide by just a few hours, in the same manner as the mad prince, then Howard would have died a very wealthy man indeed, albeit that while I lived he possessed not a penny-piece himself and his post mortal wealth would be only notional.

This afternoon, Howard's own will and testament will be read to me by his solicitor; I have never seen this document so I am mightily curious as to who his chief beneficiary will be . . . certainly not *me*, of that you may be sure.

I asked Delphine to accompany me for moral support, but she twitched a nervous smile and declined.

Early this morning I surprised her in a huddle with Rex, and I overheard her asking him a lot of officious pseudo-diagnostic questions as to my state of mind, pretending to be concerned for my best interests, as if I couldn't see through them both!

'I'm not her doctor!' I heard Rex protest.

'Nor you are, my pet,' Delphine had answered laconically. 'Nor you are.' And she had chucked him under one of his many chins.

Despite her Botox bruises, she had then recomposed her mouth, I noticed, into her familiar, unfathomable, secret smile.

Since my return from the church yesterday, she behaves just as though she's appointed herself my companion-nurse to regulate my daily, routine medication; she seems to believe I'm incapable of remembering the frequency of the correct doses myself.

The fact is I am growing a little afraid of Delphine.

I have a scheduled prescription for each hour in the day; and she says that until I take the tonics she prepares for me I'm absolutely forbidden to think of leaving my bed.

So what is one to do? I wish I could get well faster; I feel so dreadfully tired. For some reason I'm sleeping a good deal now in the daytime.

I hear the rattle of the medicine tray. I must put these papers away; it'll soon be time to take my nap.

❀

Delphine thought I was asleep, but I wasn't. I must set to work to finish my task for it is with these remaining vague thoughts that I reach the dismal coda to my long and a sad tale, which has led to this pool of tears.

As I have related, a 'trial by newspaper' may well have judged Howard and myself on very little evidence and decided our complicity, but the jury is still out on the method of his death.

However, a tragical plot may yet produce a comical conclusion, so I trust I haven't entirely wasted my time by committing my thoughts to paper . . . or by making that second pilgrimage to the little granite church yesterday.

'What is death, after all?' I thought, as I returned to my car beside the lych-gate, *'when we are just brushed off like flies from a wall.'*

The one-eyed gravedigger removed his cap to scratch his head and watch me depart. I refrained from putting coins in the poor box; I felt it was tainted money.

The snow lay with a thin covering on the new-dug earth of the empty grave.

Howard had read somewhere that it is statistically proven by insurance companies that, to avoid road accidents, the safest colour for a car is yellow.

So I turned round and drove homewards in my husband's little yellow car.

My future, I fear, is still coloured by Howard's idiosyncratic prejudices.

❀

'It is an offence for a person to aid, abet,
counsel or procure the suicide or attempted suicide of another. '

Section 2 (1) Suicide Act (1961)
Offences under the Law of England and Wales.

ELEGY FROM A LOCKED DRAWER

(*Marianne E.* — Clonidine)

Assessment Summary (extract): Drug dependency is no respecter of age. The baby-boomer generation who were young in the Summer of Love will be of pensionable age in 2010 when it is estimated that a significant proportion of an ageing population will be addicted to drugs (2.2 per cent). Like the 4,500 NHS patients suffering from 'flashbacks' due to LSD (Lysergic Acid Diethylamide) clinically administered (treatment of alcoholism, etc.) in the 1950s and 1960s, many of the future elderly 'acidheads' will continue to experience psychotic responses resulting from self-administration of hallucinatory agents in their youth. The experiences of Marianne E. are not untypical.

ELEGY FROM A LOCKED DRAWER

Patient ID CPN0326030844: Marianne E.
Occupation: Hospice administrator.
Drug: Clonidine hydrochloride.
Drug class: Imidazoline derivative. As an anti-hypertensive agent, it can inhibit severity of flashbacks associated with LSD use and Hallucinogen Persistent Perceptual Disorder (HPPD).
Common side effects: Drowsiness, dry mouth, headache, possible rebound hypertension.

THE NAME ON the worn secondhand spine was of a well-known poet. My hand trembled and, seemingly of its own accord, refused to take the book down from the tightly packed shelf. The mule-faced bookseller glanced up and considered me curiously, so with a fierce effort I disengaged the paperback and flipped open the last page to read the index to first lines.

'There was no vaccine proof against our love . . .'

I did not need to read further; I knew the words by heart; because (and this is a fact I had long withheld from all but myself) it was I, as it were, who in my wild girlhood had been their 'onlie begetter.'

My teeth numbed as though there was no longer any solid reality to bite on.

I tried my best to resist them but disturbing memories of that distant episode came flooding back.

My hand refused to stop shaking so vivid was my recall of my wayward and overweening younger self; so acute was my recollection of that desk in the publisher's office where I had once sat and of the view from my window over Grosvenor Square; so alive, after all, was my remembrance of the locked drawer.

For, you see, I had inherited that desk from its last incumbent: the Great Poet.

And what—you may be asking—as I was to ask myself, too, all those years ago—does the locked drawer of a great poet hide? Before my tale is done I shall tell you.

❁

My new job had been won on the strength of my handwriting, I afterwards learned from the chief editor who had read my letter of application.

I was young and pretty; he looked me over not without interest, as though he were a cavalryman measuring me in hands (my height is actually 16½ hh).

I remember exactly my dress sense that day. A heroine invented by Jean Rhys (whose novels I had just then discovered) could not have achieved a more convincing Left Bank look.

I was wearing a nipped-waisted, ciré satin, salon blouse from the nineteen-thirties belonging to my mother, with thirty-one glass buttons and narrow stripes of dark emerald and indigo. My hair was tucked under a basque beret, and black, thigh-length, high-heeled boots tapered from beneath a new, button-through, indigo skirt I had bought for the occasion from Bazaar.

It seemed the editor regarded himself as something of a graphologist for he unfolded my letter under his anglepoise for closer reinspection. He said my rapid, connected script indicated a logical mind and mental agility; the 'deep garlands' of my downstrokes, he added, meant I was 'contemplative'; but my script, he warned, was 'arrhythmic' in certain places which could indicate a certain 'intellectual disturbance'; in fact, in my haste, I had written parts of the letter on a train. I nodded earnestly and refrained from mentioning this detail.

His instructions were brief: in preparing my précis of prospectuses from the publisher's Spring Poetry List I was to conform to active sentence structure and to strictly eschew the passive form of phrasal verbs.

'It's a device there is no longer a need for.'

He then handed me a fat bunch of papers for my immediate action. He shrugged and bared his teeth in a smile.

'I know it's a fast ball but . . .'

'. . . it's in my court,' I remembered my English idiom to pronounce crisply.

He nodded and appeared satisfied.

'I'll take you over to your desk,' he said.

❁

'Hello, Miss Blue Pencil.'

A pale face beneath a furball of dark frizzy hair looked up from the next desk. A haggard youth grinned at me, eyes unnaturally bright. He had the same costive pallor of the fully cultivated habit, I noticed, which betrayed the appearance of my permanently stoned elder sister.

I took to him instantly. His name was Toby Freemartin, the editor's copy assistant and general progress chaser. Opposite him, seated across the aisle, was our office section leader, Desmond, a small, fussy, mild-featured copywriter who could, nonetheless, unsheathe kittenish claws to rake his victims with a lacerating wit.

Toby made a long arm and boldly withdrew from my grasp the cloth-covered writing-case I had brought with me which bore my name. He untied the tapes and riffled through the thin sheaf of poems I had not dared to show the editor.

'Audenian,' he sniffed, passing each sheet ponderously to Desmond.

'*Macspaunday* without the audacity,' Desmond purringly demurred.

They were both absolutely right, of course.

Soon a spirited argument developed which centred on my indictment of a number of curious imprecisions which, in my own view, annoyingly marred Auden's phrasing; I was soon citing '*. . . a solitary truck, the last of shunting in the Autumn . . .*' as a particularly glaring example of such infelicities. Their protests were silenced when I mentioned my great-uncle had been a locomotive engineman hauling French sleeping cars on the Continental Express for more than twenty years. He had shown me his railway company's pre-war Signals Manual, I said, which proved conclusively that shunting in sidings was not exclusively seasonal work.

'"During darkness, fog or falling snow,"' I quoted, '"the track-loading in either direction must not exceed ten goods-wagons and a tail lamp must be placed on the last truck by a handsignalman."'

My great-uncle and his Marxist footplateman agreed that Auden's phrase was ultimately meaningless, I assured them airily, and simply a case of seductive euphonious assonance.

Toby and Desmond exchanged thoughtful glances.

I think I must have succeeded in impressing them.

❁

The telephone on my desk rang almost at once.

A heavily accented male voice wheezed on the line and began to cough.

'I wished I would not have rised so early,' he exclaimed peevishly. 'I am not enthusiasted by the weather in England. All these days I have a flu and that did not let me to finish the work.'

I murmured a token of sympathy.

'Even a cat is happy to hear a kind word,' said the voice.

The voice became conciliatory. He announced his hallowed name.

'Plis study carefully the passage what I read,' he pleaded.

I listened reverently.

'My guiding spur, my goading star.' He sneezed. 'I ask of you only one plain service, which I with all respect dare to beg. I hope it is not of a very great problem but plis to look under the blotter,' he continued, 'I have a well fundamented guess there is a line on it where better I succeed to bring forth the meaninks.'

And, yes, indeed, there, under my blotter, a textual variant was written in a cramped spidery hand. I read it to him.

He sighed.

'Thank you. There might be no excuses for such carelessness. We must practice hard,' he growled, 'or we cannot arrive at our aim.'

His voice was drowned by pips on the line and he rang off. He was evidently in a call box.

Desmond stroked his chin with feline fingers.

'Hmm, our resident poet, I wot, or I'm not a tree full of chickadees.'

At my urging he and Toby sketched in the reasons for the great man's absence from his desk.

There had been a double tragedy I was told. The poet's wife had been taken ill six months earlier and he had rushed to her sickbed. (I gathered they occupied a grace-and-favour cottage in a writers' colony in the Pennines.) The poet had hired a nurse to tend the wife. Then the wife had died. It was whispered the grieving poet had delayed his return to London because of his infatuation with the nurse.

'A good occasion for courtship is when the bereft returns from the graveside,' I reflected, remembering one of my grandmother's many censorious axioms. A man but lately come to widowerhood, she thought, was like a new-born animal. ('The first person it sees it regards as its protector,' she would say.) For some reason, I had a sudden vision of the nurse running to the chemist in the rain, wearing the wife's coat.

I asked for a description of the poet.

Toby teasingly said I would easily recognise him because the poet wore 'fast glasses'; Desmond said the poet resembled an 'overblown cabbage' as he had the habit of arriving at the offices buried inside the wind-tangled remains of his scrunched-up daily newspaper.

'And the *double* tragedy?' I asked.

They looked grave; the poet and the nurse had been pony-trekking on the fells; the nurse had been thrown and killed.

That silenced me.

I opened the inner lap drawer of the poet's desk. Inside was not the poet's encrusted bottle of fountainpen ink I had expected, but a mouldy sandwich with a single bite taken from it. Beside it was 'a' cigarette butt coated in bright lipstick.

What else does a poet's drawer contain?

Enquire not e'er what is in another's drawer.

I remember there was a box of those sugar-covered, nut-filled, glorified gum-drops from the East— *rakhat loukoum*—and fingers of nougat, a tribute, according to the label, from a brother poet, Yevgeny Yevtushenko. If I ate one, I wondered, would I be gifted with a lyric tongue?

Underneath the box was a 1939 first edition of *Auf den Marmorklippen* ('On Marble Cliffs') written by that pioneering experimentalist in ololuiqui and LSD, Ernest Jünger.

Toby's shadow fell across the page; he leaned in very close behind me.

'A notable anti-Semite, Jünger,' he observed. He then asked half-seriously, 'Are you one of the *Yehudim*?'

I declared I was not a Jew. He sat on the edge of the desk and swung his legs.

'I am.'

He told me his mother was a naturalised Briton who had succeeded in escaping to England from occupied France with her unborn son by adopting the name of Mrs 'Freemartin' which, for some obscure reason, she knew to be the term for a sterile pig.

When Toby laughed so easily I felt at liberty to laugh, too.

'How desperately odd!'

We then discovered we had a shared passion for the humorous Jewish tales of Arthur Kober. It was clear we were hitting it off.

'What is your favourite colour?' he asked.

'Iridescence,' I answered quickly (paying homage to Marianne Moore).

'And your favourite poet?'

'Anon.'

His smile was wary. I suspected he was more than a little struck on me but puzzled by the immature elusiveness I often contrived to make myself more fetching.

Desmond observed our growing closeness with a jealous disapproval which began to manifest itself in an unreasonable tetchiness.

He was reading the latest issue of the *Times Literary Supplement* from which he was culling reviews of authors under our imprint.

The *Supplement* had recently announced its intention to change its mast-head to the *TLS*.

Desmond stood up and shook the paper in exasperation, condemning the reform as '. . . a sop to grammar-school boys who haven't mastered the pæonic foot and can't say "literary" with three unaccented syllables.'

With a sneer, he tossed the paper on to Toby's desk.

'Here, see if you can read the damned thing!' he flung over his shoulder petulantly as he slammed out of the room.

The next day, for reasons of either exigency or malice, Desmond asked me to assist him with the summarising of his Academic List.

He showed me a pro forma exemplar he had prepared as a demonstration of the house style. The titles, he explained, were mostly of rather dull doctoral theses deemed too specialised for publication by the universities which had fostered them. Our own publishing house profited from certain nourishing literary grants, he hinted, which promoted the works into print.

'There's a dread pattern to all the titles, I'm afraid.'

Desmond shuddered.

'Unavoidable. A lofty quotation followed by a portentous convoluted subordinate title. See for yourself—here's my latest wee abstract on the horrid, hooting stanzas of the Belle of Amherst.'

I examined Desmond's specimen piece.

(*She Quotes the Leaves—Mythological Leitmotif and the Metonymy of Nature in the Poetry of Emily Dickinson*. I began to see his point. The quotation, incidentally, was from *Titus Andronicus*, I later learned.)

Indeed, in the bright spring days of that distant year I was to learn from my two colleagues much else besides which I would later savour as truly new to me. For, little heeding the deeper resonances, I heard for the first time many curious expressions then gaining currency, such as 'male chauvinist', 'bamboo curtain', 'hanging loose', 'liaise', 'psychodrama', 'mixed-up', 'uptight', 'acidhead', 'flipping out', and 'chasing the dragon'.

But hear me to the end.

I had just prepared my first batch of copy for Desmond when his phone rang.

'It's your friend again,' hissed Desmond, carelessly cupping the receiver with his palm. My persistent caller must have heard because his first desperate words on the line were: 'But I *am* your friend, aren't I?'

I assured him he was.

'I hope it is not of a very great misconvenience,' the great poet said, breathlessly, 'but I am working with the second draft today and I feel some barrier to do anything besides what *first* came to my mind. I am in this place since half a year so, plis, it would be good to have that text immidst my papers I forget.'

The voice directed me to the upper right pedestal drawer (the lower file-drawer was locked) and I retrieved a packet of his correspondence.

Under a callow fan letter (in German) from the young Libuse Monikova, and a book, *The Problems of Lieutenant Knapp*, inscribed in Czech by fellow exile, Jīř Mucha, I found a pair of two-guinea tickets for a cello concert given by Jacqueline Du Pre at the Festival Hall the previous year.

Scribbled on the back of one ticket were two words: '*Secretest raptures.*'

I read them to the great poet. I heard a hoarse laugh.

'So! That is the way how it was!' He sounded suddenly elated. '*Lyrisch!* Perfect! Once more you are not less kind. For today much thanks but I am certain of our meeting in due time.'

He rang off.

As I returned his notes to his desk, I idly rattled the catch of the lower locked drawer but it would not budge.

❁

In those days I slept in an unheated conservatory with a fernarium in Brunswick Gardens, W8.

I should explain.

My half-basement was connected to a vast echoing house I rarely entered composed of a ground floor and three empty stories.

While the owner was away at a health farm in the south of France I lived there rent-free to tend the ferns. My sister, Victoria, had made all the arrangements. She lived in a suite above.

The conservatory was stone paved and cool, and smelled of a dank wood.

Around my shake-down bed were three fig trees.

There was a gas-ring on the tiles for my kettle. I could draw only cold water from a floor-level scullery sink which was fitted inside with a retractable hinged grid for supporting garden buckets and washing gumboots; in this rudimentary basin I would attempt to bathe.

On my return that evening the brass taps were newly gleaming and I saw there was a note from the cleaning woman, Mrs Grady:

> <u>FLOOR WET</u> as passage slused down with cloth and no soap. Ask Miss Victoria please to repay the three and six whats owing for new bars of soap or I get behind with my bills. Have you seen the key I give to Miss V to mind, what fitted the big wardrobe?

You being her sister should tell her not to borrow them things as Madam likes to keep her things private to herself. Taken laundry in bin.

For the first time in several weeks, I ventured upstairs into the principal drawing room.

On the mantleshelf was propped—against a silver snuffbox—an invitation from the Suffragette Fellowship addressed to the lady of the house.

Mrs Pankhurst's Jubilee
Flowers will be laid at her Statue at 5.45 p.m.
R.S.V.P. by June 21st.
(Some Jubilee stamps are available 9d each.)
50 Years of Votes for Women • 'Deeds, Not Words'

Beside the invitation was a picture postcard of a sanatorium in Hyères addressed to Victoria. I looked for the message. An infirm hand had written, in dainty, arched arcades, these words:

Victoria Dearest

You're not my first love—
I loved before we met.
You are my last love—
The dearest, sweetest best—
My heart has shed its outer leaves —
I give you all the rest.
M N-J

My own heart thudded; my cheeks burned; Victoria has always had the gift to command powerful emotions, especially in myself.

' "You are my *last* love," ' I whispered. '*Another* superlative! How entirely bloody typical!'

(Because Victoria is the elder, my father would say he could not but aver that he had loved her the *longest*. Yes, an acute word cuts deep—particularly as my father had abandoned my mother at her childbed and left her entirely dependent on her own exertions the day after I was born.)

I heard a step in the hall. I guiltily returned the card to its place.

A footfall behind me.

'Wotcher,' Victoria said huskily. 'Gimmee five bob, my sweet, I'm stony.'

I gave her ten shillings; she is as close as my skin.

She was wearing a vintage tea-gown of yellow Chinese silk hitched up by its sash—very high over her pale thighs—like a Greek tunic. Her face was ashen, an effect heightened by her heavy eye make-up and absence of lipstick.

Her mouth, I could see, was dry, with white flecks of spittle in the corners.

Swaying, she almost stumbled as she drew the curtains.

Her photophobia and her blurred vision, I knew, were symptomatological signs of her addiction.

In the new darkness, she moved towards a stately radiogram of fumed oak and satinwood. I think she must still have been mildly 'tripping'.

A record was on the turntable and she touched a switch.

Marianne Faithfull began to sing: *'Is this what I get for loving you, baby?'*

A great languor stole over me.

Victoria took my hand in her hot, dry clasp and we began to dance.

She led. I followed.

(When I was no more than five years old she told me I must call her *The* Miss Victoria. Whether I cared for the fact or not, she asserted, I as the younger daughter was destined indefinitely to be merely *a* Miss. Even then, please understand, she had conferred on me a subordinate title.)

'Vix,' I began, 'you know, you really oughtn't to be wearing her things . . .' but she pressed her fingertips to my lips. I did not resist.

The song ended but Victoria sang and danced on.

(Once, years before, at one of her college parties, Victoria had introduced me to Marianne who had been invited to sing. Marianne must have noticed the disdain written on my face when I listened to the embarrassing insipidness of that early versifying because afterwards she came up to me and said, very charmingly and modestly: 'Darling, I apologise *not* for my singing but *unreservedly* for the song.')

Victoria's repetitive, hypnotic singing; a picture on the wall (a drawing by Corot of a girl in a beret who resembled me); the odour of damp ferns rising from the floor below; the dim light; the whirling yellow silk; all began to disturb my senses and I was assailed by bizarre thought patterns.

It was as though Victoria was speaking a private language and willing the dissolution of my inner self, intent on my transcendence to share the paradisal visions of her drugged state.

Perhaps, at that moment, you may think, I was experiencing my first 'contact high'.

Maybe. But I had known Victoria all my life, you see, so I was unable to judge such distinctions.

When her energy flags Victoria invariably becomes childishly tearful, so, in the event, she insisted I stay to sit at her bedside and hold her hand until she slept.

The matter of Mrs Grady's note was, in consequence, quite understandably forgotten.

❁

It was a perfect May morning when, next day, I walked across Kensington Gardens to the office, but an aching loneliness descended on me.

In London, a crowd is not company, for in a great city there is a great solitude.

The sun seemed to shine on every leaf but through the bright unthreatening greenness I saw a bird was sharpening its beak on a branch.

At the Serpentine, I remember, a tourist was seated on a park bench listening sombrely to a World Service news bulletin from a transistor radio.

'Czechs resist Soviet blockade threat . . . shortlived Prague Spring . . . radio and press muzzled . . . 12,000 Soviet troops massing on Czech borders . . .'

The foyer to the publisher's offices was empty when I arrived and entered the tiny lift—it was a two-person affair—a 'Waygood', with a lattice door, and floor area no greater than a dumb waiter.

Then Toby tumbled in before I had a chance to close the gate.

Toby—eyes alight with mischief—refused to share the fragile cage until he had calculated my counterweight; an insistence I viewed as immoderately impolite.

He soon established that, fully laden, I weighed just over fifty kilogrammes.

In a dumb waiter there is no need to speak.

Taste, touch, sweat, sight, his breath in my hearing . . . maybe I had been deprived of my senses too long . . . because, weakly, I did not resist with any great conviction when he suddenly kissed me. I felt I was rediscovering the rules of a forgotten game or some lost tincture of alchemy.

In the office we found Desmond mournfully eating a chocolate bourbon biscuit, reading *The Times*.

My face was flushed.

Toby was whistling tunelessly through his teeth.

Desmond examined our faces very carefully then ate another biscuit.

'That's the trouble with this country, if you like something it's either illegal, immoral or fattening. And if you like some*one*, he's bound to be . . .'

But I cut him off swiftly by pouncing on his paper's morning headlines.

'A trick question. Who took the first steps to building Communism? Scientists or the apparatchiki?' I asked

'Taking a scientific wild arse guess, I'd say . . .' Toby smirked.

'Wrong,' I said. 'Scientists would have tried it out first on dogs.'

The phone rang on my desk.

The great poet sounded distressed.

'A call from Prague I have just a few minutes ago,' he announced excitedly. 'My brother-in-law is first party secretary of our district and he counsels my return.'

From the slight shift of auditory quality on the line I formed an impression that he was closer to London than hitherto, perhaps even in the capital.

The poet's voice was competing with a background hubbub and I had a sense of animated salon gossip in foreign tongues —*salonlöwen*—other social lions roaring, like him, from the margins of governments-in-exile—shadow cabinets of purged politicians, relief fund organisers, armchair strategists, and the diaspora of banished Czech patriots who had fought with the British forces, or of German irredentists agitating for the restitution of their Sudeten enclave.

'It is not easy that you can imagine,' the poet bellowed, 'to get use to live in a foreign country!'

He asked me to refer to a ruled jotter under a jam-jar crammed with his pencils.

Markedly underscored, with deeply depressed pencilling on the note-pad, were the words: *'I owed Death nothing then Life intervened.'*

I read them to him.

'Phantastisch!' he shouted with relief above the din. 'It is worth to do everything well. I hope my poem will be for you great interest! You are very kind!'

He rang off.

I thought, then, with a disappointment more profound than I considered possible, that *that* phonecall would be the very last time I heard from him.

I replaced the pencil jar. The ends of each pencil (there were five) were gnawed and showed his tooth marks and I imagined the poet's finger-nails bitten to the quick.

❀

'"Tonite let's make love in London,"' Victoria quoted, speech slurred, on my return that evening. Those liquid eyes were again distilled to needlepoint droplets of narcosis, I noticed, and her flesh lacked skin tone.

Three years before, when I was fifteen, our mother had been shocked when she learned I had accompanied Victoria (at Vix's insistence) to hear Ginsburg recite at the Royal Albert Hall. ('Infantile scatology,' was Mother's verdict.)

Now in the darkened drawing room Victoria beckoned to me and extended her palm.

She held a small cube wrapped in metal foil.

'A sugar lump to gild the pill,' she said tenderly.

I recoiled but she seized my arm and pressed the object firmly into my hand.

'Know what this is?'

'Haven't the faintest,' I whispered fearfully. But I knew.

'A tab. A dot. For dropping acid, silly,' she said.

She unwrapped the cube and placed it on my tongue. I tried to spit it out but she sealed my lips with her fingertips. Involuntarily I swallowed.

'Tune in, dearest heart. I will be your guide,' she soothed.

Marianne began to sing from the radiogram: *'I always needed you to look out for me . . . oh, baby . . .'*

At first, the rubberiness of my gums from the anæsthesia I found frightening.

Soon, however, I began to sink into an hallucinatory reverie.

It is true that during those psychedelic hours with Victoria I learned the meaning of Ginsberg's 'Blake-lit Mohammedan angels' —because, for two eternities more ancient than Chaos, I stared at a milliard of those lucent homunculi in the reticular texture of the drawing room wallpaper—*yet* . . . I also stared into that purgatoried place where every monster has its own multitudes.

By looking through the fissures of the old house, I seemed to see not only the stars but to penetrate upper chambers I had never fully explored.

At an unknown hour I found myself floating some distance above Victoria's bed gazing into upcast and darkly oracular eyes to contemplate a voluptuary pythoness wearing my face whose every sensuous uncoiling convulsion was suspended in an aphrodisiac prolongation I, also, shared.

Over her seraphic nakedness a swarm of furry bees hovered which slowly resolved itself into a shock of tightly crinkled hair . . . the frizzy hair of . . .

Toby Freemartin lay across her—a supersexual being of extraordinary radiance and beauty hewn from an heroic age.

Colours intensified. Light diffracted. Objects distorted and shrank.

Somehow, a yellow paper rose twisted on a wire hanger in the big wardrobe seemed to acquire an enormous significance.

Time warped. Joss sticks were lit.

As from the edge of a great divide I observed a distant simulacrum of my being receive the tributes of the flesh . . . he-she and he-I and I-she, all interconnected by a glowing force field which seemed to strike sparks as lips touched, and melded into a totality of incorporeal sensation.

The bed had dematerialised, as had those affirmers of mortality, our teeth and gums.

I learned too late all trips are braved *sans* gritted jaw.

The foundations of the house had dissolved into the infinite void and our flesh seemed to be tingling with electric static as we brushed the dark velvet of deep space . . . a friction which seemed to transmute that insubstantial velvet into aurorean ripples of charged silk, billowing in waves, stimulating my-her-his-their-our senses with the glancing touch of a thousand quickening fingers, until we knew ourselves as one flesh, a single skin, slick with sweat, yearning like a fierce rolling tide to break together on a nearing shore.

What I-she-he-they-we felt-saw-tasted-*knew* there-next-before-then was spasm after spasm of burning white light, which overwhelmed selfhood, as my-her-his-their-our senses were pierced by darts of super-refined pain.

Then the wave receded and—beached—we lay together, struggling for breath as though we had just swum the infernal regions' Hellespont.

By unspoken agreement we avoided each other's eyes, and before our temporal lives fully reasserted themselves, I remember, we three were next sitting cross-legged—Victoria, Toby and

I—watching in wonder the slow-motion, frame-by-frame, glittering parabola of a silver snuffbox we pitched from hand to hand.

Drug-induced synæsthesia I mused, was like a problem in grammar, where the active and the passive voices become confused and there is a difficulty in distinguishing the moment of action from the resultant state, and no one knows whether they are the object of the action or the subject performing it.

A new word for my lexicon I learned that night was 'freakout'.

❀

'Here, take it.'

I groaned in protest. Toby stared down at me with eyes like live coals.

'Fifty milligrams of Thorazine,' Toby persisted, 'it'll bring her down.'

His words cooled me better than cold water.

'Precious, my poor precious,' Victoria cooed, smoothing my brow.

Reader, I have to tell you that, even adrift in a drug-induced nirvana, the deepest love can turn to deadliest hatred. I confess to you now that the not-so-beatific emotion I brought back from the Other Side was a revived green-eyed envy towards my identical twin sister, Victoria, the Firstborn-by-an-hour.

I should also add that an out-of-body experience is a daily occurrence for an identical twin. Philosophically speaking, of course, no two persons can be identical for, if they were, they would be one and the same.

I, the last born, was ever mamma's darling; she was daddy's.

The mind-unhinging power of the LSD took many more hours to wane.

I recall Victoria and I walked, at midnight, hand in hand, up the north end of the Portobello Road. Inside a tallnineteenth-century tenement building we lingered—two escapees from reality—transfixed before a tiled mural depicting the Dignity of Work. A little girl in a nightdress scampered from the head of the stairs and laughed nervously in the dark.

Somehow, to me, it all seemed quite natural that passers-by bore the heads of wild animals, telegraph poles were hydra-headed, television aerials were tarantulas, and lamp-posts writhed like serpents.

I thought I, alone, understood the secret of Allen Ginsberg's universe where 'angelheaded hipsters' dwelt 'in the total animal soup of time'.

❁

The following Monday—the 18th—I crossed the abandoned battlefield that was Grosvenor Square. On the pavement outside the American Embassy the tinders of the stars-and-stripes still smouldered.

Anti-Vietnam war protesters had hurled red paint across our entranceway but it was the window of the neighbouring office which was smashed.

The Passover, I thought.

The Angel of Death has passed over and the Firstborn will be saved because the lintels are painted with the blood of the lamb.

I imagined the missile as a transitive verb, nimbly skipping the Indirect Object immediately following, and taking the Direct Object in its path.

❁

My editorial office was empty and eerily silent.

'Henceforth, words, not deeds,' I vowed silently to myself, toying with my pen as I recalled the miraculous transference of sense impressions the previous night and the freakish distortions of time and space.

Now, as I examined the cap of my fountain pen, the inside of the screw-top holder did not, somehow, simply *seem* metaphorically to be the sour-tasting ribbed roofcage of my mouth's palate, but indeed *was*, in every physical respect, a reamed cavity between my jaws, and *was* my ink-stained, furred tongue, and *was* the inner narrowing shaft which terminated below my tonsils.

I meditatively re-screwed the cap and tasted the grooviness inside my mouth; because, you see, only the influence of a psychoactive drug, or the art of super-mystical oriental calligraphy, can ever ordain that a scribe *becomes* her pen.

Seated at the great poet's desk, I stared uncomprehendingly at an unfinished abstract in my pending tray, which attempted to assess a critical essay on George Eliot (*A Male Profession—Marian Evans and the Paradox of Duality*), and I steeled myself to resist my being overthrown once more by treacherous perceptual changes.

Victoria had warned me of the dangers from side effects such as psychotic 'flashbacks'.

I had replied bitchily that identical twins were immune to schizo-affective disorders.

The door opened and a giant overblown cabbage composed of leaves from the *Süddeutsche Zeitung* walked in.

When the outer leaves were shed, I could see the great poet was wearing blue-tinted 'flip-ups'—a double pair of dual-purpose, twin-lensed reading glasses, hinged upwards like the folding windscreen of a fast continental touring motor car.

He appeared to be in a great hurry.

His new Jaeger suit was smudged with wet paint. (*Period sartorial note:* his waistcoat of matching check fabric was cut like a one-piece v-neck sweater.)

He pointed to the red stain.

'Such things when they happen—it seems to me—have some meanink and significance for all persons involved.'

He placed a brown leather Gladstone bag at my feet, then examined a pot of maidenhair ferns I had brought for my desk from the conservatory.

'The ferns loose their leaves,' the poet observed and, indeed, the air conditioning had withered the stems.

I went to fetch fresh water, but I knew in my heart that my errand was the poet's ruse to permit his emptying the locked drawer unobserved.

His last words of farewell are still strong in my mind.

He appraised me steadily with melancholy moon-soaked eyes. I noticed he had rather Slavic features, and a slightly drooping moustache; and, curiously, he wore a thin silver bracelet around his left wrist—a relic of his departed lover, perhaps?

'It is worth to live to see a so beautiful sight,' he said and bowed to kiss my hand according to the Mitteleuropean custom of his youth; but he managed to kiss not only my fingers but further up.

I was wearing a white, sleeveless dress.

I felt very hot.

About his person I detected more than a hint of the zest from limes. As he bent over my hand I smelled his aftershave. (I am certain it was *Eau Sauvage* by Christian Dior, and his breath smelled of cigar smoke and also of a powerful, juniper flavoured hunter's vodka, or so I believe, with an undersong of resinous essences redolent of the forsaken forests he loved—an impression confirmed, incidentally, by a reminiscence I read in a *Festschrift* dedicated to him a decade later.)

'I dare to wish you good luck in your writing and all the other domains of your young life,' he said.

❀

Three months passed, and the day after Russian tanks entered Prague I learned of the poet's death, by his own hand, in London.

Desmond and I attended the funeral service in the Brompton Oratory.

A newspaper magnate read the eulogy.

There was a coronet of kingcups on the casket.

The great poet was, the press baron said, like a candle lighting others and consuming itself. From the pulpit the eulogist raised his hands in emphasis and I saw he was wearing white cotton gloves. (Gloves, particularly those of traffic policemen, have a meaning for symbolists and students of poetics but, on this occasion, they were worn as protection by a sufferer from interdigital mycotic dermatitis.)

The poet, it turned out, had been a correspondent for the weekly *Sudetendeutche*, and also filed copy to the London press. His imposed exile, the death of his Czech wife, the death of his lover (the young English nurse), the re-enacted assault on his homeland must have all compounded in his mind as a case of quadruple betrayal . . . or so I thought then.

The eulogy ended, at the poet's request, with a quotation from John Clare:

Swamps of wild rush-beds, and slough's squashy traces . . .
Flats and low vallies of kingcups and daisies . . .
Your flat swampy vallies unwholesome may be . . .
Still . . . ye are dear as this heart in my bosom to me.

But I suspect, when the poet chose those words, he must have been meditating, overcome by homesickness, on those 'unwholesome' gaseous Sudeten marshes, beloved by entomologists, north-east of Franzenbad in the former Hapsburg Empire of his birth.

❁

A great man's foolish sayings can pass for wise ones.

But what of the wise sayings from that fraudulent decade?

Reader, I have not betrayed your trust.

As I promised, the contents of that drawer I can reveal because, naturally, long before that ill-fated Friday—long before my drug-fuelled trip to the Gates of Hell—I had learned all.

Alone, one lunchtime, my colleagues absent at a book fair, I had unlocked the forbidden drawer.

(Later, I had very easily covered up the loss of Mrs Grady's key to the big wardrobe by placing it, where she was sure to find it, in her string bag of vegetables.)

The key had perfectly fitted the poet's locked drawer as I knew it must.

The contents? A booby prize, you've no doubt concluded.

Thirty-one magazines were marshalled neatly in the file-rack, their pages studiously tagged.

Adam, Bachelor, Carnival, Escapade, Gent, Harlequin, King, Man's Life, Mayfair, Men Only, Monsieur, Nugget, Parade, Penthouse, Photoplay, Playboy.

The pages the great poet had particularly marked were provocative photostories of the *Mädchen*-in-uniform variety—for the main part, young nurses of the dominatrix type, mostly out of uniform.

I noted the phrases the poet had underlined: *'Sex on Punishment Ward 10 . . .'*; *'. . . petite Nurse Stern . . .'*; *'. . . with a forward look . . .'*; *'Call for Dr Longpeter . . .'*; *'. . . the Doctor's Prescription for Love . . .'*; and so on.

His elegy, I saw, had been one of those poems that had practically written itself:

There was no vaccine proof against our love,
*Wagest du Scheusal neben der Schönheit.**
Doomed passion—a Monster whom Beauty made slave
To secretest raptures. Cold scent of delight . . .

I am sure you can recall many more of the stanzas yourself. They are often anthologised, for few can forget the memorable closing quatrain . . .

. . . Petite nurse stern—my goading spur!—my guiding star!—
Liebender Sterne!† —with forward look and burning glance
Shall press and count again our pulse's mortal dance.
Liebling, at Baltasar's I smoked my last cigar.

Yes. The great poet did, indeed, smoke his last cigar, it was whispered, as if he'd regarded himself as a condemned man who'd been granted one last request before his self-imposed death sentence was executed.

Ah! But what exactly *was* his crime you continue to ask.

* 'Darest thou, Monster, here beside Beauty.' The poet, in his grief, has consciously refashioned imagery from the 'Helena' sequence in Act III, Part II, of Göethe's 'Faust.' (The elegy, you may remember, is inscribed 'To H.D.', the dedicatee being the young English nurse.)

† 'Existent star!' The metrical foot into which German most naturally falls is trochaic; while in English it is iambic. The exilic poet expresses the ambivalence of his divided national loyalties by loosely accenting alternate lines in iambic and trochaic pentameter.

As I intimated earlier, I've long debated with myself the ethics of denouncing the poem's true begetting, and even now I hesitate on the brink of full disclosure lest you think this memoir amounts to a smear campaign to have the great poet blacklisted . . . since that locked drawer, I confess, contained a document far more damning than a collection of tawdry back numbers.

For wedged in the drawer's rearmost recess, behind the cardboard lining of the file-rack, a legal-size envelope was stashed I discovered . . . of whose contents only this memory alone remains.

But be assured my memory does not play me false.

The purplish mimeographed typed sheets I withdrew were clear enough . . . columns of addresses, listing the names in England of the poet's nationalist compatriots . . . exiled political dissidents, distributors of samizdat writings, their British sympathisers, committee members and adherent members of a clandestine Freedom Movement reporting to a secret Czech legation in London.

Before returning the papers to the drawer, I observed the top sheet was overstamped in red ink with a special divisional insignia of the *Státní Bezpecnost* (StB), the Czech state security police. (*Kremlinological Note:* The device was, I recall, a smudged heraldic lion on a banner surmounted by a red star.)

Now, maybe you regard my suspicions as sinister and unfounded but, I regret to relate, the recent unearthing in Prague of over two hundred thousand StB dossiers recording the activities of alleged communist-era collaborators suggests otherwise.

Only a fraction of those names has been published in the uncensored Prague press but, as foreign correspondents there have noted, a number of famous Czech literary luminaries have been reputedly exposed as StB agents, recruited as informants to spy on their colleagues.

Indeed, maybe by the time you read these words the poet's name will have surfaced as a clandestine Communist Party operative.

The Romans had a noble sentiment when they declared *de mortuis aut bene aut nihil*—speak well of the dead or not at all.

Of course, it is villainous to traduce the dead; and I am emphatically *not* a grave defiler. Particularly as there exists the profoundest concern that many reluctant secret StB agents were first compromised under duress, and thus recruited through extortion, or their collaboration was falsified, or forged false criminal evidence was laid against them.

So why do I persist with my doubts?

Let my modest textual analysis of the key passage from the poet's antipenultimate stanza attempt to shine a light on the truth . . .

I owed Death nothing then Life intervened,
*Verräterischer, nichtswürdiger Geist.**
So cold upon your mouth† my kiss demeaned
Our love. My song I sold, an egoist enticed,

For a handful of silver and a state riband‡ . . . etc.

So there it is.

Espionage specialists and security experts have known for almost a century that police bureaux in communist bloc countries have penetrated international academia by deploying suborned academics, awarded spurious honorifics and doctorates, to provide their political masters with local intelligence concerning the underground activities of émigrés around the world.

But whether the 'traitorous contemptible spirit', who betrayed with a kiss, similarly succumbed to such coercion I must leave you to judge.

* 'Traitorous contemptible spirit . . .' From Scene XXIII of Göethe's 'Faust, Part I.' The poet refers to the betrayal and abandonment of Faust's lover, Gretchen (whose character is said to be based on Friederike Brion, Goethe's mistress, who inspired several of Goethe's heroines).

† A line evoking Goethe's song, 'The Farewell', written between 1767 and 1768 (exactly two hundred years' earlier); a poem believed to mark Goethe's lovetorn final parting from Friederike Brion.

‡ These lines recall 'The Lost Leader,' Browning's repudiation of Wordsworth who, in 1843, was named England's poet laureate. Like many young poets who considered Wordsworth their mentor, Browning accused the nation's new laureate of betraying his radical political views in exchange for a 'handful of silver' — 'Just for a handful of silver he left us,/Just for a riband to stick in his coat.'

Certainly, by his own admission, he was no stranger to betrayal.

'There was no vaccine proof against our love . . .'

The mule-faced bookseller resumed his scrutiny of me as I returned the poet's collected works to the shelves.

My mistrust for men generally, after all these years, has not notably diminished, yet, willing-unwilling, I felt a tremor of reawakened tenderness for the Great Man.

'Apes are never more beasts than when they wear men's clothes,' I thought.

In the poet's own country there is a saying: 'Love is severe, you can love a goat.'

I smiled tentatively, remembering the poet in the heyday of his goatage . . . then my smile faded, remembering those five chewed pencils—splayed on the poet's desk—like the bitten fingers of a man inwardly bleeding, outflung in appeal.

RED COFFEE

(*Irina P.* — Carbamazepine)

'Everything is stolen, betrayed, sold . . . '

— Anna Akhmatova

Assessment Summary (extract): On examination, the patient looked frightened and suspicious. After her defection, she claims to have passed through great suffering, experiencing complex magico-esoteric multimodal hallucinations (e.g. in the last 4 days, she had sensed that she was 'possessed by a Thinking Energy', a fully sentient form of plant life which communicates with her, the roots, stems, branches, and leaves talking to her or touching her.) When these somatic and tactile hallucinations appear there is also a sensation of estrangement from her body. These 'night frights' are of such vividness that in her fever she 'leaves the impression of her body on the sheets'. She also reports a perceived male voice commenting on or criticising her behaviour to which she responds with pronounced docility. The voice, she says, is hostile and cruel. She believes that this internal voice has taken absolute possession of her, ordering every action, word, or thought and she foresees brooding disaster and catastrophic events for herself and her partner. Her Referral Notes record that she exhibits self-mutilative behaviour (palms of hands); and they suggest that carbamazepine has perhaps been prescribed unwisely as its effectiveness for her treatment is far from clear.

RED COFFEE

Patient ID CPN0287170449: Irena P.
Occupation: Legation First Interpreter, ex-*Corps Diplomatique* (current status, asylum seeker).
Drug: Carbamazepine.
Drug class: Antimanic medication used in prophylactic treatments of manic-depressive disorders in exceptional cases.
Common side effects: Dizziness, drowsiness, coordination disturbances, nausea, headache, fatigue, blurred vision or visual hallucinations.

SHE HAD BEEN passing the same florist at the same spot at the same hour for the past week, but, today, the shop was no longer to be seen; or, rather, *was not to be found.*

The sun shone cold for a second on Novy Świat.

For there was Konrad, opening a car door for his insufferably young wife.

Irina could not fail to recognise the car.

The car, of course, like everything else—even that new Jaeger jacket Konrad was wearing—was in the gift of Kristina, whose inheritances were rumoured to include not only her late father's cherished old blue Mustang convertible but an ancient title from the *Almanach de Gotha.*

Haughty *Księżna* Kristina.

If Konrad was to be believed, his wife was related to the first forty-seven noblest families through a lineage that numbered a Radziwill, an Ogiński and a Sanguszko.

Hidden by the boulevard trees, Irina gazed fixedly at her lover's wife, committing to memory the aloof over-made-up face.

She was struck not so much by Kristina's starlet good looks but by the desperate artificiality of her smile.

Then Konrad laughed outright; that characteristic, infectious laugh which curled his rather fleshy lips with that droll facial mobility which made him at once resemble Fernandel.

The lover's laugh; the wife's cheerless smile; and the mistress dismayed.

The scene was exactly as Grazhina had predicted.

Irina reeled, as from a blow. She inhaled deeply; then she remembered where she first heard Konrad's laughter.

❁

The English Soil

The approach to Stoneburgh Military Academy was through the garrison's camps, on a concrete road flanked by gorse thickets and wild heathland churned by tank tracks.

'The English soil,' she thought fondly.

For she could not deny that in her long-dreamt-of assignment to the foreign fields of England, after all those oppressive years of diligent study in Moscow, her soul had recognised what her masters would condemn as the delusions of a spiritual homecoming.

When she arrived at the guardpost she saw a soldier remove a black disc from a hook and hang an orange disc in its place on the message-board.

'Security state raised to Condition Orange,' Irina thought, suppressing an impulse to laugh, *'but surely I alone can't be the cause of their heightened threat alert!'*

The Ministry of Defence guards inspected her Cyrillic passport, unsmiling. Not until Colonel Rees-Sholter rang the gate-house was the barrier raised.

Irina drove the hired car cautiously, nerving herself to remember the rule of the left hand lane.

Where two broad avenues met she halted before a huge, black eighteenth century mortar with a mouth wide enough to fire a Landseer lion.

The Palladian façade, she observed with a pang of disappointment, was disfigured where the portico pilasters were parceled up in green plastic for restoration. She felt deprived of her proper due.

The guards had directed her to 'K' section. The college blocks for the gentlemen cadets and the great park of over six hundred acres had been laid out in tribute to beleaguered forts, border disputes and skirmishes in the Indian and Afghan wars of the nineteenth century. An entire square mile was divided alphabetically into twenty-six sectors, ranging from Alipur and Berar, through Charasia to Zulfikar. Irina was detailed to 'K' sector (the siege of Kotah, 1858) which adjoined the Residency of the Lieutenant Governor.

A cadet platoon, selected from the New Intake Group of that momentous year, jogged by with war-whoops, thighs sweating like champion gladiators.

As she parked her car, a soldier-cyclist rode up and blew the midday lunch recess on his buglet.

❁

She was next struck by an image of an enormous black boot.

When she raised her eyes she saw it was attached to a Brobdignagian colour-sergeant, whose slashed peak was forced sharply downwards like a visor. He silently escorted her down a brown tiled corridor, past polished brass fire extinguishers, and thence to the office of Colonel Rees-Sholter.

❁

Thank-God-It's-Friday

Since Irina tended to meet a person by his clothes and see him off by his intelligence, her first acquaintance with the colonel was to find him somewhat unprepossessing.

He was in civvy tweeds. The day of Irina's arrival must have been Thank-God-It's-Friday because the colonel always wore mufti checks for his weekends in the country.

'The British military has a name for such dress,' Irina remembered. *'Scruff Order.'*

The colonel's complexion was bibulous. The eyes that met and challenged hers were fierce and violet-blue but, fortunately, he preferred excessively young women so they got straight down to essentials brusquely.

Her new colleagues 'tipped their hats in at the door'.

First entered an Airedale called Beau. Woe betide the cadet who shunned the touch of that lathered tongue. Irina attempted to smooth its rough coat to the satisfaction of its master, Major Poultney.

Superfit Roland Poultney in his cypress-green beret, Irina learned, was a Green Fly from Intelligence seconded to the Task-Force as the colonel's ADC.

'Bow-wow,' Beau woofed, so it was the dog who made the introductions.

'Rollo,' the major insisted, as they shook hands.

RHIP. Rank Has Its Privileges, and one of Rollo's privileges was to be attended by his dog.

'Ma'am.' He saluted as though he were addressing a noblewoman. A charming, conceited schoolboy voice—yet those tones were sharpened by an edge of malice.

He delivered a well-rehearsed *tac-eval*, crisply summarising his tactical-evaluation of Irina's rôle in CERC, the Central European Research Committee. He passed her a bulky file for her prompt attention.

'Hard lines on your first day, I'm afraid, but we never promised to handle you with . . . '

'. . . Kid gloves?' Irina agreed cheerfully, splaying her blunt Stakhavonite fingers and weighing the heavy file in one hand.

Poultney exchanged a glance with Rees-Sholter. Their manner relaxed; they seemed content. The colonel pressed a buzzer.

Next, Second Lieutenant Pym manifested himself. Duncan Pym.

Somehow the orderly officer, unnoticed, had shyly insinuated himself into the room bearing a tray.

Irina knew, immediately, she had conquered her first English heart.

She could practically see Duncan pledge his devotion with his eyes.

'Do you fancy a wet?' He indicated the mugs.

She had taught herself to distinguish between the comfortable lived-in voices of the elect and the carefully modulated enunciation of the pseudo-posh.

Duncan smiled. A row of well-polished, crooked teeth.

'Two Harry Whiters,' he said carefully.

For his own part, Colonel Rees-Sholter unscrewed the cap of an unsteaming thermos flask.

❁

They took her to a darkened room, photographed her, and gave her a Pass Number. She could not stop shivering.

❁

Don't Crack Under Pressure

Little by little—*malo-pomalu*—Irina accustomed herself to CERC's office routine and service lingo. 'File Thirteen' was the wastepaper bin, for instance.

As for Rees-Sholter, the man seemed more anxious about etiquette at the next banner parade than the Task Force Report, fretting about a VIP's post-nominals absent from a commissioning dinner guest list.

'Some bod has lost a KG in the print room,' Rollo informed the colonel.

'Buggerance and shame!' the colonel shouted on the telephone.

The colonel conducted only one-way conversations.

She very soon learned the way matters stood between Rollo and Duncan.

Rollo was weary of Stoneburgh Academy; the same camp had seen his first tour of duty five years before. During that assignment he recorded his earliest encounter with young Ensign Pym.

'If you don't pass off the square, you're confined to barracks,' Rollo confided to Irina one day beneath the saluting base.

In the smoke-break they were watching cadets endure, blindfold, sensory deprivation exercises on the assault course. The attrition rate was high.

Adventure training was on Wednesdays—a chance to be legally scared.

Rollo revealed the second lieutenant invariably had 'a sad on', and was known variously as a 'One Pip Wonder' or a 'PITA'—a Pain In The Arse.

According to Rollo, Duncan was regarded as a 'total arse-wipe' by most of the CERC team, in response to which the young lieutenant had assumed a baffled defensive air. The sign above Duncan's desk read: *Don't Crack Under Pressure.*

Even five years ago, Duncan had been singled out as a 'utter zoob' who had been 'bounced off the square' for slacking at drill.

At the end of the Standard Military Course, the rest of his class had been given probationary Risk Passes under the Review Board, but Duncan had been back-termed to the intermediate semester.

'On Animal Night his squad got him bladdered, bound him in bodge-tape, and gave him a bit of a beasting,' Rollo gloated.

Irina thought of Duncan's misshapen teeth.

'Sometimes he's lucid. Sometimes he isn't,' sneered Rollo.

Anyhow, Duncan had been lucid enough about his golf, Irina was to reflect later. The colonel enjoyed coming off well in rounds with Duncan which his subordinate deliberately conceded.

Irina's efficient progress with her Report for T-FECS—the Task-Force for European Co-operation and Security—pleased the colonel. His trusty workhorse, he called her.

'Don't think for that I am all horseflesh!' she sparked up.

'Nor you are, my dear,' brayed the colonel amiably; thanks to Duncan his handicap had improved. At the mention of flesh, Duncan blushed.

They were entering the grand dining hall.

In the lobby the Airedale reclined *regardant*.

Beau thumped his tail when he saw Irina.

An ancient titled lady who was deaf dispensed lunch tickets.

Rollo was seated in the mess with two newcomers, one talking non-stop.

That was how she met Konrad.

A Polish Irregular

Duncan was not amused by the effortless way Konrad could cause Irina to laugh instantly.

Konrad's dining companion, Vissarion—a former KGB man—was a typical Georgian, and they vied boisterously to outdo each other as raconteurs.

The mood was delightful.

She was eating a sponge pudding when Konrad suddenly raised his glass and proposed a toast to the lucky gentleman, of all the officers present, who Irina most preferred. Ten faces in the mess turned to listen to her answer.

'Your choice plis!' cried Vissarion, cheeks flushed.

She was seated in pride of place beneath the sovereign's portrait.

'It has been a great pleasure for me to meet them all,' she said regally, 'and to enjoy their company.' She indicated her dish. 'I can compare it to biting my favourite chocolate Pavlova; I savour every piece of it.'

There was an outburst of guffawing and the men downed their glasses.

She learned, then, the power of Konrad's laugh was irresistible.

He touched her hand.

'You have not answered my question, and, as for biting, you can bite me, if you like.'

There was another roar of good humour and she could not stop laughing. That was the very first moment of their closeness.

An unfortunate wasp chose that moment to fly on to her spoon.

Konrad took his knife and attempted to dispatch the trespasser.

'Die. You deserve it,' he rasped.

The wasp escaped. The stabbed dish was inedible.

Duncan wrathfully brought her another pudding.

But the effects of the men's unrestrained drinking were growing ever more apparent and Irina was determined to accomplish a not ungraceful exit.

Keen eyes followed her as she departed.

Distantly, Irina heard Vissarion ask Konrad, 'What is your favourite breakfast?'

Before Konrad could answer, Major Poultney piped up, 'A roll in bed with honey!'

The whole table convulsed at this sally—except Duncan.

❁

Her formal introduction to Konrad was five minutes later. She had splashed cold water on her face and was taking the East Wing passage to the Chapel quadrangle for a breath of fresh air.

Irina had paused at the distinguished officers' honours board to read the motto—*'Patriis Virtutibus'* engilded beneath two tattered gonfalons—when Konrad appeared on a lightning tour with Duncan.

Duncan murmured reluctantly something about a Pole who would be working in their section.

Konrad's heels clicked smartly. As he bowed to kiss her hand, Irina could not help staring at the black-flecked greying head of hair; the two opposing whorls reminded her of schoolgirl experiments in the science lab to demonstrate the properties of electro-magnetic fields.

Duncan watched the tableau unfold with condescension.

Then Konrad unbowed and asked casually if Irina was returning to London. On Fridays the section clocked off at noon.

When Irina nodded, Konrad at once proposed taking her in his car.

'But you have a return ticket, haven't you?' demanded Duncan grimly.

Rain began to fall. Duncan lent Irina his greatcoat in a sulk.

In other words, Duncan had 'got the hump', as Rollo would put it.

Irina Regina, Palace Court

Palace Court, W2, is a haunt of Russian diplomats, journalists and émigrés.

In those days, Konrad's third-floor flat shared a landing with a broadcaster in Mingrelian from Bush House.

In the flat Irina very soon learned to her pleasure how the mobility of Konrad's smiling Fernadellian lips had a multiplicity of functions.

(Irina once noted a passage in her copy of *Varieties of Topical Interpretation* by I. S. Slovenko, Moscow 1993: *'A false transcription by an interpreter rendered President Carter's words on his arrival in Poland, in 1978, as "I desire the Poles carnally."'*)

English was their shared tongue. Konrad had no Russian, she, no Polish.

'You might have noticed,' said Konrad breathlessly, 'my student days are long over.'

They were lying naked in a shaft of late-afternoon sunlight.

His socks were expensive and bright. His shirt size was 41, continental.

The service flat was austere, except for his photos.

Kristina. His wedding party. His son.

'A happy family,' she thought. But her instinct told her there was something wrong. As if the photographs were props in a theatrical performance and soon there would be a scene change.

The only additional personal objects in the room were three bottles of 45.8 per cent proof Talisker malt whisky, and an antiquated .455 Webley pistol.

He poured her a thimbleful, rising to his feet with an effort.

Shrapnel had severed a peroneal nerve in the fibula and he had difficulty raising his foot. After an hour's driving, he said, he would tire.

The spirits scorched her mouth.

He had chanced upon the gun in a British air-drop, he said, when he was thirteen, trapped in Warsaw.

The providential packet had smashed, and the gunmuzzle had been dripping with cold blood from a burst plasma sac.

After the razing of the city, the youngster escaped and joined the Home Army—*Armia Krajowa.*

Later he defected from the AK to the People's Army; but only because he was 'whistling into his fist with hunger' and the Party promised him composite combat rations dropped by Soviet reconnaissance planes. The promises were never kept.

He was to find neither bread nor freedom. Within a month he was interned and only through the influence of his older sister, a Party favourite, did he escape deportation to a Siberian forced labour camp.

Irina was moved. But Konrad's mood lightened.

'What do you think about me?' he asked suddenly. 'Women always pay me nice compliments, saying I am very handsome.'

Irina laughed involuntarily.

'You are not handsome at all! Charming, yes. *Cuddly.*' There was something bear-like about him.

Konrad was so evidently disappointed that she felt obliged to kiss him. He invited her to stay for the weekend. An odd arrangement she never contemplated—a Polish Irregular sharing his London address with one of Stoneburgh's NRPs, herself assigned as Non-Regular Personnel.

Irina believed, then, she ruled his heart.

Irina Regina, Palace Court.

A Risk Pass

At first, she did not find strange the inquisitiveness of Konrad regarding her Report. In the circumstances, his interest seemed quite natural.

Irina had vowed to keep their affair under wraps. Their meetings were arranged by signals.

To carry two books through the office meant the lakeside boathouse for a picnic tryst.

Perhaps Duncan guessed from the start. Since her weekend in London, he'd begun to work out with tension exercises for his neck and upper arms he half remembered from combat fitness tests.

Besides, the Report was behind schedule.

The Green fly was lean and mean.

'The Brigadier's going to have a baby,' Rollo announced at one tense Monday morning pep talk. 'He'll be on us like a screaming skull if you don't start pulling your finger out.'

He was referring to Brigadier Wingfield, chief of the FFES, the Forum for Federated European Security.

'They don't give his job to any old swinging dick,' he asserted. 'The Brig's a three-star admin nightmare.'

Rollo instituted a buddy-buddy system and assigned Duncan to assist Irina with the collating.

Duncan perked up; his neck reddened.

'Right! Crack on!' ordered Colonel Rees-Sholter.

The colonel, fortified by his thermos, fidgeted with his biscuit-coloured moustache. More and more (Rollo had disclosed to Irina earlier), the old boy was 'totalled' by lunchtime.

'Is a life worth living that depends on the liver?' was a sentiment attributed to the colonel, which Konrad endorsed when he learned the colonel was invariably 'piddled'.

❁

Most Secret

From Day One of her induction, Irina had been determined to honour the supreme trust the Academy had invested in her. In those early weeks she could scarcely believe her good fortune. The six historic cannon evenly spaced along the South Terrace, the great Park, the ornamental Lake, the Piranesian vaulted library, all conspired to create a classically golden atmosphere of privilege and distinction in which she basked.

The day was warm; the month was March; Shirt Sleeve Order was five weeks away. She sat at the lakeside and wrote an airmail to her sister.

Irina described Stoneburgh as a 'time capsule'. In her own country Time and Change raced like the clouds reflected on the water. She could not conceal her yearning to *'remain always in ancestral gardens, seated on soft grass, without thinking'*.

Privately, the colonel had told her she had 'made a hit' in K section; Duncan had referred to her as 'the lady of the regiment'.

She had almost completed the blue features on her map. The scheme was classified 'Most Secret'.

Under the auspices of the IRP—the International Redistribution Plan—the conversion of military bases was proposed on a vast Central European demilitarised zone where three state frontiers met. This forested land-mass cradled more lakes than finland.

The trade-off was two-fold: admission of the former satellite states to an entente with the Powers, and development of the infrastructure for new rapid MSRs—Main Supply Routes—to their borders, in return for cutbacks in front-line military establishments.

The MSRs had been carefully assessed for vehicle choke points.

❁

Irina was cross-indexing the Report. Duncan brought in two steaming mugs of 'brew' and a 'wad'—a fried-egg sandwich. The tea was Standard, according to Queen's Regs (milk and two sugars; Irina had a sweet tooth). Sometimes, when Duncan was not thinking, he drank tea from his 'mog'; he had been raised in the Midlands. In the officers' cadre English was Standard.

His sweat was pungent; he smelled of canvas and brass polish. Beau hoovered up their crusts.

❁

Extract from Standing Orders: ' . . . maintain procedures to ensure day-to-day shredding of any draft documents issuant in the preparation of Classified files.'

❁

Rollo studied the Report's centre-fold map where Irina had summarised the Industrial Reclamation Plan with a legend keyed to her own symbols.

Lakes containing sapropel were marked with a gold leaf.

Formed by broadleaf and coniferous forests, sapropel organic matter is an aquatic carbonaceous nutrient lying in ooze on the lakebeds.

Wingfield's Redistibution Plan was to integrate a series of foreign equity-funded water sedimentation plants to yield highly mineralised compounds for fertilisers and animal foodstuffs. Fifty lakes taken together contained more than five hundred million tons of sapropel, it was estimated, based on optimal utilisation of the natural resources beneath waters surrounded by the largest undisturbed ancient forest in Europe.

❁

Konrad's stories of derring-do could not but provoke curiosity in Irina; a curiosity mingled with admiration, too. She thought: *'This is a man to trust and rely on. So many hardships in life! He has guts, he has been battlehardened.'*

All of a sudden, Konrad said, he had stumbled over feelings which recovered the desires of his youth.

Guarding his mouth, he spoke fervently just above his breath.

He called her Irisha.

A band was rehearsing on the square. Elgar.

Up to that moment she had awarded Konrad a Risk Pass under the Review Board; now she felt her soul unbuttoning.

He was working in the office next to hers, a cold, dim, musty cubicle with green metal filing cabinets. Only a thin partition separated them. She quelled an impulse to perch on the edge of his desk.

To enter his sanctum Irina had executed a fast body swerve to avoid Duncan. Duncan hovered, then he was gone.

Konrad, eyes downcast, rustled some papers and muttered he had heard a whisper of Bolkashin's arrival.

Irina's face blanched. Her breathing quickened. Her hands trembled so much that she was obliged to make a pretence of closing the window when in truth she was struggling for air.

She was seized with a fit of shivering, an intense and sudden chill that made her teeth chatter.

❋

General Yegor Bolkashin was the former Chief of Intelligence in the republic where Irina was born. They had met in the state capital where he chaired the powerful, post-separatist Land Utilisation Policy Commission whose delegates pulled the strings of puppet states still in thrall to Soviet centralism.

'He knows where bodies are buried,' Rollo had alleged at her last Appraisal; the major was itching to see more action. A visit to the republic was imperative but entangled in red tape.

That an exchange visit to facilitate matters should be arranged was not a suggestion but an order.

So, reluctantly, Irina had written a letter of introduction and Rollo's wish had been granted—the FFES 'Good Neighbours' *Kongress* would be hosted by Bolkashin's land utilisation *komissiya* in the state capital and Yegor had conceded the major's priority admission clearance.

❁

Irina was surprised to learn that the lives of Konrad and Bolkashin had more than once intersected.

As youths, they had both witnessed, helplessly, one on each side of the Vistula River, the destruction of Warsaw by the Germans.

Recently, Bolkashin had established an Institute for Security Affairs, and Konrad's own press agency in Warsaw—*Biuro K*—exchanged communiqués with Yegor's outfit in the neighbouring republic.

Cosy, Irina thought, with an inward shudder. *Too* cosy.

She had reason enough to recall Yegor and their last meeting; her mind shrank from memories she had endeavoured to suppress.

The semi-retired general had been a career intelligence officer in the Soviet military security service. Konrad understood Yegor had very little money.

An elegant, cultured man, the general was a womaniser she had cause to remember, a charismatic intriguer with well-kept hands as though he washed them often. He had graduated from several universities. She could not forget the self-imposed virility of his commanding voice, and that heartless, imperturbable gaze which characterises a long-lived commissar. He was said to have a glass eye. You could tell which eye was the artificial one; it had something kindly about it.

Konrad grinned slyly. His *biuro* had learned that the General was fishing around in Warsaw for details of the secret sapropel programme.

At which point Irina's face darkened and Konrad was summarily dispatched from her NRP accommodation quarters.

She took the phone off the hook.

The next morning she found a note thrust under her door. An invitation to a weekend in Brussels and an infelicitously scanned love poem:

'You are asking me where you're going to, where you'll find your way. Forever we'll walk the future together and from our love we'll never stray.'

❀

The collegiate Library was in 'L' sector (Siege of Lucknow, 1857).

The library's Custodian-Marshall had asked Irina to sort out some books in Russian. She stacked the volumes on the belvedere window-seat.

In the mirroring pane of the open casement Irina examined her reflection. She liked her black lashed, large dark eyes, small snub nose, mischievous lips and shadowy slavic cheek bones.

Cheek bones were 'in'.

But what of her slavonic chin?

On the shelves labelled 'Anthropometry' she found an early monograph on Slavonians. *'The tribe of Slavons is characterised by darker hair and eyes than the Saxon.'* There was an engraving of a house set far apart from others. *'An Anglo-Saxon, if possible, always stands detached.'*

Rees-Sholter passed beneath the window and threw her a jaunty salute.

She discovered the books were extremely rare.

A treatise in Russian on breeding hybrids! What was the purpose of instructing Russians in the mysteries of cross-breeding a camel and a llama, two species reproductively isolated for eleven million years?

Irina studied an authentic early vellum map of Vrangel's route across the frozen sea to the island which bears his name, then she unexpectedly opened a volume on a botanical expedition to the Amazon River basin in the early nineteenth century led by Count Aleksandre Voronetskiy.

Voronetskiy!

She could not subdue a trembling in all her nerves.

Konrad, she saw, was crossing the main square from the car park with General Bolkashin.

Konrad was limping. He glanced up and saw her. She was carrying two books, her face pale and resolute like that of an ideological statue.

The Department of Lost Files

Brussels smelt of hot milk chocolate, she thought.

Konrad leapt out of his skin to show Irina how generous he could be. The best restaurants, presents and compliments. He drank heroically; he suddenly appeared to have a good deal of money.

He was full of ideas and optimistic about the future. Major Poultney had entrusted him with the *Kongress* arrangements; Konrad was liaison officer for negotiations with Warsaw.

At last he felt vindicated in the eyes of his Polish compatriots, Konrad confessed, as he had tried many times to convene such a 'Good Neighbours' congress and failed bitterly because of acrimonious jealousies and suspicions.

In his own country, the higher authorities falsely assumed he was a wealthy aristocrat, he laughed, and they had not wanted to deal with him, even though the Polish flag had regained its crown after the fall of Communism.

Hence, Konrad had been black-listed.

The newly whitewashed state officials, who were desperately trying to distance themselves from the Party, asked why they should share the Peace Dividend pie with a man suspected of being a Kremlin plant or, at the very least, wobbly.

'Now,' Konrad declared, 'when I speak, Warsaw will listen.'

They had reached a time in 'the dawn of their love' (as Irina would afterwards recall this passage of their affair) when she was capable of observing him judiciously, as an outsider.

She was conscious of his compulsive name-dropping.

With equal ease he would sprinkle his talk with important officials in the Headquarters of the Powers as well as ex-Party bigwigs who governed in Warsaw. Irina could not be sure whether his swaggering braggadocio was typical Polish exuberance or the laconic two-edged tongue of a double agent.

On Sunday morning he said he had a business meeting and asked her to accompany him. There was a look of appeal which she could not refuse.

She had a presentiment of impending misfortune.

They crossed the Parc de Bruxelles to the hotel and took a lift to the penthouse suite. The carpet was deep and springy. They entered unannounced.

A clean-cut silhouette at the desk was writing, face dipped in darkness, flanked by two urn-shaped zinc containers planted with vigorous specimens of Voronetskian mimosa.

She recoiled, heart pounding. The multi-tendrilled fronds quailed, refurled and withdrew.

General Bolkashin arranged his face into a smiling mask behind which he studied her with shrewd, impassive speculation.

Irina stood motionless, her eyes fixed in a tranced frozen stare, and wondered in a distant region of her mind whether Bolkashin's teeth were also as false as his charm.

Yegor's voice detonated.

'I hear our friends in Moscow have invented a device for reconstituting shredded documents stolen from careless embassies. Why do they bother . . . ?'

' . . . When the original papers could be stolen intact,' Irina finished coldly.

'Exactly.'

She felt a wave of helplessness and betrayal engulf her; she could not be sure whether she trembled from the most craven fear or blind anger.

'A mistaken assemblyman known to us lost an arm in a shredder once,' the general observed in a voice of politbureaucratic suavity.

The general's nonchalant bloodthirstiness brought an evil taste to her tongue and tightened her throat.

Since they had entered the hotel, Konrad had evaded her eyes.

Grinning sheepishly, he'd departed to an anteroom in search of Coca-Cola.

(Konrad drank whisky and Coke which Irina considered ruinous.)

The general zeroed in and expertly squeezed Irina's well-shaped knee.

'Irinka. Your knees are the property of the republic. So is sapropel. You should think carefully about what you are doing.'

He jerked his head in the direction of Konrad in the next room.

'Your comical *pshek* has many women; he'd settle for one less. You're worth better than him. Remember your duty to the state.'

Irina thought, *'I have heard the second warning bell,'* but she tried to pretend she had not heard it ringing.

❁

'Remember your duty to the state.'

The confusion in her mind took a vague frond-like shape and she shook her head to be free of dark unfurling tendrils of dread.

She was impatient to return to her own unhappy motherland but her plane was late.

Irina was waiting at passport-control behind a tall young man whose smallness of head was infrahuman in relation to his long red neck where a muscle was pulsing madly. His features seemed vaguely familiar.

He suddenly faced about; then his lips trembled and began to move convulsively. His English was heavily accented.

'I beg your pardon. Our courier has been delayed. Could I prevail upon you to take this pouch. Medicine for sick animals. A colleague will be waiting.'

'Find someone else,' responded Irina crisply.

He pressed the envelope into Irina's hand. Before she could again protest he had gone.

She was preparing to call after him when Konrad appeared through the crowd.

Even at that distance she could see him extend a forefinger and tug at his lower left eyelid. Then he shrugged heavily . . . helplessly.

His gestures were unmistakable: *You must be alert. I am powerless.*

She scowled and slipped through the gate.

Dawn found her haggard and weak.

Irina at last allowed her thoughts to dwell on Konrad's outrageous deceit. He had clearly misunderstood her loyalties as an intermediary between East and West.

Not for any gingerbread would she betray her new friends at Stoneburgh who had treated her only with affection and respect.

Tears threatened, but her tears were dried by indignation. She could forgive Konrad his cowardice and greed, but—at the very moment when she was most happy—she could not forgive a duplicity that had reduced her to the profoundest despair.

She remembered the odd whimsicalities of Colonel Rees-Sholter when he drank too much 'red coffee'.

(Red coffee was 'office code' for the colonel's claret, and by the late afternoon his mood would become more expansive.)

A trumpeting herrumph would precede his pronouncements.

'Take my word for it, Someone Upstairs has banjaxed my barometer!' His utterance of the word 'barometer' resembled a general purpose machine gun.

The colonel had once explained in a blurred voice his 'Theory of Lost Files' whereby Someone Upstairs was intent on spoiling the lives of mortals below. Sometimes the files of mortals were lost and, for a short time, they could enjoy their lives unburdened, but as soon as their files were found mortals were doomed to pay for their brief moments of pleasure.

The explanation for her unhappiness was simple.

Upstairs, clearly, Someone had found a lost file with her name on it.

The Phobokinetic Polygraph Machine

In the early morning light, as the plane touched down, she saw the envelope had her name on it, recognisably in the general's handwriting.

Reluctantly she withdrew the contents:

Confidential Memorandum: Agronomy Dept.
re. Sapropel-A Polygraph Experiments.

Memorandum to the First Secretary, Land Utilisation Policy Commission, copied to the Director of the Research Institute for Agricultural Sciences.

Sapropel-enriched soil samples, from the conservation region, exhibit excellent alpha-horizon crumb-structure yielding a significantly accelerated growth-cycle for a-series plants.

Hypnosis was induced in Subject X-1, an attractive, intelligent woman selected from 1st-category legationary candidates under observation for overseas assignment. She was placed 18 centimetres from a-series plants connected by electrodes to the phobokinetic polygraph machine and layered-voice analyser.

General Bolkashin suggested to X-1 that she is very pretty. (She is.) A childlike smile of contentment appeared on the subject's face, upon which the first reaction of the a-series plants occurred. The Y-axis plot-pen synchronously responded to her emotio-physiological reactions.

Similarly, when the general suggested to X-1 that she should 'envision' a hooded male figure drawing near behind her, and a harsh icy wind approaching, the subject recoiled in fear and she commenced to shiver with terror like a person violently thrust into the Arctic cold in a light, sleeveless, summer dress. The trial plants at once registered this abrupt change of mood.

All current indications confirm the sensitivity of a-series sapropel as an effective biogenic agent for regeneration of the sentient a-series seeds from the Voronetskiyan mimosa specimens identified in the Amazon Survey (1847) deposit cases.

The next subject, X-5, a 5th-category fiscal management trainee . . .

Irina simply could not still her shivering limbs.

That day she had presented herself at the Agronomy Department she had truly believed she was to be briefed by Bolkashin for an imminent trade mission.

The lights had been dimmed in the research laboratory when she'd entered and, as her eyes had become accustomed to shadowy forms around her, she'd slowly become aware of a room enwreathed in mimosa foliage of unexampled luxuriance whose exploring tendrils trailed over her mouth and hair and tongue.

The mutual revulsion of a sentient plant and a sentient being had occurred some two minutes after the commencement of Bolkashin's experiments in phobokinetic lie detection, as the memorandum summarised.

Now, as she prepared for touchdown, Irina's chilled frame was shaken by confused recollections and her breath was drawn in rapid gasps.

That Irina was the 'property of the Republic' was a truism that required no further debate when even a tropical shrub, as Bolkashin had demonstrated, could be surborned by the will of the state.

She was reminded of an orang-outang in the state zoo who had been taught by his keeper to smoke cigarettes.

She noted that the memo was addressed to the general's private offices in the old clerical quarters of the defunct ComIntern. Irina was aware the building had been refurbished quite recently for occupancy by commercial enterprises. Quite obviously, the general's former masters still haunted its halls.

At home, she retired to her childhood room without delay, complaining of a stomach ache. Her parents shook their heads, sighed, and exchanged long, significant glances.

She lay down on a schoolgirl's narrow sofa-bed. The room had remained unchanged for twenty years; a small room with a tall ceiling and view over ancient roofs. The family flat was high above the old quarter; a pre-war apartment block with long, spacious corridors smelling of bees wax.

(In Irina's republic the priests secretly blessed the bee-hives on the first day of August.)

Her sister's bed stood where it had always been, under the window.

A wardrobe. Bookshelves. On her bedside table were her university studies from the lectures she had attended on recidivism among the Western bourgeoisie.

Irina restacked her favourite titles in their correct order.

Foremost, of course, *The Forsythe Saga*. Who could forget Soames and Irene? Who could forget two ruthless, tenacious magnates bickering over a woman whom they regarded as their property, as might a patrician own a slave. It was not only in unscrupulous bourgeois society where money ruled, she thought bitterly, questioning her reflection in a large antique mirror, a relic which had survived miraculously intact after the war.

On the window sill there still remained in its place the tin collection box in the shape of a house brick into whose slot she would slip a coin each week, a child's contribution towards the building of a national monument to celebrate the Dawn of Socialist Plenty.

A curtain draped the secret corner where her mother kept the family photos and icons. When an infant, Irina had been baptised clandestinely by her grandmother who'd harboured a priest.

In this room Irina had first started on her journey to understanding.

The red kerchief of her Young Pioneers uniform hung in the wardrobe. Its three corners represented the unity of the Pioneers, the Komsomol and Communism.

To qualify for the standard Physical Education badge when she was thirteen, she had been required to throw a 500-gram hand grenade 25 metres. The Pioneers had taught Irina to be honest and truthful; to respect her teachers; and to be loyal to her country.

Irina abhorred betrayal.

❀

The family meal had just begun. There was a timid knocking at the door. On the step stood the general's messenger, teeth chattering.

His hands were continuously shaking so Irina placed the envelope into his open, quivering dossier-case.

'So kind, so very kind of you,' he stammered.

Then she remembered where she'd seen him before. He was the eager 5th category trainee, X-5, who'd been waiting his turn outside the door to the experimental laboratory in the Agronomy Department.

Her mother had prepared her favourite dish of potato pancakes with sour cream and mushrooms, but Irina had no stomach for it.

❀

A day later, Konrad and Irina were reconciled.

He had arrived at the family apartment abject with contrition.

Irina's parents liked him very much. Somehow he managed to look younger, leaner; his face shone with boyish charm.

Irina thought: *'After all, even at his age, he remains no older than a boy. Irresponsible, changeable, yielding to temptations, but Oh so charming, and with such an irrepressible zest for life.'*

He denied all knowledge of the general's inducements and Irina chose to leave it at that. Before the eyes of her adoring family Irina could no longer appear indignant.

❀

Irina would never forget the tempting smell of French pastry after their sleepless night on the train to Warsaw.

Konrad had managed to drop a word in the right quarter and she was installed in a flat on the top floor of a nine-story apartment block resembling a Russian wedding cake, once a prestigious address for the *nomenklatura.*

The landing of the staircase smelled of naphthaline and of homemade cakes.

The lift did not work and Irina could not rid the bathroom of spiders. Yet she was happy.

Piano scales from an inexperienced hand rippled down the corridors; a signature of bliss.

Konrad bought her an eternity ring.

And in the *pâtisserie* Irina met Grazhina.

Grazhina

She had arrived to collect her birthday cake ordered by Konrad.

As the girl at the counter curled the carton's ribbons into ringlets, a voice with the resonance of a hog-caller announced: 'Aries! How fortunate to celebrate the pivotal sign of the zodiac!'

Grazhina's eyes were larger and more mesmerising than the general's; and her voice, coarsened by chain-smoking, was a register deeper.

Arians are thought to be leaders, not followers, but Irina, unresisting, followed her new acquaintance to the mesmerist's salon.

The fortune teller's looking glass told her every day that she had been a beauty in the past, and her black eyes were still enormous and fathomlessly deep, and would be so, the glass averred, on into the untrod future.

She lived in an elegant four-room apartment with a pitted stone frontage which was all that upstood to recall the site of an old city mansion. The furniture was solid and valuable.

On a baby grand piano were photos of her long career as a colaratura contralto at the State Opera House where she remained as a voice coach.

Grazhina could see the past very well, but when, sometimes, the future was obscure to her, her knowledge of horoscopy helped her to make unequivocal predictions.

Without preliminaries, Irina was told that she and 'the-man-in-her-life' were 'written into each other's destinies'.

An enchantress can see into the coming day.

'You'll be linked to the end of your lives,' Grazhina foretold huskily.

❁

There then followed an interval of tiffs and rifts. (Grazhina called the love affair 'stormy'.)

Irina had discovered Konrad was exceedingly vain; he began to boast about the multitude of women he had loved.

Hurt, Irina had responded in kind; she told him of the men she had known.

Then, of course, he began to blame her for first preying on him and initiating their affair.

After one of their periodic dust-ups, she slammed the phone down on him. Two minutes later he rang again to condemn her for deserting him for another man.

Duncan! Ridiculous!

❁

You Cannot Hide an Awl in a Sack

From the day of his arrival at Stoneburgh, Konrad had been jealous of Duncan. The feeling was mutual.

One day, not long after the wasp episode, Duncan invited her to a picnic with two colleagues from the Ministry of Defence.

She made a polite but feeble excuse.

When Konrad heard about Duncan's advances he was outraged.

'It's unforgivable! The oaf imagines he can seduce you!'

Later, as matters turned out, Konrad was correct.

(Rollo had told Irina that the eyes of 'that khaki-brained sad sack' travelled after her like 'heat-seeking ferrets'.)

But you cannot hide an awl in a sack, as Irina would say in her Russian tongue, which meant any secret will become known.

Duncan had obviously expected Irina to stay overnight and actually booked a hotel in advance. The reservations desk had rung Duncan's wife and asked for confirmation. His wife knew nothing of the picnic and rang Rollo, so Duncan's secret became public property.

God! How they made fun of him in the mess.

He stood apart, with a red face, until he could bear Rollo's malice no longer.

'Chuffing well sod off!' Duncan yelled in incontrollable fury, cracking under pressure.

❀

In the gallery in Novy Świat she saw the canvas immediately.

A sub-genre of French Expressionism in the style of Vlaminck (*wasn't he the artist who was a professional racing cyclist?*), the painting was in Irina's colours—warm greys and a deep vermilion the hue of *Kievskoi nalivka*, a reddish liqueur she adored.

The artist had depicted a man and a woman, walking on a quay, enveloped in a mist of unknowing.

When she presented him with the picture, Konrad said he had been thinking of her, too.

Irina said, 'If you were so worried about me why didn't you phone?'

He could not answer that question, and Irina realised he was afraid of his wife.

'Tell me the truth, Ataman,' she quoted, 'why do you need my love?'

He said he loved her.

She thought he loved her.

On the evening before he was due to leave Warsaw he took her to see a film called *French Kiss* and imagined he had consoled her.

❁

Two Emissaries

Irina was alone. The flat smelled of good food and cigar smoke. They liked to cook together and savoured the ritual.

She gazed out from her balcony to the plaza below where the moon cast a greenish light on the awnings of the shopping arcade in which a manager was counting his stock.

The time had arrived for her own summing up.

Since their return, Irina had not mentioned to Konrad the general's heavy-handed warning.

From Rees-Sholter she had learned that the date for convening the FFES *Kongress* was to be brought forward.

Rollo had 'worked a flanker, PDQ' among his 'oppos' in the state *komissiya* and 'zapped some logs' (logistics) into their 'organised chaos'.

The *Kongress* was now only five days away.

Her palms were hot as they gripped the balustrade. No more than a week remained for her to evade the sinister depredations of Bolkashin, and then, thankfully, the most secret Sapropel Report would enter the public record.

The full-throated roar of an exhaust drew her eyes to the street.

A young woman stood beside a vintage American convertible.

She gazed up at Irina's window.

Kristina.

❁

She had expected a showdown with Konrad; she had not expected two emissaries from his wife.

Their English was perfect, their manners were imperfect, and they did not stand on ceremony.

The taller of the two, a full-lipped, heavily pockmarked young man sprawled instantly at the table, sniffed Konrad's cigar still smouldering in the ashtray and lit a cigarette from it.

They were too careful to give their true names.

The squat heavyweight with the insolent smile, who stood with his back to the door, was addressed as Dombrovich.

He stared at her with an intensity which felt like a magnetic field, striking his palm hard with a heavy rouleau of coins packed in a cardboard tube. He was sweating. With a look of unrelieved lust he stared continually at her breasts.

The studious-looking young man introduced himself as Mikhalski.

He swung his legs up on to the dining table. He commenced to gnaw a wishbone from Irina's plate as he surveyed her with calm, practised effrontery.

'Don't imagine the *Księżna* has been unaware of your subversive activities. Nor have your movements passed unnoticed by the New Kingdom Party.'

(The New Kingdom Party was an extreme nationalist organisation founded by the military elite of the aristocratic old guard.)

'There are two tasks you will perform for the *Księżna* and her party. When Bolkashin . . . '

'Don't deny your relations with the Moscow general!' Dombrovich yelled, watching her with a heat that oppressed her like a heavy embrace.

Mikhalski cast a vituperative glance at the other, and continued.

'When Bolkashin contacts you—as he surely will—you will promise him the T-FECS Report. The location of your rendezvous and a copy of your Report you will convey to me.'

Mikhalski scribbled a Warsaw telephone number and impaled the card on a carcass congealing in the meat dish.

'Fail to inform us and the *Księżna*'s traitorous husband . . . '

Mikhalski snapped the wishbone.

'Smacznego!' (Only he could make *bon appetit* sound like a curse.)

When they had gone, to calm herself, she began to apply one of Duncan's tension exercises until her head was rhythmically pitching like a ship in a gale.

On the first day of May the *Kongress* would convene; she could think only of Konrad's safety, and of how to prevent this unforeseen catastrophe.

❁

'The Court cards are the significators.'

First Grazhina dealt the King of Diamonds.

This suit, apparently, represented Irina's fire sign, and contained the divinatory titles for interpreting her path-workings under Aries.

'This king symbolises an older man, usually a dark, stern person.'

The King of Hearts followed whose element is Water. (Konrad was born a Piscean).

'This king signifies a friendly, charming man, also somewhat older.'

Next appeared a Four of Diamonds.

'A Rest from Strife,' divined the cartomancer.

The Queen of Spades made no appearance.

❁

Kristina had flown unexpectedly to London for a shopping spree, Konrad informed Irina. Irina was to pack an overnight bag he said; they were to journey together to his beloved forests that spanned the disputed lands at the border.

❁

The Duchy of Kristina

There were said to be elks in those parts of the forests.

Certainly when Konrad had fought in the forest detachment of the *Armia Krajowa* he had heard them coughing at night.

They drove in Kristina's doughty blue Mustang to a wild region of post-glacial lakes surrounded by the last primeval forests.

The bottoms of the lakes were lined with ancient sedimentary sapropel.

At a quay, they halted at dawn. The sun was vermilion.

Vapour from the lake clung to the water; they walked through the mist to the landing's brink and saw the shadow of a pleasure boat approaching.

They crossed the lake with other excursionists and arrived at 8 a.m.

❀

The horse-shoe shaped manor house was a sixteenth-century fortified dwór for a feudal suzerainty, Konrad explained.

When the border between the two republics had been redrawn, after the war, the house had become a health clinic for faithful Party members.

But the house was shuttered and empty when they arrived.

In the dining room hung early nineteenth-century oil paintings; one, a portrait of Kristina's ancestress. The resemblance was striking, especially the artificiality of her smile.

From the ramparts the view of lake upon lake cascading across the frontier deep into Irina's republic was truly remarkable.

'But how do you have the key?' demanded Irina. She was disturbed by the sumptiousness of the furnishings.

'Don't you see? We are now standing in the Duchy of Kristina! This is all that remains of her title, and these lands aren't *hers* but the *state's*!'

Konrad's hands reached out to clasp her waist.

She thought: *'The chase has ended. I cannot outrun a hunter in his own forest.'*

Surely he must wear his old hunter's jacket from conscious choice; yes, of this she was certain.

Konrad had told her he was a perfect dancer and she believed him. He boasted he was a popular partner much sought after by women. But because of the secrecy of their affair, Irina had never once had the chance to gauge the truth of his assertion.

Yet she believed him. It was one of the few things Konrad told her she did believe.

He kissed her.

She was overwhelmed by a sense of release from strife as though she were melting—in her own private lexicon the word was almost *smelting*—a fusion in the fiery furnace of fever, at the same time both *smiling* and *melting*.

Sometimes to an interpreter there is no equivalent word.

Sometimes there is only a sign. A fire sign.

In her private lexicon the word was *radtayat*.

In no dictionary will the reader find this entry.

❁

She realised that, in this forest stronghold, Konrad briefly reinhabited the noble *cytadela* he believed to be his wife's lost heritage. Kristina's family had once owned twenty-five thousand hectares.

Irina suggested they collect mushrooms.

They walked barefoot on a carpet of pine needles.

The wild mushrooms grew just as she remembered from childhood. Little chocolate caps peeping from beds of pale lichen.

The roots of the trees writhed deep under the frontier that separated her from her homeland; burrowing with the quaquaversal instinct of some powerful kind of racial memory, she thought fancifully.

Konrad pointed to a six-hundred-year-old beech tree.

'That's where I first met Yegor.' She was stunned.

Aged fourteen, Konrad had seen a German parachute-rifleman fall from the skies, and he had stalked the *fallschirm-jäger* for eleven hours before Yegor rose from behind the tree and broke the silence with his short horse laugh.

Yegor led him to the spot where he'd killed the parachutist.

They had lived off beech nuts, mushrooms and moss. Somehow Yegor trapped rabbits.

Konrad considered he owed his life to Yegor.

'Somehow, the debt must be repaid,' he said moodily.

He folded his arms and looked straight at her.

'I took Bolkashin's advance for our Brussels' trip, but, I swear, I could not sell out to anyone.'

He spread his arm with an all-embracing gesture which encompassed the swans on the rivers, the forest fringing the sparkling lakes, and a Polish eagle hovering above a crag.

'I could never sell my country,' he said simply.

And Irina could not tell him all she knew.

The night of her return she received a drunken telephone from Duncan who was flying to the *Kongress* via Warsaw.

He asked her to meet him at the *InterContinental Warszawa*, where half an hour later she overheard him in the hotel bar mawkishly toasting her name.

'To the lady of the regiment,' she heard him proclaim, as he clinked glasses with his drinking companion, a signalman from Electronic Warfare.

'Sorry and all that to turn up like two bad pennies,' Duncan mumbled apologetically when she appeared.

He swayed and clenched her wrist.

'We wanted to get some shuteye before our flight, so we thought you wouldn't mind putting us up for a few hours.'

Strangely, Duncan did not smell of liquor. (Rollo had told Irina that the subaltern 'drank like a budgie with a chipped tooth'.)

She refused a drink and said she would wait for them in the lobby.

On the way out she met General Bolkashin entering, carrying an attaché case and travelling bag.

He barely paused but gripped her hand so hard she thought it must bleed.

'Tonight,' he grated, before releasing her.

❁

The rigid formalism of what the mess called Duncan's 'uptightness' was only matched by her own when she showed the two men her tiny two-room, ninth-floor flatlet.

Duncan insisted he and the signalman would bed down in their 'scratch bags' in the kitchen and they'd leave without waking her at daybreak.

'I never thought we'd sleep on a scullery floor and be thankful for it,' Duncan assured her, overcome by a fit of yawning.

She summoned a smile, her thoughts clouded with anxiety.

'I'll make you breakfast,' she said gravely, 'but I can promise you no more than black coffee.' Her deadpan expression caused Duncan to blush.

When she was satisfied the two soused dishevelled Englishmen were in their 'Bed-fordshire' (as the English say) she rang the general, then dialled Mikhalski and whispered, *'InterContinental.'*

The envelope marked *Sapropel Report Most Secret* she packed tightly into her Young Pioneer's tin collection box then closed her fist on the handle. When she hefted it the weight felt reassuring in her hand.

❁

The Breaking Point

The rain lashed the pavements as she neared the hotel entrance.

She was confident Mikhalski would observe her enter the slipway into the hotel's underground carpark.

At the end of the ramp, Bolkashin was approaching her without haste; his eyes seemed abnormally large, burning with the basilisk glare that could compel the surrender of another's will to his.

The brick-shaped tin collection box swung loosely in Irina's grasp.

As the general extended his hand for his prize, Irina saw Dombrovich, hair bristling in wet spines, emerge from a dark entry, his rouleau of heavy coins raised, preparing to strike.

She ran forward at a half crouch and with the heel of the palm, the full weight of her body behind it, she struck Dombrovich under the base of his nose.

She heard the nasal bone snap.

With an agonised howl Dombrovich buried his head in his hands.

Bolkashin, breathing heavily like a broken-winded satyr, ran towards the ramp, then paused, fixed her with his severest gaze, and nodded.

She heard a soft footfall behind her and glimpsed Mikhalski, pockmarks dimpling to shadows in the gloom.

'The eyes may fear, but the hands do their duty,' she remembered. 25 metres, in a poor light, is no mean distance to hurl a tin box weighing 500 grams, but with a fluid motion of her arm Irina flung the box in an arc to fall at Yegor's feet.

She only knew, as the English say, 'It seemed the right thing to do at the time.'

Then Mikhalski struck—a sickening rabbitpunch that felled her—and in her ebbing sight she saw Dombrovich and Mikhalski running at astonishing speed in pursuit of the general.

A moment later she found Bolkashin, empty-handed, half concussed on the rainswept pavement.

For some reason, Irina thought of Rollo and his parade ground litany: 'If it moves shoot it; if it's on the ground pick it up.'

She was stooping to retrieve Yegor's false teeth when she saw Duncan rapidly crossing the road towards them. There was blood on his shirt and he was nursing a bruised fist. In his other hand he held Irina's brick-shaped tin box, weighing it in his palm.

'We Salute the Dawn of Plenty,' Duncan grinned crookedly, slowly spelling out the Cyrillic slogan on the band that bordered the box.

'I've seen better days,' General Bolkashin groaned. He opened his eyes just at the moment Duncan removed from the box the envelope marked *Most Secret* and the Sapropel Report fell into the young lieutenant's hands.

The shredded paper unfurled in the wind like party streamers, like curls of wood shavings, like ribbons of excelsior.

On Duncan's lips was a smile of immeasurable, childlike cunning.

The exhilaration of violence can cause fatigue.

The brisk rustling of starched skirts as the ward nurse passed her, and the rattle of a bedpan in an enamel basin, roused Irina from her doze.

Bolkashin was hooked up to a morphine drip, his face contorted by pain from a shattered pelvis.

She approached him, unheard.

His toothless lips parted in a rueful collapsed grin when he saw her so close.

'My ears aren't as sharp as they were, Irinka . . . '

' . . . Neither are your teeth. I know.'

The general grunted in anguish as he raised his arms to replace his dentures.

'Did you really expect to bend me to your will,' she said, 'trembling in the laboratory like one of your trapped rabbits?'

The general sank back into the pillows.

'Nevertheless, I nominated you for Stoneburgh and you did as you were ordered. Today I had word from your upstart republic. Your renegade parliament has thrown out the lakeland privatisation programme. Wingfield's hopping mad. His sapropel scheme's well and truly sunk before the *Kongress* has even convened. So now my own plan is . . . ' he spat out the word, '. . . *kaput*.'

His voice broken by age and defeat, Bolkashin admitted his desperate need for ready cash had driven him to devise the sapropelian regeneration experiments with the sentient mimosa *voronetskiana*.

Bolkashin was to have been paid well by Military Intelligence; he'd led them to believe he'd stumbled upon interrogation techniques superior to intravenous truth serums.

'You know, it was my own initiative to experiment with that cache of seeds brought back by Count Voronetskiy. It was our great good fortune they weren't eaten.'

Irena shivered as she recalled how the Research Institute for Agricultural Sciences had been beseiged by the German invaders for six months in the harshest winter for decades, yet the starved technicians, close to death, had forborne to eat their priceless seed reserves and botanical specimens.

'And what of Subject X-5?' The fate of the young fifth-category student preyed on Irina's mind. The general had a chasm for a heart.

'We conducted another special experiment with *him*.' Yegor opened his mouth in a silent laugh, at the same time stroking his chin. 'The conditions were a pitch-dark room with two polygraphed sapropel-enriched mimosa seedlings and one human subject. We cast lots as to which of the plants he should uproot in the dark. The only witness to the crime was the second mimosa plant monitored by the polygraph. Later, as Subject X-5 passed the rooted specimen, the pen practically shot off the graph when our little green witness recognised its companion's "killer"!'

The general's cold eyes narrowed, as he grinned.

'The young devil hasn't stopped shaking since.'

Rapidly chopping each sentence, Bolkashin outlined his covert scheme, now scuppered by the National Assembly's narrow-run vote.

In a double blow, the general had planned to both subvert the military supply routes of the Powers, *and* secure the sapropel excavation concessions for his puppetmasters in Moscow.

'We'd lined up Subject X-5 as a front man for a joint stock company.' The general then acknowledged how the true ownership of the company would have remained veiled; his masters in Moscow had been captivated by the seemingly miraculous properties of the sapropel-bearing sediments under the lakes.

The general smoothed the bed sheets as he prepared for rest.

'And is there truly a machine that reconstitutes shredded documents?'

'You know better than to ask,' the general hissed. He paused and drank feverishly from a plastic beaker. 'In our country Miss Curiosity has her nose torn off.' He had endeavoured to speak with his usual cold imperiousness, but his voice had lost its firmness.

Irina remembered the general's own words from her indoctrination in his counterintelligence classes.

(*'The classic candidate to consider for betrayal is a man who has descended from his physiological peak, which is very often the breaking point in an operative's career.'*)

His eyes locked with hers and Irina strained every fibre of her will to break awayfrom that basilisk stare.

'You cannot break through a wall with your forehead,' she thought

She searched her pockets for some hard or pointed instrument, and her hand closed on the pin of a medal. (The award of Meritorious Culture Worker had been conferred on her before her assignment to Stoneburgh.) Her fist clenched until her palms bled. She displaced her fear with self-inflicted wounds.

She could not resist one last sharp riposte.

'Then who had the casting vote in the Assembly?'

He countered with a hoarse laugh, harshened by threat, then sank back on the pillow and closed his eyes.

'An assemblyman with one arm who'll learn of his mistake.'

❁

Irina sought the refuge of unreason.

Dreamily she listened to Grazhina as, cigarette smoke curling above her temples, the enchantress described Irina's destiny as a voyage of two lovers set adrift into mists of uncertainty.

Irina had never once mentioned the picture, but Grazhina saw the painting clearly, as if it hung before her innermost eye.

Irina thought: *'Vlaminck and Grazhina are two kindred spirits. She is conversant with the wiles of psychiatry and, after all, Vlaminck was a trick-cyclist, too, in his own way.'*

❁

The sun shone cold for a second and the florist shop disappeared.

At that moment she saw Konrad and Kristina.

There was Konrad, opening a car door for his insufferably young wife.

The makeup of her face was flawless. The sort of girl, Konrad had laughed, who would not blink for fear her eyelids would gain an uneven suntan. Yet Kristina was colder than the sun which shone so cold on Novy Świat.

❁

'You repress the cause of your mental suffering,' explained Grazhina. 'The florist is no longer to be found because your lover no longer sends you flowers,' she continued fondly. 'Whilst you suppress your memories of this man, more erroneous actions will surely follow.'

This Viennese reading of Irina's palm seemed for Grazhina to be a source of considerable pleasure.

But Irina was thinking only of the oppressive humid atmosphere of the florist shop, shuddering as her thoughts teemed with shadowy forms, her senses reawakened to the clamminess of the experimental chamber enwreathed in mimosa foliage whose exploring tendrils trailed sentiently over her mouth and hair and tongue.

❁

In Konrad's bachelor-apartment (his description) she stretched her legs on the studio couch.

Her slavonic legs were long; she knew her ankles were shapely. They were her strong point.

'Kilometres of leg! They grow from the armpits!' Konrad had once observed. 'Is it because of the Chernobyl disaster?'

That remark was *before* he had learned of his cancer.

In the next room she heard him sigh in his sleep.

The *Kongress* had been adjourned, the negotiators withdrawn.

Rees-Sholter had recalled his Liaison Officer and Inter-preter for a review.

Cats were scratching at her soul; she felt sick at heart before the prospect of a drumhead enquiry to establish her guilt.

When she arrived in London she swore she would end the affair and return Konrad's keys. But, of course, just as she approached the flat, his door was flung open and there stood Konrad, the heart-throb. Hearts were trumps.

'Please do not say anything,' he said to his interpreter. 'It is too good to put into words.'

Irina noted he was wearing the special tie from Jermyn Street. In the past he had not worn the ties she bought him—Kristina might have asked awkward questions.

As Grazhina foretold, 'The Queen of Spades is more concerned with the *appearance* of a happy reign than the reality. In truth, she is cold, calculating and tyrannous.'

Irina tiptoed to the bureau where the wedding party photo-graph stood. Kristina's frozen artificial smile had not changed.

On the bride's left, Kristina's sister-in-law stared at the camera with her dark, brilliant, inwardseeing eyes.

Grazhina!

Why had she never noticed her before!

Perhaps Grazhina had not intended her to notice.

Then the memories flooded back. Konrad had once mentioned his older sister. He regarded her as a very *perceptive* woman.

Irina packed her bag and crept from the flat. Konrad did not stir.

❁

The telephone was ringing when she reached her quarters at Stoneburgh Park.

On the line she heard the Dead Man's Click of his pistol—the hollow blown-egg sound of no rounds in the spout. If the pain became too great, he told her, he knew what he would do.

'What will you do?' she asked in a passive voice.

Konrad bawled in the earpiece, 'I'll come down there and shoot every last one of your unillustrious lovers!'

❁

Irina remembered the pitted façade of the fortune-teller's elegant apartment block, pockmarked like a mobster.

The enchantress had interpreted Irina's dream of a handgun floating from a parachute canopy, its muzzle dripping with cold blood.

'He's completely harmless, of course,' Grazhina had smiled fondly. 'You were dreaming of your lover.'

Konrad once said to Irina: 'Our love was against the odds.'

He had shown her a press clipping that reported the unearthing of a young couple who had lain buried for over 5000 years. Scientists believed they were locked in an affectionate embrace at the time of death.

Irina concluded happily that she was in grave danger of becoming Polonised, eating dainty profiteroles in the cafés of the *emigracja*.

❁

The façade of Stoneburgh was at last revealed for what it was.

A New Intake Group jogged down the wide avenue. A Commonwealth contingent, she noted.

Except she knew the drill pigs called them chocolate drops or chimps.

Irina followed the colour-sergeant's enormous empire-crushing hob-nailed boots to the Orderly Room.

The colonel rose to greet her.

Irina stared at his moist sensual mouth.

(Rollo had once said: 'I would not trust him as far as I could throw an elephant.')

Duncan was seated at the colonel's desk, polishing a set of golf clubs. He wore a new Number One dress uniform. He could not suppress his cunning childlike smile. On his epaulettes the two pips of a full lieutenant glittered.

'Meet our new Lt. Pym. He's been booted Upstairs. Psy-Ops.'

(Psy-Ops was the Special Division for Psychological Operations in Int & Squint—Intelligence and Security.)

Rollo whispered rapidly, 'Things have changed around here. Since Duncan's wife left him he's ponced himself up like a poof's hen party.'

A trumpeting herrumph preceded the colonel's pronouncement.

'A mention in dispatches. Thanks to Duncan's exceptional vigilance in Warsaw, that shining example of *homo sovieticus*, the *so-called* General Bolkashin has been well and truly trounced!'

'So-called?' Irina whispered to Rollo.

'A Russian general only ranks as a colonel in the British Army,' Rollo murmured in a muted undertone.

Duncan opened the envelope he had wrestled from Dombrovich and Mikhalski.

The shredded paper fluttered into 'File Thirteen'.

'Bolkashin stole the Report right here from under our very noses and we never knew it. Duncan tells me the Russkies have developed a machine for reconstituting shredded paper.'

Irina glanced at Duncan who returned a furtive wink, a mere tremor of the eyelid. Rees-Sholter peered at Rollo reprovingly from under his bristling minatory brows.

'Duncan acquitted himself rather well and gave the fella a pretty thorough pasting, I understand.'

Duncan's eyes were modestly downcast now. The lines round his mouth twitched and he twirled a Number One club between his fingers. A Number One iron is designed for the longest shot.

'Bolkashin knew the New Kingdom Movement was a façade party with a secret agenda to destroy our scheme and he tried to hijack the sedimentation project to his own profit.'

('So,' Irina thought, '*all the time, Kristina was trying to preserve the disputed lands from industrialisation before their restitution.*' Konrad must have known that fact from the very beginning.)

'I regret that Duncan's intercepts were too late to alter the course of events. All the same,' concluded Rees-Sholter, rubbing his hands, 'Duncan showed exemplary initiative in tapping Bolkashin's telephone line.'

Irena caught Duncan's warning look and, as their eyes communed, he pressed his finger to his lips enjoining her silence.

Apparently theirs was to be a secret shared by them alone.

His maloccluded mouth broke into his cunning childlike smile, as he rose and caddied the colonel's golfbag.

❁

'Maggots!' spat out Rollo with unrestrained malevolence.

Irina was observing Duncan teeing off on the Governor's lawn. The colonel was advising his subordinate on his swing.

'I can't believe the general would have succeeded in his plan,' Irina protested disingeniously. Yet she knew only that Duncan had saved her from exposure by confiding to Rees-Sholter the general's conviction that he could magically reconstitute deconstructed documents.

'No doubt we've not seen the last of him. The Russians have three strong principles . . . '

' . . . "Perhaps", "somehow" and "never mind". I know.'

She could not cease twisting compulsively the gold eternity ring on the third finger of her left hand.

Rollo lowered his voice.

'If you ask me, I'm prepared to believe this whole debacle has been dreamt up by Duncan to gain his promotion. Not only that, Brigadier Wingfield's been sacked from chief of T-FECS and Rees-Sholter is in line for his job.'

The colonel on the distant green demonstrated the follow-through.

Rollo stifled a yawn.

'The colonel plays a pretty long game, you know.'

Irina nodded, thoughtfully. The fire of demagoguery burned more fiercely in the colonel's eyes than in the general's, Irina decided.

She thought of the moment when Duncan suddenly stood before her in the Orderly Room on her first day at Stoneburgh.

Like an apparition.

Duncan, she thought, had turned out to be a spook of a kind.

Someone had tipped off Kristina. Duncan's jealousy was ample motive.

Beau bounded to the major's heels.

'The colonel's still keen on the Sapropel Project going through, incidentally. This time he's wooing a consortium of German oilmen. If the krauts can't take central Europe by war, they'll take it by stealth.'

He saluted smartly and his glance sought her complicity. 'But not while I'm still on strength.'

He squared his shoulders.

Superfit, resolute, he strode off for his twice-daily visit to the gym.

❁

On the Governor's Lawn the colonel's Number One iron tore out an ugly divot from the turf.

The English soil everything they touch, Irina thought.

She kept thinking of the staff sergeant's monstrous black boot.

A 17½ Imperial.

So far as she knew there was no equivalent continental size.

❁

So, after all, Konrad was to continue as Staff Liaison Officer while she would be his Int., with time enough to explore their love in a language that was not their own. (Int. can be read as Intelligence or Interpreter depending on the sensitivity of context.)

Irina had never rushed to put labels on human behaviour. Who to label 'good'; who to label 'bad'. Irina had listened to the counsel of her mother who, despite every hardship, still believes there are certain eternal verities which remain above the realpolitik.

❁

Nearing the great library Irina looked up at her belvedere window.

'Love isn't like a potato, you can't throw it out the window,' she thought. To be denied Konrad's love was like being deprived of her senses.

Konrad was seated reading a book bound in old buckram covers.

He was tracing Vrangel's journey across the Frozen Sea towards the island which bears his name.

Grazhina had told Konrad—in the same words as she told Irina—of a distant island, as yet clouded by unknowing, where the weary traveller will find landfall.

He was imagining snow billowing like white smoke and the traveller journeying towards a terrible uncertainty.

The solitude would be like a place where no sun ever reached.

Then Irina raised her hand and waved.

DISPOSSESSION

(*Mary H.* — DESIPRAMINE)

'. . . since thy original lapse, true liberty is lost . . .'

—*Paradise Lost*, JOHN MILTON

Assessment Summary (extract): Rarely, I believe, has a personal account of the inner life been written, which enables us to see so clearly the processes of suppression, repression and complex-formation during the impressionable years of pubertal development, as these experiences recorded so vividly by this patient, whose severe behavioural problems first came to the attention of mental health professionals after a *Fête de Noël* organised by her French Circle. The patient has been referred because she presents delusional thinking, claiming to have unusual perceptual experiences, interpreted by odd beliefs, and magical thinking, in which actual childhood events are continually being confused with a false chronology of unconscious fantasies. Her eye-contact is poor and her attitude is mistrustful, compounded by a histrionic personality and by a tangentiality and circumstantiality in her speech. She reports auditory hallucinations, and has a bizarre delusion of being possessed, perceiving the physical presence of living beings (a 'bird' or a 'snake') in her fingers. She attaches great importance to divination by dreams and claims to be in contact with the hereafter. Four years ago, following repeated episodes of grandiosity and impulsivity, of extended duration, the patient was admitted to a general hospital for an eating disorder and depressed mood, and treated with antidepressants.

DISPOSSESSION

Patient ID CPN0312110842: Mary H.
Occupation: Manageress (drapers & ladies' outfitters) rtd.
Drug: Desipramine.
Drug class: Tricyclic mood elevator.
Common side effects: Blurred vision and nightmares. Use with caution when driving; can cause drowsiness.

I CAN REMEMBER in every bright-etched detail the precise moment I first decided to murder my brother.

I had returned to our family home, the day after my mother's funeral, to discover he had changed the locks.

I knocked on the bay window for several minutes before he emerged, obviously hungover, yawning lazily like a sated cat.

He stretched his arms and barred the hallway.

'Don't come anywhere near this property again!' he shouted. 'I don't want even your damned shadow falling on this house! Understand?'

He then slammed the door with his boot.

❀

The explanation for his intemperate outburst was contained in our solicitor's letter, which arrived the following week.

Dear Mary [*he was a friend of my mother's*],

<u>*Your Late Mother's Estate*</u>. We were consulted recently by your mother in respect of her bequests, and the last Will we drew up is available at our offices, a copy of which may be requested by your goodself for your perusal. A letter of administration was received from your mother appointing your brother and myself as her Executors and Trustees. In which capacity I must inform you, as to her estate, that her house, her personal chattels, and greater part of the residue of her monies, after disbursements and the payment of funeral and testamentary expenses, are bequeathed wholly to your brother.

I sank limply into a chair and began to cry. Unseeing, uncomforted, I crushed the letter with tremulous hands that could not be stilled.

I then made a pot of tea and protracted the drinking of it as if to delay the necessity of reading any further.

At length I took up the wretched letter once more and continued to read:

A small packet, deposited by your mother at our chambers, explains the reasons, I believe, which determined her decision; and your brother, on his part, would prefer these matters to be resolved amicably; nevertheless, you may wish to seek independent legal advice in respect of the Will's provisions and of the instructions of the Testatrix. May I express my sincere condolences at the sad loss of your Mother.

I remain,
Dear Mary,
Yours most respectfully, etc.

I felt neglected and vulnerable, held together weakly by will alone, like a house shored up by its own shadow.

I remained for some time breathless and motionless in my chair. I was nonplussed as to how to proceed. Then I picked up the telephone and arranged to see the solicitor in London that very afternoon.

❁

At the railway station I was in a foul mood and I had to reprimand a counterhand who overcharged my train fare at peak rates to London.

'Young man,' I said, 'I could buy a pair of shoes for that money and walk there.'

On the train, to distract my attention from disturbing thoughts, I idly flipped though the travel supplement of an abandoned newspaper until my hand was stayed by an announcement: *Special Offer! Six nights at deluxe hotel in Biarritz.*

Biarritz!

My memory these days is like a leaky pitcher, but one of the oddest effects due to my medication is discovering that events in my distant past are far more vivid to me than most events viewed in the present.

I remember so well the little gift shop in the Avenue Victor Hugo when, as a girl of fifteen, I bought that box of almond macaroons—*mouchous*—for Mother, a pungent potted cheese for Father and, for my brother then aged eight, after a considerable amount of soul-searching, a painting-by-numbers set, with enchanting miniature punnets of oil paints set into a cardboard palette.

Peinture par numéro
idéal pour enfants et débutants

In the box were five overprinted canvases: a Parisian *café* scene, a circus, matadors, ballerinas, and a group of tropical hutments on stilts under palm trees somewhere in the French dominions, the kind of exotica I thought Boy would particularly favour.

I am, myself, addicted to jigsaw puzzles and in the shop I'd been strongly drawn to those lively scenes; to my untrained eyes each canvas resembled a puzzle of a complexity that would challenge the most sophisticated enthusiast.

But when I arrived home Boy's response to my thoughtful gift had been entirely characteristic. A surly look and not a word of thanks. Yet, you know, without my gift I doubt very much whether Boy would have taken the first step on the road to his modest fame as a painter in the lower pantheon of the so-called 'School of London'.

As it is, I recall his only artistic impulse at that early age was to reverse the sized canvas and paint on its unprimed rough side between the wooden stretchers, a technique which he later adopted to ease the flow of his brush.

In the train the bitter recollection of Boy's infantile churlishness drew from me a convulsive sigh which caused the other passengers in the carriage to start.

Up until that frosty reception, my first unaccompanied trip abroad, quit of a kid brother, had been so blissfully perfect, do you see.

I'll always remember my wide-eyed early morning walks alone, the greetings from the *jardiniers municipaux* and from the cleaners hosing down the streets, and watching the men raking *La Grande Plage* while, on the water, the *bateaux nettoyeurs* trawled for weed and seawrack before the berobed bathers descended for breakfast on the terraces of their shimmering white hotels.

And I certainly cannot forget my last day in Biarritz when one of my father's overseas business representatives arrived at the hotel with a mysterious wicker hamper which I learned belatedly I was charged to carry on my return flight home.

In that year the currency rate had been pegged artificially to 980 francs to the English pound, but on the black market the going rate was over 1200 francs to the pound. On my first day in Biarritz, my father had made an appointment for me to meet, in the hotel lobby, this same overseas rep who'd surreptitiously changed my pounds at an advantageous rate.

Only later, homeward bound, on board the small English twin-prop, seated precariously on a Lloyd Loom cane armchair, did I learn that according to the consignment note the hamper contained an extremely rare venomous *snake* destined for London Zoo.

When we touched down Father was there, waiting, a lone figure at the end of the airstrip, standing apart from the apron, to commend me for my courage, and to bestow on me a kiss for a mission successfully accomplished.

Arriving alone, I had the pleasure of Father's company all to myself that long afternoon. I hung on his arm there with no thought of Mother to blight our happiness.

In the presence of Father I always felt stronger because we were so alike.

I suppose I could see my own weaknesses in Father: our shared familial timidities and nervous laughter under the dominion of a woman to whose supremacy we cravenly kneeled.

Without *Her*, dearest Mama, life possessed so much more light-heartedness and joy.

❁

Before the Light Failed

Our family solicitor, I perceived, had the grace to act shame-faced when he greeted me, and placed in my hand the packet bequeathed by my departed mother of unhappy memory.

He escorted me to a cheerless anteroom with a view over the backyard of a butcher's shop. Washed muslin cloths were draped over the intervening fence.

The grey cloths were steaming in the chill air, and I thought of pasture animals and slaughter and blood and abattoirs.

After I'd finished reading my mother's letter a red mist swam before my eyes.

I append her letter entire, because, for pure self-serving sanctimoniousness, I believe its style does not have an equal.

> Mary [*there was no salutation or endearment*],
>
> There was a time, I recall, when you and I were more best friends than mother and daughter but now I wonder, over and over in my mind, what have I done to have such a thankless unnatural child? As you grieve for your mother, so I grieve for my daughter—what a sorrow you have been for me. I have always had trouble with you.

> I don't need to explain everything to you, because you know yourself you have acted unwisely in attempting to set your brother against me. If your father were alive he'd be terribly angry and aggrieved to learn of the mischief you have done. You can plead, you can coax, you can threaten but I have nothing but bad memories of your meddling.

Readers may wish to skip the next few pages as this letter has little bearing on the idiosyncrasy of my disorder, but there may be some curious enough to be desirous of knowing the full extent of my mother's perfidy, and I see no reason to deny them that satisfaction.

> Even by your own long record of petty tantrums, since the time you were a little girl, your recent unconscionable behaviour brooks no comparison, when I think of how Boy does his best and listens to what I tell him. Why it should be that you always want to stand between us I truly cannot say.
>
> But my care for you has cost me dear, that I do know, and now I would not ask for my life to be lengthened except for Boy's sake.
>
> All I can think upon now is that Boy, my only son, will be an orphan until his death and will never again see his mother.

'Poor lamb,' I thought, *'condemned to be the oldest orphan in the county!'*

> So, for Boy's sake, I beg you to settle your differences. Since you were children, it's always been six of one and half a dozen of the other, and today nothing has changed in your apparent mutual mistrust, I'm sure.
>
> Someday, you'll understand that these legalities have been more painful for me than for you, Mary. You may be stunned initially, but deep down you'll be profoundly grateful.

> Even now the thought of this decision weighs heavily upon me, but I remain unwavering in my resolve because from my own daughter I have had no comfort at all, and any tender feelings for you I may have once known are outweighed by my desire to protect Boy with a roof over his head. Ergo, I can foresee the possibility that there will come a time when he will be unable to continue his important work due to ill health at some future date.

'Important work!' I yelled inside my head. *'Huh! That's rich!'* In my own view, Boy's crapulous canvases duped the art market with their cynically inflated price-tags only because Mother hired fashionable galleries to exhibit them in. *'And as for his "ill health", if you please! Couldn't Mother see his drug-induced respiratory condition was largely self-inflicted!'*

There's none so blind as those who will not see and none so deaf as those who will not hear.

> I wish I could help you understand how deeply your thoughtless unkindnesses have undermined my health. The accumulation of years wearies me, but today I improved sufficiently to take my place at the table to do justice to Boy's 'devilled egg surprise' and, before the light failed, to settle to my task to give you as good an idea as I could of the disfavour you have earned.
>
> It is getting dark so I will say good night. I have nothing more to write, only to beg you to take care of Boy and be your brother's support, and to bid you goodbye,
>
> M.
>
> P.S. Please accept the enclosed clasp. The 'Scots' brooch you once said was 'me' is now yours.

'Good Christ! Mother's memory was elephantine!' I almost laughed aloud, and a sob nearly undid me. It's true that the hideous penannular bronze brooch I took from its tissue wrappings was more suited to the cloak of a Scottish chieftainess rubbed with woad, and I'd once told her so.

I reread my mother's letter and reached a decision: I would not contest the will; my efforts would be futile. To contend Boy's ascendancy in the family was like a dwarf threatening Hercules.

As I walked out of the solicitor's office I heard one of his typists whisper to another: 'What's up with her? She looks as if she's swallowed a wasp.'

The cat. The spiteful cat.

I pocketed the injury and softly shut the door.

The Malodorous Flower

Curiously, an earlier event—the fall of the Berlin Wall which ended the Cold War—was when the dam first burst in my emotional life or, rather, more accurately, was when I set about contriving the Fall of the House of Us (without *Her*), so to speak, to evoke the shade of Edgar Allan Poe. Those early amateurish machinations of mine you may now read in my personal history recorded here in these pages.

The crisis point was reached when I read one day a newspaper item filed by a Frankfurt correspondent reporting one of the odder consequences of East Germany's reunification with the West:

Murdered Man's Lover was his Own Sister

Killer freed . . . wife's sexual relations with refugee brother.

The court in Frankfurt today acquitted a self-confessed murderer when it learned that his wife had been conducting a long-standing affair with the murdered man, her own brother. An extraordinary story emerged as the court learned the killer's brother-in-law was a refugee from the East Zone. The wife's older brother, Friedrich, was just seven years old when, sixteen years earlier, their mother had escaped to the West with the infant Elsa, leaving him in the care of the maternal grandmother and

> trapped in the Communist State. Giving evidence, the grandmother said, 'Friedrich always used to say he wanted to marry Elsa when he grew up. They were always so affectionate with each other before the split in the family.'

To understand the strange resonances of an echo this story sounded in my memory I must take you back to an event early in my schooldays which was to stain my innocence with the blackest doubts as to my parentage.

The recollections of my earliest years are connected with our village schoolhouse, for in a classroom of infant pupils my sorrow was born.

As an exercise in our History lesson we had each been instructed to draw our family trees.

In the Sussex downlands where we farmed, the leading families had boasted settlements for more than four hundred years. In my class register you could read their children's names: the Bournes, the Brookeses, the Combes, the Hursts, the Steads, and the Wickses.

'Don't talk so ignorant,' said the village schoolmistress when I showed her our family tree which demonstrated that both my *maternal* and *paternal* great-grandparents shared the *same names* and dates of birth.

'Take a hundred lines!' she ordered. So I copied, from my nature book, 'The Stinking Iris, *iris fœtidissima*, has purplish flowers and an unpleasant smell.' My mother's name was Iris.

Even while I gazed at those lines, the spirit of change swept over me as I realised a most singular and appalling distortion had been wrought in my personal identity.

If my mother had thought nothing of marrying her first cousin, what other accepted taboos was she capable of violating?

How erroneous the belief that 'like' blood makes the happiest marriages when the blood of my mother and father was as alike as that of siblings, blended in a consanguineous marriage, which had reproduced in their children, I had no doubt, their own morbid irritability and doleful maladies.

Yes. There was a striking similitude between my parents; they could have been brother and sister. I think they both must have inordinately admired the image in the mirror and married twin versions of themselves.

But, you know, self-love can very often change to self-loathing and those who marry from self-regard can be the first to find fault.

So that embarrassing early incident of the malodorous flower was, I think, like my own given name, emblematic of the calamities that then fell upon the wellsprings of my life.

Nomen est omen. As I was to learn, names are destiny.

❁

They say that a father is a treasure and a brother a comfort but my father is long dead and my brother is a boaster and a liar and a thief.

My baptismal name is Mary; that of my family I will not mention. I was named Mary at the priest's insistence because I was the first-born daughter; it's a name that carries a burden of duty, an allusion I have always deeply resented. (Actually, were I consulted today, I would almost certainly prefer to be known as 'Berenice'; my veneration for Poe's genius is boundless.)

My brother was called Boy from the cradle.

Shall I ever forget the night of his birth?

He was born at home in a thunder storm. There was a tremendous clap and then I heard for the first time that assertive gruff voice that was to make me forever my brother's minion.

'Your ma's a-bed and sleepin',' grumbled the District Nurse, 'and there's the wee boy lookin' as disagreeable as a dead dog in a wet sack.'

I instantly had a vision of our old sheepdog, a Border Collie. Its muzzle was misaligned so its jaws didn't fit; it sounded as though it had a worm stuck in its throat. Mother had named the dog Grasper; she had a passion for the novels of the Brontë sisters and Grasper, if you remember, was the parsonage dog.

Intermarriage between near relations, I thought, must hence spawn a being as grotesque as Grasper and from that moment a sense of insufferable anxiety oppressed me.

As you can just possibly begin to imagine, my brother's birth was a fearful page in the record my existence.

I can remember Boy in his pram, a peevish elf in a pointed woollen hat. That elfin cap concealed a skull elongated by a forceps birth, as though he had been delivered by coal tongs.

Coincidentally, Grasper the sheepdog was struck dead six months later in an altogether less violent thunder storm; a bolt aimed true and found the brass tag that honoured his name; a medal struck by lightning, you might say.

Mention of that sheepdog recalls a variant account of my brother's nativity story, a kind of parallel creation myth that relates the genesis of the Young Lord and Master. As it also concerns myself it bears retelling.

The Mandrake Shriek

A lamb, you know, can be born with eyes of a different colour and, in ancient times, shepherds believed such a lamb had two different sires. In fact, a lamb characterised by this phenomenon is one of my earliest memories.

When I was going on seven, on the way to the lambing sheds one spring morning, Wilkes, the farmhand, pointed out a tawny-eyed ram, then, in the pens, he showed me lambs with brown eyes and, later, a sickly lamb with blue eyes suckling on a ewe. Disowned, in a corner, on shaky legs, stood an even sicklier lamb with an eye of each colour.

'Minds me of the time tha' brother of yourn come into this world 'cause, true enough, he were born in a barn.'

'In a barn?' I exclaimed in wonderment.

'Ain't you never heard tell of the birth of yore brother? T'was full moon and light as day. Heard this hollarin' an' fancied diddikoy folk mostlike must of took the wrong turnin' into the yard. So afore it's light I got the lantern an', begger me, I wouldn't of belieft it if I hadn't sin it wi' my own eyes, a diddikoy babe bawlin' in the cowhouse! An' no sign o' the mite's mother.'

'No!'

'On my word. Next thing I knowed, yore ma comes hurryin' outen the gate in her nightgown so I arsts her if summat's wrong. Then the mistruss took on summat terrible—sez the diddikoys are allus up to tricks—sez they'll take away a mort of things as they've no call to have. She set up such a din, cryin' and sobbin', sayin' as how the brat'll be tarrible difficult to rear on account o' it bein' a child o' the gyppos.'

'A gypsy's child! No!'

'Then yore ma ketches holt o' the babe an' laid it on a silk idydown. "They'll be a bout o' trouble wi' tha' boy, shouldn't wonder," sez I, but yore ma jest gives it a sup o' milk, an' a crust to bite on, an' sez as how the babe is her'n.'

He rubbed his nose reflectively.

'An' nobody didn't tek it away from yore ma agin, 'cause nobody didn't know the mistruss had bin cheated by the diddikoys. Same as a cuckoo, surely. Jest 'sposin' a cuckoo come along and turned out all them blue eggs and laid a speckly brown 'un.'

('An absolute imp,' Nurse Harbour had said fondly at his birth. Now I no longer puzzled over her meaning.)

Grasper loped to his sunny spot on the porch steps.

'When yore brother were born,' Wilkes said grimly, 'that dog barked fit to kill hisself.'

'A cuckoo in the nest? A changeling?' Since that talk with Wilkes when I was an impressionable child my mistrust of Boy has not been amended.

Yes, Father, Mother and myself all shared the same traits of lineage, never mind Boy, and, moreover, in this particular family's case our eye colour was as recessive as our madness.

Of course, when I reached an age mature enough to enquire into the secrets of my paternity, I discovered the oddity of Boy's eyes—right, green and left, brown—was most likely the result of the trauma of a home birth in our grey hereditary halls. I also learned hereditarists had a name for it: *heterochromia.*

❁

According to Clara, my earliest schoolfriend, a changeling child initially resembles its surrogate parents, but gradually it grows more hideous in appearance; in looks malformed, ill-favoured, and given to screaming and biting.

Although in misbehaviour it is ill-tempered and bellicose, a changeling may exhibit supernatural cunning. To be sure of truly identifying a changeling, and certain of making it vanish, the infant should be bathed as soon as practicable in a solution of foxgloves.

So one midday I took the squalling child into our back garden where my father kept a zinc bath in the heart of a miniature boxwood maze (an austerity measure before we had the indoor plumbing fitted). Father had cut the topiary himself to accommodate a soap dish and an enamelled tin wash basin.

I'd gathered the foxgloves that morning by the stream and filled two pails with my magic potion. But my attempts to bathe the infant Boy in the foxglove essence failed; he broke out in a rash and into convulsions of weeping. Maybe I should have bathed him in moonlight.

Nurse Harbour had to be sent for.

I secreted the foxglove mixture in a jar under my bed.

That night I smelled the contents again and drank a trickle; at once I began to sink into a delightful swoon.

As I fumbled to seal the jar's screwtop lid, my fingers were all thumbs, and I remember thinking, on the brink of sleep, that so many thumbs must surely claim a natural affinity with those mittened extradigital foxgloves trembling on the banks of the brook.

❁

How to describe my brother? In appearance, when a youth, he resembled a sharp-eyed strutting crow; so unlike my placid father, an endomorph with plump hips, who had a tendency to slouch. In fact, there's a famous photo, if you've seen it, of the young Kafka with deep-set shaded eyes and beaked nose, standing in Prague's Staromestske Square—he's smiling enigmatically, much in the manner of my brother before he is about to savage me with one of his devastating put-downs.

My mother coddled Boy with special foods. She declared he had a delicate stomach. So my father and I grubbed as best as we could.

As for me, the day after I heard the mandrake shriek of that forceps delivery, Mother started to treat me as a person of little consequence as though one of lesser breed.

At the breakfast table I would recoil from the noise of Boy's industrious champing. He produced an unreproducible sound, swallowing whole mouthfuls unchomped. I would excuse myself at the earliest opportunity.

Unbreakfasted one morning I met Wilkes returning from the village. His face lit up when he saw me, and he explained his errand.

'I'd never had belieft a lad could take on like tha' brat.' He grimaced. 'Hoppin' about wi' rage he were this mornin', afore breakfass. Found the mustard pot empty so he got up an' left the table, an' banged the kitchin' door an', when I went in for my orders, the mistruss were cryin' an' sent me down to the village.'

Thus must the Infant Satan have demanded in a tantrum more sulphur from the sulphur mines.

Wilkes showed me the new tin of mustard he'd fetched from the store.

Grinning, he took me into the harness room, prised off the tin's lid and doctored the contents with powdered black mustard, the hottest and most pungent rubefacient he had in his equine medicine chest. I'd seen Wilkes apply the same mustard when preparing poultices and plasters.

'That'll learn him better'n tellin' him.'

But Wilkes's cure was without effect, for next morning Boy ate the mustard like a prize turkey gobbler with undiminished relish.

''T'would give e'en a horse a headache,' growled Wilkes with grudging admiration.

My young brother didn't seem to possess normal human faculties but the heightened senses and fearlessness you'd expect, say, of a feral child who'd never learned to stand upright or encountered fire.

Boy was double-jointed. To shock people he would bend his thumb all the way back to touch his wrist; and, like the deformed Daniel Quilp, he could drink boiling tea without blinking.

Perhaps his most grotesque party trick was when he rolled back the whites of his eyes. He'd rub the surface of his eyeball without any apparent discomfort using his thumb. Boy, *sui generis*, had no sensitivity in that department.

Insensitivity, indeed, was the most marked characteristic you'd note in that child who was otherwise unclassifiable.

❁

Boy loitered away his boyhood, and dissipated his youth informed by only the most random education.

I once heard Father warn my brother about running wild with a gang of village lads.

'When a boy's alone he's a boy,' he cautioned, 'when he's loafing with another lad he's half a boy and, when he's in a pack, he's a beast.'

Father's wise counsel was ignored.

Once, on Boy's seventh birthday, when I entered his room unannounced, carrying a long cylindrical parcel that had just arrived in the mail, he punched my breastbone then waved his fist in my face.

Taunting him, I held the parcel just out of his reach.

'Touch what's mine and I'll give it to you again, straight in the snout!' he yelled. His eyes bulged from his head with the same mad glint seen in a bolting horse.

'Big words off a little chest,' I scoffed. I was approaching my fourteenth year, then, I suppose; twice his age for the only time in our lives.

Then Boy hit me a second time and my head seemed full of clangour.

Striking and not making it felt is anger lost, so I lashed out with the back of my hand and caught him with a stinging blow on his cheek.

Even at that young age Boy was strong and agile; he held my arms and I punched with no more purpose than to beat my fists against the wind.

You cannot see the charisma that a clever criminal can cast over his victim but it exists. It's like the aura of a snake that hypnotises a rabbit before gobbling it up.

Now we were very close my nose twitched as I became aware of my brother's curious odour. Boy smelled of bitter almonds; the local mole-catcher had been teaching him how to mix sodium cyanide gas for pumping into wasps' nests to destroy them. In the parcel was Boy's new bicycle pump for that purpose.

We were both breathing heavily; his reddish hair stood up in spikes. He frightened me. In a certain light he could look quite maniacal.

Boy shouted hysterically, 'You pretend to be a visitor but you're really a spy!'

He was inappeasably indignant.

He was attempting to push me from his room when Mother ran up from the kitchen, face flushed, her mouth viciously tight.

'Is this true?' demanded Mother.

'If it's not made up it must be true,' Boy declared.

He turned up his eyes in an absurd look of entreaty which instantly won the support of my mother who sank to her knees beside him, as though he were placed on a pedestal.

Boy was adonised by Mother.

I could see at once that he'd wrong-footed me and I protested.

'You're too old to be carrying tales about your brother,' Mother said, sniffing the air, 'and now you've burnt the butter.' She dished out a lambasting with her wooden spoon.

'See!' crowed Boy. 'I warned you! Don't touch what's mine!' (But at that moment I'm certain he was referring to Mother.)

Of the rest, all I remember of my brother is him standing in that crude attitude, arms folded, exultant, in the knowledge that he could with impunity leave his trademark on my upper arms and throat and places where Mother would never look. In that encounter I'd sustained appalling bruising.

My friend Clara, when she saw those bruises, believed we'd been skylarking and I did not contradict her.

Late that night I again entered Boy's room, and soundlessly crept up to the foot of his bed. He was sleeping like the den of the Seven Sleepers.

I looked down at the utter vacancy of his countenance.

Expressionless: but he was tale-bearer, a snitch, and a faithless brother, faithful only to his own self-interest.

He had won that last bout, I conceded, but, I vowed, feather by feather this goose would be plucked.

'Nighty-night, Master Sly,' I whispered.

❀

My father, as you've probably divined from the foregoing, was a sort of gentleman farmer; but his business card declared him to be a 'Furrier' and, more sinisterly, a 'Skin Merchant'. His office and storehouse were in a dark little court down a blind alley off Regent Street.

Once, shortly before Boy was born, Father as a special treat took me aboard a recently docked merchant ship discharging a cargo she'd brought from the port of Murmansk.

At dusk, Father led me to the dock gates and, curiously, I remember, he held my hand the more tightly when the dock-policeman in a waterproof cape who stood on sentry duty examined our papers under a flashlight. Not until the policeman saluted, and waved us through to mount the gangway, did Father's grip relax.

As we descended a companionway, a deckhand in an oilcloth peaked cap grinned insolently and stood aside to unfasten tarpaulins lashed over a hatch leading to the stowage.

In the hold were bales of hides, I recall, and even goose feathers stowed in cheesecloth bags. The air reeked of disinfectant and the smarting odour of bleach—a number of metal drums containing bleaching powder had corroded and the fumes thus released had destroyed a large number of goods stowed in the same compartment.

Above us, the metal treads of a ladder suddenly rang out with a tattoo.

Rattatattat—and the burly Russian captain slid down, his high-top, fur-lined sea boots barely touching the rungs.

He wore a gold-braided peaked hat set jauntily askew, and the brass buttons of his uniform, under his arctic parka, I noticed, were green with mould.

He conferred on my father a perfunctory salute, and the two men silently consulted the consular sanitary certificates forwarded with the consignment.

Father shook his head morosely when he examined two of the broached tin-lined cases in which his furs had been shipped, now eaten away by the bleach. The white furs had been packed in disinfectant powder which now hung in the atmosphere, and penetrated our clothes.

A faint flush crept across Father's forehead as he discarded the two cases.

'Double damn,' he said with an intensity I'd never heard before.

There was an embarrassed silence.

The Russian captain examined the white dust on his gloved hand, then smiled somewhat nervously. Without turning his head, he glanced sideways into my father's face through the gloom, and winked.

'At least, my friend, with all respect I dare to say, the more damaged your goods the better we're all spared those ritual bows with your customs-men.'

Another wink.

'True, my dear fellow, very true,' grunted my father. Rising, he brushed his knees. 'Sweet memories, *tavarish kapitan*,' he continued in the same tone of irony, 'that'll be all I'll be taking through today.'

The captain removed a glove to stroke my cheek.

'Sweet memories, Mariya.' he sighed. His breath parted the shifting laden air. '*Proshchái*, my little one. Manyusya. Mashenka. Farewell.'

He pressed into my hand what I thought was a gold sovereign (it was a pre-revolutionary five-roubles coin I afterwards learned).

When I protested the Captain only brought his head closer so his beard pressed into my chin as he kissed me.

'Take it, I insist. What's freer than a gift?'

❁

The tenderness of those words, and that moment when the bearded captain stooped to kiss me, the odour of sweat-stained animal fur, left an abiding impression on me.

Manyusya! Yes. I confess for that short spell I was almost reconciled to my given name.

But, after all, do memories of past bliss simply intensify the anguish of the here and now? Certainly, after the birth of Boy, my early teenage years were occupied wondering how so strange a revolution in my family had been so suddenly brought about.

From his earliest manifestation as a malign child my brother was more a mocker than a well-meaner, and known in the village as a boy of bad character.

From the age of eight he became increasingly interested in chemistry.

He took possession of an old henhouse where he conducted his experiments. Somehow he'd learnt to combine iodine crystals with ammonia. He would leave the solution for half an hour until he'd made a black sludge, which he then dried, and scattered as a powder in the schoolyard, and once on the staircase which led to my bedroom.

The loud bang the black powder produced delighted him, but I kept my nerve and never allowed him the satisfaction of seeing me blench.

That particular experiment ended when he carried a matchbox of the mixture in the pocket of his shorts on a very hot day. The black sludge leaked and dried on his thigh and he had a large violet stain there for many months.

When Mother demanded the cause he said I'd kicked him and he'd rubbed on gentian violet for the bruises.

From iodine crystals Boy graduated when a teenager to making fireworks and a cat lost half its tail. Then, his friend, Miles Orme, lost one eye when Boy laid explosive charges inside a World War II concrete pillbox, one of a string of hexagonal fortifications in the defensive line that passed through our farmland. Boy blew out a reinforced concrete embrasure three foot thick that was supposed to be shellproof.

Playing with Pillboxes

When I remember now poor Miles's hollow ribcage, his stricken face, I remember, too, that Boy, you might say, had been playing with *pillboxes*, of one sort or another, from the earliest age. To state the matter plainly: *Miles's severe drug addiction was due directly to the influence of my brother.*

It's a fact that none of my mother's nodding acquaintances would again acknowledge her in the street after the village learned Miles had returned from a 'bad trip', his face transfigured, 'turned on' to LSD and other mind-altering substances by my brother.

A well-disposed neighbour took Mother aside and attempted gently to break the news to her concerning Boy's true nature as a black sheep and blot on the escutcheon, but criticism of her wayward only son or the least contradiction would send her into a mad tailspin, spluttering with rage.

Mother said majestically, 'It is apparent to me that I am in your way at present,' then she circled the neighbour, and continued to sail up the high street in full muslin.

Uncontrite as ever, my brother took perverse pride in claiming total responsibility for Miles's unfortunate facial appearance . . . a face some said that now looked like a death's head fixed on a mop-stick . . . and others said were the features of a crucified Christ.

Yes, like our field defences crumbling on the farm, poor Miles was simply not shellproof.

For, as I shall relate in a little while, Miles would later die in strange circumstances from one of Boy's *bombitas*—in this case, a mixture of cocaine and heroin.

'Who's to Know?'

But as I have indicated—and I cannot lay too much stress on the formative years of Boy's proclivities—my brother's taste for playing with fire had defined him from his earliest boyhood. Hence, after that juvenile phase of pyromania, his curiosity was directed towards mycology and he became a dedicated *champignoneur*, roaming our country estate, daubed in Queequeg-like tattoos, on quests for hallucinogenic mushrooms and 'magic' runic stones.

One day, my regular tennis partner, the local grocer's son, Douglas Sherrard, invited me to the cinema to see Disney's *Snow White*. Boy clamoured to join us and inevitably Mother softened. Besides, she said, he was too young, aged nine, to attend the special screening unaccompanied.

So reluctantly, Douglas and I allowed Boy—a hostile cupid—to tag along on the excursion bus.

The children's matinee was a triple-bill, and what struck that ill-assorted threesome most forcibly was the stark realism of the unsuitable supporting newsreels, two *cinéma vérité* documentaries that had us gripping the edges of our seats.

The first, extraordinarily enough, was a propaganda film, with footage of the liberation of Bergen-Belsen concentration camp.

There were murmurs of distress from parents in our midst, and some removed their children from the theatre.

But it was not the privations of those unfortunate prisoners that fascinated us because the second film was a report from Borneo showing a Dayak woman performing an erotic snake dance to the sound of native drummers.

Beside me I heard Boy emit a sigh of rapture, and I felt his shoulders tremble when the voice of the narrator explained the significance of the dance, and we learned how the dancer had gained supernatural powers from a cobra and jaguar, enabling her to move like a snake's body and fly like an eagle through her dreams.

That evening, after we retired to bed, an incident additionally curious occurred which is strikingly illustrative of the power of film to 'imprint' (I use the term naïvely) a child's subconscious with an *idée fixe* as indelible as a fast stain, and of a tragic monomaniacal character quite beyond one's reckoning.

Just before midnight I heard a light knock on my bedroom door.

The room was in darkness save for a dribble of light the length of the jamb. Then the light spilled as Boy entered. His eyes glistened unnaturally bright and with an eager imploring gesture he offered me the first gift he'd ever thought to bring me in all the nine years of our mutual antagonism.

A necklace it was, of strangely shaped charms: hollowed flints, fur tufts, bones, shrew-skulls, quills, animal teeth separated by freshwater shells, and a fossil hallmarked by eons.

Not to offend him I rose from my bed, bobbed, and permitted him to thread his offering round my neck only to meet shining eyes willing me to to further compliance.

'Now, the snake dance,' he pleaded. 'Who's to know?'

He entreated me with such devilish insistence I could see no way to refuse him.

'*Please*, Zizzy.' (Prompted by Father, 'Zizzy' was Boy's first infant pronunciation of 'Sissy'; the last time Boy addressed me so fondly he would have been in diapers.)

I insinuated the flat of my hands, palms together, into the space that separated us, moving my waist to the rhythm of those Dayak drums evidently still beating in my brother's head, heedless of a footfall on the stairs and the shadow falling across the door.

'How dare you! How *dare* you!' Mother hissed, shaking my shoulders. 'You've gone a step too far this time!'

My mother had a narrow mind and a broad tongue. She frowned on any intimacy with morbid suspicion, and with a guilt-torn anxiety that is, no doubt, the prevailing feature of interbred cousinhood. As a small child I'd soon discovered the least sign of innocent flirtatiousness in the presence of my Father was crushed.

Now Mother had stormed downstairs from her mezzanine floor on the next landing like Moses from the mountaintop to give me short shrift.

'Attractive? You?' she jeered, wrenching off the necklace. 'A more appalling sight I've never seen!'

I was close to tears but I raised my voice above the clamour to defend myself.

'Clap a padlock on your tongue, girl! And put this in the cupboard!'

(She was referring to the 'confiscations' cupboard Father ineffectually oversaw to discipline Boy.)

'Well, jump to it!'

After that episode my mother's reproofs only hardened my silent defiance.

The double iniquity was the thought that Boy had once again escaped reprimand and withdrawn to a safe distance after igniting yet another false distress flare.

Unlike the corneal surfaces of his unfeeling eyes, the remaining living essence of my brother was as supersensitive as a bluebottle fly.

Houseflies have pressure-sensitive cells that warn them of any approaching harm, that's why it's so hard to swat them. Likewise, Boy somehow always managed to dodge the bullets.

❁

From that day on the wind blew a different gale, and not a day passed without some new grief.

I carried worries like a hot brick on my head. When I was a girl I held myself in very low esteem; I used to think I'd die unknown, unkissed, which is very nearly the truth, as my story attests, should you thumb through these loose leaves to find the last missing pages of a tale which should not be told.

In my childhood, my mare Dinah was my only comfort and confidante. With my cheek pressed against her warm bulk, Dinah's belly gurgled like a huge hot-water bottle.

Dinah knew very well my family was doomed because I whispered often that certainty into her ear. She heard how I cursed myself for being so great a fool as to dream of hope at all.

So when my beloved father fell sick I was not taken wholly unawares.

'Good awning!' Nurse Harbour would greet my father brightly, as she plumped up his pillows. Those ancient *Bonsoir* pyjamas Father wore were hideously striped like a vast faded sunblind.

'Dratted woman,' Father would mouth behind her back with a roguish grin, and signal to me to hasten her removal.

I mistrusted her; I held for her physical appearance such a repugnance that on each visit I could scarcely look at her bulbous porous nose—so like a pepperpot—or allow my glance to stray to her squat frame where she stood, bowlegged, by her bicycle, as though she'd just that minute dismounted a pack pony, having ridden all the way from Samarkand.

And another thing. Nurse Harbour had always retained a soft spot in her heart for my brother, but it was during my father's illness, I suspect, that the strongest links of their unholy alliance were forged . . . probably even in Father's sickroom while he slept.

'An absolute imp,' Nurse Harbour had said on Boy's entrance into this world. The true meaning of those words now became clear; it was as though she had recognised a future sorcereress's apprentice.

The deeper connivance of these mismatched accomplices had come about by an odd coincidence. In the pioneering days of our rural telephone service, our farm and the cottage of the district nurse shared a 'party line' (our two-digit telephone number was 39). When the instrument jangled either Nurse Harbour or my mother would accept the call until the identity of the caller was known.

Boy used to lurk in a sort of butler's pantry under the stairs where the telephone was hidden . . . that he eavesdropped on Nurse Harbour's patients I was to learn only years later, when I had occasion to reinterpret the sinister trade which passed between them: *a trade in live rabbits.*

I have a memory of Boy, aged ten, at dawn, as he set out wild-faring in our woods for rabbit greens where there was an abundant supply. Along the hedgerows grew the leaves of coltsfoot, dandelion, clover, vetches, yarrow, sow thistle and that astringent tonic, shepherd's purse; and, nearer the marshy margin of the stream, hogweed and clumps of hazel flourished. The leaves of oak, elm and maple also abounded.

Later, across the yard, in the enclosure under the ash trees, a lamp could be seen swinging to cast splashes of light into the breeding hutches as Boy moved among the pens and nesting boxes of his rabbitry.

If you passed him in the house you were quickly aware the young rabbit breeder possessed an unventilated odour, a drainish atmosphere which recalled damp straw litter and bran mash.

His corner of the yard smelled of sodden sawdust and droppings from beneath the cages; yet, contrarily, from one special cage of does flowed the overburdening fragrance of juniper foliage, antiseptic and sharp.

I suppose I put two and two together when Clara whispered news of an unwanted pregnancy in the village; a girl of fourteen, who'd shared a bedroom with her elder brother, had turned to the 'districk nurse' for help.

To Clara's certain knowledge, Nurse Harbour had dosed the girl with a special julep electuary, said to be brewed from crushed juniper berries, that had acted upon her system as a powerful oral contraceptive.

But I suspected otherwise.

Boy, I knew, had experimented on animals and birds. He'd once caged a bullfinch whose feathers he turned black by feeding it entirely on hempseed.

In our forgotten corner of Sussex, the urine of rabbits fed on juniper was still considered sufficiently potent, when imbibed, to terminate an unborn child. Besides which, I'm convinced Boy supplied Nurse Harbour for another reason: the injection of a woman's urine into a female rabbit—the 'Rabbit Test'—was then a widely used technique for pregnancy determination.

Clara, unblushing, said the rabbit did not die if you were not pregnant; I never questioned how she came by this intimate knowledge.

Clara and I rode together and were fast friends but not all our secrets were shared . . . whoever reveals her secret makes herself a slave.

No. Well-mannered Dinah, my seven-year-old dapple grey mare, was my soulmate during those years of my adolescence. She was an unflappable Clydesdale cob; although her lower legs were heavy and shaggy, she could nonetheless fly over five-foot jumps.

I would exercise Dinah every day, in all weathers, with no thought to my own discomfort, and willingly attend to her stabling such was the refuge I found in her placid company.

However, my concern for my father during his decline meant she was exercised less, since I had made it my duty to stay at his bedside.

'I'm as sound as a pound,' my father averred one Friday evening, and insisted I join Clara at a saddle club show to be held the next day on an adjoining farm. Reluctantly I obeyed.

Clara and I rode well as partners in the mounted games; in the baton exchange relays our team won, and we both ran well ahead in the endurance ride.

Our horses were fit, but I grew distracted by thoughts of Father's condition, fearing it had worsened, and I took a fall when Dinah had bridled her head. The fault was minor—Dinah had been merely tittuppy—and I returned to the starting line with no worse disgrace than dented pride. But without me, my team was beaten in the run-off to eliminate riders for the last heats of the games.

So, earlier than expected, I rode home to find Boy had been sent to fetch me from the riding stables. At that time I was bonily slender with a front as flat as a washboard, and a waist Father's long pianist's hands could have enclosed with the span of his supple fingers, which reached easily to notes an octave higher.

Father once told me that, in emulation of Liszt, he had spent tormented nights as a youth with his fingers splayed with leather thongs strung from the rails of the bed head. His perseverance had been rewarded, and eventually his hands could stretch across an octave and more than two keys beyond. In fact, like Liszt, he could play an octave and two keys easily in the key of A major, which is among the most challenging of spans on the keyboard.

Father had taught me piano-playing and my hands were nimble but, the day Boy met me, the sensitive flesh between by own long fingers was blistered raw and bleeding from the reins.

Did I sense impending disaster from the very fact of my brother's unwonted appearance in that stableyard?

I had just dismounted from Dinah, when I turned to see Boy staring with a near-phobic intensity at the blood drying on my palms.

Then I saw Boy had fixed his gaze on the long buckskin leathers that lined the inner legs of my jodhpurs where they were rimed with horsesweat and flecked with lather. Certainly Boy seemed to flinch when I idly rubbed them down with a dressing-whisk of straw, and took Dinah's halter to make a step towards him.

'It's Pops,' Boy said abruptly, 'he's not in good trim.'

My heart lurched with a terrible throb of pain and my hand flew to my mouth. Soon I was sobbing uncontrollably and, as I wept, all the while Boy stared at me with unashamed curiosity.

❀

Horse and hattock, I raced home and entered the sickroom.

According to Boy, when Father refused to drink Nurse Harbour's herbal draught her patient had said in a hoarse whisper, 'There's no medicine against death,' a remark typical of his dry humour. All the same he'd drunk the dose.

Yet if I had expected any grave profundities in Father's dying breath I was to be summarily disappointed. I held his hand. His last words were: 'This haemmoroid is the first I've ever had.'

'Well,' said Nurse Harbour, with a meaningful glance as she wiped Father's medicine glass then covered his face, 'we must all have a little something to bring us to our end, and he *was* in his seventies.'

Poor Father. The indignity of being laid out by that frightful old crone!

She closed the curtains to keep the flies out.

Later, Mother and I watched her set to work.

'I may say you will not believe a man is dead until his arms are bound,' Nurse Harbour observed, then called for wet unbleached cotton wool for his eyes to close them.

Up and down stairs I carried warm water, cotton wool, towels, old night clothes, crêpe bandages, and one of Father's scarves to set the jaw.

Still later I heard her descend the stairs and murmur to Mother, 'All serene. I've tied off the old tinkle.'

I entered Father's room. Nurse Harbour had straightened and washed the body, then folded a thin, worn-out cotton drawsheet in the manner of a baby's napkin at his waist.

I bent my head to kiss my father and pressed my face into his grey beard.

I thought of the Christmas before Boy's birth, when Father had brought home the child's-size tippet he'd had made up for me from polar fox furs and pelts of white kolinski ermine.

He'd promised me a proper furcoat when I grew up, and showed me a section in the fox fur, cunningly stitched, where he said Eskimo dogs had gnawed off one of the ears.

The fur had smelled faintly of disinfectant and coffee beans.

I thought of father's five-o'clock shadow when he used to return from Town. He'd kiss my cheek and abrade my chin with his bristles.

I never saw my furcoat but, another time, he brought home for Boy a pair of caribou socks said to be worn by Alaskan trappers.

A Fall from Grace

I once overheard a teacher of mine observe my brother had 'ape personality', which I felt endorsed my own private opinion of his simian appearance—that egg-shaped head with eyes deeply set together—until I realised, with an after-burn of profound regret, that those words had been unintentionally elided with a fussy diphthong. It seemed that unlike myself he was blessed, after all, with '*a* personality'.

After father's death there was brief rapprochement, the object of our rivalrous claims for paternal affection having vanished, and for a while we decently tolerated one another, like dogs that snarl over a bone and play together when it's gone.

For almost a fortnight, in that period of mourning I remember, we shared a passion for E. A. Poe, and, in the silence of Father's library at night, we devoured those macabre tales of lunatic cousins, my brother seated before my tear-blind eyes—an Egaeus to my Berenice—as I contemplated how differently we had grown: me, buried in gloom and he, overflowing with energy, not as a being of this earth, but as an abstraction of such a being, and the theme of my melancholy speculations.

But beware of enemies reconciled. My short-lived reign, when I believed I'd found favour in my brother's eyes and won his trust, endured no longer than the nine days of Lady Jane Grey, when she too had ruled in a *règne de folie*.

The circumstances of my fall from grace were these:

In the weeks after Father's funeral, Douglas, who was on leave from the plantations of Borneo, began to quite seriously pay court to me.

In the Tropics he had achieved a modest kind of handsomeness, with his sun-dried face and deep-set eyes as brown as polished leather.

His was a decorous courtship, in the shadow of a bereavement, but maybe I cut a mysterious romantic figure in my mourning clothes because I cannot else account for his devotion.

Douglas used to say I had the ambivalent look of a docile adventuress, which is very near to the truth, as I've always been less a reluctant leader than an impulsive follower.

He regarded me, I suppose, as his Insignificant Other.

Douglas always had an uncomplicated doggy nature. His attentiveness reminded me of our old farm dog, Grasper's successor, who, if it saw me put my lipstick on, would jump up and stand by the door, believing I was going to the shops.

Douglas would meet me after my parish visits to the village poor when I accompanied the rector on his 'good works' to deliver cottage lectures on the profligacy of breeding. Mother had always regarded 'slumming' as a higher duty that could not be shirked by a person of standing.

What's more, thanks to Mother's insistence on my given name I was invariably asked to play the Holy Mother in the *tableau vivant* of the Nativity, candlelit in the nave.

I had grown plump and my legs stout after the shock of Father's death . . . a trauma I believe that stimulated my late sexual development, because that night I menstruated for the first time.

Mother was no comfort and referred to her menses as her 'domestic afflictions'. The doctor said my thickening girth was a symptom of a depressive disorder which in time would pass.

'Puppy fat,' Mother scoffed, and assured me the tubbiest grubs can grow sylph-like wings and fly. I was excruciatingly embarrassed by my appearance so you can imagine my hot-faced shame when, on leaving church one Sunday after evensong, Mother patted my plump legs proudly and said to the rector, 'Two pillars of the church! None doughtier in all of Christendom!'

'Indeed,' he agreed doubtfully, steepling his fingers under his chin.

So, I must have looked the very picture of ill luck when Douglas came calling to ask for my hand.

❁

At the farther end of our garden, behind the boxwood maze, there was a bower with honeysuckle and other creeping plants overlooking the tennis court.

That evening I sat with Douglas on the swing-seat within the trellised shadows of the arbour.

The fringes of our fingers were touching. I felt an electrical charge passing between us.

A crescent moon rocked gently in the cradle of a pine crest.

Above us, in the twilight, hung yellow roses so brilliant that for a moment I'd almost mistaken them for lanterns. Beyond the rhododendrons, the chalk lines of the tennis court glowed in the dusk, and I glimpsed a pair of bats dipping low over the net.

I nestled on Douglas's shoulder as he talked of warring Dayak tribesmen.

'When drums speak out, laws hold their tongues,' he said gravely, puffing on his pipe.

'In a remote place of flies and midges men don't need permission to smoke,' he added thoughtfully in parenthesis, striking another match.

Suddenly I felt Douglas's shoulders stiffen and he slowly reached down and I saw his hand close on a large windfall apple, which with a lightning move he hurled into the darkness.

There was a yelp of pain from the shrubbery and Boy emerged.

'Listen, chummy,' Douglas drawled, 'there's a difference between staring and being stark blind.'

Douglas was a crack shot with a sporting rifle; he could shoot the eye out of a mosquito, or so he claimed. And he also said he slept with his eyes open like a hare.

'What do you want here?' Boy asked in a shrill quavering voice.

'Your sister,' Douglas boomed.

'No one wants to marry a quaint old thing in a poke bonnet,' Boy sneered. 'Besides,' he continued, 'Mummy says she would not let a daughter of hers marry a Roman Candle.'

It was true. Mother and Boy had got up a whispering campaign against me when they had learned Douglas was a Roman Catholic.

Boy ran off up the path, shouting, 'She's got it bad, Mummy! She's got it bad!'

'Sawn off little runt,' I heard Douglas mutter.

'What did you expect?' my brother grinned evilly, when the next evening my new beau arrived looking glum. 'Rosaries all the way?'

I thought, *'A deceitful truce is more unnerving than a declared war.'*

❁

'That's all very fine and large,' Mother said sourly, when the matter of marriage was broached, 'but what are you going to do for money?'

Our painful argument over tea was prologue to a worse supper, without even the solace of a bath before bedtime.

Since her widowhood, Mother had professed to being inconsolable and she'd insisted on sharing my bed, for no good reason other than a childlike reluctance to sleep alone.

One night, I awoke to find her wildly clutching at my hair.

Her explanation was as bizarre as her actions. She'd been dreaming of an old nanny of hers who was famed in the county for having saved from drowning two children when the *Lusitania* sank. According to legend, the nanny had unloosed her braided hair and ordered her little charges to cling to her plaits for dear life until they were rescued.

Later, as my mother slept, I lay awake pondering on how few lifelines of my own I foresaw in a future of desponding hopelessness.

For the remainder of his leave Douglas and I continued meet, but those first hesitant kisses had declined into token pecks before our customary drive to the country club.

That Douglas recognised my plainness and lack of sex appeal was evident in the excessive vacuity of our smalltalk on the evening of his return overseas.

'It's a decentish bar,' Douglas said with a nod of approval.

'It's the smartest bar by far,' I replied loyally on cue.

Not until the savoury arrived was I to choke on his next pronouncement.

Douglas cleared his throat: 'I cannot be your friend and your flatterer, too, you know.'

Business-like, he then proposed that during his 'tours of duty' to follow we should correspond by 'special rate' aerogrammes and wait until, in his own words, 'we discovered the true depth of feelings' we held for each other.

Yes, that was his *proposal*.

The next day, after we parted at the airport, I bought my own engagement ring as a hedge against his inconstant, sometimish attitude. I practised the signature I foolishly believed one day would be mine. *Mary Sherrard.*

Now, of that long engagement (Oh! So long!), all I can summon from the grey ruins of memory is a bundle of airmail letters (Oh! So many!) crammed into a shoebox.

How many you ask? We wrote twice a week and one-hundred-and-sixty of Douglas's letters weighed a pound. I know this fact because I weighed a mere fraction of our correspondence once, when aggrieved, on old Mr Sherrard's grocer's scales, which did not give short measure.

And, unlike my detractors, Mr Sherrard had refused to pour scorn on the unconventionality of a love affair conducted with his son as a correspondence course. But then, did you know that Tchaikovsky had a very intellectual and emotional correspondence for about twenty years with a certain Madame von Meck? And *they* met not once!

Mother had concluded that Douglas was a shellbacked reactionary who'd never marry, so to defy her I started to earn money for my trousseau chest by accepting a job as an assistant in Douglas's family store:

Sherrard & Son
High-Class Family Grocers • Fancy Drapery & Silk Mercers
Telephone 37
No Order Too Small

As the manageress of the Sherrard haberdashery I soon developed the neutral warmth of manner that identifies the better class of saleswoman.

My saleswomanship was never obsequious but I showed proper deference to those of breeding who warranted it, and I made a special study of colour harmony so my advice to my customers would carry conviction.

Even in my earliest years at the shop there seemed to be no limit to the number of shades to each colour. In blue alone there were over sixty shades of silk—sky blue, baby blue, cornflower blue, powder blue, Alice blue, Shetland blue, midnight blue—and it was up to me to pick out the colour that would most suit my customer.

'Would you like something in a restful blue,' I might say and I'd show her a better-quality, higher-priced line that was 'a little more', since old Mr Sherrard had taught me never to say 'dearer'.

The shop was double-fronted and, in quiet periods, Sherrard *père* would shake the flour off his hands to 'cross the floor', so to speak, from the dry-goods counter to preside over the fancy linens and sewing requisites where he metamorphosed into a lace-unfurling draper.

Under his kindly tutelage I learned which shades suited blondes and which suited brunettes. The true blonde, I learned, can find her colouring quite ruined by vivid orange or cerise.

Browns, greens, and autumnal tints seem to enhance the muted glow of the sallow-eyed, auburn-haired woman, such as myself.

On the other hand, a woman with a high complexion can look positively lurid in violet or purple. My mother can be cited as a precedential case.

Mother, who rarely rode, once marched into the shop in her pre-war ride-astride skirt, her complexion even more florid than the flush of the hunting field. She was wearing a hat of a hideous bishop's purple.

'Have you a veil to match this?' she demanded peremptorily, addressing old Mr Sherrard and ignoring me.

'No!' I wanted to shout. *'No, we haven't! And if we had, I'd burn it!'*

Who was my most awkward customer? Why, my mother, of course.

Some years later, when attending to one or two commissions in the High Street shops, Mother paid another rare visit, just before Early Closing, strutting like a pouter-pigeon into the store.

I had a raging headache; the fluorescent tubes above the counter often caused me to fall into a depression.

On that day Mother wore primrose yellow stockings she'd dyed herself, and on her hat a pale yellow hydrangea fashioned from artificial silk.

She selected from my display case a skein of green embroidery thread.

'Do buck up, dear,' she chided loudly. 'You're so listless . . . so lifeless . . . why must you be so drear?'

I felt at that moment I was still held fast by her apron-strings and experienced an all-compelling desire to throttle her with them.

She yawned, her pointed tongue protruding like a gargoyle's.

I was so desolated by her heartlessness I began to quietly weep.

'Any more of that, my girl, and you'll remain a mope-eyed spinster!'

At Mother's words, old Mr Sherrard's head jerked up from his account book and he studied us both steadily over his bifocals.

'You need not marry,' Mother said with chilling calculation meant for him to hear, 'you have troubles enough without it.'

Sure enough, that afternoon, I saw Boy crossing the rickyard wearing a sports shirt designed by Fred Perry, the famous tennis champ. I noticed Mother, under my brother's direction, had all unwittingly embroidered a marijuana leaf over the laurel wreath trademark on the breast pocket, a direct slur I considered on the reputation of Douglas who was singles champion at our village club.

Boy knew perfectly well how I first met Douglas, from that auspicious day I returned home from a match with a tennis ball I'd mistaken for my own.

Douglas had written his name on it in indelible ink: DE SHERRARD (the 'E' stood for Eric, I was to learn eventually, of course, but at first I'd been willing to believe the 'de' was the nobiliary particle, because Douglas was such a perfect gentleman). I have the ball still.

Boy had been spiteful as a child; now as a youth he acted as he would when an adult, who'd sooner revenge an injury than return a kindness.

Later, after returning from an early evening canter with Clara, I overheard Wilkes talking to my brother as they led Dinah into a loose box.

'. . . An' them girls wearin' britches so tight,' Wilkes leered, 'tweren't a midge's wing betwin the seat of thar pants and thar birthday suits.'

I heard him slap Dinah on the cruppers.

'An' take tha' sister of yourn. She's a rare kiddy. And don't she smell justabout good? The things tha' girl has had give her! French scent and clo'es enough to fit out a lady seven times over.'

'Shut up!' I heard Boy say fiercely in a low, strained voice. 'Shut up, damn you! Leave my sister out of it!'

But Wilkes blithely continued; there was no stopping him.

'Now thar's an angel to find under a blanket in all her born nekkedness afore her white wings is sprouted. I would give I dunnamuch money to be the first, afore she walks out with some feller. I don't say as I ever arst her proper-like, but 't'would be a singular man who'd bed her, 'cos he'd ne're get an answer out of her but a grunt.'

My brother's whip cracked on flesh.

A hoarse curse. 'Dammee!' Then Wilkes, grinning ruefully, came into the yard. A livid welt striped his cheek.

'Unaccountable cruel, I reckon, little childern can be, missy,' he blustered. 'On my word, something cruel and mischiefful, an' carrying tales tha' be tarrible untrue.'

'I daresay,' I said cooly.

'Goo'night, missy. An' may every hair on yore head be as a wax candle to light you to glory.'

Tiresome Freudianisms

A half hour afterwards, when I'd changed, I strolled down to the stable yard to water Dinah and to freshen her feed and bedding.

That summer evening, I remember, I wore absinthe-green Capri pants, and a baggy, shapeless Breton pullover, with broad stripes, belonging to Douglas to whom, like his sweaters, I was then still sentimentally attached.

When I first entered the stables and saw Miles Orme, at once something seemed out of place somehow, like a blacksmith in a white silk apron.

On the lapel of his school blazer above his prefect's badge was another embossed with the ironical legend: *'Junkies Against Drugs'*.

His sighted eye—lustreless, and seemingly pupilless—was focused on a leaf spiralling at the end of a spider's web. He was staring with such supernaturally exaggerated interest that he did not hear me enter.

'Where's Boy?' I asked in the soothing voice I used for Dinah in tests of obedience that had won us any number of rosettes.

The eye he turned on me was that of a gangling dilettantish day-dreamer; speculative, and of a distempered vision I'd seen in unhealthy dogs.

'Easing his bladder in the bushes.' He shrugged.

A liar must have a good memory, I thought. That evening, my last sighting of Boy was in the lane; he'd been carrying bunches of dandelion leaves for his rabbits and a heavy acid-cell battery for Mother's wireless he'd had recharged at the village garage.

At that moment a pair of girlish legs in tight breeches descended the ladder from the hayloft, and Boy scrambled down after them.

'Horrid little boy,' laughed Clara. Her face was red and she rebuttoned her waist-band with flustered haste; she had the waist of a greyhound. Her lips were as bright and defined as the finest embroidery.

Boy passed his fingers through her hair, which like my own was tied back in that summer's ubiquitous ponytail. Clara responded with the absurd simpering of a burlesque queen.

'What's up, Zizzy?' my brother enquired knowingly. 'Off yer oats?'

Since that brief interlude of mourning, when for the space of a few summer days we'd been kindred spirits, he'd acted towards me like some carrot-crunching rustic.

My brother's mockery was licence enough for Miles to resume the goading.

'No sight finer than your sister in her fancy rig-out,' he said, with a smirk in his voice.

'You betcha,' said Boy.

Clara caught my eye and came to my rescue.

'Oh, do sit down, darling, you're so damnedly *unbending*! Sit down *do*.' She patted a hay bale skittishly. 'They're both high as kites on the dreaded devilweed, and your brother's chattering is driving me simply scats.'

'Speak for yourself,' Boy retorted and sat down beside her.

(There was some truth in my brother's remark. 'Little Miss Busty,' was how Mother had once pithily dismissed Clara. 'She talks for England and goes in first.')

Miles, Boy and Clara were now seated together on the hay bales. They all ruched up to make a space for me.

I could not countenance another broadside from my brother nor, for that matter, could I suffer Clara labelling me an old maid, so of those two evils I chose the least and sat down beside her.

But Boy at once nudged Miles.

'Zizzy thinks she's too good for us now she's become a naughty man's plaything.'

Since Boy as a baby had first cried in the night, boding no good, I'd endured his ceaseless narking remarks, and now I winced inwardly and drew a deep breath.

Miles's hand rested weakly on my shoulder to draw me close.

'Your friend,' he whispered dreamily, indicating Clara, 'she's a nice looking filly and frisky enough, but balls-achingly tiresome. Now, you, on the other hand, a woman of *means* . . . how would you like to play Vatican Roulette with *me*?'

Men, I had noticed, never thought to ask me how I was; they always seemed greedy to ask me what I *had*.

My hair had been fair when a child but now it was as nondescript as dust, yet I improvised and pretended to be a dizzy blonde for five minutes, a stratagem which I find invariably disarms. I was aware men began to suspect my sincerity if I laid it on with a trowel so I'd coached myself to surrender the briefest account of myself. On this occasion, however, my playfulness of demeanour seemed only to excite his ardent-eyed intentions to an overboiling flood, because he fell against me, forcing me to the ground.

'Lay off, will you!' shouted Boy harshly.

I twisted half around as Boy and Miles fought over me like puppies. I felt a pawing under my loosened clothes as I attempted to struggle to my feet.

But, before I could stand, I found myself stumbling on a crocked ankle into the thick of the *mêlée*.

'Think again, Zizzy!' Their cracked voices yelled gleefully. 'Let's have a looksee!'

Hands again swarmed over me like a nest of spiders.

(Art critics will remember the calculated perversity of Boy's earliest lithographs. One notorious print shows a reclining nude, an odalisque, whose sensuous curves are defined by a tract of virgin white paper fringed by a hundred probing black fingertips to enclose her form. Even the memory of the repellent thing still makes my flesh creep.)

Now in the stables, Clara's cheeks had changed colour, as though her face had been dipped in milk.

'Some best friend you are!' I accused Clara in a half-sob, and I thought of all the priests and guilt-instillers who'd regulated my life, when all I'd ever wanted was a scandal-proof existence free of any tiresome Freudianisms.

I found myself gripping Boy's hands together with an intensity that hurt.

An uprush of self-hatred consumed me and, in an evil moment, I threw him to the ground as though I were a mare he'd treated as his lash-horse.

'Get out!' I yelled. 'Get out, and take your ludicrous sidekick with you!'

'Shut your mouth or I'll belt you one again!'

Boy was still cursing when Miles seized his arm and pulled him away.

I seemed to be tasting the bitter lees of a once young wine and knew our childhood was over.

Miles slunk off; I made a mental note to avoid him in future.

'Good night, Miss Emma!' he called, doffing an imaginary cap. 'Good night, Mary Jane.' (Only much later did I learn from Clara that Miles was referring to Boy's morphine and marijuana habit and not to ourselves.)

Clara had risen, consumed by a silent fit of nervous giggling.

She was now wearing a snazzy flyaway swagger coat with coquettish pockets on each side. She drew Boy's arm through hers.

'Love grows bitter with treason,' I thought pityingly, *'and is only sweet for a day.'*

As Boy passed through the door I raised my fist and limped after him.

'Seeya around, Zizzy!' Boy laughed lightly, his eyes unblinking.

When they had gone I clambered up to the hayloft above the stalls.

The place smelled of an earlier year's harvest of sweet apples, with an admixture of Clara's patchouli-oil and pungent scents from the tobacco leaves Wilkes had dried there. The loft had been a child's haven, a place of innocence hidden from the grown-ups where, after so many bitter winters of post-war rationing, we'd sensed the dark clouds lifting to herald a new dawn of bright comic books and pink bubble gum, even though Wilkes continued to grow his own tobacco plants on the vegetable patch behind the farmhouse.

I was staring at the bower of straw where my brother and Clara had lain when Wilkes's head emerged from the hatch.

'There was a bit of a to-do and hurly-balloo about it,' said Wilkes with a wink, 'but don't tell me she don't want it.'

He spoke with the same relish he'd voiced when showing me the sickly lambs.

There's only one choice, I thought, when the whole stock is bad.

And, then and there, I decided to live my life by an avowed rule to remain childless.

Le Petit Peintre Maudit

Very shortly after those alarums and scarums, to Mother's dismay and my relief, Boy ran away to sea.

We learned Boy had attempted to enlist in the Royal Navy. He'd been refused due to a defect in his vision so he'd signed up for the Merchant arm instead.

Wilkes was the first to remark on the strange coincidence whereby the colouration of my brother's eyes accorded with maritime law.

Wilkes had met the postman at the gate and, as he approached, I saw he was insolently reading Boy's postcard from Portsmouth.

My face fell. I'd thought he'd brought a letter from Douglas.

'Brat's gorn to Pompey, certain, missy,' Wilkes gloated.

Then he shook his head.

'It'll be a great game, this, missy.' Then he added darkly, ''Course, sailors don't know one vice from t'other. Nor wheat from corn, nor wrong from right, nor right from left, reckon.'

He pointed to his right eye.

'Wi' one green eye for starboard, jest one look at yore brother's mug'll leastways learn 'em a lesson they'll not be fergittin' in a hurry.'

I read the card addressed to Mother; it was signed, 'Your affectionate son'.

My brother must have fancied himself to be another Rimbaud, I concluded from those brief impetuous scribblings, rejecting art for adventure, thinking he'd leave his teenage excesses behind him . . . *le petit peintre maudit*, in self-exile like the accursed poet.

Nothing had prepared Mother for Boy's absence and there were fewer and fewer lucid intervals in the settled apathy to which she then succumbed.

She refused all entreaties to permit the doctor to call; cantankerousness was her nature. I remember she had decidedly cranky views on infant health. If roadmenders were working in the street, for example, she would in my infancy make a point of swinging me over the bubbling tar vat to vent my chest with the bitumen fumes. No wonder I feared the *Brer Rabbit* stories.

Her malaise was relieved only by her consuming passion for our family's genealogy.

She had traced our Huguenot ancestors as far back as the ninth century to a warlord who'd guarded the entrance to the pavilion of Charlemagne, where the barons and the noblest knights were tented. Despite my mother's fiercest efforts, however, she had been unable to pursue our noble lineage further than the threshold of the tent flaps, yet she remained convinced we were descended from a race of visionaries and believed there was more than sufficient evidence to warrant the belief.

Agreed, there was a certain romance in my mother's tales. She liked to retail the escape of one of my ancestors after the Revocation of the Edict of Nantes when he fled as a fugitive across the frontier through the unfrequented defiles of the Pyrénées disguised as a shepherd, and with his sabots stuffed with moss.

Indeed, the mock-heroic 'shepherd' was to prove a motif that would reappear in the conduct of the fugitive's descendants, even down to the present day.

That is to say: in her make-believe pastoral, my mother bore the same relation to *farmers* as Louis XVI and Marie Antoinette to *shepherds* and *shepherdesses* in the rusticised hamlet they made their pleasureground at Versailles.

With such singular fantasies as these occupying her mind Mother took to her bed.

The application of sal volatile was to no avail, and at night she would awake in fits of inexpressible agitation so my nerves became thoroughly unstrung.

Late one night, bewildered and fearful, I kept her talking in her delirium until our GP could be sent for. I'd discovered her seated in a bubble bath, fully dressed, and when at last the doctor arrived, in his pyjamas, I had to find a complete change of clothes. Fortunately, Mother always kept an 'understudy dress' in reserve, in case of an emergency, so I was able to coax her into an identical afternoon frock she'd last worn at a Royal Garden Party.

She'd had them both run up in fabric from one of our poorer-quality lines . . . now they'd faded to a lightish beige. I'd warned her they would fade in the wash.

When the doctor persuaded her to accompany him in his car to the hospital she turned to me and said in a furious tirade, 'Why must you tell such lies, Mary? Didn't I say they wouldn't fade!'

At the hospital she was sedated and detained under the Mental Health Act.

❁

So I continued in the same quiet occupation, visiting mother, supervising the shop and running the farm.

'Your every line is nectar,' Douglas wrote from Borneo. 'Dearest, I have been a bit seedy. I'm a famished wretch and quite lost without your company.'

He hinted at a 'spot of bother up country', and in words disconnected he wrote of the stirrings of his Kaffir-pot as though he were still back in Kenya, which had been his first posting. I was troubled by the weakness of so few rambling details and their utter triviality.

At night I dreamt of Boy's ship foundering, dead eyes under.

One morning, very early, I was awakened by a scream and ran down to the lawn to see a fox tormenting a frog. I'd had no idea a frog could scream.

Boy had once caught a fox cub. Its teeth were like a row of pins. He'd caged it near his hutches to frighten his rabbits.

The frog was seemingly unharmed so I placed it near the rushes by the lily pond.

The scent of the fox still hung in the dawn mist and I tracked its paw-prints in the dew to my brother's long abandoned rabbitry. Between the hutches the odour was more intense, and I remembered how Boy would feed his rabbits on scraps from our table and old tea leaves.

His practice was to empty the leaves from the teapot into a jar he kept by the kitchen sink, until late one night he'd surprised our housemaid salvaging them in her own container for reuse by the parish poor who lived in the tenements at the far end of the village. Boy had remained silent following his discovery, but next day he'd had the maid dismissed on a trumped-up charge of theft, when he accused her of stealing a coin he'd planted himself on the backstairs.

I shuddered at this recollection of my brother's gross deceits, which pressed upon my mind the full weight of his other betrayals. I felt the little hairs on my forearms and nape rise.

His very presence seemed to fill the air I breathed, so when I returned to the house I was not altogether surprised to smell a wisp of a familiar tobacco odour, just as the first threads of mist can whisper one's fear before the approach of a storm.

In the kitchen Boy looked up and stared at me intently (if you dared to look into his eyes for long you'd notice his irises were black-rimmed). He was razor thin and smoking one of his marijuana cigarettes—his 'African Woodbines' he called them.

I felt a maddening desire to shriek aloud. I shivered and clutched the collar of my dressing gown closer to my throat.

In a voice husky and low with menace he said, 'Look at you! You look about as innocent as a tart at a christening!'

You can sense the threat of domestic violence. It's like the powerful hum you hear from those electric sub-stations in the suburbs, discreetly screened by flimsy rustic fences. With slow deliberation Boy opened the jar of honey I'd set on the table for sweetening my breakfast tea.

'You've been rumbled, Zizzy.'

He paused and stared insolently at me and then resumed licking out the honeypot with his little finger.

'I don't understand.'

'I've just had a most illuminating little chat with Mummy at the funny farm.'

'The devil you did! What did she say exactly?'

Boy threw back his head and closed his eyes as if to better recall a cruel jest.

'Her exact words were: "When I return home I don't want to find Miss Sourpuss there casting a spell over the place. After what she's done she is no daughter of mine."'

I felt I was being lied to, and I sensed a metallic taste in my mouth, as though my teeth had closed on a counterfeit coin.

'She's coming home, you say? So *you* intend to cook her meals, do you?'

'It's a stroll, doll,' he said.

I reminded Boy of his fecklessness. At a pinch, he could maybe whistle up a scratch meal for Mother, say a mixed grill with devilled kidneys, but a balanced diet was quite beyond his abilities. I also stated bluntly, drawing on past experience, that when he was drugged silly, on one of his euphoric 'highs', one could not expect his powers of reasoning to be otherwise than low.

He at once gave tongue to an incoherent rant, a series of blistering quarterdeck expletives as crazed as chain lightning.

'D'you think we'd listen to you?' he raved, shaking his fist preparing to strike. 'You! *You* with a mouth tighter than a witch's . . .' but at that moment Mother walked in.

My brother led her to her customary chair. A thronelike perpetration covered in purple brocade he'd bought her long before he'd shipped out.

So there Mother sat, a sullen haunch of cold mutton, viewing me with undisguised disdain.

'Liar!' she said, narrowing her eyes. 'Liars end up deceiving themselves, and until you learn that lesson, my girl, there's no penalty in this world that can be punishment enough.'

Boy grinned smugly and handed me the empty honey pot.

Banishment

In consequence of my mother's return there were changes in the household arrangements.

When I remind you that mother and son had been hand in glove since Boy's birth—and I've dwelt upon their most striking peculiarities—I trust you'll *believe* these final broken sentences of mine; as I strive to describe the last epoch of my life; these hesitant words are *not* the product of an excited imagination.

For there now followed an unusual day, during which the pair conceived a plan whereby they'd subsist by selling off plots of land to augment the new council housing estate, then marching up the hill from the village.

My father's last wishes to transmit the paternal acres to his children were interpreted by Mother as though the right of male primogeniture had never ceased to exist, and thus I lost my hereditament and was humbled once more by their denial of my *firstness* . . . a fledgling dispossessed of the nest.

One of Mother's first actions was to send for Wilkes on quarter day.

'As for Boots,' my mother said to Boy grimly (she referred to Wilkes as her 'Boots'), 'one may well keep a thing for seventeen years until one finds a use for it, but in the case of Wilkes, I think *not.*'

So after seventeen years' service Wilkes was dismissed on Michaelmas Day, and I, Mary, Our Lady of All Sorrows, was banished to the tied cottage from which Wilkes was expelled.

'Yore ma 'ud skin a rat for its hide,' Wilkes said to me after our dismissal.

''T'was a reg'lar oration,' he added as he carted my belongings across the yard. 'P'raps, arter all, we're a mort happier somewheres quiet.' Wilkes seemed to accept this new turn of events philosophically, I was relieved to learn. 'There's always those as is never happy 'cept when they're findin' fault wi' folk.'

'At any rate, there are two less of us to take to task,' I laughed, 'now we've both been sent packing.' I asked him what his future held.

'Folks is makin' an unaccountable fuss 'bout lads leavin' the land. But there's big money up in Lunnon. Look at yore brother. He've bin all round the world an' sin all manner o' things an' here's me, like a sparrer wi' clipped wings.'

A sudden shower drove us into the cottage.

'If I had my time over agin, I'd git out o' this place an' see a bit o' life.'

'I'll not be hounded out of my own home.'

'Well, there's no accountin'.' He gave the suspicion of a sigh. 'Best shift yore pianna afore the mistruss puts the bailiffs in.'

Father's piano was the one article of my patrimony I would take with me to my new home. Wilkes nodded in the direction of Boy who, impatient to see me dispatched, stood at the farmhouse door, surveying my little stock of baggage I'd dragged to the porch.

'If you was to arst me, girly, you can't help tha' brat 'cos he don't help himself an', if anythin' happens to yore ma, he'll feel the miss of her, certain.'

For myself, I felt—none too soon—I was cutting the ties that bound me to Mother and I was at last standing apart from the apron.

❁

Classical tragedy, according to Douglas, should be composed of five acts and have three main characters of noble birth. Well, I've dealt with three phases of my early life, which leaves only two brisk acts to follow. I think, by now, the three ignoble principals are known to you, so I shall allow myself the space of these few remaining pages to wonder at the extent of human credulity, and to smile awhile at the madness I hereditarily possess.

❁

So numbed were my emotions by this banishment, so deeply did I take to heart my family's rejection, it appears to me that a very long interval of years elapsed before I quite collected my senses, so I can take but imperfect note of time.

Of all those lost years the return of Douglas from the Tropics is, perhaps, most vividly brought to mind. I refer to his final aerogramme from his palmoil plantation in which he informed me that, years after his first posting to Kenya during a mild malaria outbreak, he'd 'bought a packet of the same trouble' when exploring for his company a malarious forest region of Borneo.

In the rains his malaria tablets had dissolved in his jacket pocket. Teeth chattering, dehydrated and near to death due to constant diarrhoea, he was saved by his nightwatchman—a witchdoctor—who'd treated him with herbal antimalarial cough drops consisting of dried snakewort. 'Now I can't trust the company's own medical men,' Douglas wrote, 'tho' they say if I am to be restored to my former health I must lay off the juju jujubes because there's no known antidote!'

On the day of his return I went to meet him at the farm gate.

At the entrance to our lane my father had erected a sign:

PRIVATE VERGES.
No Admittance.

As a teenager, standing at that exact spot, I'd once observed my French tutor passing the same sign. I'd heard him snicker delightedly: *'Les vierges privées! Hélas! Vive l'Angleterre!'*

That my virginity, long preservèd, was intended as my private tribute to a reluctant fiancé at his homecoming is, nonetheless, perfectly true. I was quite confident that the intimate conjunction of minds Douglas and I had once enjoyed would survive our everlasting engagement.

So there I stood, untainted by impurity, and there soon arrived Douglas, driven in a taxi . . . *my Douglas* whose appearance was so altered by time that I hardly recognised him.

A convalescent nursed by a herbalist in a waterlogged village in the heart of the Borneo rain forest is an unlikely lover, and equally, no doubt, Douglas regarded me as an improbable object of desire, not that *desire* was exactly his forte, since one the great evils of blackwater fever is impotency.

The day of his return we became lovers of a kind . . . notionally, at least.

'Nothing doing,' Douglas sighed. I felt a feeble pulse, as of a foamless wave, and Douglas groaned.

'The spirit's unwilling, darling, confound it. In future, I fear, you must take the will for the deed.'

In truth, my unweddable fiancé's redundant 'wedding tackle' (Douglas's term) had puckered and shrunk, and nestled quite passively in my palm like one of those drowned worms you see in the base of a tequila bottle.

I resorted to every guileful expedient to conceal my distaste but from the day of our reunion I saw clearly that, unlike Poe's 'Berenice', it was not a *disease* my family had transmitted down the generations but a legacy of *sexual guilt*, and in time I lost my longing.

❀

The new drug the pharmacy dispenses from my latest scrip has, so I'm told, the effect of deadening the patient's auditory sensitivity.

Nevertheless, my charm bracelet chatters, *chink-chink*, not unlike a chaffinch perched on my wrist (my flesh is blackened from sterling silver reacting to the acidity of my skin).

Each 'lustrum' (Father's legalese for a half-decade), on my birthday, Father would affix a new charm to the chain . . . an inscribed cross for Faith, a gold heart for Charity, an anchor for Hope . . . and even the gold five-roubles coin the Russian captain bestowed.

In some extreme cases, the persistence of filial love, particularly daughterly devotion, knows no bounds, and after my father died I maintained the tradition and continued to attach a new charm on the anniversary of his death . . . an aeroplane . . . a violin . . . and, more recently, a tiny chastity belt fastened with an even tinier padlock.

Now I walk around my tied cottage like a belled cat.

But oppressed, as I was, by the strange alteration in my circumstances, I was not so unwise as to dare call attention to my presence by the merest sound when observing the farmyard and my brother's activities through my peephole in Wilkes's pantry, a brass grille on the inside of an air brick. Nor did I allow any light to shine to alert Boy to my observation post.

Indeed, a strict watch I kept upon his movements, yet, as the lustrums flew by, and I advanced in years, I experienced no relief from a thousand conflicting anguishes, in which depressive moods and periods of forgetfulness and confusion were predominant; not least because all went well with Boy who, having inherited his estate, lived like a lord unburdened by any weight of anxiety for simply years and years and years.

And watch him I did, with—I admit—an unhealthy interest, though, despite his antics as an irreclaimable drunkard and cocainist, the idea of his death never once entered my brain.

During all those years my piano and my jigsaw puzzles consoled me.

I have no patience with kitchen-sink novels and their oh-so-tidily milled-down reality nor with powder-and-wig bodice-ripping romances. No, a jigsaw puzzle allows the mind to float free. A famous mathematician, you know, was a jigsaw addict and believed in the therapeutic power of ludic rituals that energise the mind. However, a recent case of a notorious kidnapping of little girls revealed the abductor to be a jigsaw enthusiast.

So my fate having been decided, I settled into my new quarters. The place was scrubbed and stripped of all furniture but I furnished it well enough; there were few relics of Wilkes's tenancy to speak of all his years at the cottage.

Tucked away inside the fusebox I found an unopened packet of rubber preventatives and Wilkes's childhood Sunday School Attendance Book with stamps of biblical scenes stuck into blanks for every Sunday attended. I noticed the unbroken series of his good attendance record had ended where the School Superintendent had written, in the third Sunday of Epiphanytide, *'Absent, father dcd'*. The note was followed by ten remaining blank pages of absenteeism. A lump formed in my throat. Poor Wilkes must have been twelve, I guessed, when his father died, and boy and man he had laboured in the fields ever since.

My brother, on the other hand, was a stranger to diligent work. Yes, he laboured over his paintings, but too much care in the opinion of his tutors was as bad as downright negligence and Boy was awarded a third-class degree. His obsessive, overworked canvases and his gloopy impasto technique—the colour and consistency of mushy green peas—had found favour only with Professor Deverill-Hewells, the court painter, under whose patronage Boy for a brief term flourished.

The 'Prof' was said to have 'more opinions than the Queen has soldiers,' Boy once repeated admiringly.

But Boy scoffed at his other art college tutors and seriously maintained that one of his professoresses, a celebrated novelist and philosopher who actually died only the other day, tragically from Alzheimer's, was, in fact, clinically colour blind.

'Can you imagine it? Listening to that woman declaiming on art,' I believe he said, or else he chose similar words. 'It was like a guided tour of a brewery organised by the Sally Army!'

I don't think the general public is aware that art for art's sake is a privileged pursuit often underwritten by family trust funds or that, immediately after the Second Great War, art was considered a gentleman's profession very like the practice of publishing, and infested with remittance men.

The Audit of Fame remains a book that begs to be written by an aesthetical chartered accountant. I repeat, had not Mother progressively sold off parcels of land from my father's estate—including Wilkes's prized vegetable plot—Boy would not have had the wherewithal to mount his one-man exhibitions, nor would he have garnered that minor entry in the current guides to British artists, under 'H' (my maiden name is the sole inheritance we share).

Mother had fitted out a studio for Boy's student vacations in the double garage where father had once moth-balled his two Bentleys. The broad doorway had been sheeted with glass to admit the north light.

Once, at the South Kensington Civic Museum of Antiquities, my brother showed me a private entrance to his art college next door. The arch opened on to a broad flight of stairs where the stairwell and pillars were decorated with glazed ceramic vine leaves entwining incribed panels dedicated to Aristotle, Galileo, Newton and Linnæus, above which were two tablets, *Honos, Salus*. I was impressed by these secret backstairs in a public building, and envious of Boy's evident freedom to roam those galleries with an unchallenged *entrée* into an exclusive world to which my own access was denied.

I cannot help remarking, however, that Boy's secret world was not entirely closed to me because his work in his studio was directly within view of my covert spyhole, so none of his nocturnal transactions escaped my notice.

Open a chink and daylight will peep through the smallest hole.

Boy could often be seen late at night dividing the dibs with two tattooed lunkheaded junkies who I'd hear chattering like pied-magpies through the wall.

Douglas had warned me about my brother's police record for drug offences. Boy claimed to have left no trace of his dodgy activities after his naval discharge but Douglas had made some discreet enquiries and hinted otherwise.

'He has a file so thick that only a very long arm can begin to circle the bulk of it.'

So you can guess the Long Arm to which Douglas referred.

Douglas was more amused than outraged by Boy's antics at sea. I learned my brother had been demoted, confined to ship at Aden, and denied shore leave for 'serious crumpeteering'. On his second sea trip, the shipmaster purported to be on the lookout for a personable lad to squire his daughter (photo of decoy furnished) as his 'protégé' for preferential elevation to first Mate. The crew took Boy aside advising him that the captain had been practising this chicanery with the same fake photo for a number of years, and had duped some takers into signing on for many more voyages—Boy wasn't one of them; he jumped ship at Perth and was arrested outside a hotel, so he related to Douglas, for the crime of 'possession of a suitcase without a rear light'.

When he was frogmarched aboard, Boy said he could hear the crew laughing five decks down in their quarters.

My brother's devil-may-care escapades as the Wild Colonial Boy did not cease when he returned to shore.

He continued in the same madcap, lawless manner, finding among the younger tenants of the newly constructed council houses a willing clientele for his drug dealing. In short, Boy became the friendly neighbourhood dope pusher—the local 'Candyman'—for whose transgressions I hold myself indirectly responsible.

How?

Like a generation of women who were prescribed amphetamine-based pills for weight reduction as teenagers, I was aware that dextroamphetamine diet pills had all the properties of 'speed', the kind of performance-enhancing 'go-pill' issued to pilots or the military on long missions to assist their remaining focused and alert.

Shortly after my father's death I was prescribed Dexedrine, my 'black bombers', for pubescent obesity.

In the third week of treatment I was alarmed to notice the depletion of my 'Dexes', and suspected Mother—herself overweight—of the theft.

The true culprit, of course, was my brother, then eleven years old.

'I can explain everything,' he protested when I caught him reaching into my bedroom cabinet. Well, his theft certainly explained his heightened aggression and sparkly-eyed hyperactivity as a youth.

'Qui s'excuse, s'accuse!' I shouted. 'Shut up, will you! For *once*, shut up! When you *excuse* yourself you *accuse* yourself, and this time there are no excuses!'

Boy never satisfactorily explained that episode, so I can only assume it was yet another example of how he always yielded freely to childish temptations, by way of experiment, like his appetite for toadstools.

Later, as I have intimated, he brazenly smoked his 'Mexican hay' around the farm, in the presence of my ever-complaisant mother, and even went so far as to sell quarter-ounce wraps of cannabis to a troupe of dusky Moroccan tumblers performing in a travelling circus pitched on the village green.

The scent of the circus lions had stirred memories of Kenya for Douglas, who while visiting the animal compound had observed Boy behind the cages weighing out some matchboxes of Moroccan hashish.

Afterwards, he'd overheard my brother's proud boasts.

'It was like selling refrigerators to the Eskimos,' he'd bragged, 'and even the strong man wept.'

Psychoses Passionels

One afternoon, as I crossed the farmyard, I noticed a young woman in a riding habit leaving my brother's studio and entering the house.

I hung back, unwilling to enter the farmhouse should Boy be at home. Where my mother was concerned, Boy saw to it that I was the last to know of anything amiss at home (you'll note that I still referred to the family farmhouse as 'home') and he'd forbidden me to approach the house without his consent. He'd once surprised me tidying mother's sitting room upstairs.

'I don't want you tear-arsing about cleaning our rooms, d'you hear?'

Now, drawing back into the shadows of the stables' entrance, I reflected on that first glimpse I'd caught of the girl, for I had seen that she was singularly like myself when young, both in contour of person and outline of feature.

The resemblance was uncanny; it was as though she'd perfected an imitation of myself. I recalled an odd remark of Clara's who'd only recently asked, 'Taking up riding again?' She had insisted she'd seen me in a riding habit entering the farm. *Did I have a double?*

A vigil of two hours in the cold was rewarded by the girl's reappearance wearing her street clothes and carrying a small suitcase in a bandaged hand.

I was aware my brother had a very effective method of ridding himself of an unwanted 'lady guest' from the previous night's carouse; he would send her off in the morning with a hundred pounds, say, to settle a gambling debt, or to square the account of one of his numerous dunning creditors, in the full expectation that the money would never reach them, and she would never return. But the poise and apparent character of this girl hinted she was somewhat different.

I saw there was a bruised and swollen mouth beneath the bright lipstick. She'd put a brave face on it. On closer inspection, I now recognised her as one of the girls from the steam laundry beyond the village.

I touched her sleeve encouragingly and cleared my throat to speak.

'I've worn myself to a shadow worrying about my . . .'

'*You* should worry!' she interrupted curtly. '*He's* the one who's got to be taken care of!' She dabbed her lower lip and winced. 'For *this* he's gonna be shot!'

She shrugged off my solicitude, glancing up at me curiously from beneath her long lashes.

'What's up wiv loverboy? All he wants is to spout halfbaked nonsense and drink himself even stupider at my expense.'

I shrank away from her as she began to explain in exhaustive detail the exact nature of their recent debaucheries, dwelling at length on the more objectionable scenes.

Unwilling, I listened, blushing in an agony of shame. I remembered all his former deeds of cruelty, my disgust rising into the bitterness of hatred.

Strangely, her account of Boy's sexual predilections recalled an incident long before in my own youth, when I'd attended a girl-guides' meeting on a chill autumn evening in the church meeting hall. The fumes from the coke stove had overcome our entire troop and when Boy arrived to accompany me home he'd encountered the rather bizarre scene of two dozen girls in uniform laid out in a dishevelled frieze, comatose, on the grassy border of the graveyard.

Certain details in the girl's account corresponded to this *tableau morte* and Boy's morbid preoccupation as a painter with the death-like passivity of his subjects. (He has a modest fame as a dab hand at the daubed *instantané*.)

However, I do not wish to trace the wayward course of my brother's profligacy here, nor his rooted habits of fetishism and vice. Rather, suffice to remark that, during all those years of exile from my rightful home, I became something of a connoisseur of *psychoses passionels*, as you'll maybe appreciate when the whole of my narrative is done.

After that ill-starred meeting, I dreamt regularly of a secret family of abnormal siblings, locked away by Mother, their features deformed by interbreeding, their eyes sightless, their faces blank and as mouthless as mayflies.

Just as they say that the eyes are the windows of the soul, so it could be said the soul of a house is revealed by its windows. That is all very well; but I believe, and this narrative does not contradict it, that the true spirit of a house is glimpsed very often through its front-door fanlight.

I would not have contended this notion had I not, one midnight watch, heard the approach of my brother from the lane.

A songbird is known by its note, and I recognised my brother's whistling at the end of the yard, and saw a familiar figure jauntily sauntering towards our gate. There was a half bottle of liquor in his hand, which he paused to polish off before falling heavily into a puddle that reflected a thrice-ringed poacher's moon. My brother dropped anchor at every pub in the village on Friday nights.

('A rough diamond, your bruvver,' that girl of his had observed through swollen lips. 'Or a half-cut one, at least.' Boy's twin gods, she affirmed, were alcohol and narcotics, and when he was 'bevvied up', she'd added, he was' . . . meaner than a cornered snake and twice as nasty.')

I glanced up through the illuminated glass panels in a semicircle above the farm's front door—they were like segments of a truncated orange—and espied Mother in her best starched nightgown descending the stairs to admit the prodigal son.

And next morning, when I forced open the front door and entered the house at dawn to enquire after Mother, what did I find?

In that huge farmhouse I'd imagined my mother and brother rattling about like the proverbial two peas in a pod, but I was mistaken. My mother lay pinioned on the bristly door mat, on which she had evidently toppled the previous night, while Boy still slept prone upon her mountainous breast.

'Sh-sh-shush! Don't wake him! Such tremendous larks!' she laughed. 'I should take a strap to him!'

So, with a whispered imprecation on Dr Freud, from off the vast mound of my over-indulgent mother I rolled her foundling son, still snoring like a prize pig, his breath strong enough to knock you down.

A Scarcity of Friendship

These days I find I can't even summon the strength to rise each morning, and I lie abed till noon, but that Saturday those Freudian grotesqueries at daybreak drove me into the fields to gulp fresh air.

It was one of those unseasonably warm, calm, and misty days and the sleeping land, dreaming in the sun, seemed to breathe with gentle prolonged exhalations.

I stood by the river bank under the withies. Reflections of mooring ropes dangled in the water, and I considered again how fate found Boy still dwelling in the mansion of my father, while I languished, an outcast of all outcasts most abandoned.

Behind me, in the lane, I could hear the bees haunting the linden flowers, and I admitted to myself a scarcity of friendship. I was aware I was subject to the wildest caprices, and prey to the most ungovernable fears. And I'd grown self-willed, a cause of serious disquiet for my few remaining friends.

Douglas—who, after all, had received very little compensation from his company—was, I discovered, practically penniless like myself. (His kidney failure, due to his dependency on snakewort, was deemed a self-inflicted condition and disqualified him for receipt of medical benefits. His savings, like mine, had dwindled frighteningly fast.)

For many years, I admit, yes, we'd conducted a sort of meretricious relationship, which had branded me, I suppose, as a species of 'kept woman', for there was a lighthearted understanding that we should assist each other financially from time to time, when low on funds.

Hence, when Douglas stole from the warmth of my bed in the small hours, I would often run to the piano to vocalise my penniless state in a patter song of my own devising. . . .

Lament of a Girl Led Astray

Put a tenner on the table as yer leavin',
Put a tenner on the table won'tcha, dear.
Put a tenner on the table if yer love me,
'Cos a girl 'as gotta live . . .
'Cos a girl 'as gotta live . . .
'Cos a girl 'as gotta live on more than
cold and *bit*ter beer.

Lament of a Girl Led Astray

© 2006 GJW/MRB/CIE

The mock pathos and jangling honky-tonk beerhall accompaniment had generally been productive of more than a tenner.

Then, a change fell upon all things, when, in the light of one exceedingly feeble dawn, he confessed he was leaving me for a younger, more provident woman.

'After traipsing after you all these years! You . . . you . . .' I stuttered, quite beside myself with anger. 'You . . . you . . .'

Douglas turned slowly at the threshold.

'Well?' There was a peculiar twist to his lips as if he were pleased to be hurting me.

'You . . . you . . . bally bastard!' I finally managed weakly.

He gave a derisive little laugh and slammed the door.

'I don't care a blind fig who she is,' I shouted after him senselessly, I was so angry, 'or a brass farthing for your petty fornications!'

Even now, his desertion, in retrospect—as I gazed in a reverie at the river's oozy bed—prompted a bitter taste in my mouth; his laughter had simply added wormwood to gall.

A factory hooter blared from the Sanitary Steam Laundry to rouse me.

From the upper meadow I could look down at the loading bays. I envied somehow the laundry-girls in their knotted kerchiefs, hair-curlers and factory clothes, strolling arms-linked carelessly in the sun.

A skein of clouds like geese in flight was reflected in the farm pond below, an ancient excavation contained by the remainant spoil of a cutting and embankment for a railway enterprise long abandoned.

From the marshes the distinctive sound of the lapwing—'peewit!'—seemed to call 'Biarritz-Biarritz!' and invite me to a rest cure.

Far beneath me, at the head of the valley, I saw Mother bowed at the farm's kitchen door. Mother would skim the cream for the feral cats she called, with a cloying insipidness, her 'little waifs and strays'.

My brother once went to Harrods with Miles Orme, and at Boy's urging, between them they bought a monkey. You could buy an elephant there in those days. Miles very soon tired of the novelty and Miles's father gave it to his stable lads who released it into the Members' Enclosure at the next race meeting. The unfortunate creature escaped into the woodlands and was shot next day by a gamekeeper who mistook it for a feral Siamese cat.

My mother was dreadfully upset and predictably raged at the keeper instead of blaming the bad seed of her litter, young Master Sly.

The farm's dinner-gong sounded far off. My mother had evidently prepared lemonade for the haymakers. Boy, I saw, lounged in the yard smoking—a rooster on his own midden—then he tossed away the butt and entered his studio. He was, I knew, completing a posthumous portrait of Miles whose distraught parents had commissioned it. Each day from my spyhole I could distinguish indistinct brushstrokes slowly resolve into a death mask.

I'd heard Miles had thrown himself off the fifth-floor window of a recording studio.

I'd asked Boy what possible explanation there could be for such a desperate act. Surely they'd been some sign of Miles's emotional distress? What had been his last words?

'What do you think he said?' Boy had grinned wolfishly. 'One minute he was lying there, all sniffed up on the finest Bolivian Marching Powder, next minute he said, "I'm the Queen of the Fairies" and flew out of the freaking window.'

A Study in Sable

I'd last seen Miles when he'd quite unexpectedly sent me a ticket for a dress rehearsal of *La Bohème* at his opera festival. Miles actually had a very sensitive ear and was a much-sought-after *répéti-*

teur. The details on my ticket also conferred above-the-line billing on my brother as the set designer.

I was apprehensive. Either Miles's influence in the music world extended further than I'd ever suspected or their joint presence at this production was a beastly fluke. My indecision was resolved by Clara's insistence that tickets were as rare as hens' teeth, because a friend of a friend of hers had expired the very day her name was picked for the first time from a waiting list for rehearsal tickets on which she had been registered for twenty-five years.

So I accepted.

In the event, backstage, Miles charmingly introduced me to a vast Russian *basso profondo* whose sepulchral timbre was sustained, I was told, by his eating, daily, a dozen baskets of ring doughnuts with pink icing dusted with powdered sugar.

When I took my seat for the performance I found the singing was almost uniformly excellent and I was very soon enraptured, though Rodolfo had a throttled tone and there were some intonational lapses.

I began to relax. Happily, Boy's avant garde-ish *décor minimaliste* provided no distractions.

My mood changed, however, to one of uneasiness when, remaining in my seat alone in the longish interval after Act II, I observed the lighting director switch on a spot above the darkened proscenium and saw Boy amble across the stage with his dog, Bounder, walking on hind legs behind him, for all the world as if they'd never left the farm.

Boy and Bounder were as inseparable as Bill Sikes and his bull mastiff. I believe Boy had acquired the dog in settlement of a debt. At the time I'm speaking of, Douglas had reported sighting Boy in a local spit-and-sawdust saloon where my brother stood tipping his elbow with a Dirty Shirt Club of regulars while, beneath the bar, the dog was taught to sup on a draught of beer.

('Never a kind word heard against him!' Boy once declared cheerily when Bounder chased one of Mother's cats. Bounder was a repulsive looking brute with a prey-directed eye as if it carried about with it an evil conscience. *'Two of a kind,'* I remember thinking.)

Now, as the lights in the auditorium dimmed, the third act opened on the snow scene with, stage right, a consumptive Mimi coughing and slumped against the arch of a city gate.

The audience warmly applauded in wellbred recognition. I expect you know that theatrical set designers often compose their scenes with reference to celebrated paintings. But you can you imagine my horror when I recognised the composition of Act III as that of my brother's most discussed canvas, *A Study in Sable*, exhibited the previous year.

I knew what my brother meant by that bravura set-piece well enough—and only I knew what he wished to make me understand.

The sable coat in Boy's *painting* was one of Mother's many furs, of that I am certain, but the girl wearing it was *me*. I know this fact because the sitter *en déshabillé* put me in mind of nothing so much as the night Douglas left me, when I'd drunk half a bottle of sherry, and I'd lolled by the cottage hearth in a stupor, my naked legs splayed and mottling in the heat of the electric fire.

Douglas seemed to prefer my breath sweetened by sherry; he liked to hit me sometimes for he seemed to have convinced himself that I liked to be hit, and he knew a certain sense of shame prevented me from physically defending myself.

Befuddled as I was by wine I had, nevertheless, heard a scuffle outside the cottage and the darkened room was bleached suddenly by a flashbulb from the window, then I sank into blackness as though that extinguishment were a candle snuffed by a puff of Boy's breath.

I now feel I've reached a point in this narrative at which every reader will be startled into positive disbelief at the next fiendish torments contrived by my brother, that tyrannous metaphysical puppetmaster.

As those bitter thoughts of my brother's devilment possessed my mind, I heard from the stage Mimi's heartbreaking farewell, and I'm certain I heard, too, amid her tear-jerking coloratura, ' *. . . torna sola Zizzy al solitario nido.*'

And so it was *not* Mimi that night who returned alone to her nest of solitude.

❁

Thus on the hillside above the farm I mused, with half-shut eyes, while the sun sank to rest and thunderclouds threatened.

Very soon I grew deaf to Time.

The shadows lengthened into evening, crepuscular long fingers that reminded me of the emaciated hands of poor Father in the weeks before his death.

I would have remained in this twilight state for some hours had I not been surprised by a pack of beagle hounds followed by huntsmen in green livery. A hare bounded past me, eyes starting in fear.

So I rose and smoothed my skirt and followed their halloos down the track to the farm; but what now caused me further surprise was the fact that I had no sooner seen them pass from view than my brother appeared, pacing with long strides up the lane.

'Charlie's dead!' he warned as he approached me. Involuntarily I glanced down at my skirt in expectation that my slip was showing. It was a euphemism both Miles and my brother would employ often as boys to provoke Clara and myself.

'No,' Boy corrected, with an unpleasant little laugh, 'I said, *Douglas* is dead.' He sought my eyes with a fixed fascination.

I gripped his unshaven throat, fiercely kicking his shins to drive him away, yet he did not recoil but craned his neck to turn upon me those hungering particoloured eyes, and attempted to enclose me in an embrace.

He crushed my mouth with a rough kiss.

'Oh in God's name! We're *through*, you sicko! Once and for all, we're through!' The words bubbled to my lips in defiance of my own will.

He released me from his grasp, his chest wheezing like a broken-winded nag.

'You're no better, flaunting yourself like an alien sex fiend,' he jeered.

'Go away, damn you! Just go away!' I heard my own voice, muffled and broken, like the sobbing of a child.

'Yeah. Well, look,' my brother said with the same gleam in his deep-set feral eyes, 'Mummy asked me to deliver the message, that's all. Don't shoot the carrier pigeon.'

There was exultation in his voice.

'Mummy says she'll lend you her black coat.'

As I watched him depart, I thought: *'It's time to fight cunning with an equal guile. In an indefinite future either I can let him be the architect of his own downfall, or I can engineer a speedier demise.'*

It seemed to me that, if dying was as natural as living, then killing was as natural as birth; and I reflected on the trump card I held in my hand, but I was too skilful to play it then, as the rain fell like the balmedest balm.

Deleterious Effects

Although every *why* has a *wherefore*, for every *maybe* there is a *maybe not*, and I would have remained in an agony of indecision had I not seen, from my window that same evening, Boy prancing through my mother's sitting room in his Y-front underpants like a participant in a prize-fighting Mr Beefcake pageant.

That night I dreamt of Boy as a Janiform monster, one green eye and one brown eye looking two ways.

Next morning, at first, I made an effort to shake off this nightmare of the soul, but soon I actually realised it was a waking dream no sane person was at liberty to doubt.

Douglas had died of a fever. 'Pneumonia, the old man's friend,' nodded Nurse Harbour sagely but, of course, I knew the calamitous asphytic condition of my inconstant lover had another cause.

So some days of bitter grief having elapsed, an observable change came over me and I set out one dawn, along the abandoned railway, to gather more mushrooms.

The grass in the meadows was dappled with sparkling frail nets to catch the dew, where cobwebs hung above dimpled turf.

A horde of flies led me to an object stippled by their whirl.

The dome of a psychoactive—*pointilliste*—fly-agaric toadstool.

That morning, the third of October, my brother had made a trip to London's Green Park to celebrate the two hundredth anniversary of the first recorded account of mushroom-induced hullucinogenic behaviour in Britain. Wild mushrooms which grew in the park were a customary source of breakfast for the eighteenth-century family that had picked them (according to a scientific paper sent to Boy by a fellow dopehead); and, on that occasion, stated the journal, the family's delirium was due to the *'deleterious effects of a very common species of agaric mushroom, not hitherto suspected to be poisonous.'*

I recognised their smell; the gonadic stench of dogs rutting.

Boy bragged that he and his fellow mycologist, Miles, had ingested six dried caps of agaric; the Laplanders, he explained, fed the fungi to reindeer to induce docility when rounding them up. This agaric, I learned, contains tremendously potent psychotropic compounds; so, to be sure, I gathered a round dozen of the white-spotted red caps.

That day, the mode and the hour were all that occupied my mind, for I'd chosen the afternoon of Early Closing Day, a Wednesday, on which to prepare Boy's doom.

When I entered our farmhouse I at once stumbled over a row of empty wine bottles lining the passage to the kitchen.

My mother tapped on the ceiling with her stick and called down the stairs, assuming I was Boy: 'Take them away, dear. They're all dead men.'

The bottles clinked as I loaded two crates outside the scullery door.

That afternoon everyday noises sounded excruciatingly loud.

My nerves had become so jangly that in my own kitchen, for example, I'd see a scrap of tinfoil fall to the floor and hear its crash louder than a skipload of breaking glass. In fact, I haven't visited the cinema since I was a child; the crackling of cellophane sounds like rifle fire.

I was suffering, like Beethoven, from hyperacusis,an acute sensitivity to everyday sounds. But whether Beethoven was hit over the head when a child by a younger brother's seaside-sand-pail I cannot say. I still have a ragged scar under my hairline where Boy struck me with his metal bucket. And, yes, that bucket was filled with sand. Isn't a sand-filled stocking the favoured modus operandi of prowlers and thugees?

I'm prescribed 75 mg of Desipramine daily and without my medication I'd cringe away from a world where even the sound of leaves blowing in the woods is utter torture. (Actually, my doctor confirms I have suffered a serious neurological injury, and to enhance the drug's analgesic efficacy I have secretly increased the dosage of my other neuropathic medicines.)

In my brother's drinks cabinet I rummaged some shelves and found, beyond question, the hiding place of his own pharmacopeia.

I recognised a flacon that had once belonged to my father.

In my childhood, when Father wanted a salad dressing, he'd take himself off to the Chemist's for a tiny flacon of olive oil. (In those far-off days he could buy courgettes only from Bewick Market in Soho, you know, and his beloved French cuisine was a distant dream, to which his only other practical homage was to reprimand me if I did not rest my wrists in the French manner on the table edge between courses.)

Now the flacon bore the label of a quack nostrum of local origin, *Nurse Harbour's Curative Syrup*, a strong tonic and 'nerve stimulator' Boy regularly had made up for his own consumption by his earliest mentor.

Into this mixture I added my own ingredients of dried and powdered fungi. Shaking the sediment, I observed the liquid remained the same murky tint as the original. I tasted a tablespoonful and found the flavour agreeable, suggestive of liquorice and aniseed oil.

But, as I returned to the kitchen, I caught my breath and I felt myself sucked into a void and swallowed by blackness. Seven minutes later I awoke in a cold sweat, and found myself staring intently at the mist that had bubbled on a glossy, newly painted garden gate, as though I were consumed by a lucid monomania, my attention riveted to the unparalleled beauty of the cosmos condensed by vapour to a tiny bead.

I saw some mischievous devils in the night had cunningly fitted sheets of glass into every cart rut and they'd glazed every puddle with bevelled oval mirrors. Clumps of fiercely glowing flowers grew everywhere, luxuriantly, in the interspaces.

Clearly I dwelt in an alternate state of consciousness, and inhabited my lost realm. And, truthfully, I'd have been quite content to have remained in that magical promised land had I not heard my mother's call, demanding I make her tea.

My mother adjusted the table lamp to clear a space for the teacup. A fan of light, as though spilled by an hourglass, was cast upwards on the wall. She arranged her hands and commenced to make shadow-creatures above the bed as if I were a child again.

A hook-beaked bird.

I was terrified and ran from the room.

Weak-minded, and beset with constitutional infirmities akin to my own, my mother, I saw, could do but little to check the evil propensities which also distinguished her daughter.

Perhaps it's that small taint of heredity which is in the blood that makes it thicker than water.

I will attempt to bring my story quickly to conclusion by stating that, two days later, my brother stormed up the cottage path to beat madly on my door.

He told me he'd dosed Mother with his nerve tonic, as she'd complained of feeling 'tuckered out' (his term) by my ill-advised visit.

Now, he said, her face was swollen, and she was hallucinating in her dementia, convinced that little people and giant insects were dancing on her medicine tray.

Clearly, I had shot at the crow and winged the pigeon.

Boy started to call down maledictions on my head as if they'd been dinned into him by some mad djinni.

I protested my unequivocal guiltlessness.

'Bilge! Utter bilge!' he recited. I could only assume Boy had once been bawled out by a senior naval officer in this fashion and now he was taking it out on me.

I learned later that Boy had discovered the medicine's substitution when he later drank his own dose. But my mycological Mickey Finn appeared to have had as little effect on him as that of lysergic acid in the case of LSD's failure to reportedly change the heightened consciousness of a Tibetan sage.

To cheer up my mother, Boy had the blue shutters of the farmhouse painted a deep sunflower yellow. 'Like the Yellow House at Arles,' he explained. The surest means to invite a plague of madness, I thought, for it was there that Van Gogh splattered the yellow walls with his blood.

So in my dreams of my lost domain the shutters remained bright blue.

To mock the memory of my musician father, Boy then ordered from a magic shop a novelty electronic violin (batteries included) with which he serenaded my mother. As he drew the bow across the strings the instrument responded with all the true notes; he could even control the vibrato with his fingers—every inch the 'instant virtuoso', just as the salesman had promised.

Mother, who had a tin ear, beamed as Boy played *You Are My Sunshine* endlessly below her sick room.

'I do hope to be able to pull through for another five years at least, for your father's sake,' Mother said to me one day, 'but it is vanity for me to think it.'

You see, she believed Father was *still alive* but his absence was due to his having been sentenced to imprisonment for a term of five years, the 'lustrum' by which he'd taught me to count the daunting stretches of my own questionable life.

For, now, suddenly, all the dirt was coming out.

Vague suspicions slunk from the shadows into the light and, heeding my mother's ramblings, I at last understood why Father had lived in such fear of the law.

Mother's disconnected utterances hinted at enough skulduggery to expose my beloved father's feet of clay: from 'foreign currency fraud' and 'fake manifests' to issuance of 'fraudulent bills of lading', and 'stolen cargos' abetted by his illicit 'warehousing of perishable freight' in his refrigerated fur store.

That odour of coffee, for example, clinging to those arctic pelts borne home by our tribe's hunter to adorn our cave . . . how well I recall its taint whose origin I can now assign.

Father used to insist the rooms in the farmhouse were strewn with dried lavender to discourage the moths; while in London his chilled lockup afforded ideal conditions to both deter larval breeding and to stow pilfered foodstuffs.

This unexpected disclosure rather reassured me than surprised me, however, as any doubts I had once entertained concerning the unique cast of my criminal insanity were now set at rest by the certain knowledge that the maddening influence upon my reason was occasioned wholly by heredity.

For example, from sire to daughter, a patrimony of musical facility had been conveyed yet, at the keyboard, we both would stumble awkwardly in Chopin's *Valse in A-flat Opus 42*, at the same point in bar 210 where the piece halts ominously, with two notes tapped obsessively like Chopinesque *Chopsticks*.

Like my mother, I realised, from earliest infancy I'd given evidence of having fully inherited the family character.

Yet, despite her mental decline, Mother to the end maintained her cat-like observation.

'When the doctor recommends a lot of remedies,' she said, 'it means the disease can't be cured.' Her coquetteries with that young doctor were too absurd for me to now relate.

'The shameless flirt!' Nurse Harbour remarked with a droop of one eyelid. 'Faithless unto the last.'

She'd injected her patient with a heroin sedative, and Mother at once sank into a blissful repose. Her pulse was thready and barely perceptible.

An hour later, when Boy descended from his vigil at the deathbed, his own face had assumed a deathlike pallor and sunken outline. He stumbled blindly from the house as though his eyes were sewn up with red thread.

When I next saw Boy at Mother's funeral he was wearing a long Astrakan fur coat over a velvet smoking jacket with gold frogging, both of which had once belonged to my father.

The hollowness of the affair! The solicitor with my brother followed the coffin at an alderman's pace. Boy was as drunk as a boiled owl.

❁

THE GRAVEYARD SHIFT

It's true, as I have related, I afterwards became dreadfully nervous but you could not say I was entirely mad; for observe how calmly I can tell you the whole story. My affliction has sharpened my senses, not dulled them. Above all, my sense of hearing is increasingly acute. I hear many things perhaps I oughtn't, and, as Nurse Harbour says, warningly, 'What one *knows* it is oftentimes circumspect to *forget*.'

All the same, Boy's faculties apparently remained unimpaired.

After Mother's death, though, he suddenly seemed much older, with thinning hair and his teeth stained and loose, but he retained a sense of menace that continued to instill fear. *'An old wolf may lose its fangs,'* I thought, *'but not his nature.'*

And Boy's true nature, I now saw, had been to watch me with all the avidity of an erotomaniac stalking his prey.

The night after my visit to the solicitor's I once more resumed my 'graveyard shift' (my own expression) in the cottage pantry; the shelf, my handhold, I noticed was polished from my grasp during the long years I had obstinately persevered in my solitary observation.

But since my previous night-watch something unusual—some change which, at first, I could not appreciate distinctly—had taken place in the studio.

I discerned a *statue*. Boy stood with the stance of Masai warrior, *in puris naturalibus*, foot sole on shin—in an attitude of the profoundest attention—as if listening to some imaginary sound.

He was staring across the yard towards my lookout with long and very deliberate scrutiny.

I gasped for breath. My brother had the habit of mesmerising the person who beheld him.

The anxiety that seized me can be understood only when you appreciate the fact that—as you'd expect—I would invariably make a special point of extinguishing the lights in the kitchen so none shone from my spyhole.

But on this occasion a freak of fate had decreed my forgetfulness.

Now my brother wore a ill-natured smile of peculiar meaning.

Next minute he took up a zinc dyeing pan, once used by Mother to steep her stockings in a new and more ghastly hue. Then, as naked as the day he was born, he strode across the yard and hooked the pan over the air-vent to shield my view.

'Think again, Zizzy.' His voice rang hollowly through the vent.

❀

I have just written of that morbid condition of the auditory nerve which rendered some sounds intolerable to the sufferer.

Next morning I awoke in pain to a multitude stamping in the farmyard beneath my cottage window, and wild music from an amplified record-player seemed to echo their steps. I parted the curtains.

A threesome of doltish grooms from the neighbouring livery stables came cavorting from my brother's studio in a *quadrille en grand rond* with their thumbs in the armpits of their greasy biker jackets for want of fancy waistcoats, whereupon they lost their balance and, guffawing, slapped each other's backsides, speckled with chaff-seeds where the trio had fallen.

The noise steadily increased, the music drowning their heightened voices. My brother, wearing a Rastafarian woollen hat on his pointed head, danced while singing in a high key with violent gesticulations, eyes starting from his head. He was dressed in a hairy salt-and-peppery tweed suit a rag merchant would have disdained.

Bounder trailed at my brother's heels, snuffling.

On a farm you're never more than five yards away from a rat.

I threw on my wrap and escaped swiftly from my kitchen door, through the backyard gate, into my mother's garden.

But at once the shrill and piercing shrieks of female voices rang in my ears to overstring my nerves and put to trial the acuteness of my senses.

'What's with Lady Muck?' someone said. I recognised a group of ex-laundry-girls. They were seated drinking pint-glasses of beer at trestle tables that had somehow mushroomed in the night on the lawn.

Shortly after the arrival of the automated laundrette in the next village the steam laundry closed. You may gain an inkling of the backwardness of our rural fastness when you pause to consider a notice that appeared, at the time of the closure, above the new washing machines:

No Horse Blankets
Household wash only

This flock of slatternly village women endlessly cackled like hens in their coops.

'Just lay your eggs and leave, damn you!' I raged mindlessly under my breath.

My mother's once formal garden, bordered by lavender, was heaving with the lowest forms of pill-popping riff-raff, as though my brother had laid out a banquet and invited all the County's hawkers to squire the drug peddlers' trulls.

My brother, I saw, had mounted painted goat's horns above Mother's trellis arch where she'd cultivated her climbing summer roses; he'd hung a tablet above the entrance, incribed: *'Lasciate Ogne Speranza, Voi Ch'Intrate'*.

Abandon all hope. Yet what business had I with hope?

A fool woman was laughing at me quite openly, shaking unrestrainedly. Evidently she was Boy's latest 'squeeze' (to recall the demotic of the late Miles). I pitied her; her worst enemy was that she was pretty.

I turned and fled, ashamed of the contemptuous familiarity.

The beer flowed freely; their profanities were heard until the grey rising dawn of the following day, urged louder by my brother, who roared like a madman who'd eluded the vigilance of the madhouse.

From my window I gazed down at his moonlit laughing face in his Saturnalian beer garden.

'An evil destiny has pursued me,' I thought, *'as if in exultation.'*

I knew the inside of my brother's mind fully, as if I'd gone through it with a lighted torch. When he signalled his intentions they were about as subtle as a cartoonist's thought-bubble over his head.

The rabble was at the gate.

Our idyllic farm had passed from *pastorale* to *bacchanale* in one generation but, I vowed, that act of desecration would be avenged.

Not Strictly Street-legal

A word was scrawled with a laundress's indelible pencil on a brown egg.

Today.

Every weekend, for as long as I could remember, a rush basket of hens' eggs had been deposited on my cottage doorstep by faithful old Wilkes from the village. He always marked the freshest egg.

Today.

There's a critical minute, the psychological moment, when there seems to arrive a time when we act as if chosen.

Today.

Fortune only knocks once. I removed the eggs and arranged them in the sunlight on a blue dish. The basket, I noticed, was lined with old newspaper.

Then the light shifted and the bright rays fell vividly upon the basket, and my eyes, at the same moment, fell upon a headline:

Ex-Para Dies in Charity Skydive

15,000 ft death plunge as crowd watched in horror . . .
tributes paid to Falklands veteran.

A former lance corporal in a parachute regiment, a veteran of the Falklands landings, died on Friday after his reserve parachute failed to deploy due to a freak wind gust while making a sponsored parachute jump to raise funds for charity. Charity organisers paid tribute to the 52-year-old bachelor, etc.

I thought of him plummeting to his death, his chute his winding sheet, and I laughed and wept, wept and howled with relief, for I knew him well, you see, and we'd shared an oppressive secret.

Hope long deferred can enervate the spirit but I bucked up when I read of that death, for a reason I'll explain.

The previous August I'd answered a small ad, inviting offers to purchase a 'nippy, very economical' little car, 'some scuffing on bumpers, two small points of rust, suit single lady.'

The house of the owner was in the midst of a smallholding, I discovered. Cucumbers and melons, and chilli peppers the size of shoe trees, were arrayed in the sunlight on a warm low wall where, chalked on a slate, oddly, were these words:

BUY Cu's Melons & Squashes
Support Ex-Parabasher!

I simply had no idea what a 'parabasher' was so I asked the car's owner.

'I see you are a market gardener,' I continued idly, nodding to his vegetables on display.

He bristled.

'I'm not that ancient, surely?' He manner was stiff; I'd obviously offended him.

And then the truth of the absurd misunderstanding struck me.

Of course! 'Operation Market Garden' was, I remembered, the catastrophic airborne assault by Allied paratroopers in 1944 to capture the bridges over the Dutch rivers near the German border.

'Oh. So that's it! I understand perfectly.' The conversation had become idiotically self-referential. 'I was *correct*, but you're just not that *particular* generation of market gardener!'

He nodded, smiling, and his manner melted.

'Never mind my age.' He pointed to his stained red beret proudly. 'We're still the Red Mafia, and don't no one forget it.'

He then elaborated on how certain mechanical deficiencies beyond remedy made the car particularly suited to a single lady owner.

'It's not strictly street-legal, ' he cautioned me.

He then sold me the car at a knockdown price, because he couldn't be 'shot of it quick enough'. I suppose I must emanate a special odour of sanctified spinsterhood.

Earlier, at the gates of his smallholding, I'd encountered two disappointed respondents to the advert, a young couple walking away whom the ex-parabasher had rebuffed.

The young wife had a babe in arms and I'd envied them intensely. But when the despondent husband turned towards me in the unforgiving sunlight, I noticed his face was profusely bleeding from the pores, and was infected with clusters of boils.

❁

For weeks, for months, I had pondered upon the means of murder. And I'd rejected a thousand schemes, because their accomplishment involved a chance of detection. But to enveigle my brother into that car was a challenge that could be met, I was confident, by sufficient presence of mind to avoid revealing the ceaseless agitation of my own base thoughts.

However, there is nothing more easy than for a woman to deceive a vain man; gross flattery and praise, those unsubtlest of persuaders, will yet see him surrender to an illusion like a child.

'I owe you money, or what?' Boy asked sarcastically, when I proposed free driving lessons in my latest car. (Encouraged by

Father, I had, wholly unassisted, learnt to drive in an Austin Seven on the private tracks that once criss-crossed our estate. Father's early death had denied Boy this advantage.)

'So what's the drill?'

Boy smirked—dreaming of more dangerous seductions—and arched one eyebrow when I stated my terms. They were quite simple. In return for Mother's sable I'd instruct him in the Highway Code and in the rudiments of what he was vain enough to dismiss as child's play.

'I can learn in no time flat. As easy as falling off a log.'

We agreed to meet next evening when the sable he assured me would be mine.

❁

That night I completed a five-thousand-piece jigsaw of a scene from *A Midsummer Night's Dream*. I'd been working on this puzzle for months. The scene, curiously enough, depicted the custody battle between Oberon and Titania for her little stolen changeling boy and only after my meeting with my brother did I distinguish clearly, it seemed to me, between the gossamer-winged faeries and the nodding violets and eglantine. The very last piece revealed the camouflaged face of an enwreathed Puck grinning out of the shadows of the shrubbery like a monkey with two tails.

There is an old country saying Mother would repeat which states that 'No carrion can kill a crow', meaning, I would guess, that the ghosts of our roadside carnage—the spirits of a flattened vole or hen grouse or hedgehog or rabbit or even a shrew—could never return to threaten the remorseless equanimity of that sinister bird.

'I would beg to differ,' I almost breathed aloud, for not a single impediment now lay in my way to reverse this natural law.

Anthropomorphically, my mother believed there should be shrines to our animal 'roadkills'. You've no doubt seen that floral shrine to squashed fauna she erected at the blind corner just above the gravel pit.

At the stump of a lightning-blasted hanging tree, the site of a gibbet, there Mother chose to honour her dead with posies of wild flowers.

'Nodding violets and eglantine,' I murmured, and packed away the puzzle.

Across the farmyard I could see, against the dimly lit bay window, the silhouettes of the mescaline cacti in their pots that Boy had been cultivating since his early teens.

Above the farm, the moon hung like a pitted metal dinner gong, too much beaten.

I was sick of it all. Dreadfully tired and sick unto death.

I became irresistibly drowsy. Soon a deep sleep overtook me —a sleep like that of death.

❁

Boy was three sheets to the wind (his favourite pick-me-up was 'Snakebite') and smoking one of his 'herbals' when, the following night, I invited him to take the wheel of my nippy little car. He was wearing my father's Royal Artillery tie, a dark blue silk with zig-zagged red thunderflashes.

'I just adore the jazzy abstractionism,' he explained.

Seated beside him, I wore Mother's sable and carried her ebony walking stick.

I tapped with the stick on Boy's left toecap to remind him to plant his heel firmly on the floor, and not to hover with his foot over the clutch pedal as there was likelihood of cramp.

'This was dear Father's patented method,' I said, which seemed to reassure him. But I thought: *'Chance is a dicer, and the die's been cast.'*

There were a few glitches at the beginning, of course; the embarrassing clashes and engine seizures preceding Boy's engagement of a gear. (His left palm was always slightly out-thrust—a perpetual sideways gesture with pronation—a testament to the struggle of his difficult birth.) But within the hour my brother was driving with wild aplomb at a furious pace as each moment added to the car's speed and to his headlong career.

Very soon our progress had acquired a monstrous velocity.

I turned and saw my brother, heedless of our perilous position, was now frantic with every species of uncontrollable excitement, and his hand fell upon my right knee. The fingers that now slithered up my inner thigh neither relinquished nor contracted.

I am slow to anger but you cannot guess what my hot blood may do in a passion. As we approached the blind corner for a brief moment I hesitated, trembling.

In another minute, I thought, I'd be looking at a lost opportunity and—too late—I'd grieve for a chance that had passed, so I raised the stick and directed pressure with all the strength I could amass into the driver's footwell.

Boy writhed, and made strenuous exertions to free his foot to reach the clutch but I denied him every attempt to move.

'Hey, what's the big idea?' he shouted in apprehension, feverishly scrabbling to fasten the buckle of his seat belt.

'The big idea, brother dear, the *big idea* is quite the biggest it will ever be your privilege to hear.'

The dark trees that hemmed the corner rushed up to meet us.

The scream which escaped his lips was the authentic primordial cry of psychical pain.

'You blanked me out! Don't you know that, Zizzy?' he yelled.

His eyes seemed to start from their sockets.

'You've *always* blanked me out! All my life!' he managed to shout before he was hurled into the hereafter.

I heard a crunch like that of a crushed cornflakes packet, terminated by a metallic, clangorous, but muffled reverberation.

'Bleeding everything,' I heard him moan. They were his last words, as though his last thought was of a world weeping blood.

❀

I thought I was in heaven because all I could see were fleecy snowflakes; all I could see was falling snow.

I thought I saw a glowing tablet inscribed 'Salvation'.

The sky was a midnight blue, a restful blue.

I thought I could smell aviation gasoline.

The raw night air breathed on my face and I quite believed I was seated once more in the semi-pressurised cabin of the private twin-prop and would very soon meet my father.

But I had not erred in my calculations: the smashed windscreen, the clots of blood on the steering wheel, the grumous matter spattered on the dashboard, all resembled the visceral effect of one of Boy's own theatrical spectacles.

'Well, what's done can't be undone,' I said. In that instant, all Marian virtue dropped bodily from me as a mantle. From comparatively trivial wickedness I had passed, with the stride of a giant, into the enormities of fratricide.

'No carrion can kill a crow,' Mother had said, but she was wrong; it was I—the listless, lifeless child—who had survived.

I was practically unscathed, apart from bruises round my collar bone, but these were no more severe than the bruising Boy used to inflict when we were children.

My right foot felt unnaturally heavy and sodden as though I were shod in a wooden sabot lined with damp moss. I looked down and saw my shoe had filled with blood from a deep transverse gash on my shin where my leg had struck the edge of the storage rack beneath the dashboard.

My brother once boasted he had nine lives but now, as I gazed at his sunken head, I reflected that he'd just jumped out of his ninth skin—his *next-of-kin* skin—and was clinging to a life-belt which was no longer there.

His gaping jaw hung witness to a permanent suspension of disbelief.

I was in no doubt at all that he was dead.

Around his neck was tangled limply the driver's malfunctioned airbag like the folds of a placenta; unlike the passenger's airbag, it had never inflated, just as my ex-para had warned. It had been earlier breached, the man confessed, and had simply been repacked by an unscrupulous dealer.

There was a powerful fragrance of fresh sap like flattened woods after a hurricane. We had struck a tree and I thought I could detect the scent of wild violets.

I examined the white dust on my gloved hand and pressed my burning forehead against the cool glass of the side window.

I thought I saw a scavenger crow circling.

Then I shrieked, I raved, I keened. My words were like goose feathers tossed in the wind. I held the shattered windscreen with the same nervous tension with which I would grip the reins, until my palms bled.

A blizzard of snow-like powder had settled on my brother's once so alive but now defunctive flesh. The body was now dressed in dissolution, dusted with the white corn starch designed to sheathe and lubricate the airbags to prevent bruising when they deployed.

I removed from Boy's breast pocket his house-key. Tied to it was a label on which was scrawled a recipe for Snakebite in case he were too drunk to recall the components in a cocktail bar.

I leant sideways and, placing my hands beside those shattered temples, I peeled back the lids with my thumbs to reveal upturned fleshy whites the colour of bruised fruits.

His eyes, muddied, motionless and unseeing, then rolled themselves slowly open.

I shuddered as the pupils again disappeared upwardly, as sightless as two points of rust.

And then a hideous thought struck me. In contradistinction to their insensitivity in life, perhaps those post-mortal eyes were no longer inured to pain in death.

As I gazed at the dead stony eyes, I buried my chin in the huge furcoat and trembled like a cat.

My long fingers played over the dark fur.

The benefit of dark furs, Mother once confided, in a rare moment of clannishness, is that they accentuate one's naked white throat to greater advantage.

❁

The fur impressed my cheek. My face flushed. I could smell male sweat.

That which is bitter to endure can be sweet to remember, and I sensed my blood quivering, and the tremor and heat of a trickling within me of honeyed pleasure at the thought of a brotherless future, and the swooning probability that I'd again relive this luminous feeling of melting indulgence I'd never experienced before.

I cannot say how long I sat there dazed by what had happened until I heard a voice out of the darkness: 'An infernally long time for the ambulance to arrive.'

'He's not of this world, that's for sure.' I heard the paramedic pronounce over the remains of my brother.

'On that matter there is no mistake,' I whispered. '*On ne peut s'y tromper.* One cannot be mistaken there.'

I stated to the police that my brother had detached his seat-harness in a fit of panic when we were about to crash. (Before the ambulance arrived I'd untrapped the buckle I had wedged beneath the driver's seat.) I was confident I'd left no shadow of a clue by which it would be possible to convict, or even to suspect me of a crime. After all, the ex-paratrooper, my single—albeit unwitting—and now silenced confederate, was dead.

You cannot conceive the depth of my satisfaction as I reflected on my absolute security.

The season was high summer so for my brother's funeral the undertakers had, on my orders, instructed young boys with feathers to march in front of the coffin *cortège* to repel flies for the comfort of the plumed horses.

My shoes were too tight; every step was like walking on thorns; every movement of my legs sent a thousand needles pricking my nerves.

'If only,' I thought, *'like a wild creature, I could lick myself whole again.'*

The raucous Misses Bagwash and Washtub from the laundry followed the parade under parasols. Two dim, hulking, tattooed knuckle-walkers who I remembered as Boy's 'heavy users' trailed after them, accompanied by a drunken landing-party of ex-Merchies. And arm-in-arm at the tail of the procession, my brother's twin oracles—Nurse Harbour and the addled, raddled-faced Professor Deverill-Hewells—followed, too, at a sedater pace, exchanging drolleries.

In the congregation there was a fluttering dove-cote of do-gooders from the Women's Institute, and the whispering of blue-rinsed biddies from the lounge bar who, I knew, could not wait to meddle in my domestic affairs.

'If the rector wants a eulogy, he can whistle for it,' I muttered viciously. *'It would be like taking a golden pen to write upon dirt. What could I say? That we were assembled in celebration of my baby brother because his warped nature formed the Missing Link between that of the human and that of the elf?'*

There are sovereign truths which guide the world, and one such is that the wake of a drunkard attracts all manner of mourners thirsty to sink a final round at the expense of the departed.

I declined all drinks, and discouraged all commiserations; I feared, of course, that in another moment I would trip over an abyss, and plunge into my mental disorder, and the long-imprisoned secret would burst forth from my soul.

I returned to the graveside. In the late evening sun, tightly wrapped flowers in a heap were decomposing, shaped like so many disposable paper cones of monkey-nuts, like those you see peddled from pushcarts at the zoo.

My own flowers, I saw, were suspended in a malodorous chaplet for all to see: the stinking irises I had gathered that morning, which still flowered by our woodside brook.

Beneath the flowers a sloughed snake-skin with zig-zag markings was coiled in the grass.

❁

A policeman and old Wilkes accompanied me to the farm. I admitted them to the lazar-house with Boy's key.

The policeman whistled through his teeth: 'Never seen anythink like it in all my born days!'

The amount my brother had hoarded in all those years was simply astonishing! Pans of sump oil from my father's old Bentleys were perched on the shelves of the Welsh dresser. Blown electric light bulbs, each one marked with the date of its extinguishment, were arrayed on my father's bookcases, together with tall pillars of pre-decimal coins that were no longer currency. Every available surface of my mother's blue and gilt Derby dinner service had been heavily pigmented by Boy with scumbled oil paints.

And the revels of the previous week still remained in evidence.

My attention was drawn to the staircase. In an ironic gesture typical of my brother, an *orchid*, in homage to Tretchikoff's kitsch masterpiece of post-party blues, complete with teardrop and party streamers, was placed on the penultimate stair leading to Mother's bedroom quarters.

Somehow I seemed to hear a violin weeping; I seemed to smell lavender.

'Mind if I poke around?' the policeman asked, but it was not a question.

He raised the hatch to the farm's roof-space and a light was automatically tripped in the attic.

But the marijuana plants Boy had thought to propagate, above Mother's sickroom, in that particular experiment had died long ago.

The policeman examined every room then shrugged and departed empty-handed.

Wilkes and I entered my former bedroom; I had not set foot in the room since my banishment.

'Well,' said Wilkes, 'thar's a queer welcome home, you won't mind me sayin'.'

Now the walls seemed to be painted with some kind of scarlet Chinese lacquer. The entire surface of this ground was crudely daubed in all manner of hideous and repulsive forms, and fearful images overspread and disfigured the ceiling. Although the colours seemed faded and blurred, the outlines of these *outré* monstrosities were sufficiently distinct.

'Quite honestly,' I thought, *'art should be treated as a pathological compulsion for which there is no known cure.'*

Above my former bed the painted figure of Time was represented, except, in lieu of a scythe, he held what, to my uninformed eye, I supposed to be a seed-endowing lingam of a suprasexual omnipotency.

'He were a sharp lad, yore brother,' Old Wilkes conceded, 'sharp, orright, 'ceptin' there's no jestin' with edged tools.'

He winked, and prepared to leave the room.

'Don't think much o' this. A filthier room you couldn't have if it were ever so. Whitewash'll fix it, sure 'nuff, an' good riddance, I say.' Wilkes grunted. 'Umph! Looks like thar's nothing for it but a bout o' bug-blinding this arternoon.'

❦

While Wilkes fetched the whitewash I thoroughly surveyed the whole room for signs of my former occupation. I saw one of my woven hairbands remained twisted round the bedknob, except the strand of hair caught in the weave was not my own.

However, above the bedhead a series of yellowing cartoon strips of 'Black Beauty', tacked up with rusting thumbtacks, had not been removed. And on the bedside table my tattered copy of 'National Velvet' had not strayed.

But I now noticed the proportions of my bedroom had greatly changed during my absence of so many years. At length my eyes, in roving the circuit of the room, fell upon a dirty loop of scarlet ribbon hanging from a little brass knob at the base of the scarlet wall abutting the mantel-piece.

Of course! There had once been an alcove there! I examined the wall with greater care.

That the chimney-breast did not present the slightest appearance of having been disturbed did not altogether surprise me. Boy's painting tutor, Professor Deverill-Hewells, like most of his colleagues on the art college faculty, had applied for the Artists'

Rifles but, instead, had been ordered to serve in a secret camouflage unit during the war against the *Herrenvolk*.

Boy had told me that the professor's raw complexion rivalled the face of an engineroom stoker of his acquaintance and, certainly, 'the Prof' never ceased to relish stoking up controversy, for the 'rummy old coot' had often claimed that he was the first practitioner of Optical Art, and that he had not only invented an invisibility cloak but had caused a battleship to disappear, in a series of trials that had excelled the Philadelphia Experiment. (You can see [or, rather, *not* see] Boy's witty *trompe l'oeil* portrait of this master of deception in London's National Portrait Gallery.)

But *I* was *not* deceived. To a determined woman such a thing as a secret hiding-place is impossible.

I simply saw that the false wall had been fashioned to resemble the red of the chimney-breast and, painter-like, my brother had varnished literally over the cracks of his secret wall-closet.

So I hooked my finger through the ribbon and pulled—you cannot imagine how stealthily—until, at length, the door cracked open and I examined its innermost recesses.

I withdrew a number of articles: a silk doll with a pocket for my nightclothes, which used to rest on my bed; snatched flash-lit paparazzi-type shots of myself caught unawares; Dinah's rosettes; faded photographs of my brother and myself as children, bathing naked in the old bathtub under the boxwood hedge (my mother, in one of her periodic fits of prudery, had cut off the lower portions of the photos and Boy must have later reassembled them); together with a small original oil portrait of myself in riding breeches I'd never set eyes on before (the title, a quotation, was painstakingly printed on the canvas's reverse: *I Had a Sister, Lovely in My Sight*); the picture was wrapped in my girl-guide uniform (long forgotten) to which Boy had attached his necklet of strangely shaped charms.

I placed my own charm bracelet beside the necklet; you don't have to be a Freudian symbolist to observe how those charms were emblematic of the arc of my life . . . the cross . . . heart . . . anchor . . . aeroplane . . . padlock . . . the violin.

But there was more. A little box with a sulphurous lustre.

It was of no remarkable character, having on the outside a pattern of nails and narrow bands of thin, white, hammered iron that looked like moiré silk.

I do not know why I shuddered in regarding it. I grasped the lid but could not force it open; and in my tremor, it slipped from my hands, and fell heavily, and burst into pieces; and from it, with a rattling sound, there rolled thirty-two glittering little black eggs to scatter to and fro about the floor.

They were of an iridescent black as though Boy wished to defy the earthbound belief that black will take no other hue.

My brother had once boasted to me, after he'd returned from sea, that he'd smuggled in his tobacco pouch a small fortune through customs . . . a clutch of the finest gem-quality black opals from Australia.

'How many?' I'd asked.

'Quite a few, if you are really after truth,' Boy had said complacently.

Now I thought, trembling delightedly in my sable: *'How contrary of the blackest hen to lay the whitest eggs when her birthright should more properly be sparkly black ones.'*

❦

I locked the farmhouse door and skipped across the yard to the cottage.

I noticed the zinc dyeing pan still hung over my redundant spy-hole. When I removed it I found beneath, clinging to the damp wall, a perfectly configured disc of clustered snails all a-shine with mucilage.

At the cottage gate a young boy approached with Bounder led on a leash of string. I recognised the lad as one of the undertaker's young attendants from the coffin cortège. My brother's sick hound, I saw, had come halting home.

'Is it yours?' the boy asked

There was entreaty in the dog's eyes, and the tail thumped on the ground.

'No,' I said coldly to the eager young boy. 'No. Not mine. Nor anyone's by the looks of him.'

The boy persisted with an insistent smiling ingratiation that sickened me.

'Then I *can* keep him, can't I?'

I remained silent.

'I know nothing about it,' I said at last, 'and care less.'

I waited to note the look of hurt in his eyes before I turned away.

The Dancer Stumbles

A minute later I lifted the lid to the keyboard and adjusted my piano stool.

I have since read that seers believe that to dream of playing a piano is a favourable omen and means the discovery of something of great value in a surprising place; so I resolved to realise my dream of the night before.

I experienced a feeling of equipoise I had not known since I last rode Dinah . . . a balanced seat, hands-free, independent of the reins.

In my opinion it is actually more difficult to run into bar 210 of *Valse in A-flat Opus 42* where the waltz 'stumbles' than *emerge* from it—one runs the risk of sounding as if one has simply walked into a wall, rather than suspending the breath for a moment—hence, this artifice of ineptitude is not easy to achieve and, even though Chopin intended to simulate a clumsy dancer's imbalance before her lost rhythm is regained, the player's assumed clumsiness must be diligently practised over and over again.

So, creating this suspension requires exceptional finesse in timing and shades of dynamics and balance, which, to my way of thinking, is the more difficult task.

In my father's case, alas, the task was performed never with consummate success, as though the passage was a nagging regret and he had to return again and again to pick a sore. (Father would tune his piano himself by feeding a reference note into an oscilloscope an army pal of his had once used for reading radar; he'd then retune the fifths until they were slightly flat. Those dancing waveforms on a monitor screen, as I told the doctors, I always associate with Chopin's waltzes.)

For my own part, my effortless arpeggiation on the evening I returned from Boy's funeral, and my faultless span at bar 255 —which had once made such demands on the extensive stretch of my Father's left hand—meant I rode the home-straight cooly through the flurry of that passionate coda, and reached the winning post at last, luckily without a fall . . . until pent-up grief all at once welled up and burst my heart.

A STRANGER IN BLOOD

(*Elspeth P.* — MIRTAZAPINE)

'Who looks outside, dreams. Who looks inside, awakens.'
— CARL GUSTAV JUNG

'Reality is that which everything is an instance of.'
— ELI SIEGEL

Assessment Summary (extract): The patient had spent her childhood with different relatives since her mother's premature death. Her general medical condition was good, but her mood was depressed, a depression which, she claims, underlies the persistence of major sleep disturbance and, in the past month, chronic insomnia. Appetite and self-esteem were diminished. She has discussed problematic relationships with the opposite sex. Currently, she is in a new relationship which she describes as 'her best ever'. She displayed features of an incomplete bereavement reaction with ambivalent feelings towards her mother. The patient also reported episodes of depersonalisation and described apperceptions of alternate identities. The anamnesis of this patient is characterised by her persisting memories of personal long-standing experiences which she denies are cultural acquisitions; a belief sustained by her uncanny ability to produce, as flashbacks, realistic accounts of events from history, as if they were her autobiographical memory, despite such episodes being clearly unrelated to her chronological age. When discussing the possibility that her memories were factitious, or the racial inheritance of traumatic experiences of ages past, she conversed in a detached tone of voice, affirming her conviction about the reality of her experiences. I would prefer to delay further psychotherapeutic interventions for this patient until her case is discussed with a family member or close friend who can confirm her accounts. Until our next consultation, I have proposed a choice of expressive formats through which she may daily record underlying thoughts and feelings.

A STRANGER IN BLOOD

Patient ID CPN0338200976: Elspeth P.
Occupation: University Lecturer in Comparative Literature and Critical Theory.
Drug: Mirtazapine.
Drug class: Tetracyclic antidepressant and mood elevator for treatment of major depression, particularly when associated with sleep disturbances.
Common side effects: Drowsiness, headache, dizziness, changes in appetite and dry mouth.

'A WOMAN WITHOUT a past has no future.' I laughed without thought. 'The question you *should* have asked is not where I'm *going* but where I'm *from*.'

I rapped my forehead with my knuckles.

'A locked room mystery for you, look.' I twisted my hands together. 'Locked inside my head the *real me* is! No way in or out! I know what I know, but no more, see. It's hopele*th*.'

In moments of extreme emotional disturbance I revert to the cadences and syntactical quirks that betray the speech of my Welsh childhood, and the pronounced lisp of my infancy again afflicts my tongue.

My therapist nodded encouragingly, then fingered her chignon to assure herself it had not strayed. She wore a false hair-piece. I did not trust her.

'I own to being a bastard,' I said. My lip did not tremble. 'Satisfied?'

An 'identity crisis' had been glibly mooted when I'd earlier confessed to the confusion that bedevils the psyche of an adoptee, and to my reluctance to delve deeper into the mystery of my true parentage: a father unknown, and the identity of my birth-mother withheld by my adoptive parents, Mam and Da.

'Self-knowledge requires more,' she put in portentously.

So I grudgingly agreed to the therapist's suggestion to keep a journal should I decide to explore that nameless dark corridor which, she assured me, could lead to the clinical glare of a 'rebirth' bathed by enlightenment.

She began to probe further into my past, alluding to childhood phobias.

At which point I clammed up. I'm perfectly aware that 'basket' is an English euphemism for 'bastard', of course, but I certainly will not *openly* admit to my compulsive avoidance in supermarkets of the *'Baskets Only'* checkout line.

Friday, March 24 (Lent Term) . . . A Loose Cannon

Da, I learned late last night from the Bursar, has been gravely ill, yet, before I could pack my overnight case, I received another message from Aunt Nesta breaking the news of Da's death in a fire that has destroyed our family home. The dizzying terror of that moment as my mind denied the words that rang in my ears caused me to cry out loud, and then I must have fainted.

Later, I remember, the Vice-Mistress in the library spoke to me in a low, calm voice—as though I were a disturbed child—and pointed out the advantage of using the Easter Term before the Long Vacation to begin a prolonged leave of absence.

'How long have you been with us now?'

'Two years, is it?' I raised my voice in panic. 'I can't be sure.' My mind was so clouded by grief I truly could not remember.

'Oh, a far longer tenure than that, you may be certain,' she declared with a bright smile. 'And quite long enough to be eligible for a paid sabbatical. Just imagine! You're free to complete your book! An entire term on full pay!'

The arrangements were all so sudden, I could scarcely draw breath. But convenience, I believe, dictated this speed, because the Vice-Mistress was far too well mannered to go so far as to state the matter plainly: that I was suffering from what is vaguely called a nervous breakdown. She took pride in running a 'tight ship' and, as I was now regarded as something of an elusive loose cannon, she was eager, no doubt, to see me hog-tied.

EASTER SUNDAY, MARCH 26 . . . HOW CAN I REMEMBERTHE UNKNOWN?

Da's little bungalow had once clung to a bleak outcrop commanding the valley with a view of the sea; it was pebble dashed with a slate roof and built directly on to bedrock. Now only the coalhouse and chimney-stack remained standing. I thanked Providence that Mam had not lived to dwell in this home promised her by Da on his retirement. The roof had collapsed and brought down the blackened walls. I could still smell the smoke.

Poor Mam died when I was twelve. She'd died in the shower from a weak heart. She had always been in poor health and terrified of hot baths.

Now, some two decades later, Da had died in a coalhouse where he had sought refuge from the blaze. I could imagine the headline: *Death of Collier in Coalhouse*; the bathos of that death scene was as inescapable as it was inexplicable, for the coalhouse not only had an inner door connected to the scullery but an outer door, for deliveries, giving on to the yard. Why had not Da chosen this escape route and fled to safety, into the open air?

I tried the coalhouse door but it appeared locked.

I thought, I've lost everything. With Da's death I've lost every clue to my prenatal identity. Now the precious memories of my birth have died with him how can I possibly remember the unknown?

Truly, I'm an artifact intact, I told myself, washed up on a strange shore with no documented provenance.

'Lost everything, have you, my lovely gel?' a voice at my side asked sympathetically.

A stranger shouldering a spade, an old tramp in worthless rags, had paused by our neighbour's gate. His hands were grimier than an ashman's. He carried a pail of onion-sets for planting. His face was travel-stained, and his boots were as dirty as the road. About his person there was a certain niff.

'A proper home I've not had since I was a boy. Aye, and nor likely to have one. But no roofs do we have in heaven, *fâch*, surely now?'

I smiled through my tears.

And equally, I thought, we might very well not demand a roof over our heads when our title to this world is so mystifyingly uncertain.

❀

The Hospital Almoner handed me Da's personal effects in a yellow plastic bag intended for the disposal of clinical waste.

Although her spareness of diction, of course, was cultivated for the best of motives, her over-punctilious textbook manner and measured tone, when I asked her for an account of Da's last hours, simply reasserted the polished counselling techniques that informed her tactics for regulating grief.

However, under my persistent questioning she somewhat thawed.

'He was found in his pyjamas and dressing-gown. Sinking fast he was when they brought him in. They had to cut away his night-clothes. Really speaking you should be talking to your auntie, because she found him. Making a fire he was, by the looks of it, from drift-wood and the ribblings, but why he should be chopping sticks when there was ten ton of coal, all along, out the back, is beyond our understanding.'

I could not account for this puzzle either. Da had no need for wood fires. He was an ex-miner with six tons of concessionary coal delivered to him every year. He had prided himself on banking up his coal fire at night with a crust of ashes, and greeted each morning by stirring the embers into life.

'I'm mystified,' I whispered. 'It makes no sense at all.'

The Almoner nodded her dismissal. 'See your aunt right off. I would.'

❁

Opposite the hospital gates, between a florist's and a funeral director's, a table, I saw, was prepared before me, sheltered by an arcade, where an Italian café dispensed, like its neighbours, the reputed comfort of cool polished marble and cut flowers. The staff served, too, with a condoling solicitude.

Why is it, I wondered, as expresso caffeine jolted my senses alert, that where there are way-stations for the departed—whether hospital or cemetery—the bereft are always pursued by ambulance-chasing chrysanthemums.

Da's yellow clinical waste bag contained three items: his dentures, his snuff box and a scrap of charred paper melded to a remnant of his candlewick dressing-gown, evidently cut from his grasp.

The oval brass snuff box was familiar to me; snuff was the only source of nicotine for Da underground, as was the case for all miners, unless they chewed tobacco. Engraved on the lid, beneath his name, were the words, FORGET•ME•NOT; a keepsake for Mam in the event of his death at the face.

I held it reverently by my fingertips as though it were a sacred relic which could inspirit me with the strength of mind to direct my reluctant gaze to the brittle paper fragment, and to the words printed on it.

But, when I shook off my fear-stricken irresolution, this is what I read:

CERTIFIED COPY OF AN ENTRY OF BIR
COPI DYLIS O GOFNOD GENEDIGAETH
Pursuant to the Births and Deaths Registration Act

Registration District ....
irth in Sub-distric .... in the

When and where born

....
....

WARNING: A CERTIFICATE IS NOT EVIDENCE OF IDENTITY.
RHYBUDD: NID YW TYSTYSGRIF YN PROFI PWY YDYCH CHI.

Truly, this page might just as well have been a Dead Sea scroll for all the evidence of anyone's identity it proved because, by a perversity of fate, the essential details of my birthplace and the names of my biological parents, and all other handwritten entries penned by the registrar, had been scorched into oblivion.

It was as though some cosmic dramatist had sketched out an improbable plot with no shred of evidence to even hint as to how to resolve the *dénouement* of that inscrutable design.

My half-suppressed moan became the senseless giggle of one who laughs to prevent too deep an apprehension of spiritual distress.

At an adjoining table, two young seminarians in solemn conclave (I recognised their scarves as the colours of the nearby Theological Training College) looked up startled, then exchanged glances, painfully embarrassed.

I thought: How characteristic of my over-principled Da! Of all the cherished possessions he could have chosen to save from the burning building, he chose, at the eleventh minute of the eleventh hour, the birth certificate he'd never wished me to see!

In point of fact I knew the exact location of that birth certificate. In a black enamelled deed box it was stowed, on a shelf above the scullery door. But, unless you are as grievously insecure as myself, and *also* an adoptee, you'll never, never understand my reluctance to open that box.

Mam and Da were loath to tell me I was adopted; aged ten, I learned the truth by accident at school. Our teacher was taken ill one day and an older girl was placed in charge of our class. She rummaged through the teacher's records searching for our end-of-term grades. That's when she exclaimed, '*Jewks!* Why did you not say you were adopted, Beth?'

(At my birth, quite clearly, the evil godmother of my misfortune had conspired to name me Elspeth. Could ever a more disadvantageous name be given to a lisping child? When addressed, I never answered to El*th*peth, you may be sure; I answered to *Beth*.)

My voice rose to a shriek: 'For shame, calling names on people!'

'Think I canna read?' she jeered.

Her contempt for me was nurtured by envy, for she'd been needling me ever since the announcement of my scholarship to a private high school.

'Proper come down, this is!'

Still I protested as I fled the classroom. 'Leave me alone, can't you!'

'There's swanky for you!' was her triumphant closing jibe. 'She canna see for lookin'!'

I will draw a veil over my homecoming that day of revelations; I locked myself in my room. Da, unbathed, came hurrying to my door from the pit, mid-shift, under a special dispensation from the gaffer.

He was contrite, holding his cap, repeating twenty times oft-rehearsed explanations, his red tongue working rapidly in his blackened face.

They assured me I was 'special', and had acted only to protect me from heartache. Da said I was 'saved for glory' and Mam declared I was their 'chosen one'.

Tears, prayers, kisses, gifts, reconciliations.

So, in all the years that followed, I never once sought to learn the identity of my natural mother. The very thought of my demanding her name I knew would profoundly upset my adoptive parents, such a fear I had of bringing down on my head the confusion of further rejection.

Besides, my greater fear—more than filling in the blanks, and laying that ghost to rest—was my dread of disappointment, the complete devastation of my persona, should I learn who my biological parents truly were and fail to come to terms with unwelcome knowledge.

You'll understand my dilemma if you've ever seen that well-known public sculpture entitled *Illusions reçues par la Terre*, which symbolises the extreme emotional pressure, no less powerful than the colossal gravitational field of a planet, say, like Saturn, under which our frail illusions fall to earth.

So the deed box remained unopened; and I promised myself I would never seriously trace my natural mother while Mam and Da were alive.

My mouth was dry, and I gulped water with an unsatisfied thirst.

For now I understood, with a terrible finality, my search for my lost past was, by far too many years, long overdue, and the last traces that could disclose the secrets of my doubtful parentage were crumbling to ashes in my belated grasp.

If only I could be enclosed in a time capsule, I thought, in which I could travel through this fog of unknowing and awake refreshed inside a clear bubble of irrefutable truth.

I sat like a Sphinx, clutching the table top, staring at the veins of marble with unseeing eyes, as the sounds of the café broke in upon my reverie.

The two seminarians, a Welshman and an African, had resumed their theological argument.

'When it's lost you're not entirely hopeless. You must talk to the chaplain,' the African urged. 'His faith is equal to any occasion, even the loss of it.'

As so often is the case in these godless times, a black convert from Africa was ministering to a novice from the mother country of their faith.

'No, man,' protested the Welsh lad. 'My mind's made up, Kwesi. When my Nan lost her memory, your medical mission doc had the cure, honest! Hypnotherapy! In a proper fix she was, but, today, there she is, right as ninepence! If that bloke can't cure loss of faith then I'll have to jack it in. Mind, it'll be a tidy spell before I get it back, the doc says, but he's promised faithful, by damn, he'll do it.'

Well, I thought, when all else fails, seemingly even that same darkness of doubt and that same cloud of unknowing could yield enlightenment through one's submission to an artificially induced mesmeric trance.

But, for the moment, I believed Aunt Nesta held the answer to the Riddle of the Sphinx.

Monday, March 27 . . . Lapsus Linguæ

Yesterday, up the hill to the top of the town I marched to my aunt's house, and here I am in her second-best bedroom.

I'd had but one question for Nesta, but when I plucked up courage to ask it she'd practically laughed (but not unkindly) in my face.

'*Rwtsh!* Shush your noise! What nonsense, child! Merely a slip of the tongue!'

(I'd reminded her of the occasion of my eleventh birthday when, returning with me from the shops, she had—much to my embarrassment—praised my scholarly successes to a neighbour.

'Passed her exams very high you know! My daughter's got a good head on her!' Then my aunt had flushed crimson, conscious of her words. 'A credit she is to her Mam and Da,' she had added hurriedly.)

This morning, at breakfast, Aunt Nesta placed a comforting hand on my shoulder and shook her head.

'Get along with you! The very suggestion I'm your *real mother*! If your Uncle Emrys were alive how we would laugh! No, I must have said *daughter*, because I was so proud of you and regarded you as my own.'

So, I was obliged to accept that my aunt's unfortunate error of speech, from which I had woven an intricate misshapen girlhood fantasy, was, after all, no more than the *lapsus linguæ* of 'a foolish old woman overfond of her niece,' to repeat Nesta's own bewildered denials.

And I was no farther forward in my quest since, frustratingly, my aunt's knowledge of my adoption seemed genuinely hazy.

I'd been adopted under a veil of secrecy, unofficially, and in great haste. My birth-mother had been very young. An art student. Single. Troubled.

'That's all I know, honest to God.' Aunt Nesta stifled a sob. 'And now your Da's gone. Would you credit it, his oddness!'

'His oddness?'

'A real case that one, even though he was my own brother! There's times I could cry when I stop to think about it all. And when he told me what he was doing I nearly had forty fits!'

'You mean the wood fire?'

She looked at me sharply.

'Bright girl. Yes. He'd been a bag of nerves ever since your Mam passed over, as *you* know too well.' (Her tone was accusatory.) 'Lately, he'd just sit in the corner by the fire. You should have seen the state the house was in, *ach-a-fi*! I wouldn't give thank you for a night in that house it were that cold.'

She took my hand, urging me to understand.

'It's hard to credit it—I never thought him old—but he'd been drawing his pension for more than a twelve-month. Except he was rare cut up, see, when they started shipping in sacks of coal from Poland as his concession. Act of treachery, he called it, seeing as how he'd been through all those hard times on strike, and all for nothing when they closed the pits. But I might as well have talked to the wall to make him see reason.'

I gasped. My fingers trembled. The explanation for Da's death hit my senses like bleach.

'You mean he stored ten tons of Polish coal in the coalhouse and never used it, but burned wood instead?'

'A real case that one! All on account of a fine principle. He said he once cut around seven tons of good Welsh coal a day, and what did he want with Polish clinker? He said I had no cause to worry, but a bigger liar I've never heard, because worry I did when I couldn't open the coalhouse door, what with all that coal stacked behind it!'

The picture of my loss was now clear: my uprighteous God-fearing Da trapped in a burning outbuilding, the protagonist of a tragic morality play of his own contrivance, holding the key to my destiny in his unnaturally white hand.

Our past was so far away that, beneath us, in the valleys, even the rivers had ceased to run black.

SATURDAY, APRIL 1 . . . A JUNGIAN MANDALA

I shall not mention the significance of today's date when I admit that *foolishly*, importunately, I located the hypnotherapist by telephoning the theological college late last night, and asking for the 'medical mission' doctor, to whom I explained in the barest terms my spiritual crisis.

Today, full of trepidation, I kept my appointment with Dr Priestly, in the grey remainder of the evening, directly after tea.

I found his door in a creeper-covered corner of an inner quad.

Claws of ivy clung to the brass plate:

KUAMINA MEDICAL MISSION

memor et fidelis

I need not have worried. The episode passed off smoothly, even when the young Welsh seminarian opened the Mission office door just as he, himself, was leaving.

The nervous glances of mutual recognition we exchanged were not so brief as to prevent me from noting that he had one smile for men and another for women. Was it so inane of me to feel flattered?

So I still wore a contemplative smile when I entered the reception room and the missionary doctor came forward to greet me, and shook my hand in a clasp that was palpably dry, harsh and leathery.

Dr Priestly bowed his close-cropped grey head, and I saw his once brown face had paled in our northern climes, and was haggard and worn, with those fever-shot eyes that told their own story of a white man's long service on the Dark Continent.

In his study, he sat me in a patched easy chair and directed my gaze to what I recognised as a Jungian mandala hanging above the fire.

He then lounged in his own armchair with his slippered feet on the polished fender. The firelight played on a stoical face whose lines were like a delicately carved bust of nut brown marble.

'Africa,' he breathed. (The largest word has the smallest sigh.) 'So near to Southern Europe, so very near, yet we must not judge one land by the morals of another. In my district it's a *sine qua non* that traditional ceremonies like marriages and funerals are performed by the magic men, as the order of precedence, then followed by Christian practices. Not everyone agrees, of course.'

His voice was soothing. I felt mind and body relaxing under his spell.

'I once knew a Presbyter,' he continued, 'who, having finished performing the burial mass, refused to bury the corpse because the native traditionalists poured a libation—*amena so énsa guo*—into the open grave right after the Christian holy water. The dead man was finally buried by the native wizard.'

'I think the least they could have . . . ' I began.

'Oblige me by refraining from thought, that is not your purpose here.'

Curiously, I did not take offence at such brusque directness but accepted his words as an instruction that, in observance, promised the reward of grace.

'No one knows what goes on in the heart of Africa,' he continued almost dreamily. 'In Africa you may inhabit infinite varieties of consciousness. And as to *belief* . . . we Europeans are not called in the night nowadays to a special vocation; we have to find it out for ourselves. There are many entrances to the truth of *being*. Tapping the unconscious by regressing your age is one of them.'

❀

What do I remember now of that *séance*?

I recollect he suggested I should picture my dilemma as like that of a princess imprisoned in a tower.

I should imagine the tower's spiralling steps (he pointed to segments of the mandala) corkscrewing down through room after room—imagine a descent through layers of Time—down, down, counter-clockwise, until the steps reached the ground floor with a prospect of a moated keep, and of a drawbridge which spanned the gulf between my childhood as an adoptee, and the special flowering garden of my unrecorded infancy wherein could be found even the earliest stirrings of my blind, pre-sentient, unborn existence.

'The door to the tower room is unlocked,' the grave voice affirmed. 'You're quite free to escape to the garden below; just walk down the stairs, and count each room.'

'I can't.' Some part of me still rebelled. 'My eyes are open.'

'That's perfectly alright. It's understandable you should want to go into hypnosis with your eyes open.'

His calm words resulted in my immediately closing my eyes.

'Now your eyelids are getting just a little heavier. Isn't it nice to close them for a little while?'

I could find, after all, no conceivable grounds to disagree. As I began my descent, I was aware my breathing rate changed because, such was the melodic quality of that doctor's unparsonic voice, I must have passed easily from a light trance into a much deeper one.

When I reached the lowest room, I heard him ask:

'How old are you now?'

'One.'

'Then cross the bridge into the garden. *Now*.'

My body writhed. There was a pricking in my left thumb. My fingertips and the soles of my feet tingled, supersensitive to stimuli like the flesh of a newborn babe. I began to sob.

'I'm not ready to go there now,' I lied.

'As I count from one to five, with each number you become more alert, more awake, more ready to return to your waking state of consciousness.'

On awaking, the sense of unaccustomed release puzzled me beyond measure. Dr Priestly brought me tea, and I drank it gratefully.

The missionary doctor smiled, his face crinkling, as his eyes seemed to bore keenly into the very quiddity of the phenomena that met his gaze: fire, woman, tears, teacup, restless shadows.

'You crossed the bridge, didn't you?'

I reluctantly nodded. Truly I can say I have not met a wiser man.

'When you're ready you'll remember what you saw—not now, not even soon, maybe, but some day when you least expect it. With the unconscious, the harder we try to remember, the harder it is for our memories to reappear.' The fire was low. It was almost dying. He helped me into my coat. Outside, the daylight had faded into deepest dusk.

As we passed into the reception room I heard the cinders fall together with a crumbling sound and, glancing back, I saw a greyness was stealing over their glowing depths.

In the darkness of the college grounds, as I approached the imposing gates, I heard the African seminarian still arguing as he pursued his young Welsh co-religionist:

'Will you stop and listen to me for one second,' the African called angrily, 'and see some sense! Can't you understand? A hypnotised patient and his hypnotist don't differ in the slightest degree from the relative position of a certified lunatic to the chief warder of an insane asylum!'

His words still rang in the night air as I passed through the gates.

Thursday, April 6 . . . Saman twén-twén

His name is Bryn! Seven years my junior! We met again by chance (?) at the café. He was sitting in the same position, but this time alone. Our eyes met.

When I was seated he walked over to my table carrying his own coffee.

'So you worship, too, at the shrine of the Okomfo?' he said with an ironic twist to his lips. He has a shock of luxuriant dark hair, and the sturdy thews and deceptive grace of an Arms Park full-back.

'The Okomfo?' I repeated puzzled, as he boldly sat down.

'Otherwise known as Dr Priestly—*Doctor Okomfo*, that's what Kwesi calls our mutual friend at the mission. Kwesi's so fiercely damnatory he's renamed it the Ministry of Mesmerism!'

Bryn's face is most attractive when he laughs, otherwise he can look rather morose.

'An *Okomfo* is a fetish priest in Kwesi's local parlance when he's back home at Kuamina. That's the township where the mission is. Dr Priestly baptised Kwesi a Christian. But now Kwesi is torn apart denying his pagan roots.'

'I think I begin to see . . . ' I began.

'Oblige me by refraining from thought,' Bryn said sternly, 'that is not your purpose here.'

We both laughed in recognition; I felt a surge of relief flow through my limbs; the sort of feeling you rarely experience except when discovering a new friend in whom you can place absolute trust.

'Kwesi may think like a Christian Rationalist,' Bryn resumed, 'but all his instincts tell him to accept the witness of his own eyes.'

'How do you mean?'

'Ask Kwesi about his pagan friend, Osei, back home in the township!'

I leant forward across the table. I saw the pupils of Bryn's eyes dilate, as if his interest had been aroused, and I wondered whether in my own eyes he saw a corresponding response. Pupil dilation, I'm aware, is said to be irresistibly attractive in women.

'No, *you* tell me,' I nodded eagerly.

'Well, one day, this old school friend, Osei, shows up at Kwesi's door. Haven't set eyes on each other for more than ten years. Since school, see? Seems Osei had got himself in some scrape or other. Banished from the town by the Elders; warned never to return. Then Osei tells Kwesi how in a far distant village he has fallen in love with a young woman who had *died* in their home town of Kuamina some three years *before*. Because he had been banished from their community Osei had not known of her death, see?

'In Kuamina the pagans believe that a person who dies prematurely can appear in another town and continue their life there.

'*Saman twén-twén,* Kwesi calls them.'

I shivered.

'Custom has it that the *Dead-but-Leaving-People* can be seen only by someone who has not heard of their death. This experience Osei claimed to have had with the dead woman.'

'He had not heard of her death, you mean?'

'Right enough! A week later, after Kwesi's reunion with Osei and his friend's departure, a report appeared in Kuamina's local newspaper.

'Seems a girl from Kuamina had been to visit friends in the Eastern region where she saw in their photo album a picture of a young married man who turned out to be a *Died-but-Leaving-Person* now settled in her Kuamina District! She was told the young man had died in a road accident two years back!'

I was visibly trembling by now, and Bryn took my shaking hand in his. Then he resumed:

'Shocked by this knowledge, this girl asked her friends to accompany her back to her home district to see this person with their own eyes! However, on the very day they arrived it was reported that the *Died-but-Leaving* young man had left with his wife the previous evening and, to date, he has not returned.'

'You mean . . . ?'

'Yes! That young man was Osei!'

We stared at each other, immersed in our own thoughts. Bryn did not release my hand.

'Hypnosis was once taboo, now it's accepted practice,' he said. 'Who's to say there are not great untapped powers of the spirit we have no words for?'

'What do you intend to do?' I asked gently.

'Me?' He grinned nonchalantly. 'I must haunt my own dreams until I learn their meaning. That's what oldDr Okomfo decrees. What about you?'

'Likewise,' I said. 'But, in my case, I haunt my own daydreams.'

Sunday, April 9 . . . A Stain of Memory

The worn-out old clock on the mantlepiece has just wheezed and struck six. Curiously, unthinkingly, I've resumed the study routine of my schooldays here in Aunt Nesta's front parlour.

Nevertheless, my emotions are mixed when I recall those years of grinding self-application, diligently completing homework in a home that was not my own.

Mam was not long dead, Da was out on strike, surviving on hand-outs of food parcels and soup kitchens, while Uncle Emrys, a colliery electrician in a different union, crossed the picket lines every day at the pit gates.

Da's double humiliation was the knowledge that each evening, after school, I sought the welcoming warmth of Aunt Nesta's household, bought at the price of his brother-in-law's 'scab' labour (an unfair view); another act of treachery recorded in his Judgement Book.

Da's funeral was last Friday. There was no inquest.

I'm ashamed to admit it, but my working materials—my coloured pens, my notes, my files, my card index box, my eraser and ruler—spread out here on Nesta's protective green baize cloth are a kind of consolation, as they always were in that time of tumult and sadness, when entire communities lost their livelihoods.

Ultimately, even Uncle Emrys himself was out of work, a defeat that occasioned a truce between the two men . . . Da and sinner reconciled . . . and a double line was drawn under their differences.

Da and Emrys still argued, of course, but both agreed that, with a free market in freefall, they were powerless to oppose laissez-faire economic policies that fostered global corporatism and the dumping of imports.

In the event, both those men, whose working lives had been spent below ground with blackened faces, found work in a factory making white goods . . . gleaming tumble dryers and spotless washing machines.

Yet a dark stain remained on my family history, however hard Da may have tried to wash it away—a stain of memory that, according to Dr Priestly, cannot be removed even by the Lethian waters of forgetfulness.

❁

Wednesday, April 12 . . . A Quest for Selfhood

My appetite has returned and has strengthened me with a renewed vitality so, today, I was prompted to revisit my childhood haunts where the playing fields skirt the foothills above the town.

Although you may imagine me to be a sedentary individual, I think I can fairly lay claim to being an athletic girl, yet not excessively developed in any particular direction—a lack of definition that is, no doubt, matched by the colourlessness of my looks (regardless of my distinctive hair, obviously).

At my college I indulge in rowing and swimming, *ad libitum*, in their respective seasons, and I can walk fifteen miles without undue fatigue so, when I breasted the brow of a hillside path and I met Bryn making the same ascent, I proposed we should strike out together in the direction of Da's old colliery.

Bryn, I noticed, seemed withdrawn and greeted me with a lifeless voice; the blue of his eyes seemed to have faded into an ashen grey, and the warmth of his flesh tones had visibly paled. Even his manner had cooled.

'I hardly expected to see you again,' he said.

'Why on earth not?' I was unaccountably stricken by his remark.

'Last week I felt you had turned a corner in your life, so you had no more use for me.'

I could not repress a short laugh. 'Then I must have disguised my feelings remarkably well, for nothing is further from the truth.'

'No,' Bryn said with a strange fervent certainty. '*No*. Though you are harder hit than I am, you're far nearer to the *truth* than you know.'

Bryn sighed. In some ways he looked stronger in spirit, in others he seemed subdued and, in his pallid diffidence, appeared quite unlike the robust stranger of our first encounter. A reverse symbiosis seemed to be at work: Bryn gave every sign of physically weakening—fading to a shadow of his former self—while I, conversely, seemed to draw vigour from his decline, all faintheartedness dispelled by a strengthened resolve to persist in my own quest for selfhood.

We trudged on in silence.

Mists were creeping westward over the hills, and the afternoon air was growing chill.

Da's colliery when we reached it was, I discovered, like a ghost town of abandoned buildings. The old mine shafts have been filled and capped, so the landscape has changed beyond all recognition.

The slag heaps, where men like Da once scavenged in the snow for coal during the strike, are now grassed over, and they stand amid wind-bent saplings like green Mayan pyramids on the sides and tops of the hills.

I was reminded of something a friend of mine once said. *Stef.*

Stefan, who works in our Slavic and East European Studies Department, specialises in Russian SciFi. It was Stefan who first introduced me to the concept of 'Terra-forming', the process of planetary engineering to deliberately modify a planet to resemble Earth in order for it to be colonised by humans.

'*Love*,' Stefan said, 'is not unlike terra-forming . . . the greening of a frozen planet can be achieved by melting the permafrost and releasing volatiles into the atmosphere to bring about temperate warmth.'

Stefan had then held my hand suggestively and traced each finger with his own until I had favoured him with a watery smile and abruptly withdrawn from his clasp.

You see, at that time, the defensive self-deception I then practised deluded me into thinking Stefan was shooting a line.

Now as I gazed at that extraterrestrial vista, the grassed over detritus, which disguised the true depths of our community's sore-toiled accretions, I could see that, in my rejection of Stefan, I had disguised my true feelings too well, and I'd concealed a quickening heart that he would gladly have read, yet could not until I chose of my own impulse to reveal it to him.

Bryn, as if he had guessed my straying thoughts, turned abruptly and retraced his steps along the path. The light had dimmed, and the mist spoiled the view landwards. Below us the sea was sluggish.

Nothing else passed between Bryn and myself this afternoon which I can now recall except, as we reached one of the many icy torrents that course down the valley, he overtook me and leapt to the further bank.

'I would give you a head start,' he called, 'but you're a long, long way ahead of me even when I'm in front.'

He was still waving when the mist enveloped him.

Friday, April 14 . . . A Prenatal Vision

The Vice-Mistress has written a note of commiseration, which I received in yesterday's post, and I responded with assurances (more or less true) that I have resumed my academic history of our pioneering nineteenth-century, women-only campus: *Voces Feminae, A Feminist Curriculum.*

But, more and more, I reflect on the paper trail of dead ends that is my own life story, and on an infancy that has been expunged from the history books.

Last night I had a richly detailed dream which has been preoccupying my thoughts all day and distracting me from my studies.

I dreamt I saw the tin footbath Da once used to carry in the coal. I saw it now emerging from a mist, floating on a stream, and coming to rest in the midst of bullrushes. Then the bath transformed itself into a basketwork cradle in which lay a sleeping infant.

How fatuous is the unconscious in its choice of imagery, I thought when I awoke. Yes. I could quite see my dream-self had stumbled upon the infant Moses in the bullrushes. So far, so clear.

Interpretation? Evidently a wish-fulfilling dream more vivid than any found in Dr Freud's *Der Traum ist eine Wunscherfüllung.*

And, *nota bene* the *basket* . . . for, of course, Moses, like myself, was a *foundling* whose legitimacy was conferred only by the *finder* since the infant was raised to be a prince. It is said that Moses stuttered, so a speech impediment is also another rather obvious signifier to identify myself, the *dreamer*, in this brief vision of my unconscious prenatal wholeness, a vision for which I'd been prepared by no less than an ordained minister of mesmerism.

At college, my lectureship and, indeed, my own books demand my analysis of themes drawn from nineteenth-century feminism, while a great deal of my critical work concerns itself with *contextualisation*, so you will not wonder if I regard the interpretation of dreams as simply an extension of this branch of study.

The so-called 'philosophico-sociological' novels of those distant times can often provide the key to understanding the social context, yet scholars like myself will readily admit to the daunting complexity of reconstituting a forgotten world.

Like the aim of novelists one reads, the critic of human actions has to thread each hidden pathway of feeling and thought that leads up to every moment of action, and account for all those intense emotions which take on the quality of action, all of which, taken together, make up the inner life which is the secret impetus of the public process of history.

Therefore, as a social historian, I despair when I pause to consider the infinitely more complex task of piecing together my own prenatal history with the paucity of data at my disposal, viz. an incinerated birth certificate.

Aunt Nesta has just this minute put her head round the door to enquire whether I'd like a fillet of hake for my tea. She's discerned no change in my habits, I'm sure, and regards me as steadily industrious as ever, bent over my books, my face composed in calm zeal.

Of course, all the while I am seething inside, impatient for another of those activations of the unconscious promised me by Dr Priestly . . . another step towards the solution to the enigma which is myself,

Jung, according to Dr Priestly, defined neurotics as *persons divided against themselves*. How very true! For clearly there are now within me two opposing psychic realities exerting pressure to be conjoined: the psychic dichotomy of my *adopted* persona as it seeks, justly, fusion with my *pre-adopted* self where it drifts in a sea of vagueness amidst hazy islands of infant memory that float with no apparent connection between them.

(*'Five minutes, love! A very nice tea I have waiting for you!'* Aunt Nesta sounds naggy and crotchetty; that's the tone she reserves for when I've failed to respond to her first call.)

Last night's dream led me *literally*, I now realise, on 'the *royal* road to the unconscious' in so far as I met one of Jung's regal *archetypes*, the Infant Moses, an unconscious, pre-existent form expressive of a universal idea . . . in this case, a motif expressive of what I consider to be my own *bastardy* but sublimated by a humble foundling's elevation to a *principality* as one of the elect.

In other words, my dream has vouchsafed me a *positive self-image*, which hints at the promise of some kind of transcendence.

At this precise moment, struck by a genuine flash of inspiration, it occurs to me that in my own history of our nineteenth-century feminist campus (my notes are stacked at my elbow) I have all the materials I need to create my own female archetype, my own private *myth* of an *Ascendant Foundling* who, cut off from the uncertainties of her past, prevails in a hostile present.

As I have repeated many times to Stefan: 'A woman without a past has no future.' And I was never so conscious of those words as when I reached the age of majority and, on my eighteenth birthday, walked out of my childhood home never to return.

(*'Tea's on the go! Time's slipping by, girl!'* That's Aunt Nesta's final warning.)

So to this undertaking I'll forthwith address myself, and after tea I shall begin.

Friday Evening, April 14 . . . An Exercise in Automatic Writing

I've decided to model my own personal archetype on those unconventional heroines found in the fictions of George Gissing, an olympian nineteenth-century novelist and feminist whose female protaganists may be seen as precursers holding the banner of post-Wollstonecraftian sexual radicalism in the last quarter of the nineteenth century.

It's appropriate that Gissing drew inspiration for his fictional adherents to female emancipation from the celebrated French anarcho-feminist firebrand, Louise Michel, herself *illegitimate* and the daughter of a serving maid; Gissing even heard her lecture at La Salle de Conférences in Paris.

(*The daughter of a maid, like the wife of a bachelor, is well taught, or so they say.*)

In my own mind, Louise is the younger, fierier, chance begotten counterpart of the gentleborn Barbara Leigh Smith Bodichon, also *illegitimate*—a founder of Girton College, Cambridge, and authoress of *Reasons for the Enfranchisement of Women.*

So, in my period text that follows, you'll note the two leading players in my personal myth are intended as two sides of the same coin—a double-headed coin, as it were—an *ego* and an *alter ego*, whose contrasting highborn and lowborn social ranks reflect Gissing's own preoccupations with class differences between feminist militants in their struggle for self-determination.

A Stranger in Blood

by Georgienne Guissant

The gravel, like grapeshot, continued to strike even after Edith opened the casement window.

'Duncie! Duncie!' a husky, youthful contralto called commandingly from the moonlit garden below.

Edith Smallwood adjusted her blue-tinted, half-moon bifocals and gazed down severely at her errant study roommate, a silhouette half-concealed within the shrubbery which fringed the cinder tennis-court.

Glossy laurels glimmered in the lamplight.

Distantly, from the chapel carolled the voices of Edith's fellow 'undergraduettes' (as they were known disparagingly by Town and Gown).

Wake, awake, for night is flying;
the watchmen on the heights are crying:
awake, Jerusalem, at last!
Midnight hears the welcome voices
and at the thrilling cry rejoices;
come forth, ye virgins, night is past . . .

A pigeon, startled from its roost, fluttered from beneath the eaves and alighted on the coping of the high wall which surrounded the collegiate gardens.

'Sh-h-h-ush!' Edith cautioned and—leaning full stretch from the first floor window of their sitting-room quarters—extended her hand to grip the elegant wrist of the Hon. Freda Nevill who scrambled up the wistaria creeper with the ease of long practice.

There was a slither of polished *crêpe de Chine* as Freda slid over the sill and subsided in silken billows on the window seat.

Edith dimmed the gas and drew the drapes hastily; at the college gates the porteress had emerged from the lodge in her nightgown and was staring malevolently in their direction. (Either by providence or low cunning Freda had never yet been 'gated'.)

'Wake, awake, for night is flying! The watcher at the gates is crying,' giggled Freda.

'Are you weak-witted?' reproached Edith. 'Curfew's been called long since! I fibbed to the Sturgeon. Said you were "indisposed".' ('The Sturgeon', a grande dame, was Miss Marguerite Sturgeon, their college principal.)

Despite her annoyance Edith could not conceal the tremor of tenderness which entered her voice when she presumed to chide her headstrong, high-born confidante.

A tin of condensed milk, and a single cup of cocoa—cold, congealed—stood on the hearth with a saucer placed on top of it, a token of Edith's long, anxious vigil. However, the pathos of this loyal sacrifice (for, such were the exigencies of her frugal budget, Edith would retire cocoaless that night) was beneath the notice of Freda who merely yawned, unbuttoned her gloves, and lit a cigarette.

'Do I *look* as though I care a rap for La Sturgeon?' Freda drawled languidly. 'I'm dead beat. Fetch me a brandy and soda, there's a good girl. And unlace my boots for me.'

Edith did as she was bidden, *but*—in removing the Hon. Freda's boots (which were damp from dew)—she could not help noticing that, though her fellow student's stockings were sheer and without flaw, the silk encasing Freda's slender left ankle exhibited a cluster of pine needles, trapped like fragile pressed flowers, *between* hosiery and flesh.

Edith frowned. Her roommate's petticoat and evening cape both smelled of cigar smoke which mingled with Freda's own distinctive fragrance of lilac-water and hair wash.

Edith brought an ashtray from the davenport on which a stack of uncut scholarly journals and yellow-back novels bore witness to Freda's abandoned studies.

The stack's height was outmatched by a sheaf of billets doux addressed to Freda, bound in red ribbon. Of the identity of Freda's ardent correspondent Edith was perfectly aware. He was a gentleman with whom Edith, like so many other young women attending the ladies' colleges, was well acquainted. His name was James Furness-Stirling M.A. (Oxon); he was one of the junior visiting tutors who instructed them under the stern eyes of the Sturgeon's ever-vigilant regiment of chaperones.

That James, a married man, was Freda's lover was a secret shared only with Freda's dutiful adorer, 'Duncie' Smallwood.

Freda suddenly threw back her head and laughed, exhaling a column of cigarette smoke.

'James told me tonight that La Sturgeon had called him an "obscurantist". I assured him it wasn't true, of course.'

'Then what did *James* say?' Duncie asked eagerly; her hand flew to her throat which had reddened in an access of emotion. Her pulse always raced at the mention of the worldlinesses of James. (He wore his hair long, curled over his collar, like Tennyson.)

Freda shrugged.

'Oh, James just laughed! Said it must be true about him being an obscurantist, because, hang it all, his *wife* certainly doesn't understand him!'

~

That night Edith could not sleep.

'*Pine needles*,' she thought, and tried to imagine sharing a coverlet of leaves with James in an enchanted woodland glade.

'*Pine*,' Edith yearned and—recalling James's aureole of fair hair, his Tennysonian mien—her ever-veering thoughts turned forlornly to *Idylls of a King* and . . .

. . . the one true knight on earth,
And only lover; and through her love her life
Wasted and pined, desiring him in vain.

Behind the curtain, dividing their sleeping cubicles, the Hon. Freda Nevill, seductress *in excelsis*, breathed in her slumber with the long, soft expirations of the blessedly satiated.

Edith wept silently in despair. '*Desiring him in vain*,' she whispered to herself. Was lovelessness ever to be her own lot? Was she never to know romance and rule James's heart?

Even the University Bookshop had seemed intent on thwarting her. The bookseller had pursed his lips in refusal when Edith had requested the *Idylls*: 'We never have had any poetical effusions on our shelves, and we don't think we shall begin now.'

Her innocent enquiry had been treated as though it were a cause of offence to the severest censors of the University's morals and manners.

~

Edith's utter humiliation and dejection were compounded the very next day.

The snub was such it could never be forgiven!

The irreconcilable rift in the two girls' relations had occurred but twelve hours after Freda's nocturnal escapade.

While attending a free Sunday Concert in the park, the Hon. Freda, surrounded by her intimate coterie, had chanced to fix her glance on Edith approaching the University's exclusive 'Honourable Set'.

Edith's timid 'Mayn't I join you?' was rewarded with the frostiest of stares and the collective disdainful silence was relieved only by her departure.

Giggles. Sniggers. Whispers. Awkward hauteur.

'A misguided creature, Duncie,' Edith heard Freda remark in an undertone. 'A pass-school's girl and an absolute prig. To be so wedded to her books is positively immoral!' The sally was greeted with unconstrained tittering. A tall angular girl with a burnished nose named Agnes laughed the heartiest.

Snared by the thoughtless cruelty of youth, Edith, on her first day at the college, had been dubbed 'Duncie'. 'Don't you *see*?' Agnes had squealed, 'Smallwood! *Small* wood! The Scottish play! Till the *smallest* wood do come to Dunsinane! You shall be *Duncie*!'

So Duncie Smallwood she was.

That Freda could 'cut' lectures with impunity, and scamped her study notes, was due in no small part to the fact that her noble grand-mother was the college's benefactress who, in recognition of her endowment, had been given a seat on the College Council.

Ad summam, in any examination sat by Freda she was unlikely to be 'ploughed'.

By contrast, Edith's three-year open exhibition scholarship (£30) to the Ladies' College had been won under the fosterage of S.H.E.W.—The Society for Higher Education for Women.

Of humble birth, Edith was registered ostensibly at the college as 'an intending schoolmistress'. However, unknown to Miss Sturgeon, Edith's true avocation was the study of Jurisprudence and Political Economy, viz. the 'Woman Question'. (Edith had been charged by the eminent suffragists who were her sponsors to submit clandestine treatises on Women's Property Rights to the Society's Parliamentary Repeal Committee.)

Edith sought the shadows of a yew-hedge walk. Laughter from the sun-lit circle of society-girls rippled after her.

'True equality is perfect freedom of action,' Edith quoted moodily, brooding on the injustices of a class system in which good breeding was valued over mastery of advanced mathematics. (*'True Equality is Perfect Freedom of Action'* happened to be the motto

enscrolled on S.H.E.W.'s banner under which Edith proudly and publicly marched.)

~

Alone at last, Edith flung herself on the sofa of the study sitting-room she shared with Freda. A fire was burning brightly but she felt no inclination to make tea.

She rose and touched a spring in a bureau, whereupon a shelf suddenly dropped down and her washing apparatus came into view. She was tired, hot and dirty, yet even a cool face-cloth on her brow and a dash of Freda's cologne could not calm her febrile agitation.

She lightly dusted her face with custard powder to conceal two livid marks of anger which now flushed her cheeks. (A want of cosmetics was another of Edith's privations.)

Edith replaced on her pinched nose the blue-tinted spectacles of the neurasthenic she affected to wear. She was comforted by the belief that blue lenses singled her out as an active intellectual among the University's professional brain-workers. She found herself twisting her handkerchief into knots.

On the davenport the college maid had placed a wax-sealed envelope.

'Mene, mene, tekel, upharsin,' Edith breathed.

Like scriptural words of flame the name of the addressee burned into Edith's mind:

To the Hon. Freda Nevill.

On the reverse, on the envelope's flap, were inscribed these initials:

I.L.Y.A.A.Y.D.

With the utmost care Edith broke the seal and withdrew the envelope's contents.

Her heart leapt.

The lines were written with James's unmistakable 'J' nib. (Edith recognised the penmanship from the marginal comments which appeared on her own respectable quantum of note-taking following James's lectures in Jurisprudence.)

My Darlingest PenELOPE,
[another intimate classical allusion, evidently!]

I have had the greatest difficulty in obtaining the number of pilules and tinctures you expressly desired me to beseech Dr Weissl to prescribe for your 'cure'. To complete your stock, he will kindly forward, under separate cover, the medicines you named on your list. There is no cash to remit as the quantity has been made up to the guinea I have rendered to the consulting herbalist.

With kisses a thousandfold,
forever enslaved,
and counting the days,
Your Ulysses

'PenELOPE!' So! Elopement! And worse! And 'Illiad?' I.L.Y.A.A.Y.D. Even Edith had heard the whispered explanation for those initials; they stood for 'I love you and adore you darling'.

Edith folded her hands on her lap in an attitude of prayer but, in truth, she was fiercely calculating Freda's long-overdue comeuppance, all the while inwardly chanting her newfound numerological spell: *'Mene, mene, tekel, upharsin . . . count, count, weigh, DIVIDE!'*

She narrowed her eyes, bitterly contemplating the passionate flourishes of James's running script, then she softened the wax with a heated poker, resealed the envelope, and returned the letter to the davenport.

Edith's mood lightened.

'And she who divides, rules.'

The following night, Edith, steadfast, waited and counted, counted and waited, seven long hours before the arrival of the moment she had chosen to exact the full weight of her revenge.

Her patience was rewarded.

Outside on the cobbles a carriage halted.

Edith consulted her watch.

'Oi'll give it foive,' she said in her best Black Country accent.

A flurry of white and the pigeon flew over the high wall.

A flurry of white and Freda scaled the wall.

A tattoo of gravel beat upon the study window-pane.

The chapel clock chimed six; dawn loitered on the horizon.

'O Duncie, Duncie, wherefore art thou?'

Enfolded in an aura of lilac-water and cigar smoke, the Hon. Freda Nevill tumbled through the window into the room.

'Damn this nunnery, my girl, I intend to fly the coop.'

(Freda's own pronunciation was distinguished by 'gel' and 'demn'.)

'Is that a fact?' Edith scolded. 'You said you'd be back by five.'

(Edith's own enunciation had a tendency to revert to 'Zarrafact?' and 'foive'.)

Soon, Edith was kneeling to unlace Freda's boots.

Edith simulated idle chatter, adopting a light, prattling style of speech.

'Tell me, dear, since we first met,' Edith asked disingenuously, 'I have never enquired, but in which year were you born?'

'Why, we're of an age, are we not?' Freda Nevill answered snappishly with a puzzled air. After the chill of the night, the warmth of their little sitting room lulled her senses, and she could think only of her soft bed. (It was from Heal's.)

'Exactly! Both born 1860!' Edith exclaimed. 'We have each passed our seventeenth year.'

'And what is that to you?' Freda demanded impatiently.

'Well,' answered Edith, relishing the moment, 'your people will take a pretty dim view of a girl who thinks to elope with a married man before her age of majority! I don't doubt they'll disinherit you!'

Each word was imbued with the venom of long-brewed spite.

'And just s'ppose the Sturgeon happened to hear of it? What then?' A harsh edge of threat coarsened Edith's words.

But, to Edith's astonishment, Freda just simply unpinned her glorious tresses and coolly commenced to brush her hair.

Moreover, the Hon. Freda was shaking with suppressed mirth.

'My poor foolish Duncie.' Freda smiled without malice. A note of compassion had crept into her voice. 'You really ought to attend more earnestly to your lessons.'

'M-m-my lessons?' Edith stuttered in confusion.

'Quite! Your studies in Jurisprudence with James!'

Freda seated herself at their dressing table and handed Edith the familiar ivory-backed hairbrush, engraved with Freda's heraldic family crest.

'Don't be fooled by *that* old thing!' Freda pouted, pointing to the aristocratic coat-of-arms.

Absentmindedly, Edith Smallwood found herself in the dim gaslight brushing Freda's long superfine silky hair while Freda threw back her fashionable pale Rossettiesque throat, from which issued an astonishing revelation.

'You should know, my dear Duncie, that my "honour" is not only irredeemably compromised by my faithful paramour, the divine James, but my "Hon." was never, indeed, conferred at my birth.'

'You don't m-m-mean . . . ?'

'Precisely, *ma petite*! I entered this world a babe *ex fornicatione*. A misadventure of my mother's! *Me!* A nameless piece of babyhood, the product of an irregular liaison!'

'In other words . . . that is to say . . . ?'

'I'm a *bastard!* There now! Aren't you satisfied? To dearest Papa, legally, I'm "a stranger in blood" to whom he can admit no consanguinity. But, thankfully, my *faux* papa is a peer of the realm who thinks it proper that his "daughter", however disgraced, should retain her honorific and her *privileges*.'

'But the law!'

'The law makes use of words in any way it pleases, you silly goose! My! How little learning has pierced that thick head of yours! Properly speaking, of course, there can be no more an illegitimate legitimate than there can be an oblique-angled square or an elliptical circle! Anyhow, my *virtuous angel*,' Freda taunted affectionately, gazing with profoundest pity at Edith in the looking-glass, 'adulterine bastardy has its distinct merits.'

Edith instantly was afflicted with remorse and shame for behaviour whose ugliness branded her unclean. She had often speculated as to why Freda was not a communicant at chapel.

'I have examined the law entirely to my satisfaction,' Freda resumed. 'I am *filia nullius*—don't you see?—a "daughter of no one". The advantages over a peer's legitimate issue are inestimable! Do you really imagine the Age of Majority applies to my case. It doesn't! Hah! *Ætas proxima pubertati!* Unlike *your* girlhood the purity of mine has been much abbreviated. As a bastard, ever since I passed the age of sixteen I've considered myself a *fille majeure* with the perfect right to marry without parental consent, you blind ignoramus!'

Edith gulped. Blood rushed to her head.

Then, as quickly, she recovered herself and recallingMr John Stuart Mill—who had once so memorably addressed Edith's sister-suffragists under their society's banner—the great man's clarion words ran away with her tongue.

'Marriage is legalised slavery,' Edith declared. 'To be the bond-servant of a husband is to divest yourself not only of your freedom but also of your fortune.' She paused to pluck a quotation from the air. *'Women must have their wills while they live, because they make none when they die.'*

'Oh, for goodness' sake!' Freda tossed her head and considered her reflection complacently. 'Grand-mama's very fond of me, you know,' she continued, 'she's promised a handsome dowry upon my marriage. I'm her sole heiress, and I may dispose of my fortune as I wish.'

'But James is *married!*'

'Marriage to be annulled on the grounds of non-consummation,' pronounced Freda in a clipped, matter-of-fact manner, and lit a cigarette.

Edith pointed, horrified, to a blue glass medicine bottle, with a bright orange label, that Freda was eagerly unpacking from a pharmacist's parcel delivered by the last post.

'Freda, tell me truly,' Edith pleaded, 'you're not—um—in a *delicate* condition! I *must* know!'

'Ever the simpleton, Duncie!' Freda scoffed. 'These are *sea-sickness* pills and powders for my rendezvous with James in Calais! Tomorrow!'

'Termorrer? Oh, Freda! Heaven be praised!'

The Hon. Freda Nevill felt a warm teardrop fall as Edith gently kissed the nape of that oh-so-fashionable pale Rossettiesque neck.

'But really, you know,' Edith murmured, almost admiringly, 'all along I never thought you anything less than a *complete* bastard!'

Saturday, Dawn, April 15 . . . A Retributive Sorority

Waking at dawn is one of the things I most dread.

I awoke slumped over my manuscript with the light streaming around me, my hand shaking like scrivener's palsy, and listening to my own heartbeats.

It had been late when last night I finished my Gissingesque pastiche and there had been the strain ofre-reading my manuscript but, however astounding the surprises thrown up by my impromptu exercise in automatic writing, that *frisson* had not been enough to jolt me back to full wakefulness.

The perceptive reader will immediately guess that 'James Furness-Stirling M.A. (Oxon)' bears more than a passing resemblance to Stefan, and that not-so-innocent ragging endured by 'Edith' from the Black Country might just conceivably be a thinly masked account of an oversensitive Welsh scholarship-girl whose true mettle had been tested by a retributive sorority.

I hear Aunt Nesta stirring; I must close here before I'm discovered in her parlour with the light on and she bundles me off to bed.

Monday, April 17 . . . An Inkling

In less than one week, since my parting from Bryn, I have passed from that involuntary flash of hope to fresh torments of doubt. Anxiety gnaws at my very being. There are circles under my eyes as though I have an illness, and each day I find a deeper core of disappointment for my dark mood to feed upon.

A portion of each day I now spend walking by myself on the hills and, when I take up my books again, it's in a desultory, half-hearted way.

These shifts in my state of mind have not escaped the notice of Aunt Nesta, because were you to poke out each eye she'd still spy a fault.

This morning, as I was reaching for my raincoat in the hall she turned from dusting a gilt-framed photo that hangs above the door: a portrait of myself as a solemn schoolgirl.

She looked daggers as she stabbed at the frame with her forefinger.

'*Ach!* It's not proper at all when a child can cry in the night without making a sound!'

Nesta gave me a quick once-over.

'Sleep is better than prayer, for sure,' she chided, shaking her head. 'There's times I do wonder will you ever alter. As thin as a lath you are, and no more grown than a child. A *child* I do say, aye, never mind your book learning.'

Her large dark eyes were brimming with tears and she fumbled uncertainly in the pocket of her apron for a handkerchief.

'I don't know what we are going to do with you. Take a brolly.' She turned away abruptly to blow her nose. 'It's raining nasty.'

❁

So, empty of thoughts, disregarding the rain, I walked in a leisurely way for about half an hour before the day brightened.

I had a bad case of Little Town Blues, to be honest.

Descending a steep shale track, which links two vales, I fell into step behind the stooped figure of an elderly man whose former sweated servitude was evidenced in every aspect of his bearing to present no real challenge for my deductive powers.

I observed at least three signifiers: his frayed trouser ends were tied up with string as a matter of long habit; he walked on bowed cabriole legs characteristic of a worker who'd laboured in a cavity the height of a child under one thousand feet of stratal pressure; and, as he walked, he was shaken by fits of coughing that flayed his lungs.

Da, too, had been a victim of 'The Dust', the pneumoconiosis that had claimed the lives of so many of his mining comrades.

According to Nesta, when she had accompanied Da to his last consultation the doctor had diagnosed Da to be suffering from a red-blood cell deficiency as a side effect of his prescribed drugs regime for inflammation of the lungs. Da, typically, had merely shrugged and wheezed: 'Damn aye, has it come to that, man? Right-o, then.' In his rich baritone he'd then sung: *'Red cells in the sunset, way out on the sea . . . '* And that was the last the doctor saw of his patient, a pure Welshman through and through! *Cymro glân gloyw!*

Now, at the end of the track ahead of me, the ex-miner shuffled across the road and joined three of his mates at a bus stop. The clincher which decided this identity parade was when I saw these infirm old men hunker down on their haunches, the recognisable posture adopted by proud colliers to whom even their children, when addressing them, were expected to bend a knee.

Yet surprisingly, as I watched, the men rose as one and removed their caps.

The object of their reverence was a sleek hearse, gliding slowly into view, followed at a respectful distance by two taxi cabs from the railway station crammed with mourners. A moment later the funeral procession had turned a corner and was lost from view.

Notwithstanding the painful associations prompted by this dark apparition I struck out in the same direction down the road, my mind now oppressed by singular thoughts.

As I passed a high-walled enclosure, a deep-throated voice called coaxingly from the gate: 'Your watch must keep a different time! You are late but if you hurry you can make up lost time.'

'I beg your pardon,' I began, 'but, you're mistaken. I'm not . . .'

A man, vigorously black-bearded to his chest, beckoned from a stone pillared entrance.

'You're not?' he laughed. 'Well, seldom I saw a better.'

His olive-skinned appearance, melodious Welsh lilt, and gentle manner, produced an instantaneous effect in his favour.

'I could have sworn you were one of our party,' he continued and looked at me keenly. As he turned, I noticed two glossy black sidecurls dangled from beneath his homburg hat.

'I'd best go on,' I said firmly. 'I'm afraid I am *not* one of your party.'

He shrugged his shoulders and made an amused grimace with the nicest shade of off-handedness. As he shut the gate and locked it, I heard him mutter: *'Don't you be so sure, indeed, it could be true.'* The keys jangled in his hand. *'Well, that's it now, she's gone.'*

When I reached a gap in the wall I recognised the place for what it was: the old Jewish Burial Ground at Crag Zion.

I could see clearly the scene at the graveside. The young moon was still well up in the refreshed morning sky, shining weakly like a candle flame in daylight.

A cantor was reciting psalms. *'As for man, his days are but grass . . .'*

A bereaved young woman in a dark toque, her face in her hands, continually bowed and sobbed, uttering at each bow a gasping sound.

The pallbearers were lowering the coffin into the grave. The casket, I saw, was the most rudimentary affair, crudely constructed from chipboard and held by cheap tin handles. And a sinister detail, this: a number of holes had been drilled around the base of coffin, for what reason I did not want to even begin speculating.

The curly-bearded gatekeeper, who appeared to be one of the synagogal dignatories, was discreetly directing the ceremony. He gave a sign and there then stepped forward a rabbinical-looking notability whose own divided beard distinguished him as a Hebraic scholar of hair-splitting casuistry.

He bowed to the principal mourner, a diminutive well-groomed elderly woman with sharp features wearing dark glasses and an expensive-looking black cloche hat, and relieved her of the little black quilted handbag she was carrying, suspended on a fine gilded chain. Whereupon, a large shovel was placed in her hands.

Another mourner called out impulsively: 'Hear O Israel. The Lord has given and the Lord has taken away, blessed be the name of the Lord.'

The little old lady helplessly shovelled earth on to the coffin while the mourners rent their clothing swaying back and forth during prayer.

The gatekeeper then addressed the burial party but, I noticed, his eyes were fixed kindly on me: 'May the Lord comfort you among the other mourners of Zion and Jerusalem.'

My last glimpse of the mourners was of the old woman ritually washing her hands at the gardener's tap below the gap in the wall from which wafted the melancholy moss-grown fragrance of her *Chanel No5*.

When she removed her dark glasses I saw she was weeping.

Before I turned to slip away from that place I took a chip of white shale from the path and placed it in my pocket.

A second later a puff of dust flew up as Bryn jumped down from the wall and barred my path.

I laughed aloud with unalloyed pleasure as I recognised the one true friend who could draw me out of myself and my self-absorbed, profitless brooding.

'You are late,' he quoted, *'but if you hurry you can make up lost time!'*

'Then you saw . . . ?'

'I saw and *heard* everything!' He broke off and laughed bitterly. He was looking far out over the valley to the sea, and as he spoke his eyes kept the same direction as though staring into the future.

'I said you were very close to a new start to your life, and, believe me, Beth, I *know* you're going to make up lost time. Now *you*, too, are beginning to believe the same, aren't you?'

There was a brief silence for reflection. He seemed to be following my own thoughts. Something was struggling to the surface of my consciousness; a lost memory was feeling its way home again out of the infinite past.

'An inkling, I grant you,' I said at last, 'but I feel nothing more than that.'

'And as for me . . . ' Bryn bit his lip.

In the five days since I'd last seen him in the mists, Bryn seemed to talk less spontaneously, and in a tone—I could not quite say what it was—but a tone that perhaps suggested the seeds of resentment.

Yet, at the fork in the road where we parted, I observed a revival of his former animation.

'I must want my head read!' he said with a half-reckless smile. 'How Dr Priestly would welcome that confession! Fact is I'm still waiting for the old sceptic to show me a sign, even though . . .'

'Even though?' I prompted.

'Even though I can't quite admit the possibility of being saved from doubt. That's why your company means more to me at present. I'm telling you straight, Beth.'

He pressed my hand then we each took a different path.

How absurdly one conjectures about unknown people, I thought, as I reflected on that mysterious encounter at the bleak hillside graveyard.

I was reminded of an occasion at my new school in the first year of my scholarship. A girl from London who had once lived in Golders Green said to me one day in the changing rooms:

'You're a schonk, aren't you?' Her smile was disarmingly sweet, but I was swiftly to learn that it's the bait that hides the hook.

'I can't think what you mean.'

'A dead giveaway! I knew you were a schonk the very first time I saw you!'

After some gauche parrying on my part, my tormentor revealed, with a greater degree of circumstantial detail, her suspicions: apparently I resembled any number of Jewish girls of her acquaintance. In short, in her considered opinion, I looked more than mildly Israelitish. My *schonk*—my *schnozzle*—I'm aware is of a delicate Hebrew model, with a breadth of nostril unusual in similar formations.

It was as though the scales had fallen from my eyes, and since that revealing moment I have remained vigilant as to further confirmation of a Judaic ancestry tying together the loose ends of my fugitive existence.

Why else, I sometimes wonder, is my face powder that special shade of pale beige called 'Rachel', were I not of Hebraic descent? When I was still a very young girl Mam had shown a curious partiality for the 'Rachel' shade, I remember, as being the most suitable for my skin colouring and reddish hair when I grew up.

We were at the cosmetics counter at the pharmacy, I remember, and my eyes were fixed on the domed glass carboys of coloured water in the shop window. The red apothecary jar was always my preference. Mam had ruffled my hair and affirmed, with a peculiar mocking emphasis, the mead of praise every girl wants to hear: that my hair was my 'crowning glory', even though my mop of Judas-coloured ringlets were said by the more malicious of my classmates to have just sprung from the curling iron.

So sometimes I wonder whether, like Disraeli, I'm 'the blank page between the Old Testament and the New', except in my own case, given my spurious origin, I should perhaps regard myself as the blank page between the Old Testament and the *Apocrypha*.

It's a comparison that's the more apt when I contrast the puritanism of Disraeli's own father with that of my Da. They are not unalike. After all, as I recall, did not D'Israeli Sr describe the castration of Heloise's lover as no more than a humiliating 'injury'?

The delicacy of the point deferred to a Victorian prurience that prevailed, too, in the valleys of my youth.Da more than Mam worshipped the nonconformist Welshman's God of the Old Testament—a punitive, unforgiving teetotal god who condemns the lewd to plagues and pestilence and everlasting hellfire.

(*'Aye . . . aye . . . that's true, very true.'* I can almost hear Da's agreement.)

Yes. Da infinitely preferred the God of the Hebrews. In fact, ask any of our neighbours, Romish practices are anathema to Welsh nonconformists, an intolerance all the more striking when compared to their regard for the Jews.

Da enjoyed repeating the story of the first Jews who came to our little town. As they passed the houses, they had looked into the windows of the Welsh and saw a Bible in every home, so they decided this was the place to stay, because the natives were so pious!

Da equally admired the piety of the local Jewish community (of late a dwindling band). Da used to relate how, in his boyhood, his anticipation of Christmas would be further excited by the sight of the Hanukkah candles shining from the windows of God's Chosen, in the dark weeks of mid-December.

Da, however, admitted to a religious dispute once, long, long ago, when the foundations of the Jewish tabernacle, by tradition the tallest building in a community, were first planned. The elders of the neighbouring chapel objected to the height of the synagogue roof exceeding their own. The dispute was craftily resolved by Rabbi Elias of the *shul* who had the plans redrawn so his congregation might worship in a semi-basement whilst the floor-to-ceiling height remained precisely the same as the original design. However, the façade, as was customary, was still oriented towards Jerusalem.

On balance, Da said, the synagogue resembled an Anderson shelter but neither party could declare their own roof was any nearer to heaven.

Like his fellow chapel-goers, the Jew never blasphemed, so Da said.

According to Da, a Jewish miner of his acquaintance—Morris—had once crushed his finger in the coupling of a coaltruck but the pious man had forborne to utter a sacred name in anguish and, instead, had cried out 'Methusalem!' in a circumspect allusion to the Holy City.

❁

SATURDAY MORNING, APRIL 22 . . . A WOMAN OF STRAW

Each night past, the same unspooling ribbon of dreams has given me no rest.

In my recurring dream I am walking in the hills when I see an aeroplane's shadow flying ahead of me, growing larger and larger as it nears the brow.

At the same time I hear a sickening thud and I am aware of crying aloud, 'There is corn in Egypt!'

Then I see a bale of straw drop from the sky a few paces ahead of me and bounce and rebound against the Jewish cemetery wall.

Two men now hurry to the scene and I recognise the bearded gatekeeper in his homburg hat and the scholar with his shovel. I appear to be merely an observer, passive, and in some way frustratingly detached from the scene, because the two men take absolutely no notice of me.

The men then carry the bale to the gap in the wall and commence to fill in the missing section with straw. Slowly, as they build, the new-dug grave is concealed from view, until I run forward and put a match to the straw. As the sparks fly upward, a great physical need to shed tears arises within me and I awake weeping.

A dream like this, interpretable though it is by various symbols compatible with the theory of the archetypes, nevertheless still does not let me escape a giddy sense of disorientation. It's true the adoptee develops an acute self-consciousness of the kind to which most legitimate daughterhood never attains, habitually studying herself, and cultivating her self-awareness and her emotions simultaneously.

So on cool reflection, I'm pretty certain my dream refers to my earliest conscious memory: a rather hazy impression of myself lying in a pram. The hood of the pram is raised so I can see the blue dome of the sky above the garden. The sun is shining. Then the vast shadow of an aeroplane, passing low, blots out the warmth and I cry for comfort but no one comes.

Shortly before she died I mentioned this early memory to Mam. Her explanation? It appears that when I was a newborn baby I would wail unless cradled in Mam's arms. Nigh to total fatigue with my clamouring, Mam devised a woollen garment with weighted arms stuffed with straw in which I was clasped as I was laid in my pram.

An unfortunate disclosure! Small wonder that thenceforth I regarded Mam as a woman of straw.

(I hear Aunt Nesta at the back door bringing in the shopping. I'd assured her earlier I would spring clean the kitchen. 'You'll have to alter your stroke, my lady, expecting me to fetch and carry when you do say one thing and then do something different altogether!')

It is time to lay aside my books for a little; apparently the fated scheme of my existence requires at this point a new experience.

Like my dreams, the process of writing this journal is entirely unpredictable and I, the dreamer, cannot prescribe for myself any predetermined course.

Saturday Evening, April 22 . . . Breaking the Sabbath

This afternoon, just after tea, I realised with a start that today is the Jewish Sabbath and thoughts of visiting the synagogue began to exercise a certain seduction.

The dominant tone of my existence has been industrious scholarship and I usually relish my books, yet I never allow them to detain me from bodily exercise; besides, my disposition to study had waned so I walked out of the stuffiness of Nesta's rooms to find the taste of fresh air after showers was sweet.

I strode briskly and very soon I found myself in the poorest quarter of the town—twisting narrow alleys through which my strict upbringing had forbidden me to stray even when I ceased to be a child.

It was a fine, warm evening when I reached Jew Street which led to the synagogue; with no map to aid me I'd found it readily enough.

As I drew nearer I noticed the doors to all the houses were open and I heard muffled male laughter from within.

From a shop doorway wafted the rotten-egg fumes of sulphur. In the window hung a card bearing the notice: *'Closed from 1pm Friday and all day Saturday'.* Not until I had passed the entrance did I identify the eye-smarting odour of hairsetting lotion, which was all the more intense for its emanating from a small circle of women chirruping merrily in a hair and beauty salon, as they fussed with their permanent waves.

Permanent wave, I thought. Another *contradiction in terms* like an oblique-angled square or elliptical circle or illegitimate legitimate.

In my parting glance through the salon window I just caught a glimpse of a many-mirrored interior where a harsh light shone on the women's hair, which hung in strong, tight curls just like my own; the kind of hair I had always imagined would distinguish my own birth-mother and attest to her being truly mine.

You see, until I was eighteen I was convinced my *real* mother lived in the town where I grew up and I believed she was continually on the lookout for a child whose corkscrew curls would so closely resemble hers. Equally, I looked at *anyone* with whom I came in contact who raised the least suspicion as to a common ancestry, virtually selecting who I'd prefer to be my mother, and panicking when I feared a woman I'd singled out, say, in a cinema queue would actually recognise me, too!

Why this panic? There are still so many people in our town, you must understand, who look on illegitimacy as shameful and any mention of the true circumstances of my birth, as I have attempted to explain, was censored by Mam and Da, just as a believer in a primitive religion is crushed by the institutionalised censorship of an officially atheistic state.

In response to such strictures, an adopted child like myself has to show her adoptive parents time and time again she's been worthy of adoption, and that's what I've been doing, I suppose: I've been trying to gain as many qualifications as I can, just to say I'm worth all that faith they invested in me.

❁

The entrance doors to the synagogue were closed when I arrived. Below me, beyond the gloom of a semi-basement area, the threshold of an underground room glowed where the vaguely familiar silhouette of a man could be seen as he paused on the lowest flight of steps.

He must have heard my intake of breath because he turned, and looked up at me with bright eyes and a sparrow-like tilt of the head.

I thought I recognised the face as that of the gatekeeper at the cemetery; his presence at the tabernacle evidently confirmed his function as some kind of officiating beadle.

But in general appearance he seemed changed, greatly changed.

Lamplight streamed from the open door of a sort of oratory. He wore no hat and, in the glow from the doorway, his black beard now appeared grey; of his frizzy black side curls I could see none. His black trousers, too, were now grey, his coat unbrushed, and his boots looked as if they had not been cleaned for weeks. Certainly, to my eye, in his attire, he appeared infinitely less like a Levite than an exiled refugee.

It seemed to have taken less than a week to change that sacerdotal beard from raven black to dove grey, and to bring a cadaverous pallor to his face and bow his limbs with sunken old age. In short, he appeared to me to be thirty years older than when we'd last met.

His voice, when he spoke, was thin and reedy and quite lacked the vigour I earlier described.

'*Shabbat Shalom!*' he said, in a low concentrated voice. 'I see you've returned. You can't take out of the flesh what's bred in the bone.'

I opened my lips, but panic altered the words I was about to speak.

'You promi*th*ed I could make up lo*th*t time,' I said. In attempting to repress my nervousness, my lisp had returned. 'I thought I would break down at any moment and go to piece*th* altogether if I didn't come at once.'

'You'd be breaking more than that,' he said with mock severity, 'you'd be breaking the Sabbath. It's the third day of Passover, you should be at home.' He examined me from top to toe. 'Have you been fasting? Rather you should taste your tears by feasting, my little *shaifeleh*.'

You cannot imagine my agitation when he smiled, accorded me a short bow, and withdrew into his subterranean chamber. Our encounter has meant nothing, nothing, I thought, and now it's as though I am frightened at a shadow.

When I arrived home, before I could reach the front door, I fainted at the gate. The dusty privet hedge saved me from falling.

'Boy trouble is it?' I heard a neighbour ask my aunt. I felt Nesta's cool hand on my brow. Then she unbuttoned my collar.

'My nerves are weak,' I murmured, 'that's all.'

(I could not tell Nesta that for the past two weeks I'd neglected to take my prescribed course of pills; they'd alarmingly increased my appetite and I feared putting on more weight. Besides, one of the dire side effects was my head feeling as if someone had rammed it tight inside a box.)

'If you ask me,' the neighbour continued, 'what that girl needs is a square meal.'

❀

Sunday Evening, April 30 . . . Walpurgis Night

It's as though I've been on the receiving end of a tranquillising dart from some sort of stun-gun that's knocked me out for a week.

When I awoke this evening I seemed to sense the presence of flowers even though the room was in darkness.

I thought I could smell an intense mossy and greenleaf odour with an undersong of a delicate floral note.

Yet how untrustworthy our instincts can prove was borne in on me when I drew the curtains and beheld a pot of blue African violets drenched in the last of the evening sunlight.

Of an other-worldly blue those violets were, of an *otherworldliness* that suggested some special meaning, because when I drew close to the flowerheads I found them to be entirely *unscented*.

The plant-label revealed the violets to be a variety named *Neptune*; a gift from Stefan. On the tag he's scrawled, *Per Ardua ad Astra*.

The reference to Neptune does not escape me. Stefan would discuss endlessly the challenges of colonising the Blue Planet, undaunted by its dense white rind of frozen gases and its sunless frozen atmosphere.

Yes. Stefan's own instinct had guided him aright.

A *scentless* flower was a befitting tribute from an interstellar voyager to a coldblooded creature from another planet totally out of her senses.

An envelope was tucked within the plant's leaves.

Dearest Beth,

I heard you were out of sorts and I suspect you're having a dull time of it. I trust you're not working yourself to death. That will never do. I'm certain you'll pick up very soon and, meanwhile, I thought this potplant just the thing, as it thrives in artificial light . . . but, caution: overnourishment can destroy the roots.

Yours in more than camaraderie (I dare to foresee),
Stefan

How characteristic of Stefan, the SciFi buff, to have underscored his prescient certainty that he was mine! A daring foreseer! Not that I've provided any evidence to support his view.

Although science fiction is his strong suit, Stefan in his academic researches is ever a pragmatist who usually does not accept claims that the evidence supports claims which it does not.

Yours. A *possessive* pronoun. Mmm. The triumph of hope over experience, no doubt.

Boy trouble. Nesta's neighbour spoke truer than she knew.

As I earlier remarked, I've always regarded myself as a blank page whose history has yet to be written so, as a critic ever in search of her subtext, I'm aware that no one can read between the lines when the lines simply aren't there.

Except . . . in my teenage years, one older boy in particular reckoned an unfair advantage could be had from persistence in his mistaken belief that my unassuming youth was, like white paper, disposed to take any impression.

He was an adept at applying emotional pressure.

That first callow boyfriend I privately labelled *Briareus.* We were both studying Greek mythology at the time. Briareus was one of the hundred-handed ones—the Hekatonkheires—whose appearance at birth was so disconcerting it was pushed back into its mother's womb.

Something has always seemed to me amiss in the bounty of the gods.

Someone always has to be punished.

Apropos . . . Aunt Nesta has just poked her head into my sickroom.

'Proper chalky you are!

She examined the flowers and read the card with a raised eyebrow.

'Blue I do like, but pink I do rather.'

'I feel so wretchedly weak. I hate to feel weak.'

'Overwork it is, my silly goose.'

A *silly goose* was my aunt's favourite epithet when she considered I needed reproof as a child. I suspect her words were calculated to discourage any snappy rejoinders from a niece hampered by a speech impediment. As it was, thwarted by the frequently recurring sibilant, I would never have attempted *thilly goothe* as a retort, as she knew perfectly well. In fact, having lived with the problem of a lisp since my infancy, I vowed to avoid whenever possible any words with the letter 's' in them, a practice I maintain to this day with varying degrees of proficiency.

❀

'On *Th*unday, of cour*the*.'

This was my impaired reply when that schoolmate from Golders Green asked me the day reserved by my family for divine worship. A look of malicious pleasure had lit up her face upon learning the shibboleth that would defeat me.

The lisp slander with which I'd then been taunted, I now realise, was nothing less than a sly variant of the gross blood libel that once impugned my alleged race; not that I can pronounce the millennia-old 'shibboleth' even today, were you to ask . . . an archetypal speech defect that would doubtless resonate with Dr Jung or, indeed, a speech pathologist, since Moses, too, as I've remarked, had an afflicted tongue.

However, my journal was never meant to be an exercise in free association. My introversions can be honestly explained, and in these pages I've attempted to trace the source of many of them, but I do not shrink from admitting that I intend to give no further hint here as to my current state of mind.

Let me just conclude by noting that, against the humiliating sense of my own weaknesses, I am consoled by the reflection that I have been fortunate in meeting two men, out of thousands, who have touched my sympathies, for each, I now realise, exerts a strange fascination I find difficult to express.

Bryn, the recusant seminarian, faithful to the paradox of questioning doubt; and *Stefan*, the astro-scholar, who for constancy of belief finds comfort in the inconstancy of matter and imploding stars.

Sunday, Midnight, April 30 . . . Walpurgis Night (cont.)

I was still considering the *coseigneurie* of Stefan and Bryn as two prospective suitors, each with a claim on my heart, when I must have sunk back again into grateful repose.

Now midnight has just struck. The ball of my left thumb is pulsing with a humming node of pain.

The world seems to me very dark, and life a dreadful penalty.

It is as though there's a gnawed hole where my heart should be.

It's been seldom these past weeks that I've given attention to my book; so despite the grim hour I'm resolved to resume my note-taking.

There's a stack of *The Blue Book* from the 1920s, unread. *The Blue Book* I should explain is our Alumni Association's annual report, and it's a fertile source of anecdote, incident and quotation when charting my college's early history and its struggle for equity in higher education for women.

Its emblem on the title page is a sprig of blue rosemary for remembrance.

Later! Much later!

Twenty past four o'clock in the morning! When I peered at my watch I had to search for a missing hand.

Outside my window it's as black as the grave.

Yet I'm elated!
It's happened!
I've remembered!
Remembered . . . just as Dr Priestly promised me I would a month ago!
This is the entry I read in *The Blue Book* for 1928.

A Remarkable Memory

Slapped wrist for infant militant!

It's hard to believe that only ten years ago women voted for the first time in a General Election and, from this March, women could vote on the same terms as men. Even harder to believe, as our alumni's celebrated militant suffragette MARGERY NAIRN-JARDINE records in a recent note to your Editrix, that despite being only six months old when Queen Victoria died she remembers vividly the funeral procession at Windsor! Margery explains: 'As a band of sailors hauled the gun carriage with the coffin along the High Street, my mother slapped my wrist so severely that I burst into tears. "There!" she said, and bestowed a kiss, "that's to make sure you remember the day the old empire died!" '

My left thumb is throbbing so I can barely write!

It seems that after all I am not so wholly alien to my birth-mother's blood that I cannot recognise the immemorially known, and recall in my visions my head laid against her shoulder . . . visions that seem to me very strange and yet strangely familiar . . . visions of her black hair, falling in frizzy finger-waves against the olive complexion of her cheek, quite different from Mam's doughy jaw . . . I can see, even now, her hairline, her throat, with its darkly pigmented skin, and her elegantly convoluted ear.

It is as though she belongs only to me, as though we are connected in some way with other *mysterious things* I cannot understand . . . a *painting*, in a vast ornate frame, for example, and a tank swarming with *tropical fishes* . . . a *singer* from carnival . . . and all the while she's pinching my left thumb so I cry aloud in pain.

Monday, May Day Holiday . . . By the Pricking of My Thumbs

It was really too much to take in all at once. I walked the streets of our little town, but I didn't see the world around me for indeed my world was changed, and would never be the same again. I knew that I had been enriched beyond my wildest hopes and, though my head was reeling, I felt as though only now I had properly joined the human race.

My dream, I was confident, had changed my fate and given me a new commencement of life.

That dream! I dreamt I was being cradled in the arms of a warm presence who carries me into the lobby of an imposing building. There, under the atrium, to one side, stands a long, low, shelf-like table bearing a brilliantly lit aquarium in which swim violet-blue iridescent tropical fishes. My face is held up to the glass and I'm entranced, suspended in delight, until an intense pain seizes me in the pad of my left thumb. Then up a grand staircase we proceed, down a long corridor to enter a handsome vaulted room, its walls lined with old paintings and fine tapestries. In glass cabinets are displayed precious *objets d'art*.

Next, in quick succession, I am shown a vast oil painting of a bewigged statesman in flowing baronial robes (*likewise in acute pain*), and then a canvas theatrical backdrop painted with a figure from carnival (*intense pain, ditto*).

❀

Now, I told myself, as I briskly walked the sunny streets, I march with purpose.

The current of my life was slowly but surely carrying me towards the disinterment of a buried memory . . . I was in thrall to the inevitable . . . or was it merely my own personal *gestalt du jour*?

Suddenly, Bryn fell into step beside me.

'If you hurry you can make up lost time,' he said breathlessly.

His appearance startled me. His hair was tossed into disarray and illness unmistakably blanched his face. In a fortnight the change was very marked.

Without offering to shake hands, he took my arm.

His eyes, I noticed, had dulled, the lids half-clenched together from exhaustion and, beneath their sunken sockets, his cheekbones stood out the more starkly in the bright sunlight.

'You look at me,' he said, forcing a smile, 'as if you have a dread of me.'

'Are you not well? I said carefully.

We were not quite at ease together.

'I'm not feverish—at least I don't think so. Fearful head.'

We had reached the steps of the Municipal Art Gallery.

'When the world weighs too heavily,' he said, 'I come to you for strength.'

'Well,' I said, 'now it's *me* who's seeking *your* good advice.'

❁

The gallery lobby was just as it appeared in my dream, but there was no fish tank. This was a terrible blow.

My limbs began to tremble, and my heart beat heavily once more.

'I fear we're wasting our time,' I faltered, 'I've got myself into a thoroughly morbid state of mind, that's all.' Then my unsettled thoughts ran away with my tongue and I told Bryn all that was troubling me.

Straightaway he led me to the upper gallery. The gigantic room was unchanged. Two vast paintings faced each other.

'See!' Bryn exclaimed. 'They hang together, just as you said!'

I stared in perplexity at those symbols of my unknowability. In truth, I was simply shattered by a confrontation with my unconscious made manifest.

I shivered as though there was suddenly no sun.

The prickings of my left thumb were unrelenting.

By the pricking of my thumbs . . . open, locks, whoever knocks!

Through my tears I endeavoured to speak. I pointed to each canvas.

'But whatever they meant *then*,' I whispered, 'they've lost their meaning *now*.'

But Bryn merely stroked his chin and read a descriptive catalogue of the exhibits.

'The Marquess of Carmarthen,' he said pointing to the brooding aristocrat.

Then he indicated the figure on the painted backdrop by the notable weish portraitist, Deverill-Hewells.

'And that's not a *carnival*, that's a *pantomime*.'

He glanced out of the window to a courtyard below, overgrown with grass.

'And as for your vanishing fishes . . . I have an idea.'

❀

In the courtyard, Bryn tumbled on to the nearest bench. The colour of his flesh seemed to be fast draining away.

He passed his tongue across his dry lips.

'Ask Old Ifan,' he said. The hazily familiar figure of a gardener was bent over a flowerbed.

A lean dog with a muzzle shaped like a boat's prow approached, sniffed Bryn's trouser ends then, with a yelp, ran fearfully away.

The gardener turned at the sound and I recognised my ragged-trousered sympathiser whose plight, like mine, was spiritual homelessness. His face was as begrimed as when I'd first met him. Under a tree he'd cast down his pilgrim's burden—a cheap cardboard suitcase with straining locks so frail I felt all his worldly possessions would spill out at any moment.

Ifan shrugged in the direction of Bryn whose face had assumed a baleful and spectral appearance.

'Not quite like you and me, now, *fâch*! Dear me, no!'

'He's not himself today.' I glanced at Bryn with uneasiness but, I regret to record, I pressed on a little too eagerly and asked Ifan without ceremony whether the fishes once in the lobby were discoverable.

'All drowneded they were in your young day on account of a cold snap. Perished they were. Heating not up to the mark, see. Shameful. No end of a shindy there was about it. Beauties—pearl Danios they were.'

'Praise be!' I heard Bryn cry. 'That's it!'

I ran to Bryn and knelt beside him. I searched his face, trying to imagine the thoughts that had ruled his outburst.

His face was a ghastly white. His blue-grey eyes met mine.

'Just suppose, just suppose . . . ' he muttered and, rising, he led me by the hand.

❁

Despite the sunlight of the town, the mists over the treeless hills gave no sign of lifting and spread inland to the horizon, a cold grey.

The old Jewish Burial Ground at Crag Zion was hidden in a cloud.

To take the road to the hills we'd passed the General Hospital where we paused while, without thinking, I bought a bunch of blue anemones.

Before we reached the cemetery entrance we saw the gatekeeper walking away down the hill.

'Bring no flowers,' he said. 'flowers are for the living.'

He placed a large iron key in my hand.

'Be sure to return it. There is but one key,' he said, as though of its own accord it would unlock all mysteries.

Bryn stood aside to let him pass. The gatekeeper raised his homburg.

'May you live to be one-hundred-and-twenty!'

I saw Bryn attempt to suppress a shudder; on his face was the pallor of unassuagable mental suffering.

I laid the flowers by a rotting timber lych-frame propped against a wall.

❁

I closed the gates and withdrew the key from the massive lock.

Evidently the gatekeeper's caution has been prompted by the recent spate of attacks on Jewish cemeteries. My heart was shaken by thoughts of such desecration having despoiled all memorials before the object of our quest was reached.

I have failed, I thought. It is a race I cannot win. Then I crossed a path between two shrubs and breasted the winning tape of a spider's thread.

The tombs in that Golgotha were simple white engraved stones, standing in neat rows, undisturbed by anti-Semitic vandals.

When we drew near the burial site I was struck by how aged and stained the headstone was. How in the space of a fortnight could a new inscription have grown so indistinct?

✡

Our Beloved Daughter
Rachel Danievsky
At Rest • Age 18 Years

The date of her death was seven months after that of my birth! I could have cried with gratitude!

I thought: If it were not for hope the heart would break.

'*Dan*ievsky!' Bryn struck his fist against his palm. 'Immense, man!'

My voice failed for a time before I could speak.

'I have a *name*,' I murmured. 'What a strange thought that is!'

'*Dan*io tropical fish!' Bryn's voice broke with emotion. 'And *Dan*dini . . .

'Prince Charming's valet . . . !' I laughed.

'And *Dan*by was the Marquess of Carmarthen . . . *Dan be!*'

'So *that* was the message.'

I examined my left hand. The throbbing in my left thumb was like a pulsing signal of intolerable joy.

Bryn pointed to my thumb's blunt fingernail.

'See . . . the half moon growing out of the cuticle is shaped just like a "D"!'

'It's simply amazing,' I gasped.

'Very simple. Very amazing. I agree,' said Bryn. 'It's difficult to believe, but you have to believe it. It must be believed. You have to believe it, see.'

He suddenly caught his breath and coughed violently, and a tiny drop of blood glistened on his lip.

His face was colourless, wasted and, as the thick mist rolled in from the hills, he smiled suddenly, and as suddenly faded away into the gloom.

'If all this leads you to the true path,' he said, 'don't altogether forget me.' And then his voice fell silent.

From my pocket I removed the white stone and placed it on that grave wherein my brightest hopes lay buried.

❁

But in the town the sun was still shining.

I read in the evening newspaper that today was the sunniest May Day in Britain since 1909. No, I thought. The sunniest day since the world began!

I felt like a newborn baby for the rest of the afternoon.

❁

Tuesday, May 2 . . . A Lapsus Per Foramina Temporis

The lights in the chapel at the Theological College were ablaze and shone on the leprous bark of a eucalyptus tree when I entered the gates.

A tenor was rehearsing *The Messiah*.

Comfort ye, comfort ye my people . . . Speak ye comfortably to Jerusalem, and cry unto her . . . Every valley shall be exalted . . .

Yet no comfort was I to find when I vainly sought the corner of the inner quad and saw no longer any trace of the door to Dr Priestly's mission.

Beneath the creeper was a blank wall. No brass plate.

In the chapel porch I stared at a memorial commemorating a century of 'propagating the knowledge of the Gospel among the Heathen' by missionaries overseas.

I experienced a most intense *sentiment du déjà vu.*

Somehow I was unsurprised to learn that Bryn, Dr Priestly and Kwesi, with sixteen other converts, had been killed in a tribal uprising on the Dark Continent almost one hundred years ago.

Unlucky Kwesi. Born on Sunday, buried on Monday.

'Look at it well,' an inner voice spoke, 'it is wholly real and it always will be so. You cannot doubt it.'

I remembered Dr Priestly's words: 'Many things are not understood by patients until some time has elapsed; only then can they take effect.'

I mourned for Bryn, condemned to be a dream-guide seen only by those who not heard of his death. *Saman twén-twén* Kwesi had called them.

From my critical perspective it was a narrative discontinuity I could not explain; it reminded me of a widening fissure, say, in a hastily written nineteenth-century novel, serialised in weekly parts, which would ultimately separate an underdeveloping character from a fully developed one.

Or, rather, had some kind of warp in the cosmic fabric caused Bryn to pass through a time tunnel to dwell in a timeless state?

'You're a long, long way ahead of me even when I'm in front,' Bryn had once said. And the gatekeeper had said, 'Your watch must keep a different time.'

Was he a victim of a time-slip—a *lapsus per foramina temporis* —a wormhole, which fate had opened up for him in the space-time continuum, where he, too, was to wrestle with the meaninglessness of his apostasy until his neurosis was cured?

Whereas I had been spared the anxiety of self-searching and my secrets had spilled out at last when every lock had proved too insecure to hold them.

Unlike the tramp, Old Ifan, I'd carried no baggage but that which bore down on my mind until dreams had unlocked all the flood-gates of my heart.

Wednesday, May 3 . . . The Sphinx is Satisfactorily De-jinxed

Aunt Nesta called me to the phone. She was smiling contentedly.

'Funny article he is! Says he's speaking from a train.'

It was Stefan. I carefully shut the door to the kitchen.

I murmured into the mouthpiece; I thought Stef, no more than Nesta, would believe my answer to the Sphinx's riddle for which I had thirsted so long, and that he'd find my recent journeyings to seek its solution to be as whimsical as they were tragical.

However, his reply was typical of a proof-reading, academic comma-hound. For him, it seemed, the Sphinx was satisfactorily de-jinxed.

'Not quite my line of country, but I'd rather I married a Jew than a Protestant,' he said robustly. 'At least they have a history.'

I laughed. I realised I not only missed the collegiality, I missed his company.

I remembered Stef's fingers tracing mine.

'When we have all our tomorrows why dwell on the past?' he said.

(I knew there was an unspoken caution in his words. He'd made it clear he suspected me of choosing dry scholarship and dusty tomes above the life force. *It thrives in artificial light*, he had written, but he might just as well have quoted *redolet lucernam*: that my texts smelled of a lamp burning midnight oil. *Overnourishment can destroy the roots*, he'd also remarked. Was that a warning, too, against the perils of too zealous ancestor worship?)

'The tribe of Dan, eh?' he said ruminatively. 'Thank goodness you're not named after the tribe of Gad.'

'Why ever not?'

'The word "Gad", in Russian, suggests unsavoury associations.' The Slavophile then began to expatiate on thediaspora and the ten tribes of Israel scattered across Russia.

'Asherovich, Ephraimov, Isakovsky, Levitsky, Manasevsky, Naftolovich, Rabinovich, Simonovich, Tsebulov, Venjamsky . . . then . . .'

'Enough already!'

I saw the kitchen door had opened a crack.

Stef's voice was breaking up. I strained to hear his fading words.

'I'm entering a tunnel.' The disembodied voice of the SciFi buff echoed hollowly down the line. 'Remember. Don't let your future be swallowed by your past.'

MONDAY, SEPTEMBER 11 . . . THE BREATH OF LIFE

Suddenly it's upon us, Autumn, and I'm walking in leaves.

'Gracious! Take a hat! The wind plays havoc with your hair!' Those are the words of Nesta when I set out.

It is two overcoats colder than the Sunday before, but I shrug.

'A right little Madam,' I hear her mutter.

For today I'm exultant. The years of scribbling in the margins are over; the last line has been blotted, and only the indexing of *Voces Feminae* remains.

And no more journal! Through travail I've reached my star*.

Yesterday, Stefan asked on the phone: 'Now you've finished the book, you're not going to write a sort ofnineteenth-century "Condition of Britain" style of novel are you?'

* The *Magen David* ✡ (Star of David) is sketched beside this passage of Beth's m.s. in the margin. *C.E.*

'You mean with England as the Counting House of Empire and the Welsh, your poor cousins, shivering in the chill west wing?' I smiled at the thought. 'Hardly!'

It may seem difficult for a non-adoptee to understand but, after those Maytime revelations, I was disinclined to pursue my putative ancestry and far from eager to immerse myself in a new life alien to, and in some respects irreconcilable with, the existence in which habit had confirmed me.

Besides, my disposition to study had returned and, during those long days toiling over my manuscript, I seldom exerted myself to wander far from the house. So the summer passed before, despite misgivings, I felt able to revisit the scenes of my reversal of fortune whose impetus seemed now to have been the excitement—dare I say hysteria—of overimaginative moods or of a morbid susceptibility to shadowy impressions.

It was like looking back on the day when I had first laid the foundation stone of an edifice whose ultimate design I'd never visualised. Now it was erected it was astonishing to see it had no recognisable shape.

In Jew Street, I saw the sign in the hair and beauty salon now declared the business to be *Open*.

I decided to join a queue at the general store next door.

'Pastrami, salami, rolled beef, bologna, pumpernickle, coleslaw, chopped chicken liver, celery tonic . . . ' The litany of the storekeeper seemed without end.

The customer in front of me turned from checking her shopping list and I recognised the bereft woman from the cemetery who'd worn the dark toque. But her hair was now uncovered and I saw the glossy reddish ringlets falling about her olive-tinted face had streaks of grey.

I looked at her and found a warm presence not dissimilar to the fleeting vision of memory.

'Oy vey!' she cried. 'No blinis!' (Yes, incredibly, these were the words I first heard.)

I must have been staring brazenly because, when she saw my eyes had rested on her face, she evinced both startlement and curiosity.

'I swear to goodness, you're . . . ' She stopped and bit her lip. 'Only once in a lifetime I say this, maybe . . . '

She took a deep breath. A wisp of a smile appeared.

'Such beautiful skin! But your hair! Looks clean like a clinic but it seems to me you could use a little *uplift*. You know what I'm going to do? Look. I've got a wonderful suggestion!'

I started instinctively as she took my arm.

'Don't make yourself such a stranger.' She smiled and led me to the salon. 'You like maybe a *new you*? Let me. One-two-three, I guarantee when I've finished the job you'll look positively another person. *Nu?*'

I did not resist. It was as if we had walked away with her blessing into the sun.

❦

It seemed unbelievable that I was seated in the salon and soothing fingers were passing through my hair yet when, once more, I opened my eyes, the objects around me were visible, just as I remembered them.

And around me the same lively chirping of women at ease. The lotions, the hairdryer, the styling scissors, the manicure bowl, the polish remover, the orange sticks.

Hanna Danievsky examined the fourth finger on my left hand.

'A single girl, huh? A spring chicken can afford to be choosy yet. Stepping out with someone special?'

I saw no reason for not confiding in her.

'A college lady and a college professor!' Hanna exclaimed. 'So smart! So refined! Regular love birds, I bet.'

I stifled a sigh of contentment as she brushed my hair with prolonged languid strokes.

'*Tchk, tchk, tchk!* Real nice it is, real nice. But never use a brush to comb out wet hair,' she scolded.

Above the mirror hung a faded photograph.

'May I see?' I asked.

Hanna reached above me to remove the framed family group. As she released the frame from the wall its hook clattered to the floor.

'A first class *klutz* I am!' A piece of plaster fell from a crack in the wall.

I examined the photograph with rising excitement. Two adults. Two little girls in white smocks as alike as two drops of milk.

'See. *Onkel* and Momma and me.' I recognised from the burial ground the scholarly, rabbinical-looking man with the divided beard and the diminutive well-groomed lady in the cloche hat.

When Hanna leant over me I could smell she wore the same melancholy moss-grown fragrance as that of her mother.

'And the other girl?'

'Rachel. My cousin. A sweet darling kid. May she be of eternal memory to us all!' I thought of the portrait of myself as a glum schoolgirl. In features and expression between our two solemn faces there was no discernable distinction.

Hanna blew lightly on her palm and pressed the flat of her hand thrice on my mouth.

I sneezed with astonishment.

Hanna laughed fondly, a distant look in her eye, and explained that, since she had survived the death of a cousin who was so like a sister to her—in fact, they were born ten days apart—the rabbi had assured her she possessed, in consequence, a double portion of the breath of life, the power of which she now imparted to me.

I felt inside of me the last of the building blocks of my identity falling into place.

Can such heartache, I thought, be transmuted into an anguish healed?

Suddenly, Hanna turned and addressed a hunched figure seated under a reading lamp in a book-lined rear parlour.

'*Onkel* Moritz!' she called. She spread her hands in mock despair. '*Ai, ai, ai!* It pays yet to run a business? And him not lifting a little finger even!'

Hanna raised her voice and pointed to the crack in the wall.

'This is strictly your department!' She held up the wall-hook. 'So who is here, the serving girl? Did you ever! Reading all day, his nose in his books, and says not two words together.'

An ancient white-haired man, with the divided beard of a scholar, shuffled towards us on those bowed cabriole legs so characteristic of a worker who'd laboured under one-thousand feet of stratal pressure.

He was bearing a hammer.

Beneath his shaggy white brows the pupils of his deep brown eyes dilated with a lively sympathy. He seemed to be the kind of man who would inspire affection: grave but benign, strong but tender, amiably diffident, with a web of lines wrinkled by mirth about his eyes and lips.

Hanna winked.

'Look, a big crack there is, in the wall,' she said, 'like there was some accident.'

Her uncle went to smartly tap the hook but hit his thumb with the hammer and cried, 'Methu*th*alem!'

THOUGHT POLICE

(*Theresa O.* — Temazepam)

'The death sentence and the life sentence are equally immoral, but if I had to choose between the death penalty and imprisonment for life, I would certainly choose the second. To live anyhow is better than not at all.'

—*The Bet*, by Anton Chekhov (1888)

Assessment Summary (extract): It is almost four years to the day since the strange disappearance of the celebrated novelist, Theresa Ollivante. Few have not heard of the case of the missing writer and of the unresolved disputes arising out of the manuscripts she wrote in this period (in particular, the litigation brought against her by her literary agent, Seymour Dane) since they have made news headlines around the world. She has been admitted to our care because she has become hostile and combative, obstinately demanding that not for one minute should she occupy a room alone. These extreme reactions are scarcely remarkable given her intense abandonment fears following the trauma of her disappearance. Without factual confirmation, we remain uncertain whether the patient's sudden and dramatic changes of behaviour, shifting from apathy and perplexity to anxiety and agitation, are expressions of an uncontrollable fantasy proneness or genuine concern for editorial control of the immense volume of writings amassed during her three-and-half years of solitude.

A paradox has arisen as to the transcription of the estimated two million words Theresa wrote in those years of isolation, a period not dissimilar to the length of incarceration suffered in Sachsenhausen concentration camp during World War II by the son of the Norwegian polar explorer Nansen. The published diary of Nansen fils runs to 600 pages yet this bulky edited volume, recording in detail those years of daily witness to unimaginable horrors, amounts to only one third of the original manuscript.

Like the wartime diarist, Theresa has found the task of distillation is more time consuming than the task of composition. As she says despairingly, 'It's as though I have all the concordances to the Bible and Shakespeare but not the Works themselves.'

But what profundities, international literary figures do not cease to demand, did Theresa Ollivante herself record during her involuntary incarceration in that grim oubliette?

Of course, we have the oft-published photos of her subterranean makeshift study, alas, trampled over by heedless newshounds soon after her astonishing reappearance—a wanton act of destruction that at the time drew comparisons with the behaviour of Press cameramen who overran the jungle hideaway of that Japanese lieutenant who had holed himself up for thirty years on an island in the Philippines rather than accept the dishonour of surrender.

As it is, frustratingly, the occasion of Theresa's *disappearance*, corroborated by a number of witnesses, has been more closely documented and reported more faithfully than the bizarre circumstances of her discovery.

You'll surely recall the scene outside Theresa's apartment house, four winters ago, when a police patrol car halted beside her as she stood immobile in the snow, dressed in a thin housecoat, staring fixedly at a drain cover where the snow had melted in a perfect dish-shaped concavity.

The cops were friendly and polite. 'From where we're looking, seems like we're talking to a lady in distress.'

They had merely put to her one question: 'Something on your mind, maybe?'

'No. It's nothing,' they both remember her answering dryly with a false smile. 'Unless, perhaps, you're a deputation from the Thought Police.'

A day later she vanished without a trace to reemerge four years later, still enveloped in a mystery that continues to perplex the minds of her loyal readers and to confound her critics.

Yet, despite Theresa Ollivante's refusal to satisfy our curiosity as to the content of her impressively weighty manuscript, we can quote a few passages from her current diary into which she has copied extracts from Chekhov's sinister cautionary tale, *The Bet*, whose unnamed young hero, as you may remember, has himself incarcerated voluntarily for fifteen years in a well-stocked library—in solitary confinement—to win a bet of two million roubles wagered by a banker.

Self-narrative (extract): 'The prisoner (writes Theresa), amazingly, in four years, reads over *six hundred volumes* and when, after fifteen years of confinement in which he imbibes the world's classics, he emerges into daylight, his appearance is almost spectral. His face is yellow, his cheeks are hollow, his hair is streaked with silver, and no one can believe that he is only forty! He is a skeleton with the skin drawn tight over his bones and long matted curls like . . . like, well, like my own, if I'm honest. But what does the prisoner declare upon his release that I would not myself assert were I to meet that hateful unconscionable banker!?

'"Your books have given me wisdom. All man's unresting thought from the ages is compressed into the small compass of my brain. I know that I am wiser than all of you. And I despise your books, as I despise wisdom and the blessings of this world. It is all worthless, fleeting, illusory, and deceptive, like a mirage . . . as though you were no more than mice burrowing under the floor . . . "'

Diagnostic Impression: Theresa evidently empathises strongly with Chekhov's disillusioned bookish captive, but she herself denies a Freudo-Marxist view of alienation to explain her own anomie and other related neurotica. Despite admitting to severe psychological adjustment problems, she claims her sense of dislocation from a once familiar world is due, essentially, to the extreme mistrust and suspicion with which she now regards her literary agent, Seymour Dane. Specifically, she accuses Dane of *ghostwriting* the major portion of her novel, *An Auroral Stain*, which was published to mixed reviews during her enforced absence. 'For Seymour, it was more than a case of *corpus delecti* when I disappeared,' Theresa says, 'it was a case of a missing opus whose inconvenient absence was remedied when he presumed to "complete" the work without my authorisation.' She is insistent that she does *not* harbour delusional beliefs, yet her apparent disoriention makes her present personality functioning even more difficult to diagnose, requiring an unbiased and full assessment by the appropriate multidisciplinary team to validate her claims.

Therefore, when even the Press have so far failed to uncover clues to solve the mystery of her disappearance, tantalisingly, the publication of a full account of her astonishing story must be delayed until the next edition of this work.

THE ELEVEN SURVIVING WORKS OF L v. K

(*Isolde B.* — Diazepam)

'And thus forever with reverted look
The mystic volume of the world they read
Spelling it backward, like a Hebrew book,
Till life becomes a Legend of the Dead.'

> The Russian-born American modernist pianist and composer, Leo Ornstein, lately rediscovered as one of the most daring and original figures in twentieth-Century music, has died, aged 109. *Daily Telegraph* 08/03/02.

Assessment Summary (extract): Results of a preliminary psychplogical evaluation reveal a relative integrity of thought process and verbal content shows a broad range. Yet the patient appears to remain extermely distressed and anxious, despite self-reports to the contrary. Since her recent bereavement the accumulation of grief appears to have partially precipitated the current extreme guardedness and withdrawal and, at present, though she is believed not to be a physical risk to others, there are psychiatric indicators of self-harm. This case is unusual insofar as it is rare to be privileged to compare and cross-reference the cases of two siblings in which the effects of the same traumatic event are documented by two distinct subjectivities (see younger sister Grete's account, *Cousin Ludwig's Subtraction Game).*

THE ELEVEN SURVIVING WORKS OF L v. K (1902–1939)

A Memoir of a Numeromaniacal Futurist

Patient ID CPN0318211042: Isolde B.
Occupation: Portraitist.
Drug: Diazepam.
Drug class: Typical benzodiazepine derivative for relief of anxiety and panic disorders.
Common side effects: Drowsiness, fatigue, light-headedness, loss of balance.

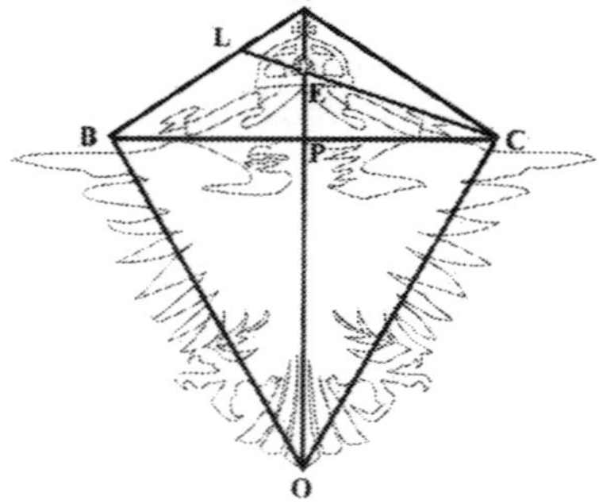

DARLING GRETE,

The death of Leo Ornstein this week, aged 109, severs the last link with that extraordinary closeknit Futurist coterie with which Fa was so intimately connected in the interwar years . . . Father, Ornstein, Seligman and, of course, L v. K.

Ma doesn't mention Fa much these days so I thought you should have a copy of this as it explains quite a lot. I've reconstructed L v. K's catalogue from Fa's private papers which, a fortnight after his death, as I wrote you, Ma tore into quarters and scattered for disposal in his war chest, that padlocked packing case (you'd be too young to remember) whose mysterious recesses held the booty he had looted in France, and which—since all demobbed soldiers were ordered, he once told me, to 'disembark with only those articles they were able to carry,' and he (typically pigheaded) chose to burden himself with a deadweight of 100 lb—stood in the cellar as a mute reminder of the root cause of his persistent back pain and short temper for the remainder of his life.

Fa's war chest, in the event, contained much more besides the documents I have edited in the enclosures: a parachute harness, a Luftwaffe aerial map of the Dover Straits coastline, and a complete black museum of the most monstrous anti-Semitic propaganda imaginable—a brightly coloured kindergarten picture-book, for example, with Reynard the Fox snarling on its cover, entitled, 'Never Trust a Fox in a Green Meadow and Never Trust the Word of a Jew,' overstamped Volksschule Neider-Ramstadt—quite evidently exhibits assembled when Fa was a translator with S.H.A.E.F. at the Nurnberg Trials.

It must have been shortly after Ma came here to stay at the Lodge—and was oversleeping a good deal because of those new pacifiers she would persist in taking against my better judgement—that I repaid a visit in the small hours to her cellar and retrieved in a plastic bin liner the whole sorry mess of torn and mangled leaves which for so long now I have wearied to piece together. The bundle's hidden even now on top of my wardrobe and the reason (no one needs to seek far to explain) for a hideous recurring dream, the details of which—even though it's a heavenly Monday morning and the sun is shining on the lawn and Ma's happily pegging out the chemise she insists on washing herself—I cannot bring myself to describe, even to you.

As it is, Ma believes I followed her instructions and burnt the entire kit and caboodle in the incinerator at the end of her kitchen garden. Now I'm wishing I had.

Your Loving Sis
Isolde

Encl: 'The Eleven Surviving Works of L v. K'

Read This First

From sifting through all Fa's other occasional commentaries on his friends it would seem L v. K travelled widely in his schooldays, studying at Herder Realgymnasium, Berlin; Escuela Alemana, Barcelona; Institut Minerva, Zurich; Handelsscule Weiss, Vienna; and the Institute of Musical Art, New York. A polyglot, like Fa, he was a gifted pianist (see Study IV, 'Padereweski's Dogs', New York, 1924) and collaborated with Ornstein on many impromptu works. Ten years younger than Ornstein, L v. K was no more than a twelve-year-old when he first heard 'Suicide in an Airplane' and, as events proved, the recital made a profound impression on him. (See L v. K's nihilistic schoolboy essay, Study I, of the same year, 'A Short History of Alsace', a territory held in contention with France by L. v. K's forebears since 1871. L v. K was born in Mulhouse-Riedesheim, Elsass/Alsace.)

L v. K was, we learn, also an accomplished watchmaker (see Study VI) to whom his small circle of friends (including Ornstein) brought timepieces and metronomes for repair.

Each momento mori that composed these eleven works was exhibited, so Fa tells us, in the reception room of L v. K's apartment in Avenue d'Iéna, Paris, at the time of his death, following the signing of the German—Soviet Non-Aggression Treaty (see Study XI).

According to Fa's notes, L v. K took his own life on August 24th 1939. Fa's solitary allusion to the identity of L v. K hints that his friend's 'ambivalent religiosity and congenital stammer owed much to his illustrious forebear whose twin strains of patriotism and rebellion found release in bringing to frenzied life the most tormented egregious hero to be found anywhere in our literature,' referring, seemingly, to a descendant of H. von Kleist (author of the incendiary novella, 'Michael Kohlhaas').

Dearest, I've sent you one or two of the smaller items related in Fa's journal; the little enamelled canister that Fa pocketed in Paris you're to retain as a keepsake. Likewise keep the child's-eye-view ('Kinderblick') picture postcard of Hitler garlanding the infants, postmarked 7-8-1937 Berlin NW7 (the message on the reverse, by the way, appears to be from L v. K himself—and gives us more than an inkling that he foresaw, even then, that 'another show' was about to begin, i.e. his last remark, 'Das Theatre fängt an!').

Yes, L v. K's caustic postcard is as characteristic of the man as these antemortal exhibits, a product of a fixated numerologist whose mordant slant on the world is unmistakable.

THE ELEVEN SURVIVING WORKS OF L V. K (1902–1939)

Juvenilia

ESSAY (1914): English composition in L v. K's own hand entitled 'A Short History of Alsace.' L v. K (aged 11) has penned solely the essay's title on a sheet of British foolscap above the stationer's imprint where appear the words:

Ruled Feint
with Narrow Margins

His tutor has scrawled in the margins in red ink an admonitory 'No more mischief!'

I

'*Creed*' *(1935)*: Handmade Glass/Chromium Case (Internal Area: Double Imperial Quarto 15" × 22") containing privately bound 1935 edition of Mein Kampf opened fully outspread at page xxiv to reveal secret cut-out compartment (internal area: Demy Octavo 8⅜" × 5⅝") containing 1917 pocket edition of Das Kapital spread open at page xxxv to reveal secret cut-out compartment (internal area: Demy Sextodecimo 5⅝" × 4⅜") containing copy of 1884 Lutheran Bible outspread at page xlviii to reveal secret equilaterally 1⅛"-sided triangular cut-out compartment (volume 5 1/16 cubic inches) cut to depth of 1⅛" to Book of Revelation (see Appendix II). Compartment unoccupied and purpose unknown. Signed in indian ink with initials L v. K on green satin ribbon bookmark stitched in spine.

II

'*Polymath*' — *Leitsatz** *(Juli 1932)* Defaced frontispiece photogravure portrait of Rudolf Steiner (embellished with doodled moustache and forelock) torn raggedly from introductory notes to an Anthroposophical Course on Curative Pedagogy, overwritten with fountain pen:

Polymath

Giftflaschen haben eine Mehr-Facetten-Form, so daß sie Dunkeln leichter zu erkennen sind.

(Poison bottles are many-faceted, too, so you may recognise them in the dark.)

* *Guiding thought*

III

Imperial Roman Bust (1923): Inside- out rubber mould of imperial portrait-head inverted. Bust mounted on upturned shoulders, on account of the head being turned inside out by withdrawal through the neck cavity; exposed inner mould's inverse depressions of eyes, nose, ears and laurel crown infilled with mosses, lichens, soot, dried woodlice, etc. Signed L v. K and titled Imperium in imperio. (Size: 17½" high.)

IV

MS Score Of 'Padereweski's Dogs' (NY 1924): L v. K's personal note admits that: '. . . at the stagedoor in the press of admirers I was unable to approach my idol so I plucked a tuft of hairs from one of his dogs which had strayed in my direction. Later that evening, I scattered these cherished curls on a sticky flypaper I had inscribed with a stave. Inevitably, a wire-haired bass clef determined the passage's notation.' Fa records that this dirge-like score was played many times, 8va bassa, by L v. K, with the flypaper unfurled with mock solemnity above the keyboard with the assistance of Leo Ornstein and two indulgent drinking companions (Fa?).

V

'Feldschusterei' — Sonnet In Metrical Feet With Masculine And Feminine Endings (1938):* 112 miscellaneous unmatched items of abandoned footwear, including children's slippers and orthopaedic boots, arranged in 14 rows of 8 items, with additional line endings as follows: Lines 1, 4, 5 & 8 — knieschützer †; Lines 2, 3, 6 & 7 — women's satin dancing pumps; Lines

* Field shoemaker's shop

† Parachutist kneepads (half rhymes noted by L v. K)

9 & 12—schaftstiefel‡; Lines 10 & 13—wooden clogs; Lines 11 & 14—young girl's gilded sandals.

VI

Fantastical Captive Clock (1935): An ingenious clock face with fixed hands bound by barbed wire. By a system of rotating dials, the hours and minutes adjust position in relation to the motionless hands. Inscribed:

Was uns fehlt ist nicht Hoffnung,
Was uns fehlt ist Glück

*(We are not wanting of hope.
We are wanting of luck.)*

VII

Euclidian Proposition (1917, aged 15) Theorum I: This prescient figure is neatly superscribed in ink over the blazon of Church and State on the embossed cover of L v.K's copybook for November, the month of the storming of the Winter Palace. L v. K seeks a syllogistic proof: 'An isosceles triangle Δ denoted **ABC** is inscribed such that **AB** = **AC**. Assume A is Ausspringender *Winkel* [Salient Angle]. The mid-point of magnitude **BC** is **P**. Let **P** be *Palast Revolution* [Palace Revolution]. **AP** is produced to **O** [Origin] in such a manner that Δ **BCO** is equilateral.

'∴ ✠ can be cut only at mid-point of **AP** at **E** *Entweihung* [Desecration]. Hence, a transversal to connect opposite sides joins **C** to **E**, and is produced to meet in **L**. Let transversal terminate at **L** point of contact. Suppose **L** is Leninismus [Leninism]. Demonstrate under these conditions that Δ **AEL** is isosceles.

‡ Jack boots or Marschstiefel

'∴, *à fortiori*, **A** : **E** = **E** : **L**, which is ∴ true.'

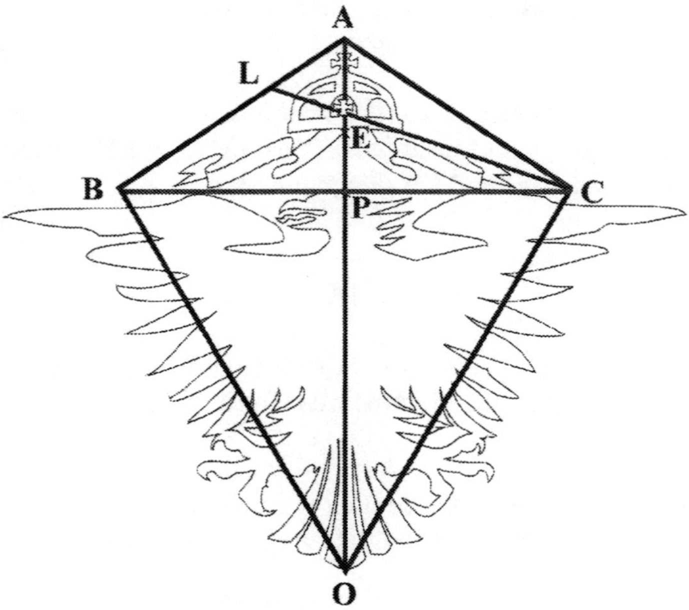

L v. K further intercalates the legend:

Geometrie ist ein **P.L.A.C.E.B.O.**
um das Chaos abzuwehren.

(Geometry is a P.L.A.C.E.B.O.
To ward off chaos.)

VIII

Theorem II (1937): Unmounted photograph of unidentified sunlit Spanish town square with fountain and townsfolk, inscribed—

$(a + b) = (b + b)$

Para ellos, la palabra más bella desu léxico era 'fuente.'

Declararon que la palabra más temida
era 'tortura.'
Vea aquí en esta foto
las personas que fueron torturadas
en aquella fuente.

(For them the most beautiful word in their lexicon / was 'fountain.' / They declared the word most feared / to be 'torture.' / See in this photo here / these people were tortured / at that fountain.)

IX

Bibliotek (1932): Picture Postcard with photograph of Königliches Bibliotek, Berlin, inscribed in slatecoal Leichner pencil—

Die Zufriedenheit der Gelehrten
ist die Enttäuschung von Explikationen.

(The happiness of scholars
is the disappointment of explication.)

X

After The Christians Overran The Circus (1938): Steel engraving of the Coliseum with scrawled legend —

Circo Perfuso Christianis
Postremo monstravit gladiatori finis
modo esse arenam metam fato sanguinis

(Last, the fallen gladiator saw,
simply, sand is what blood is for.)

XI

Theorem III — 'Sudetenland' (1938): This is the last 'composition' in L v. K's hand. Page 540 of the *Statistisches Jahrbuch für das Deutsche Reich* 1933 has been annotated with calculations derived from the total electoral returns of the N.S.D.A.P., see *Zusammen*, column 5, (17,277,180). The page is covered with many spidery formulæ and equations (see Appendix I) prompted by his arithmomania; including one cypher heavily underscored—

$$\text{INT (integer)}\ \frac{17277180}{1933} = 8{\bullet}9{\bullet}38$$

That L v. K chose September 8th 1938 as an auspicious date upon which to write to Prime Minister Neville Chamberlain can be adduced from the following correspondence:

<u>Personal and Confidential</u>

*Thursday 8th • September • 1938**

(Post restante) Studio Harcourt,
49 Avenue d'Iéna,
Paris - XVI

The Rt. Hon. N. Chamberlain, C.H., M.P.
10, Downing Street,
London, S.W.1.

Sir,

In consequence of recent correspondence with your Foreign Office I am flattered to know my name is not unfamiliar to you. In your most recent speeches you allude with prophetic utterance to a truth of such gravity,

* Fa notes: 'L v. K's own species of gematria determined not only the date of his first letter to Chamberlain but also eerily prefigured the time of death of his beloved only sister, Isolde, killed later the same day in the rioting in Prague that heralded the September 30th Munich Pact.'

which my research has now brought to light, that I would not dare breath it to a soul before exhausting every effort to establish contact with those responsible for guiding the conduct of your great nation.

My first appeal I naturally direct to you in your official capacity as Prime Minister, and in the name of God I beseech you not to refuse me an interview.

Just as I do not doubt the sincerity of your beliefs, so I implore you with all the earnestness at my command not to doubt the sincerity of mine.

The providential, dare I say, momentous computation whose recursive progression I have to communicate to you posits an astounding expression of numerical behaviour known only to . . . (letter incomplete: see Appendix I)

September 21st 1938

House of Commons
London SW1

Mr Chamberlain has asked me to reply to your letter of September 8th inst. and to thank you for the copies of correspondence enclosed.

It is felt that the subject matter of your letter should more properly be addressed to a member of the clergy or to a logician than to a layman, however great his national prestige. Under the circumstances, I am returning the copies of your calculi in case you should wish to pursue the matter with a dignitary of the church.

Yours faithfully
G. P. Humphreys-Davies
Hon. Secretary
pp. Prime Minister's office

Postscript

An additional sketch appended by Fa states:

'L v. K was born in Mulhouse-Riedesheim (Elsass/Alsace) in 1902, the son of a director of the Rheinische Creditbank. Up to the age of 16 his studies were in German until the political overthrow of 1918 and his teachers changed to French (to which his long and willing sojourn in Paris can be attributed). In this year he attended a private school at Belfort. At the age of 19 he was invited to enter the first written examination for the both the University of Strasbourg and the faculty at Nancy; however, by his own decision he spent a brief period at the Technical School at Rosenheim in Upper Bavaria which explains his abiding interest in horology and mechanics.

'In April 1939 L v. K returned reluctantly to Berlin at the behest of his parents to consult a psychopathologist with the aim to treat his compulsive obsession for numerology and his impassioned belief that only a numerist could break the bonds that held him captive of his own private cabala, whereas a doctor could not.

'A defaced souvenir, entitled *A Nation Honours its* Leader, suggests that L v. K was witness to the *gigantischen Truppenparade* of 20th April 1939. (See photospread captioned 'The flags are dipped in salute' and 'The Führer thanks his armed forces', above which, in L v. K's familiar Leichner pencil scrawl, are dashed the words: *Ave Caesar, morituri te salutant.*)'

No further details are recorded in Fa's Journal other than the description of the apartment in Avenue d'Iéna*, its exhibits and the circumstances of L v. K's death, noted by Fa in the spare terms of his final entry he headed The Etiquette of Death.

The Etiquette Of Death

(Fa writes) 'My dear comrade, the Futurist L v. K died by his own hand on August 24th 1939, the day following the signing of the Nazi-Soviet Non-aggression Pact.

'Since 1934, L v. K had suffered from profound insomnia and neurasthenia compounded, no doubt, by an increasing absorption in his numerological mania. From that time a dosage of 1.5 grams (24 grains) of Veronal per day had been prescribed and

* Fa comments: 'Studio Harcourt by 1943 had successfully re-established itself as a photo-atelier specialising in "Erstklassige Porträts" for the Wehrmacht.'

despatched by his family physician in Mulhouse-Riedesheim. The autopsy found the cause of death was an overdose far in excess of 3.5 grams, the lethal dose.

'When I was finally admitted to his apartment I was struck by a waft of Benzine mingling with the poignant pervading fragrance of Esprit de *Fleurs de Cédrat*, which he so often caused to fill the room from the font-like electric perfume burners—*cassolettes*—he had fixed to his salon walls.

'L v. K had often spoken to me about what he regarded as The Etiquette of Death and in this he had not neglected his duties to the living for the officiating doctor told me that, when found, L v. K showed signs typical of a "suicidal baptism", having recently bathed and shaved with care, attired himself in a freshly laundered nightshirt, and arranged himself on the bed with averted face*, considerately covering his head with a large cotton handkerchief.

'His left hand held a copy of *The Mausoleum* †, opened at the title page, his forefinger pointing to the book's legend: *Resurgam in Astris*.

'His right hand grasped a cylindrical tin of *Tetkum* ‡ solution with its label annotated *Après moi le déluge* AD *20•5•2011—2113*.

'It appeared his last act had been to smear a pair of his boots with this aromatic gum.

'The MS of *Exhibit IV* he bequeathed to his friend Kurt Seligman, whose *Ultrameuble* had been exhibited in the Paris Surrealists Exhibition of the previous *year*. To me he left the curious *Captive Clock* which he knew I had long coveted. The bulk of L v. K's estate went to Martin Niemöller's Pastors' Emergency League, to assist the sustenance of opposition to the de-Christianising of Germany under the Third Reich.

* Fa comments: 'A Cheremissian belief is that the sleeper is bound to die if he composes himself facing the wall.'

† 'Dreams and Reflections concerning Death and the Grave' by Amraphel. Marchant Singer and Co, 1864.

‡ Benzine-based water repellant for the proofing ('imprägnierung') of rainwear, manufactured by Schmidt & Magnusson, Kopenhaven — tradename underscored in this wise: T.E.T.K.U.M.

'It is not entirely untenable that L v. K's Latin valediction *Circo Perfuso Christianis* referred to the unequal contest between the militia Christi of the Old Church and the suborned German Christians' Movement of the Reich, and, in particular, to the statement by the Reich Minister for Church Affairs, Kerrl, delivered on February 13th 1937, dismissing: ". . . the question of the acknowledgement of Jesus as the son of God. That is ridiculous, quite inessential. There has now risen a new authority as to what Christ and Christianity is. This new authority is Adolph Hitler."'

Appendix I

Fa further notes: 'Despite the fugitive copies of L v. K's correspondence, the recreation of the missing fragments can be essayed by reference to his remaining significations. An annotated copy of a 1912 edition of Isadore Kozminsky's account of Rabbinical prognostication, *Numbers—Their Meaning and Magic* §, hints at L v. K's intentions since Chapter II on the arcana of the Hebraistic "Quaballastic Art" is well-thumbed with a web of marginalia in a familiar hand.

'Having first made the observation that ADOLF ([23] = 2+3=5) HITLER ([23] = 2+3=5) share the same puissant numerical values as NAPOLEON ([41] 4+1=5) BUONAPARTE ([41] 4+1=5), ibid page 59, L v. K , at length, records the significationof this concordance: 5 = the number of fire and struggle; combines as 10 = the number of rise and fall, of prophesy and futurity, of manifestation and power, etcetera.'

§ Fa notes : A holograph treatise on the concealed mysteries of occult mathematics by the French adept, the 'Quabbalist' Eliphas Levi, was itemised in the inventory of L v. K's remaining effects but it was subsequently removed from the civic depositary by an unidentified claimant (Fa??).

Appendix Ii
(Endpapers)

On the endpapers, almost overlooked, Fa remarks a Pentacle constructed by L v. K which Fa supposed could point to the substance of the elusive page of correspondence with Downing Street and the meaning of *Study I*.

In accordance with the Quaballah of Pythagoras (ibid. Chapter III), L v. K has assigned the system of '9-potency'(A–I = 1–9 ; K–S = 10–90 ; T–Z = 100–500 ; J–Hv = 600–900) to the Führer*, the import of whose name can be judged by the following numero-mancy:

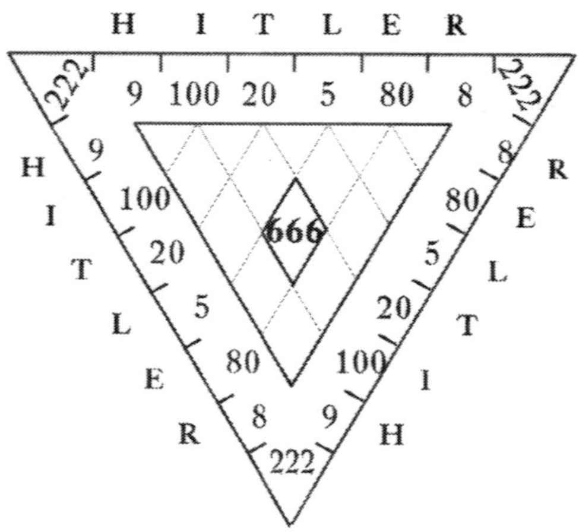

Afterword

Grete Dearest,
You'll be pleased to learn that now that I've burned all Fa's papers I'm sleeping easier at nights. On reflection, I suspect Fa's entries might have been his own odd way of tracing the fever chart of his crackup after the war. Do you remember Fa wouldn't allow

* Fa notes: Diagram labelled 'Trinity'. As is well known, the Number of the Beast in the Book of Revelation ('Here is wisdom. Let him that hath understanding count the number of the beast; for it is the number of a man, and his number is six hundred, three score and six.') was configured by Peter Bungus to correspond to the name of Martin Luther when expressed in half German and half Latin. Bungas, himself, wrote a book on occult numerological symbolism.

us to play with that girl called Beverly we liked because she went to the Steiner School? 'Too much dogma is the ruination of the soul,' he growled. You know that Fa's own father was born in Neider-Ramstadt so you're probably thinking, like me, that Fa's jottings amount to nothing less than a naturalised Englishman's protracted act of exculpation. Or is the more likely explanation that poor old Fa's observations were, like him, of such an unusual kidney that anything he wrote would invariably seem Fa-fetched?

Yours Aye,
Sis

THE THREE-TIERED GRAVE

(*Roberta J.*—PAROXETINE)

Unedited Notes for Seminar on
the Secret Catechism of the Stoneburgh Eight
to be held at Stoneburgh Ladies' College,
Michaelmas Term.

'I saw that everything, all paths I had been following, all steps I had taken, were leading back to a single point—namely, to the mid-point.

In the secret hour of life's mid-day the parabola of life is reversed: death is born.'

— CARL GUSTAV JUNG

Assessment Summary (extract): The patient told me she had consulted her Community Psychiatric Nurse informally without significant benefit. She is aware she has been labelled an 'overanxious mother' by concerned friends who describe her, she reports, as a neurotic, and a negative thinker. She says she feels isolated and has been depressed for approximately twelve years since separating from her husband. She acknowledges she holds imaginary conversations with herself, blaming herself for his desertion. Rationally, she knows the obsessiveness of her rituals are illogical, and she has discussed situations that can lead to repetitive rituals. She accepts theoretically that behavioural therapy has a number of strategies and techniques from which she can learn how to monitor intrusive thoughts and evolve a gradual approach to reducing their frequency.

THE THREE-TIERED GRAVE

Patient ID CPN0000280862: Roberta J.
Occupation: Community Psychiatric Nurse.
Drug: Paroxetine.
Drug class: Selective serotonin re-uptake inhibitor (SSRI) antidepressant for treatment of obsessive compulsive disorder, anxiety disorder, post-traumatic stress, panic disorder, and social phobias.
Common side effects: Drowsiness, nausea, apathy, sweating, tremors, insomnia, dry mouth, dizziness, decreased appetite.

Medice, cura te ipsum! Physician, heal thyself!

Please don't imagine the delicious irony of writing my own 'Psychological Report' escapes me, nor am I unaware of the possibilities for self-pity when pondering a 'Diagnostic Impression' to describe my own case.

Yet, now I've been banished 'for the duration' (my Team Manager's useful euphemism) to this cramped back room behind the Records Registry, I've seized my chance to open this (unofficial) file under the pretext of my general task, which is to correlate a decade of psychiatric evaluations against each patient's ethnicity, place of birth, gender, social class, sexual orientation, spiritual beliefs and symptom complexes (a pet project of my boss!).

So to be sidelined behind my *cordon sanitaire* for three months has proved not entirely unprofitable, after all, since I've had time enough to review my own cases (see Patient IDs 0268191058, 0291070651, 0304290749, et al., in the preceding pages).

They're the prize essays of only my 'most promising pupils', you might say, and each has a place on my own private honours board.

As to *why* I've been 're-deployed as a short-term measure' (the officialese of the letter from the Occupational Health Adviser), well, I note a more or less objective pen portrait of myself (see Elspeth P., ID 0338200976) gives the lie to my own disorder, however hard I may have tried to conceal the symptoms. 'She fingered her chignon to assure herself it had not strayed.' How well observed!

Yes. The repetitive rituals of a severe case of obsessive compulsive disorder are eventually impossible to conceal, and Elspeth P.—albeit with a motive wholly unsoured by malice—was evidently not the only only person to have reported them, because I can think of any number of personal and professional rivals within our Management Team who could have shopped me, actuated by envy, ambition, and manipulative self-interest . . . not to say downright spite.

Even Straight Trees Have Crooked Roots

I'll say this much. My retiral each day to this dusty back room to analyse these case notes has, indeed, granted me, as my boss promised, 'a period for quiet self-reflection', and a chance to 'reach a deeper understanding of the therapist's role by experiencing cognitive techniques from the patients' perspective.'

And, as you have no doubt noted, the examples I have chosen from my patients' cases are characterised, if not by a favourable resolution of their underlying psychological conflicts or by a remission, then by some seeming possibilities of therapeutic change.

So you can guess that, in the case of my own disorder, I still tend to clutch at straws, except I would probably have to wash my hands twenty times or more before I came to grasp them, and by that time any advantage to be had would have been lost.

Let me be perfectly clear, although it's hard, so very hard, to admit it, *I confess I've been growing steadily sicker ever since that fateful day my only daughter failed to return home.*

Ever since that fateful day . . . these symptoms of overscrupulosity (my cleaning compulsions are such that my flesh has peeled where my hands are washed raw) and my 'touching rituals' (I will allude to these fixations later) have become the major preoccupations in my life to the point of sheer exhaustion.

However, as R. D. Laing so comfortingly wrote, the unsound mind 'need not be all breakdown. It may also be breakthrough.' For it's true to say that now, when I reconsider the cases of my former patients, my new knowledge of my own disorder has yielded unexpectedly valuable insights and conclusions. And particularly noteworthy are apparent common threads or concordances running through these narratives that suggest not only the mutuality of women's experience but a redemptive path to inner healing.

Consider, for instance, the curious concordances between Eveline M., ID 0241090556 and Esther G., ID 0319141245 whereby the former's mother was taught elocution by the elocutionist of the latter's husband. The same name crops up in both case notes: the Speech Therapist of the Imperial Bedroom, as it were, or 'the Kammerherr-Doktor-in-Waiting for the Royal Hanoverian Stammer', as Esther so acidly phrased it.

Then there's the recurrence of near identical incidences of repressive graphology in these patients' longhand narratives indicative of vulnerable emotional states.

Compare Miriam R., ID 0198271154, and Mary H., ID 0312110842; observe how both patients repress certain symbols that represent feelings of shame and sexual guilt: in the first case, Miriam writes 'bd' for 'bed' and a 'candleholder', more tortuously, is twisted into 'cndlhldr'. Likewise, Mary refrains from writing '*cock*erel' in favour of the tamer 'rooster'.

On first acquaintance you'd be struck by the self-possession of these two sophisticated women, little suspecting the infant fears and phobias that have conditioned their adult responses—but even straight trees have crooked roots.

❀

Unreliable Narrators?

Of course, although these occasional unconscious slips of the pen can be construed as the erroneous actions of Freudian 'parapraxis', in point of fact, the acute self-awareness of my 'unreliable narrators' very often brings to their writings a candour that, despite such *vergriefen*, makes many of the histories I've selected not only refreshingly opinionated but witheringly honest.

Critics and debunkers will no doubt question the veracity of these accounts and dismiss them as confabulations—and, yes, I own to having, in the files of this Registry, unreliable narrators *in spades*—but I can cite many examples of astonishing perception that would dispel lingering doubts.

But, for the moment, the words of Miriam R., ID 0198271154, must suffice.

One day, while we talked, I observed Miriam for the first time fired up with outspoken righteous anger, especially when she questioned the supposed incongruity and randomness of early Surrealism expressed by Buñuel's cinematographic art. Miriam's left eye twitched as she condemned the notorious episode in *Un Chien Andalou* in which Buñuel himself appears to slice the left eyeball of the actress, Simone Mareuil.

'The foundations of surrealism,' Miriam fumed, 'are supposed to be premised on dream-like images or *objets trouvés* whose presence cannot be explained or *rationalised*. The only thing shocking about the sliced eyeball scene is that the first surrealists could not escape their own male chauvinism because, surely, the violation of a woman by a man can be very easily *explained* and accords with a Neanderthal male rationale that females are physically inferior and, thus, natural victims. All in all, a highly misogynistic view. Besides, Buñuel could not have made the film without his mother's money. *Très bourgeois!*' (cf. Mary H., ID 0312110842, and her remarks concerning *The Audit of Fame*.)

Wounded by a Shooting Star

So I think you now begin to recognise the truth of my belief that curious concordances abound in these patients' histories, yet none is more strange than that connecting the case of Marianne E., ID 0326030844 (cf. her sister, Victoria, ID 0332030844, cross-indexed) with the case of Elspeth P., ID 0338200976, as I'll now explain.

First you should know that the process of making a correlation between the medical information of one patient and the medical notes of another, when the patients are closely related, is accepted psychiatric practice provided both patients agree. In the cases of Marianne and Victoria, consent to disclosure was given.

Secondly, you should know that Victoria died eight years ago from an overdose of cocaine and morphine.

As Marianne has remarked, Victoria, from infancy, was always the 'wild child', a perception confirmed by Victoria herself when she later became my patient, too.

These are Victoria's own words. 'You know, when I was sixteen I was once almost arrested for soliciting because the policemen thought I was prostitute! Do you know why? I must have been the very first girl in London to wear a miniskirt made of black shiny plastic . . . I'd sewn it myself by stitching together two industrial waste bags! I was all tarted up. That's why they wanted to run me in!'

Victoria was a nostalgist for a very early beat drug scene (see her sister's reminiscences, *Elegy from a Locked Drawer*) and, once, she showed me a crumbling folded blotter of LSD that was more than twenty years old, which she kept in her pocketbook purely for reasons of sentiment.

Tragically, that pocketbook and the contents of a small valise were all the possessions that remained from her tragic life when I was called upon to identify her corpse. She had died alone in her squalid feme-sole Bayswater bedsit.

It was a duty I undertook reluctantly but Marianne was so torn up by her sister's death that I felt it was an obligation I could not refuse.

In the circumstances of both cases, Marianne's refusal to attend was understandable. Distraught, she said: 'Vix was a mirror of myself in looks, as you know. We even had the same shaped birth mark, except hers was on the opposite temple, so to see her laid out like that, were it only for a fraction of a second, would be like looking at my own deathbed!'

As even a superficial interpretivist approach to Marianne's self-narrative indicates, Marianne had resented the ascendancy of her older sister, and the powerful influence Victoria had exerted over her young womanhood.

'Since the moment of birth I think I must have always regarded her as dark shadow robbing me of sunlight.'

Marianne had then gone on to describe the precise instant she had sensed her sister's death.

'I believe Vix had come to accept that one of us had to die so the other could be free. I felt sure she was dead even though I was over a thousand miles away in Naples. I was crossing the Piazza Bellini on a cool evening when I suddenly felt an intense heat over my chest and heart as though a thousand acid-emitting insects were crawling under my skin. I stumbled towards a bench, my mind stunned by a blinding light, as if I'd been wounded by a shooting star.'

Octavia's Protégée

I made an inventory of Victoria's personal effects to send to Marianne.

Despite her squeamish refusal to take possession of them, I felt sure she would one day come to cherish those few articles of her sister's remaining estate as mementos of sunnier times before their severed siblinghood.

So that's how I came to stumble upon the Secret Catechism of Stoneburgh Eight.

The 'Stoneburgh Eight' requires no introduction; any history of the women's suffrage movement in early twentieth-century England is incomplete without mention of them.

Only the other day, in an English broadsheet, photographs appeared from police files of militant suffragettes:

Police Spy Photos of Suffragist Pickets

Covert pictures reveal birth of police state surveillance

> To mark the centenary of the Women's Social and Political Union photos have gone on display showing how secret police photographic surveillance was used to keep watch on the movements of activists in the votes-for-women movement. Scotland Yard detectives compiled photographic files of key suspects with the aim of forestalling arson attacks, sabotage and conspiracy, and to combat other acts of civil disobedience by increasingly militant suffragettes. The remarkable police mug shots show sixteen long-lens paparazzi-style photographs of London's Most Wanted, including (opposite page) 'Octavia' the youngest and most infamous window-smashing member of the 'Stoneburgh Eight', otherwise known as Margery Nairn-Jardine, Marxist theorist, Russophile, and the spirited debutante granddaughter of a Liberal peer.

The identities of the remaining seven are equally well known: 'Prima', 'Secunda', 'Tertia', 'Quarta', 'Quintina', 'Sestina', and 'Septima' . . . all once either prominent residents of Stoneburgh or members of landed families from country houses in the fenlands that surround our ancient garrison town.

Margery, as the news clipping records, was the youngest of the group. The same age as the century, born in 1899, she— ironically— was not old enough to vote when partial suffrage was granted in 1918.

The infirm handwriting of 'dainty, arched arcades' observed in letters to Victoria at her mentor's home in Brunswick Gardens, W8, was evident now in Margery's manuscripts preserved in a folder by her protégée among the pitifully few garments in the valise.

The dossier was marked:

Catechism of the Sisterhood

But the first item that fluttered from the packet when I folded back the cover was a note in Victoria's own distinctive hand (not unlike her sister's):

I remember! I have seen the garden. I am unafraid. I shall die tomorrow.*

The fragment of paper was dated a day earlier than her death. Curiously, her asterisk (*), stiltedly intrusive in a suicide note, indicated another date, stated as 'The Year of Grace I.M.', identifying the year in which she was twenty-seven years of age, exactly half her age when she died, a detail whose profound significance I would later learn only from a complete reading of Margery's dossier.

I delved deeper into the folder. Margery, the youngest of the 'Stoneburgh Eight', had retained faded, brown-edged newspaper clippings of a number of obituaries, including seven recording the deaths of her fellow Eightists.

From ingrained habit I began taking notes on my jotter. Above the dates recorded for the deaths of those seven older women Margery had superscribed a date of her own, in each case a month and year exactly midway between the deceased's birth and death, each annotation terminated by that ominous.

For one vertiginous second I suspected, like any bewildered reader, that these were the scribblings of a diabolical occultist or of a depraved murderess.

But then another bundle of notes of a more literary character caught my eye, labelled . . .

Prognostications, Egregore and Proofs

and I thought I saw a degree of rationality reimposed.

'Median Days' of Prominent Women

Two days of absenteeism have passed since I last wrote of the reassertion of reason, a vain presumption on my part as, stupidly, I had another relapse immediately after writing the words, 'rationality reimposed'!

Ever since that fateful day my only daughter failed to return home, whenever my thoughts of her intensify to an insupportable load, I have to replace 'bad thoughts' with 'good thoughts' by retracing all the words and sentences I have written and rewriting every one, and then retrace every action of the previous two days until I have neutralised all disturbing memories.

Those two days were occupied on a principle akin to the Paradox of the Complete Map, whereby speculative cartographers attempt to reproduce a terrain on a scale of *one mile to one mile* (1:1!), in which every feature and contour of the terrain, no matter how minute, has its own correspondence on a map of equal proportions . . . an impossible task of imitation like trying to trace with the point of a pencil the shadow of the tracing pencil.

I am calmer now. The packet of Margery's *Prognostications* is open before me and I've resumed my note-taking.

The first item, evidently a key text, is a quotation Margery cites from a work by Dr Tchékhov (I retain Margery's spelling in her French manner).

> 'There is a great deal that is enigmatic and obscure in nature . . . phenomena which are absolutely incapable of explanation. I know, for instance, of several strange, mysterious deaths, the cause of which only spiritualists and mystics will undertake to explain; a clear-headed man can only lift up his hands in perplexity. For example, I know of a highly cultured lady who foretold her own death and died without any apparent reason on the very day she had predicted. She said that she would die on a certain day, and she did die.'
>
> *The Examining Magistrate by Anton Chekhov.*

To this quotation Margery appends a chronological list of over fifty notable women of modern times. Against each name is a date of birth and death date and the median date of each subject's middle age, practically to the median day, if calculable . . . followed by the now inevitable, sinister.

An epitaph for this sheet is Margery's own rendering of *The Wisdom of Solomon, 18 v 14–15* (her italics) . . .

While all things are held in the *middle silence*, and
The night *halfway in its course*,
Thine Almighty Word, *O Eternal Light*,
Came from Heaven, from thy divine Throne.

There is not space in this brief discourse to itemise all of those citations, but I was soon made aware of the meaning of Margery's idiosyncratic numerology as it applied to several women not unknown to me.

In short, Margery's researches related wholly to personal documents, diaries and correspondence in which women had *divined their own deaths!*

For example, a celebrated name which instantly leapt out of those pages is that of *Anaïs Nin*, diarist, bigamist and eroticist, whose own unexpurgated journals, published just before Victoria died, provide evidential data sought by Vix to corroborate her mentor's beliefs.

Anaïs's median day (she died at the age of seventy-three in 1977) occurred when she was thirty-six and living in Paris:

> This summer I was the strongest . . . Returned [from St Tropez] fully aware of my weakness, of the prison I have made from which only the dream can deliver me.

Victoria has encircled the word 'dream'.

Margery in her own citations has travelled somewhat further back in time. Please note this extraordinary extract from the diary of Mariya Konstantinovna Bashkirtseva, Russian feminist writer, painter and sculptor (she died from tuberculosis in her twenty-fourth year in 1884, in Paris).

Her median day, *in medio* (I.M.) occurred in 1873 when she was just entering her teens:

> I went to the garden, and put my chair near the fountain; it made a magnificent picture, for the fountain has tall trees round it, shutting out heaven and earth . . . This is a day rather different from the others . . . I had a horrible dream last night . . . I saw the sun growing bigger and covering nearly half the heavens, but it emitted neither light nor heat . . . then half of it was covered by a cloud. We all cried out, 'The sun is standing still!' . . . Then the sun began to turn round like two wheels, one within the other . . . the bright sun was covered at intervals by a cloud as round as itself . . . What is the meaning of this dream?

On this passage, more sun-faded than the other clippings, Margery has encircled the words 'garden' and 'dream'. These commonalities are cited, too, in Margery's far-reaching researches into the 'median days' of prominent women, many of them Russian feminists. Here's a selection of her translations; please note the reappearance of Margery's key words, 'garden' and 'dream' and 'death':

> I cannot sleep in the bed my husband [Count Tolstoy] has abandoned . . . but it was next day before we made it up . . . and I realised to my joy that his love for me . . . was not dead. I shall never forget the heavenly cool morning, the dew sparkling on the grass, as I walked through the garden after a sleepless night in the bath-house. Rarely have I seen such a dream of natural beauty. I sat for a long time in the icy water, hoping to catch a chill and die.
>
> *Countess Sofia Andreevna Tolstaya, 1882. I.M.*

> My best dreams are of childhood . . . and in my thoughts . . . I breathe the air of the fields. I remember how nice it was there: a shady mysterious wood . . . I remember that garden—it was an oasis which has taught me to love the country life, nature and the soil.
>
> *Vera Nikolaevna Figner, Russian revolutionary, imprisoned in solitary confinement, 1897. I.M.*

This penultimate citation of Margery's I have chosen for its representing an even earlier period in Russian history and the diarist's sojourn in London in 1820.

> Only in Kensington Gardens can one breathe . . . Last year they took from its lake the body of a very beautiful woman, expensively dressed, who had probably been a whole week in the water.
>
> *Madame de Lieven, wife of Russian Ambassador to London. 1820. I.M.*

But Margery's final translation from a Russian feminist's schoolgirl diary is, perhaps, the more fascinating because here, as in no other citation of hers from the Russian, the first mention of the 'secret' appears.

> Oh my God! What a day it was today! . . . I got acquainted with a girl of the 6th class, Manya L. She has a great secret, which only Manya B, knows . . . All these days of mine are now full of doubts and alarm for myself and for the others. There were joys also. But the joys are rather rare . . . You are my secret of which nobody knows.
>
> *Elizaveta Alexandrovna Dyakonova, authorand feminist adherent. Aged 11, 1886. I.M.*

All these extracts are recorded in the middle passage of the writers' lives, in the secret hour of life's mid-day when the parabola of life is reversed and death is born, as Jung records (an apt quotation once cited in another context by my patient, Elspeth P., ID 0338200976, whose fleeting acquaintance with Margery had fortuitously shifted the trajectory of her own life).

About Anjelika

I still haven't completely fathomed the mysteries of Margery/Octavia's Prognostications File and her secret practices to divine things to come. So I reserve judgement. As it is, she's not the only woman I've encountered in my professional work who's had a turn for prophesies and presentiments.

No, I am no further advanced with these notes because I, too, have been troubled by a momentous dream, a dream that has compelled me to take another day's sick leave. Still, the boss has already written one damning sick note; he hardly needs another. He probably believes that my absence from the office is a component of an alternative treatment. Maybe it is.

❁

This morning in the early hours I awoke from the dream in a fever of apprehension. Halfway through the course of the night I'd dreamt I was adrift under water, with dim sunlight filtering down to the lower depths.

Even at this moment of sleep's deepest submergence, I was conscious of my cousin managing somehow to telephone me from her beach cottage with vital intelligence about my daughter. Half waking, I remember how the orange sodium glare from a street light dissolved in the rain rapping on the windows, but this morning the pavement was quite dry.

Was it a dream within a dream?

Before the hands of the kitchen clock had reached a civilised hour, I was dialling my cousin's number.

I should explain that Cousin Hildie is my first cousin and closer than a sister to me, an empathic bond all the stronger since she is a single child like myself. The sympathy may be only a matter of blood.

'But that's truly incredible!' she shrieked, 'I was just this second about to call *you*!'

'You *were*?' I was both astonished and relieved.

'You must come at once,' she urged excitedly, 'I have to talk to you about Angie!'

❁

Angie.

That's the name Hildie would use when discussing my daughter, Anjelika. And Anjelika, on her part, from her earliest childhood, would refer to my cousin by no other name but *Swan*hilda . . . and I grudgingly concede the length of my cousin's elegant neck is universally admired, so she is not altogether undeserving of the soubriquet.

Throughout our girlhood and married lives Hildie has been the cynosure of all eyes; she seems to attract good fortune.

Nowadays she manages a holiday cottage-letting agency with her third husband, a minor tycoon, in an enchanting fishing port five hours drive from here.

Not that I intend to take the car to travel there.

Ever since that fateful day my only daughter failed to return home, I've been afraid to drive my car for fear of causing a crash. I'm always afraid that I will be held to blame. I have terrible feelings of anticipatory guilt.

Even when I take the train I have to employ all sorts of avoidance behaviours so as not to watch the train pull into the station for fear that, just by looking at it, I'll distract the train driver and bring about a fatal rail disaster.

I'm aware these rituals make no sense at all and I'm deeply ashamed of them.

This morning, in an effort to ameliorate the worst excesses of my irrational routines, I forebore to buy a newspaper . . . a newspaper that would take me an infinity to read because I'd touch every line in each paragraph, then compute the total sum. Fortunately, there was a space for me to sit in the first seat of the fourth carriage, another compulsive habit I can't shake off.

Mild distractions are recommended in a case as severe as mine. That's why I've brought Margery's notes with me. I've been advised to study the passage of time on my watch as a means of remaining focused on the here and now. Failing this, I'm to focus my thoughts on something visible and non-threatening.

So, as we leave the town, I gaze at the backs of grim houses hard by the railway tracks.

A starved cat yawns dispiritedly on a windowsill.

Anjelika.

Before that fateful day my beloved only daughter failed to return home, she had started to sleep all day in her room, and refused to eat, the culminative signs of a disaffection I failed to recognise.

I've been accused by Hildie of overpossessiveness. She says that ever since my daughter's birth I've been an overprotective mother, but you'd think that I, if anyone, would have recognised any morbid predispositions of my own towards extreme postpartum obsessive compulsions.

It's true that even after Anjelika's infancy I'd still visit her room sometimes up to five times in one night to check if she was still breathing, but I never once suspected these actions were anything more than entirely natural in devoted motherhood. But Hildie insists to this day that my behavioural tendencies have strayed into frenetical ritualistic routine.

'Let's face it, darling, you've teetered *way over* the *acceptable* edge of the spectrum. No wonder you drove that poor husband of yours to cut loose, as no sane man could live with your never-ending, namby-pambying twitchiness.'

Agreed, years later, when Anjelika attended senior school she resented my stalking at a discreet distance behind the column of pupils walking the half mile to the main gates. But my presence, I insisted, was simply to protect her from any bad influence that would surely have exerted itself freely without my vigilance. Anjelika was a bright girl, and the class swots, I noticed, formed the head of the column, exchanging mnemonics to pass exams while the laggardly juvenile smokers dragged their feet in the rearguard.

And so the years passed.

Did Anjelika wholly blame me for the breakup of my marriage?

Certainly she took to ridiculing what she termed my excessive 'mummying', addressing me invariably as 'Mumsie' in her most sardonic manner.

This ferocious 'mumsifying' I recognise is yet one more example of how the intensity of a familial relationship can be concentrated in one powerful word—as my preceding cases have shown—and, like my patients, I am not immune to the emotions such words invoke. You'll note that the varieties of parental rule are all represented: Da, Dadda, Fa, Papa, Pops, Ma, Mam, Mummy and, even in the case of Eveline M., ID 0241090556, her 'schoolma'ama' is frighteningly indistinguishable from her mother, (nor should we forget her spiritual 'Mother', 'father' and 'sisters' at the convent whose oppression shaped her infancy) while Miriam R., ID 0198271154, addresses her father as that daddy of them all, the 'Old Man'.

In Hildie's opinion, *when my beloved only daughter failed to return home* Anjelika was not to blame, for it was I who was entirely culpable.

I'd entered the house from work at my usual hour and Anjelika's car was no longer parked in the drive. She'd stripped her room of all her belongings.

'You smothered that child by overmothering,' Hildie snorted when I rang her in panic. 'What on earth did you expect?'

Two agonising months passed before I heard briefly from Anjelika that she'd taken up with a young drug addict—*Van Schuyler*—she'd met near Soho.

Anjelika was just seventeen years old when she was seduced by that creature.

One of Anjelika's schoolfriends encountered them by chance in Oxford Street: Anjelika was riding pillion on Van Schuyler's motorbike.

'A skinhead kid in a skidlid.' That was the first description of Schuyler.

Van Schuyler, I was told, had called me 'a dangerous woman'.

This Dutchman had chatted up my daughter at the junction of Great Titchfield Street, my informant continued blithely on the phone. He'd been enchanted by the coincidence because that precise spot, so Van Schuyler claimed, beside the 'great Mediterranean' of Oxford Street, was the notorious rendezvous of the arch-drugfiend, de Quincey.

The tragedy was that neither my daughter nor 'Van' Schuyler was content with de Quincey's metropolitan Mediterranean for long . . . very soon they sought the real thing. And that's how my beloved daughter with the druggie Van Schuyler came to be stranded in Spain, detained by the *Guardia Civil* under suspicion of attempting to smuggle ten-and-a-half kilogrammes of cannabis resin across the French border.

(Incidentally, Elenore S., ID 0268191058, the cartographer, once confided to me that whenever she looked at a map of Europe she still, senselessly, could not help perceiving Spain as a 'quasi-self-similar fractal' of France.)

❁

Hildie, as promised, was on the station platform to greet me.

She was wearing a flaring black velour coat with a marigold-coloured silk scarf at the throat. Swanhilda looked less like a swan, I thought, than a beady-eyed blackbird with a bright orange beak.

Hildie at once bundled me into her car and we rode together to the seafront.

Soon we were seated in a seafood restaurant overlooking the promenade.

I raised an eyebrow. Her blouse was buttoned slightly lower than usual, displaying to advantage a new sparkly necklace. She spends like an heiress.

I pinned a smile on for Hildie's sake.

'So . . .? And . . .? Out with it!' I prompted eagerly once she had settled at the table.

Conscious of admiring side-glances from neighbouring diners, my cousin then, to my surprise, began to recount her *own* dreams.

'If this dream persists I think I shall have to consult a nerve specialist!' she laughed with an impatient motion of her hands. 'It's just that for three nights in a row I've dreamt of Angie. She's in a house—not *yours*, I'm certain—in a kind of garret room under a roof. It's a clean place, with a purple blind over the dormer window, and on its walls are coloured prints of mountains or, perhaps, prints of the *same* mountain. They're quite distinct.'

'*Unreal!* They must her Hiroshige woodcuts of Mount Fuji!' I could not believe the astonishing vividness of Hildie's recall.

'There's a recess between the chimney breast and window with fitted shelves; it's practically a small library.'

'Her study books!' I put in. 'She'd almost completed her A-levels for university.'

A young waiter poured mineral water from a chilled beaded bottle.

'Oh! And that was the strange thing!' Hildie narrowly watched the slim youth depart. In that speculative look she still remains something of a vampish tramp, despite a socially advantageous late marriage.

'The strange thing?' I urged impatiently.

She toyed with her glass.

'That attic room. I remember it felt so hideously cold! There was frozen condensation on the water pipes.'

At that moment I was shaken by soundless sobbing and further speech was impossible.

I fled from the restaurant towards a stretch of beach where a row of white bathing huts hemmed an ornamental garden and a railed-off Krazy Golf putting green.

The past had come back upon me with a shock. I stood amazed at Hildie's power to conjure up a room in which I'd never set foot, yet whose every detail seemed to be preternaturally vivid.

For *when my beloved only daughter failed to return home* I found an empty room bereft of not only her presence but of every personal article that had given substance to her being. Of Anjelika's clothes, cosmetics, books, pictures, music . . . her essence . . . not a trace remained.

After the first sighting of Anjelika in Soho I'd grilled that schoolfriend of hers mercilessly until she finally confessed to her knowledge of Van Schuyler's 'squat'.

I'd found the place with little difficulty: a shuttered-up, mud-coloured terrace house near King's Cross station.

Van Schuyler's room was on the second floor. The house was fearfully cold.

The door was open. He sat alone, lounging in a vast, grubby corduroy-covered floor-cushion. His arms were clasped behind his head, which rested on a soiled lace antimacassar. On his sharp chin, upthrust reflectively, there grew a celestial beard of tobacco smoke.

The smoke's sweet fragrance reminded me of rich brown spices. I assumed it was his strongest skunk; my head swam.

'Mr Van Schuyler,' I said, my voice trembling, 'I demand to know where my daughter is!'

'*Fun*,' he corrected, emphasising the fricative like some finicky moralist, 'it's *Fun* Schuyler. Is not it funny?'

He pointed to a cockroach scuttling over the bare floorboards, and scooped it into his palm.

'On my horizon your daughter means as much to me as my friend here,' he continued dreamily. 'She means *everything* to me.' He blew a stream of smoke which settled in an ectoplasmic canopy above him. 'In the domain of eternity are only *fillings* and *emotions*,' he sighed.

I turned away in disgust and, at the same time, I noticed, placed on the mantleshelf, Anjelika's shoe.

Anjelika's Shoe

The abandoned Cinderellan shoe was like a poignant leitmotif of her sudden flight and long absence. The strap was broken.

'As you see it is not a problem for me but just a pleasure to mend it,' the Van Schuyler fellow mumbled. Now the smoke had cleared I saw an absurd spike of hair reared up from his skull like a dishevelled aigrette.

I opened a cupboard. Empty hangers; no sign of Anjelika's belongings.

I thrust the shoe into my coat pocket.

'Tell Anjelika,' I said very slowly and distinctly, 'from now on her mother will be mending things. There is more to mend than this shoe.'

Van Schuyler's eyelids barely flickered when I slammed shut the cupboard door and stomped out of the room.

Now, as I stood on the seafront, the salt breeze drying my tears, I was assailed by dark thoughts. The shock of Anjelika's absence had affected me physically more than I had allowed Hildie to see. I could not frame words to tell Hildie the depths of my suffering.

There were public lavatories nearby. I washed my face in a basin beneath an open window. I let the gusting Atlantic scour my mind.

Gilded clouds had gathered over the bay like a kind of offshore baroque.

In the mirror my face looked sinister when I powdered it under the blue overhead light.

I knew what that blue light was for.

Blue lights prevent drug addicts finding a blue vein into which to inject drugs.

❀

Sleeping Arrangements in the Afterlife

The afternoon was well advanced when Hildie drove down the lane that led to Ocean Villas.

Abruptly she halted beside an ancient church. She opened the car door and gestured to me to join her.

'Shift your carcass,' Hildie ordered.

Shielded by sombre yews, the churchyard was warm and the air still, so it seemed as if the chill of the evening was yet far remote.

'Look!' Hildie indicated a massive stone family vault mounted atop the sloping end of the surrounding lawns.

'The last resting place of all the Symes's,' Hildie pronounced smugly.

The monument resembled, I thought, a vast Gothic four-poster bed, which on closer inspection I saw had four inscribed panels round its periphery each bearing the Symes armorial crest.

'Reggie wants me to share his *eternal* sleep as well, you know. His insistence is really rather touching, so I've agreed to be buried here, too.'

I noticed a smaller stone memorial nearby, the size and shape of an hors d'oeuvres trolley, dedicated to the memory of the Symes family's deceased servants.

A faithful old retainer, I noticed, was watering the flowers and tidying the grave.

I fretted at my cousin's insouciance. How typical of Hildie, I thought, to marry an elderly rich man for whom she had no real preference just to allay his fears of sleeping alone in the afterlife.

The church clock tolled the hour.

'In many ways,' my cousin murmured with a veiled sidelong glance, 'Reggie acts like a small child still afraid of the dark.'

The Isle of the Dead

No. 1 Ocean Villas consists of a modest stuccoed terrace ranged along a little plateau of marran grass, facing west, above the sea's edge.

The foreshore smells of tarry ropes from broken moorings.

There is a distinct change in the light, where it shines on the sea, when you enter Reggie's house. Fussy copper trinkets from the Orient wink and gleam from every surface. Reggie inherited the house from his great-uncle, a flamboyant Edwardian impresario who had the place built as a love-nest for the innumerable young actresses he lured there.

Hildie and Reggie live in the larger of the villas, where two adjoining homes have been knocked together into one, leaving the remaining villa set apart for offices in which Hildie presides over Reggie's property portfolio of over one hundred holiday cottages dotted along the westward coast.

After a large supper, Reggie likes to retire to the verandah and his steamer lounger where, idly waggling his toes on the footrest, he lies with half-closed eyes, dreamily contemplating the fading of the light.

I think Hildie overfeeds him. Since his marriage, he's become a bellygut, an appearance that is not improved by an enormous pendulous lip that juts out like a shovel. The man's digging his own grave with his teeth and doesn't know it. Hildie pretends not to notice when he lets out another reef in his waistband to show the lining of his tropical shorts.

❀

The pouring of postprandial liqueurs by Hildie invariably gives rise to our most intimate and agreeable time together, attended by the reassuring sound of Reggie dozing . . . *offstage*, as it were.

So when Hildie lowered her voice, heralding a confidence, I leaned forward in alert anticipation.

We were discussing the Symes family vault.

'Don't you see, dearest coz? This changes *everything*!'

'But I still can't quite grasp how it has anything to do with *me*.'

'Of course it has. It means Granny Lucy's tomb is *free!*'

Hildie and I share a paternal grandmother—*Granny Lucifer* is how we both remembered her—an autocratic matriarch who'd died when we were infants yet who has assumed a legendary stature in our minds.

'Dadda told me Granny Lucifer predicted the precise day of her death, that's why she bought the plot in Stoneburgh cemetery the week after her wedding . . . even in those days they had practically run out of spaces.'

The burial ground at Stoneburgh is on a mound overlooking the fens.

Because the tombs are arranged in orderly marble avenues over a raised area, on moonlit nights, according to Anjelika, the place is not unlike the *Isle of the Dead* in Venice, painted by Böcklin, one of her favourite pictures.

Anjelika had once expressed a wish to be buried there.

'Granny fully expected granddad to marry a second time so she bought a multiple grave with three levels, because space was limited.'

'You mean there's room for more?'

'Abso-bloody-lutely! It came to me in a dream! Granny Lucifer's in the bottom berth, grandad and grandma are snug in the middle berth, and the upper berth is free. Dadda said, as I'm the eldest grandchild, I should really have it by rights, but now all that's changed.'

'So . . .?'

'It's simply perfect! I should have thought of it before. Granny always loved that spot; now it's free for Angie.'

My glass fell from my hand and shattered. Then I broke out into hysterical weeping and woke up Reggie.

No Owl Ever Loved Darkness More

Dream or psychodrama? *Traum oder Trauma?*

On the train, returning home early next morning, I tried to suppress thoughts of Hildie's symbolic dreams as they replayed in my mind.

It seemed to me I was trying to escape, not so much from her dreamscape as from a foreglimpse of a future that summoned me to its horrific fulfilment.

Sitting there, gazing out, was like staring into a terrifying distance.

Indeed, the shock of her revelations quite shook me out of my persistent fidgeting and tic-like compulsions for most of the journey.

I gazed at playing fields fleeing past my window.

The football pitches seemed stapled to the grass by pairs of goal posts, I mused, and I was reminded of the bulldog clip which held together Margery's bundle of papers.

I felt that somehow a considerable time had elapsed since I had started on my annotations of Margery's dossier. When I had spoken to Elspeth about them, she'd begged me to prepare a talk for her Alumni Association.

Yet even the few hours which had slipped away since I'd last examined those clippings on the outward train now seemed to be long past.

Elspeth had been amazed when I'd revealed that my Granny Lucifer was 'Tertia', one of the original Stoneburgh Eight; she'd insisted on convening a seminar.

Thus far in my researches, Granny's name has been absent from Margery's file, apart from a tombstone announcement cut from our local weekly, the *Stoneburgh Examiner.*

'No owl ever loved darkness more than does the Consorority of The Secret,' Margery writes when recording the secret mystic ceremonies that bound the Stoneburgh Eight to avowed silence.

Alas, Margery's words are a mischievous understatement, for I now accept that to fully penetrate the dark veil of the Sisterhood's secrets is a task beyond my own feeble reach.

However, though I regret there is not space here to record the higher degrees of the invocatory arts practised by the Stoneburgh Eight's hermetic order, I *can* sketch out Margery's early impressions of her initiation as an aspirant.

> The Sisterhood, I learn, has an archpriestess and subpriestess, Prima and Secunda.
>
> My instruction in the lore, Secunda tells me, follows an ancient form of catechism that has been passed down through generation upon generation of Sisters by memorisation.
>
> When I asked the history and age of the Sisterhood, Prima averred that the Consorority sprang from the unwritten pages of darkest antiquity, and so it followed that no written tradition survives. Prima forebade me, on pain of expulsion and worse, to disclose, either in speech or by written record, a hint or merest whisper of what I shall learn in our secret ceremonies.
>
> Regardless of such *decreta*, tonight I decided to jot down some notes, despite the aims and methods of their occult rituals, on their path towards a higher consciousness, remaining somewhat blurred in my memory due to a heavy head cold.

I, too, could not prevent myself from shaking as from a chill, even though the morning sun streamed strongly through the carriage window and radiant waves rose in the dusty air.

How extraordinary, I thought, that the Sisterhood's very existence had been sealed by strictest secrecy—not even a mention in the National Archive—and the true objectives of this shadowy organisation had never once been committed to print or to writing by its postulants, until doughty young Margery had summoned the nerve to describe its origins!

Margery's exemplary summary should impress on anyone the virtue of keeping short notes at the time of life-changing events for further reflective study and self-therapy:

THE CONSORORITY OF THE SECRET

Demonesses, Doctrines and Conjurations.

Mythopoeic origins: Circa. tenth century BC. Temple of Solomon.
Beliefs: Worship of Sumero-Babylonian *FEMALE SPIRIT*, daughter of *LILITH* (?), Mother of Demons, (cf. *ISHTAR, ASTARTE, INANNA, APHRODITE*, etc.). See also, sister demonesses, the harlots from Hell (?): the *Lilim*, *Lamiae*, *Empusae*, and *Daughters of Hecate*.
Cults: Too numerous to record; see autonomous Russian Republic of Mari El and Cheremissian worship of goddess, *YUMYNUDYR*, Divine Maiden Spinner of the Thread of Fate, and the demoness, *ONOSKELIS*, weaver of ropes for Solomon's Temple and, according to a number of sources, feared as a daughter of Lilith and considered one of the *Empusae*.

Margery records a special note here that 'Prima' and 'Secunda', the Chief Adepts of the Order, both believed—quite erroneously—that the name for those Lilithean demonesses, the *Empusae*, was cognate with the Cheremissian goddess, *Yumynudyr*. On the most fragmentary etymological evidence, they asserted that Cheremissian egregore and occult practices could be compared to the ritual worship of the impudent spirit they'd identified as *Onoskelis*.

As to doctrine and prayer, Margery concludes:

Doctrine: The Sisterhood believes that their Divination Spirit, ONOSKELIS, can be invoked to foretell the *dies mortis* (D.M., the day of death) of the Supplicant. The divination is performed by taking a length of fuse-rope, knotted in the centre, and coiling the fuse in an invocatory mystic circle. Both ends of the a slow-burning fuse are lit simultaneously, and the duration of the ceremony is measured by the time observed for the knot to burn. The glowing knot is obviously symbolical of the secret hour of Life's mid-point between Birth and Death, whose Disclosure is the object of the Divination, revealed in the Dream of the Garden vouchsafed to the Supplicant.

. . . *and so on.* Well, you'll be pleased to learn that I don't intend to record *all* their *arcana* at any great length in these pages when, as Margery points out, the hypotheses and speculations of the Stoneburgh Eightists were so fundamentally misguided and flawed by epistemological inconsistencies.

My concerns are for rather more mundane, not so say moribund, secrets.

This morning, for example, I could hear my cousin blithely singing an aria in the bath when, in the flurry of departure, it somehow turned out that it was Reggie, rather than Hildie, who ran me to the station in time for my early train.

In parting, Reggie clasped my hand rather longer than was entirely decent in a married man. He appraised me with bed-rheumy eyes.

'Why don't we meet up for lunch sometime in Town?' he suggested.

'That would be nice. I'll fix it up with Hildie.'

'I wasn't . . . erm . . . thinking of Hildie . . . '

'I *see*. Well, if *you* won't think of Hildie,' I said firmly, withdrawing my hand, 'then *I* shall.'

I pinned on my public smile and seriously contemplated Reggicide.

Reggie fumbled for a cigarette and turned away to shield the match and hide his discomfiture. He was wearing a double-breasted cashmere blazer with little bobbles round the collar and cuffs where the wool had pilled. His collar was frayed and there was fag ash on his necktie.

As I boarded the train I was thinking of when I'd last seen Reggie in Town. Only a fortnight after his marriage I'd spotted him flirting outrageously with a blue blooded young cutie from his Knightsbridge office who was fondling a new Hermès scarf in the restaurant at Dickins & Jones.

Now my tears of the previous night had betrayed me. Reggie had caught me with my defences down, so he'd pounced. I suppose I should have felt vaguely flattered by the old philanderer, except I remembered Zoë W. (see Patient ID 0291070651) once telling me of her brother-in-law making a pass at her on the very day of her husband's funeral.

'My brother-in-law is a notorious wolf,' Zoë had shrugged, 'and when an alpha male dies it's the instinct of the pack animal to just take another mate.'

❦

Such Things as are Necessary to be Known

Intrusive thoughts have delayed by one hour the completion of these notes.

I was again compelled to touch each line and count the number of paragraphs I've so far written. There are two hundred and forty-six, by my reckoning, the sum of whose digits is twelve, a number which my patient, Isolde B., ID 0318211042, has repeatedly insisted is 'a powerful number because it's the triad multiplied by the quaternion'. Very good. Now I am reassured, I may proceed.

In speaking of Zoë and Isolde, I am reminded of a character I have not yet mentioned but who nonetheless is everpresent in their case histories and, indeed, in those of all my patients.

A mutual friend.

Hence, in each narrative you'll observe how a psychotropic drug has come to be regarded as a character in the dramatis personae, obtruding slyly into the life of the patient like an antagonist introduced into the tale by the psychodramatist as a companionable deceiver or treacherous friend to control events or even to propel the plot as an auxiliary ego enacting different facets of the patient's mental distress.

By contrast, the mental distress of the early members of the Stoneburgh Eight is not so comprehensively documented, but Margery records the sexual nature of the manhandling by the police when the Eightists were hauled off to Holloway prison, where they endured the great ordeal of hunger strikes and violent forcible feeding.

In her *Prognostications File* is a glossy photograph of Margery under arrest being led away, escorted by six beat bobbies and five mounted policemen, pursued by a mob of working men.

She is wearing a crocheted woollen helmet over her Eton crop.

In the photo I count thirty-eight men and one suffragette.

So maybe, like myself, you begin to accept the divinatory rites of the Consorority as an essential preparation in their struggle against the subjugation of women, and as an initiation ceremony to steel them to face unimaginable indignities and suffering under restraint.

'To know the hour of one's death is to know strength.'

Those are the words of Prima, quoted by Octavia (Margery), at the head of what I believe is the only known transcription of the Consorority's First Altitude of Divination to invoke the shape-shifting demoness, Onoskelis—a spirit, it should be noted, that assumes the guise of a fair and pretty young woman:

(The ritual is performed at midday on a Wednesday. The Supplicant kneels within the burning mystic circle; her Interlocutor stands hitherward of the mid-point knot and commences the conjuration.)

THE SECRET CATECHISM
FOR YOUNG MAIDENS

Containing Such Things as are Necessary
to be Known at a Early Age

What is it to be wise?

To understand rightly, and act accordingly.

How is a woman wise?
She is wise who is mindful of her life in time.

Then how should the wise woman use time?
Take time when time is, for time will away.
And what should a wise woman oft consider?

A wise woman considers well and oft why she came into the world and when she must go out of it.

Then sayest how shall she know what years her life has?

Her life shall be half spent before she shall know what years it has.

Then how shall she know her life's half-span?
Preknowledge of death is a second light.

Where shineth the second light?

In a bright garden. A garden enclosed shall be our Sister; in a bright garden the wise woman shall see the second light that shall show to her all things.

And when shineth the second light that shall show her all things?

Between waking and sleep at her life's half-span a vision of a garden she shall see; her head in heaven and her feet on earth. And, even though the sun shineth not, yet doth the Garden seem all in flame; for a garden enclosed shall be our Sister to show us all things.

And what is our Sister's name who showeth us all things?

Her name is *[here the Supplicant covers her eyes]* Onoskelis.

And how shall we know [here the Interlocutor covers her eyes] Onoskelis?

She weareth a crown of gold and she leaves aromatic perfumes behind her. Ye shall know her by sweet music played from hidden pipes.

And who shall know the Secret Councils of Onoskelis?

Ye who are wise women shall know the secret, regardless of time.

(When the flames meet and flare at the mid-point knot the Invocation is complete. The Supplicant eats a piece of singed bread and takes a container of the Water of Life—water drunk by a raven—and drinks half of it, the other half to be drunk when the sun comes up. She will then die at the appointed time.)

These lines of my note-taking were halted when a refreshment trolley rumbled down the narrow aisle of the railway carriage to jostle my elbow, causing Margery's folder to slip from my lap to the floor.

When I'd gathered her sheets into their former order I noticed a pink slip of paper had scudded across the aisle and was lodged under the opposite seat.

The moment I retrieved it I felt a shock of recognition judder through my veins. Anjelika used to have a lined foolscap writing block of that precise tint; I brought the scrap close to my nose. I could smell her perfume. Anjelika's handwriting was unmistakable:

> Dearest Mumsie,
>
> I never guessed such a thing could be known just by dreaming! Do you remember when I was nine I woke up crying because I'd seen burning lights falling out of the sky? I, too, dreamt then of walking in the Garden and I smelled that heavenly perfume. Do not blame yourself for what will happen. Because in the Garden every seed knows its time.
>
> With my most tender love
>
> Anjelika

A sinister tick (✓) and the ominous abbreviation, D.M., appeared alongside a date no more than two weeks after Anjelika's eighteenth birthday.

My hot tears fell on the paper and turned the pink tored.

The Penguin Lady

So Anjelika, too, like Victoria, had read Margery's secret *Prognostications File*!

There was a sudden pain in my heart and my stomach made repeated requests to pay a visit to my throat.

Anjelika must have found the packet by rifling through my bureau one day when I was out at work. Driven by a mood of resentment, she'd no doubt been determined to trace the source of her mother's rancorousness and erratic actions.

Yet Anjelika's memory of her ninth year had not played her false.

She had, indeed, woken shrieking, shrieking in the voice of another creature.

'The penguin lady! The penguin lady!' she'd sobbed. 'The lady was sitting at the end of the bed!' To calm her, I'd asked her to draw a picture of the apparition. (I don't believe I've noted in these pages that Anjelika's talent for drawing was remarkable from the earliest age.)

I remember so well her picture of a garden in flame, and at its centre stood a beautiful young woman in the black and white habit of hooded nun.

Something Nasty Happened

I'd observed a nun not unlike my daughter's crayon sketch only a fortnight earlier in Spain—in the secure side ward of a small *hospital psiquiátrico* at the foot of the Pyrenees.

The nun was wearing the habit of the Sisters of Charity, black and white, and had a rosary in her hands. I was aware of the symmetries of her face and a radiance expressive of exceptional beauty.

She sat keeping vigil at the bedside of Van Schuyler who lay in a deep coma hooked up to a ventilator and an intravenous drip.

He had been washed and shaved. His hair had grown over his scalp.

'Those who say the devil is not so frightful as he is painted,' I whispered to myself, *'are plainly wrong.'*

When I gazed down at that hated face my utter contempt for the man and the abhorrence in which I held him was so strong

I thought that, under the pressure of so intense an emotion, the room would vapourise.

Harsh words trembled on my tongue but I remained silent.

Above the iron bedstead hung a crucifix.

I imagined that weed-smoking woodlouse spouting his existential, fair-is-foul/foul-is-fair, relativist claptrap to impress my daughter and, as I dug my fingernails into my clenched hands, I felt my palms bleed.

The nun shifted in her chair and recommenced telling her beads.

'Mater omnipotens,' I heard her mutter. *'Immortalitas, Sapientia, Principium et Finis, Veritus, Aeternas, Infinitas, Amen.'*

Then a white-coated porter came to escort me to the morgue.

'Something nasty happened,' was the British Consul's infuriatingly threadbare account of the accident when I'd telephoned him from the airport.

He apologised for what he called 'the paucity of details' and the Consulate 'regretted the delays but the Spanish authorities were being difficult'; yet I suspected from his tone that the humiliation of the British by the Spaniards was some kind of diplomatic game in which my daughter had become an expendable pawn.

'Van Schuyler and your daughter were attempting to cross the border at La Junquera. It was 'a' routine check by the *Guardia Civil* and French agents with search dogs. Actually, they were on the lookout for bigger fish than Van Schuyler, who's known to be small-time, but he made a break for it and led a chase up hairpin roads into the mountains. They found the car at the bottom of a ravine with four duffel bags of cannabis resin he'd somehow brought over from Tangier or Casablanca.'

I heard an impatient sigh, preparatory to the Consul replacing the receiver.

'Until Van Schuyler regains consciousness the entire investigation is on hold,' he said in an aggrieved, half-absent manner.

'I'm afraid the charge of drug trafficking makes our negotiations very awkward.'

'So! La Junquera!' I thought, as they led me into the mortuary. *'I will always associate Van Schuyler-the-Junkie with that name.'*

The phenolic odours of the morgue are familiar to me from my duties to the dead, as I earlier explained.

Yet that odour of unceremonialised death was not in my nostrils when the mortician removed the white sheet and I gazed at last upon my Anjelika's placid countenance.

In that chamber of death I smelled only the aromatic perfumes of a rose garden, and I saw only that my daughter wore a wreath of gold.

I stared fixedly at her profile to retain an after-image in my mind.

Her teeth were perfect, you know; I never allowed her to eat sweets.

Ever since my only daughter failed to return home, each day when I think of her, I light a candle in my heart.

The Secret Talisman of the Sisterhood

My mind is clearer now.

The example of Mariya Bashkirtseva, the nineteenth-century feminist painter quoted by Margery, explains *why* my daughter was not deflected from her resolute path to cram all worldly experience into an epoch of two hundred hedonistic days. I cannot find it in my heart to blame her.

Mariya, I note, in 1881, wrote several articles under a nom de plume for the feminist newspaper, *La Citoyenne*, and she was a Parisian contemporary of the 'red she-wolf', the anarcho-feminist Louise Michel (mentioned by Elspeth), also cited by Margery on her alphabetical and chronological listings of prominent women who had divined their own deaths. Her name is two places above that of another celebrated Parisian, Anaïs Nin.

However, a question remains as to Mariya's initiation into the Consorority of the Secret, although Margery confidently proposes the case for her inclusion in the roll call of celebrated Adepts.

Margery's thesis for this supposition is too lengthy for me to here relate. However, her notes on the Consorority's pervasion of early feminism reward further reading.

In particular, Margery's concluding short notes on the significance of the secret talisman, by which the Sisterhood identifies its adherents, not only direct the dedicated reader to further study but explain her curious defacement of an early edition of the Bashkirtseff diary inherited by Victoria.

> **Talismanic symbology:** The Consorority's ritual day of Wednesday is no accident, I am instructed. The Day of Wisdom, 'middle weekday' (cf. German *Mittwoch*, Russian *Sredah*, etc.) correlates to the mid-point of the burning thread, the Thread of Life woven in Solomon's Temple by their Divination Spirit, *ONOSKELIS*. The *TALISMAN* is clearly derived from the sacred form of the mirrored Hebrew 'M' or *Mem*, the Kabbalistic cardinal middle letter of the alphabet signifying the Water of Life, which suggests the antiquity of their talisman. The later refinement of the symbol in the fifth century AD reflects the Sisterhood's sophisticated knowledge of the mathematical expression of the Parabola of Life as a *semicircle*, and their proof of the perfect equality between the triangulated projection of Life's Span and those two over-arcing crescent moon-shaped figures: the After-shadowing of *Birth* and Fore-shadowing of *Death* bisected symmetrically at Life's *Mid-point*. Their geometricised Hebraic 'double-M' faces Future and Past, etc. . . .

Mathematics in the Fifth Century
MARIE BASHKIRTSEFF, 1876.

Open Secret

Here I drew breath, my mind whirling with thoughts of my beloved daughter's own precognition of her *dies mortis* and tried to imagine how Mariya Bashkirtseff's foreknowledge of death had empowered her to produce such a remarkable body of work in a lifetime so short, albeit that she allegedly learned of the secret somewhat earlier in her youth than Anjelika.

I reexamined the engraved portrait of Bashkirtseff that decorated the frontispiece of her published diary (*Journal de Marie Bashkirtseff, 1889*).

Mariya's hands are clasped in an attitude suggestive of the talisman, I noticed, a similarity emphasised by Margery's crude scribblings, and plottings on graph paper. That Mariya attaches significance to this pose while gazing meaningfully into the camera is made clear in Margery's concluding observations:

> **Demonolatry and Cults:** There appear to be few Europo-Asian cultures where the Sisterhood's Divination Spirit, ONOSKELIS, is not invoked, even today, nor where traces of the cult cannot be found. The Consorority has evidence (which my own field trips to the Cheremissian peoples of Yoshkar-Ola in the Republic of Mari El confirm) that the Cheremissians remain a conduit of the secret knowledge, and I myself have observed (1932) their Onoskelisian talisman openly displayed under the noses of the Soviet ideologues who escorted our party of Western anthropologists.

Here Margery introduces a paradox: *'To hide wisdom it is necessary to make it available to all,'* and concludes . . .

> The Mari peoples were greatly influenced ancestrally by Iranian forerunners whose steppe tribes penetrated the Mari habitat and their adopted Semitic symbols have been preserved to this day. The secrets of ONOSKELIS, having survived the destruction of Solomon's Temple, similarly continued to be transmitted. In latterday Mari mythology a thread symbolises the path between the world of the living and the world of dead; and the double Hebrew *Mem*, which is its talisman, can be observed often as a *tamga* (clan totemic symbol) of the Cheremissians and their

> neighbouring Bashkirs. It is even possible to distinguish the same symbol in the steps of Mari folk dances!

Here Margery has sketched the dancers of the Mountain Mari womenfolk, with linked arms arched to make the 'parabola' of Life and Death. This *tamga*, she notes, is *literally* woven into the fabric of Cheremissian women's lives.

> These symbols, literally, surrounded me! *An open secret!* Just look attentively, and you will see them. Here is a Mari woman passing by; she has the symbols embroidered on her dress! Here we are given a scoop of *kvas* [beer], and there is the symbol cut on its handle! In the carving of window frames, in ritual dippers for beer, in the embroidery of Mari costumes and woven belts they can be observed! In the Ethnography museum in Budapest there are three such patterned belts, found by Kuznetsov in a Mari village in 1879.

As to how the underground 'conduit of secret knowledge' continues, unabated, to flow down the centuries of womenkind to the present day, Margery begins to hint at an answer. ' "The Cheremissians say their Book of Destiny is the book written on human flesh," my Mari guide informed me in a low whisper out of earshot of our Russian colleagues. And not until my return to England (1933) did I begin to understand the import of her remark.

'I believe now that, like so many of her fellow-Adepts, Mariya Bashkirtseff perceived, as an artist, the transmittal of the Consorority's concealed truth to be a semiological phenomenon: the "distaff sign" of *The Spinner*, if you will. The talisman, indeed, was a subtle feminine equivalent of the sacred name which in Judaic texts is often represented by a character that in English looks like a "W" whose ritual importance is its resemblance to the position of worship— arms raised above the head. Thus, Mariya's posture is mimetic also of pagan talismanic prayer.'

THE TAUNTING EVIL

I broke my journey at Paddington, and sped at once by underground to King's Cross.

At Euston Square, however, a feeling of hideous oppression came upon me and, faint with a sudden nausea, I sought fresh air.

Sickened and disoriented, I soon found myself wandering in the rain down Tottenham Court Road near the Hospital for Tropical Diseases.

Outside the hospital, workmen were resurfacing the road; I could smell the tarry odour of broken moorings.

I sat on a wet bench.

Crouched at the far end, a ragged-looking woman captured my professional attention. She had discarded her surgical stockings and was cutting her toe-nails, her drenched feathered hat pressed down over her brow.

My God! I thought. *Would I end my days like that woman, with no lodging for the night?*

I looked around me for the talismanic sign of Onoskelis but saw only the impression in the mud of a gumboot's heel-tread moulded in the shape of the Cheremissian *tamga* . In some respects, I thought, the tamga resembles a primitive knot; and I began to fear I'd fallen prey to another obsessive compulsion, and that the remainder of my life would be spent attempting to decipher a pagan cryptography in every manifestation of my daily life no matter how trivial the detail.

I remembered my patient, the spurned mistress, Mary H., ID 0312110842, had visited her boyfriend at the Hospital for Tropical Diseases shortly before his death, and I thought of Van Schuyler lying powerless in that little whitewashed side ward in Spain, while a voice of taunting evil echoed in my head.

According to Margery Nairn-Jardine, who had read *The Testament of Solomon*, Onoskelis bestowed certain powers on those who worshipped her.

'This demoness was born out of an echo of a black heaven,' she wrote, 'and her purpose is to avenge wronged women by killing men.'

No Ashtray

There was no difficulty in entering the shuttered-up, mud-coloured terrace house near King's Cross station.

Van Schuyler's room seemed just as he had abandoned it a month before. The place appeared ransacked.

A strong trapped odour like sour breath deterred me at the threshold. Unwashed socks, underwear, and stained tee-shirts were strewn across the bare floor.

By the look of his room he'd completed his rudimentary toilette in haste because the floorboards were dusted with little heaps of talcum powder where he'd dressed on the hoof.

An unfinished letter from Van Schuyler was crumpled in a ball on the mantleshelf. Astonishing intimacies addressed to Anjelika caused my cheeks to flame.

'Sugar babe, it seems like I've known you forever . . .'

I was faint with weariness and hunger; I cut a small piece of bread from a mouldy loaf on the table and stared at it uncomprehendingly.

On the table, coated with grey dust, a frosted glass night-light with a half-melted candle stood ready, with a box of matches on a wax-filled saucer.

For the dozenth time I was reminded of Hildie's prophetic dream.

Hildie had vividly described a room with a purple blind over a dormer window. 'Hideously cold,' she'd said, with 'frozen condensation on the water pipes.'

In the dimness of the shuttered room all was very quiet except for the sound of running water somewhere within the inner wall.

I reached for a light switch and then remembered I had entered a squat and, in such places, invariably the electricity supply is switched off.

A smoky black patch on the ceiling below a frosted water pipe showed at which position, on a shelf, 'Van' Schuyler's night-light had burned.

I lit the candle then carried the light to the closet and opened the door.

Of course! How could I have been so foolish!

With eyes unclouded by tears I now saw the 'closet' was nothing less than the entrance to a set of narrow backstairs, hidden by a door designed to resemble a wooden panel wall.

The candle flickered as I ascended the steep flight of steps which led, I was now certain, to a maid's garret room at the top of the house.

A washline was suspended over the dusky stairwell.

My head was hurting, my throat had dried; a pair of striped legwarmers Anjelika had once worn for workouts hung in front of the door at the head of the stairs, which was locked.

With an action as inevitable as my daughter's own instincts I reached into a bag of clothes-pegs hanging on the line; at home we'd had recourse to the same hiding place for concealing our spare house-key.

A shield of icy air met me when I unlocked the door—the killing cold of a chill cabinet—and I entered a chamber considerably smaller than the room below.

The door, it seemed, was frosted on its fastenings and I found myself in an atmosphere so benumbingly glacial it was as if my breath was condensing in an ice-house.

The candle blew out.

In that void the twilit abysses around me dissolved into those of a fourth dimension to turn consciousness inside out.

When I scraped a match and relumined the room I saw frost crystals shone on the windowpane beneath the purple blind of the dormer.

Anjelika's woodcuts of Mount Fuji were pinned on the garret's sloping ceiling, just as Hildie had predicted. And prominent above her bedhead was her favourite print of the *Isle of the Dead* painted by Böcklin.

The recess between the chimney breast and window held fitted shelves, and the candlelight glittered on Anjelika's chipped inkstand and her collection of broad-edged dip-pens she used for her calligraphy.

The ink I noticed had a frozen film on it.

My fingers shook; from apprehension, from the cold, and from a grief so intense that it shook the raw fabric of my being. In the chill air the liver spots on my hands had grown more distinct. I remembered a saying of Granny Lucifer's; her generation considered age spots 'the blooms of death'.

The chill was gaining on me.

The room smelled of not having been smoked in.

There was no ashtray.

In an odd way I can't explain this fleeting little insight pleased me.

No, definitely no odour of hashish unless I added anosmia to the list of my other failing faculties.

A lay on Anjelika's bed and pressed my face into her perfumed pillow. My cup overflowed with bitterness and I wept.

She was the light of my life, my only child, and now I live in darkness. I exist but I am not alive.

There is never a day when she is not my first thought when I awake.

I feel like my heart has broken into a thousand pieces. I can't believe she will never walk through our door alive again.

Never will I forget her. Not until the end of my life.

There is no reason on God's earth for this.

Honest to God, I wish there was justice.

❁

The last time I prayed was in the Lady Chapel at Ely cathedral where all the statues in their niches and the 'superstitious' shrines are destroyed. They were smashed by the iconoclasts following the Dissolution. It's a barren, soulless spot to choose for prayer. I wonder what Jung would have thought?

A Knot Worthy of Being Loosed

How long I lay on Anjelika's bed I cannot judge but when I later woke, and rubbed off the frostwork from the windowpane with my sleeve, the stars were of an extraordinary brilliancy and the horizon hinted at dawn.

A day of startling perplexity was beginning; yet a day, I thought, that would solve past riddles.

In that tiny bedsittingroom I now perceived Anjelika had arranged a worktable in an alcove under the eves.

The candle was guttering when I lifted the first sheet from her sketch book.

I drew a long breath and my heart throbbed when I saw she had been drawing and redrawing in coloured inks the primitive talisman of her great-grandmother's ultra-surreptitious ritualists and their occultic circles.

'It's a peculiar thing and so very much like a knot,' I murmured to myself, idly tracing its outline with my finger while giving thanks to Granny Lucifer for her supreme wisdom and foresight in having chosen her peculiarly providential interment in a three-tiered grave.

'A knot worthy of being loosed by Lucifer's hands,' I added, as though my grandmother had clearly foreseen the *dénouement*—the unknotting—of her wretched grandchild's tangled dilemma.

Behind me I heard a low whistling sound, hardly audible, rising to a eldritch shriek that sounded like a wet squeegee on glass.

It seemed to inhabit the upper air, and scarcely a breath was felt but it lifted the top sheet of Anjelika's sketches and spun it half round.

With a shudder, this is what I saw:

Suddenly my senses were drowned by aromatic perfumes and the eyes of a demoness seemed to bore into my very soul.

Postscript

And how on earth do you tell people about this? They would just think you either had a hyper-sensitive nature or were going nuts.

The funeral director was sympathetic when I explained the delayed funeral arrangements. He reassured me he was familiar with cases where the body is withheld abroad for legal reasons.

I'd met him almost two decades earlier when I had gone to the Stoneburgh burial ground to seek a name for my child from the gravestones.

He'd directed me to a nineteenth-century tomb that bore Anjelika's name.

The cycle of birth and death is his *métier*, so to speak, and since unusually he was present at the very beginning of Anjelika's existence I felt confident in entrusting to him the final passage of her life.

Anyhow, the death of Van Schuyler has resolved the wrangling between the Consulate and the Spanish authorities over the issue of the retention of my daughter in that dreadful morgue.

Van Schuyler, despite his injuries, had been making a good recovery, so the funeral director informed me on his return from satisfactorily tidying up the whole matter in Spain.

Needless to add, Van Schuyler's death had occurred on the night of my visit to the drugs-den at his De Quinceyesque London squat.

A charitable nun, her face radiant with beneficence, had been praying fervently at his bedside all through his last hours, I was told, so I could be reassured that the soul of my daughter's friend had been commended to God.

Captious critics and sceptical debunkers may well dismiss the Jungian synchronicity of these past events, and point out, for example, that Marie Bashkirtseff's disease was of that character which would admit of exact calculation in respect to its crisis and termination in death.

But in the minutiae of this affair it is possible to observe the continuity of themes that surface in the lives of my patients mentioned in this book.

Indeed, the theory of 'six degrees of separation', I surmise, hardly applies to the *connective unconscious* which links the protagonists of these narratives and gives their lives unity in the spatio-temporal causal world.

Since the funeral of my daughter and the putting to rest of so many of the fears that gave rise to my disturbing obsessions and compulsions, I have decided to draft a confidential questionnaire for my patients.

In this Self-Analysis Questionnaire I intend to apply my boss's latest ethnomethodological computing program for 'best match' retrieval to determine further the unconscious connectivity between my patients, and to identify direct causal connections between variables.

I don't wish to alarm my patients, obviously.

But should you be reading this you should be aware that, primarily, the incidence in your dreamlife of the prophetic Garden, and its divination of your *dies mortis*, will be the substance of a future edition of this work.

Provisional Conclusions

Impatient for proofs, I have combed and backcombed these pages of clinical vignettes to seek further insights and to trace Onoskelisian threads in my patients' narratives.

For example, in the case of Eveline M., ID 0241090556 (see *Confessions of a Kissee*) I am not mistaken in observing that, at the pivotal moment in Eveline's formative life, she is wakened 'from a dream portending her salvation in the garden'; and, moreover, in the very first case selected (see *Soft Skin*), I note Felícia F., ID EP0841060170, at the most critical turning point in her life, is struck by a vision of her family's *vinhinha*—the enclosed garden of vines and flower gardens from which she had been banished a quarter of a century before.

Then, of course, I shall consult Zoë W., ID 0291070651 and that highly obsessive Poe fanatic, Mary H., ID 0312110842, both of whom speak of the Expulsion from the Garden of Paradise. (Incidentally, it is curious, is it not, that when Poe wrote to his cousin, Virginia, his future wife, on August 29th, 1835, his cousinly affection had been supplanted by forbidden brotherly emotions. 'I cannot express in words the fervent devotion I feel toward my dear little cousin—my own darling . . . My love, my own sweetest Sissy . . .' i.e. Poe regarded his first cousin as a *sister*. However, to apprise Mary of this revealing oddity would be, in the circumstances of her special case, most unwise.)

So I wish Eveline and Felícia and Zoë and Mary long life, and I wish the same for all my other patients mentioned in this book. To live twice as long is their destiny . . . of that I'm certain.

And I, too, awoke this morning to a memory of the Dream of the Garden. My work is unfinished, and I've much to do, for I have many more years to live.

Medice, cura te ipsum!

ACKNOWLEDGEMENTS

'ALWAYS ENCOURAGE', THE lesser known of E. M. Forster's wise and balanced maxims, is kindly advice that I can confirm has been heeded by the many early readers of these works. So I would like to take this opportunity to acknowledge the encouragement and valuable guidance I've received from the following discerning writers (some, I regret, no longer living to accept my heartfelt thanks): the late Jon Silkin; the late Dr Alexander Gorbovsky; Dr Martin Bax and Kate Pemberton of *Ambit* journal; Carole Buchan of the Asham Literary Endowment Trust in memory of Virginia Woolf; Melanie Ashby of *MsLexia* journal; Kate Clanchy; Sally Zigmond of *Quality Women's Fiction* journal; Grace Jardine-Wilkinson and Mark Bannister for their sensitive scoring of *Lament of a Girl Led Astray*; Kerry West for her Benesh notation of *Fugue for Two Misfits*; Neville Marten of Ink journal; Prof. Pierre Coustillas, the authority on George Gissing; Konstantin Sitnikov, the Cheremissian encyclopaediast; Gerald Jacobs; Matthew J. Reisz; Katie Gilmour; Mark Pilkington and Ali Hutchinson; Alison Moir, Louise Ward of *Stand* journal; Chief (Nana) Otuo Acheampon; and, of course, my constant encourager and editor, Jen Hamilton-Emery.

A number of the *Sister Morphine* case histories, in very slightly edited forms, have appeared in the following publications: *The Catch* (Asham Prize), *Ambit* journal, *MsLexia*, and *Stand*, whose editors we thank for permission to republish.